SamSara

BY THE SAME AUTHOR:

LeRoi

Menopause Man

SamSara

MEL MATHEWS

FISHER KING PRESS

Fisher King Press
P.O. Box 222321
Carmel, CA 93922
www.fisherkingpress.com
1-800-228-9316

SamSara

ISBN-13: 978-0-9776076-2-4
ISBN-10: 0-9776076-2-3
LCCN: 2005937568

Cover photo by Ajna Lichau

Cover design by Charles Thomas

To my parents, who have never been, nor ever shall be, the villainous characters that I have unrelentingly made them seem; to the rest of my family and friends who have, also, often had to endure my distorted perceptions and impositions; and to Joseph, for loving me in spite of myself and showing me the way back home.

We never really leave home:
Just return from different directions.

Malcolm and I first met in a coffee shop in downtown Carmel just a few weeks after he turned thirty-six. Six months later, by chance, we bumped into each other again. He'd returned to the Peninsula for the weekend. A close friend of his had just died and he seemed quite shaken. He explained that he had been raised a Calvinist, had suffered from life's normal existential beatings and, at twenty-five years of age, had checked himself into a rehabilitation center for alcoholism. I mentioned the possibility that he might some day be able to accept that his life and what had happened to him was simply just the way it was. Malcolm's response to my suggestion was that he needed a new image of God and of Woman. He said that he had no idea what that meant; yet he knew it to be his truth.

We discussed a dream he'd had that day, and once a week from then on over the next few years, until just a few days before he left for Europe. The last correspondence I received was an e-mail message from Malcolm while he was still in Ireland. The letter said that it was time for him to get on with his life. After that, he never replied to any of my queries. A few months passed and I received a hand-written copy of this manuscript in the mail, along with a note of thanks. What precedes and follows this brief introduction is solely the work of one: Malcolm Clay.

Adam Sinclear
Monterey, California
December of 2001

In the Beginning...

December 21, 2000

It seems that I am dying; yet I have something to say. My greatest love affair has been with my neurotic victimhood. My grandest infidelity has been to myself. I write about me, and I write with many an 'I'. Any other way of expressing myself seems unauthentic. I can only tell you about me and what has happened to me in this life; at the same time, I reserve the right to be wrong or to lie to you, as well as to myself.

The lies will be honest, as everything I'm about to report was seen through my eyes and experienced with the senses of my singular body, and that in itself will bring distortion to the reader. I'm distorted. Like every human being, I have experienced the physical as well as the psychological trauma of birth: being spit out of the womb - expelled from my personal Garden of Eden. I also carry a personal heritage, one that is divided between the ancestry of sperm and egg. In addition to my own genetic make-up, I also have a universal lineage, the collective heritage, in which everything that is unfathomable and mysterious is contained.

It is so hard to wait. I've been waiting for forty years to start living my life and something still has me shackled. Don't ask me what it is because, if I knew, I'd be out living my life instead of sitting here writing about it. I wouldn't be living in this little studio apartment, playing solitaire on my PowerBook until two every morning.

If I wasn't an alchy, I'd be drunk; if I wasn't drunk, I'd be high; if I wasn't high, I'd be bedded down with some sweet young thing who was twenty years my junior and saw me as God, and if not God, then at the very least, the father she never had, or the opposite image of the father as the object of her rebellion. But no, it seems that consciousness has a way of robbing a man of the illusions that once served him, that once led him to believe that he was really living life to its fullest.

Now, having said that, I shall begin my lie:

I need a new lie, a noble lie, a lie that I can believe in. It's as if I've been robbed of all truth and have a desperate urge to once again believe in something: something so mysterious that it can actually entrance me.

Yahweh, the wrathful God of my youth, no longer sits enthroned in heaven. I have been robbed of this belief as well. Yahweh, too, has become an inner phenomenon, a part of my psyche, and I can no longer blame him for my victim's role in life, just as I can no longer blame and punish all women for the sins of my mother, grandmother, Eve, or Sophia.

It has taken forty years for me to learn that Yahweh rules from a throne within me and that I am actually my own judge, jury, and executioner. It has also taken forty years for me to realize that the mother of my youth, my physical mother, and all that I learned from her about woman and how a woman relates to a man is not the gospel truth. I've learned quite the contrary. It now seems that my inner image of mother, who for years I've been toting around in the recesses of my soul, is blasphemy. I'm not telling this to be rebelliously irreverent or to discredit and dishonor my physical mother's humanity; I'm writing this in reverence to myself. I'm writing this in an attempt to exorcize my demons, or most certainly to expose them in hope of developing a conscious relationship with these unseen deities.

I believe that my mother's image of man is distorted. I say this because of all she had to endure in the innocence of her youth: her parents fought like Zeus and Hera. I also believe my mother's image of man is distorted because of her Calvinist heritage. I believe that her whole view of man could quite possibly have been seen through the eyes of my grandmother, who, undoubtedly mother-fucked my grandfather in the presence of her four daughters, pointing out every one of his human imperfections, and his inability to measure up to the dogma of her puritanical standards.

My grandmother, fearing Yahweh's wrath, has suffered dearly her entire life. At eighty-six years of age, she's still preaching damnation from an omniscient, omnipresent, omnipotent, punishing God who stands ready to deliver his just wrath upon the unjust. Now, if she's that way to her grandchildren, multiply it ten times to get the degree to which she drilled the dogma into the souls of her own children. Hell, at least the grandkids got an occasional peppermint Lifesaver on Sunday mornings while enduring the infectious splinters of those hard-ass wooden church pews.

So, my mother suffered that shit and then handed it down to her four boys. We were all baptized as infants. Mom's four boys were sprinkled with the droplets of the church's puritanical dogma, and we continued to have shit-heaps of belief, which were literally translated from ambiguous symbols, shoveled upon our developing innocence as we attended Sunday School and the same private Christian grade school that our mother attended in her youth.

I believe that my mother's image of God, and in turn Man, is skewed. Think about it: how could she spend her waking hours waiting for Yahweh, her heavenly father with whom she was constantly on guard against invoking His imminent wrath, without becoming a little disturbed. Then there was her earthly father who, in spite of his well intentioned piety and affiliation with the church as an elder and a consistory member, had one hell of a time staying sober, winning a bet, or keeping his poker in his pocket. And, Lord knows, that all the pissin' and moanin' my grandmother did over the injustices of my grandfather did nothing but add to my mother's confusion about Man.

It is my guess that deep down inside, my mother is deathly afraid of Man in spite of how she may present herself to the waking world. It seems she married my father as an unconscious compensation. My father is nothing like my grandfather, not that he won't have a pop or two now and then. He's just a very fine man who likes people and likes to help them out in any way he can. Dad's now retired after forty years of service. He started out in the District Attorney's office and worked his way up to Superior Court Judge. Everyone knows Dad like they knew my grandfather, but enough of that. Let's return to my mother and her relationship to my father.

You see, I'm just now coming to terms with the fact that for my entire life I've seen my father through my mother's eyes.

My image of Man, and how woman relates to Man, has all been translated to me through her eyes. The poor guy could just never measure up. Believe me, she spent plenty of time mother-fucking him to us boys just like her mother did her father to her. She cut his fucking nuts off, and I must admit, as much as I love my mother, if I had been my father, I'd have divorced her ball-busting-ass years ago.

I recall the early years before she went to work. My father was the breadwinner and Mom took care of the house and us kids. She'd charge things and then hide the bills. The creditors would end up calling my father at work. He'd come home at lunch, embarrassed and pissed off about the call, to find the bills stashed in the bottom of the stereo cabinet. My mother was sneaky. She still is, or at least my image of her is.

Mom turned eighteen only a few days before I was born. She was still a girl: a little princess who believed her husband would treat her like his daughter. She probably got away with that kind of shit with her daddy and was bound and determined to act out the same behavior with my father. It's hard to grow up; I know.

For years, money was what they fought about, but after she had the first three boys, she went back to school and became a nurse. She got pregnant with the fourth child when my father accompanied her on a trip to the Bay Area to take the State Boards. Once licensed, Mom took the evening shifts, working just short of a week before having Angus, her fourth son. Within a month of delivering my youngest brother into this world, she was back working the same evening shift, leaving us four boys at home, motherless, and in the hands of an emasculated father; the same man she mother-fucked by day. Truth of the matter is, they both mother-fucked each other.

So I had a pissed off father and a mother who hid from her family by night. That's why, had I been my father, I'd have divorced her ball-busting-ass long ago. But, I guess, my father was too much in love with her or somehow still a needy little boy who could recycle his unfulfilled need for a positive mother-image and/or the missing feminine within his own soul. Then again, maybe not. Maybe I'm the only one who is doing this.

I don't know if this is true, but it appears to be something like this: I knew my paternal grandmother, but I never knew her well enough, nor did I have the conscious awareness while she was living, to analyze the heritage of my father's youth. My paternal grandparents were of Irish and American Indian descent, Cherokee Indian I've been told, and my grandmother was of very few words.

Mother couldn't leave an unfulfilled marriage because Yahweh's cloud of wrath was floating around in her heaven. Yet, it appeared that she could sneak around the Old Boy, by taking the evening shifts and using the nobility of her profession to excuse the abandonment of her husband and family. She cloaked all this behind a veil, justifying her flee from Egypt in the name of economically contributing to the family, much of it to pay the tuition of our puritan education. This is why I say she's a ball-buster, sneaky, and dishonest. Had she been honest, she'd have faced Yahweh and her marriage, or divorced my father in spite of hurting him; she'd have at least handed his balls back to him in the process.

Fuck! I'm getting pissed just thinking about all of this. They needed each other to carry on a tradition. It wasn't the injustice of just one; unconscious forces run them both, just as it still runs me, but it pisses me off just the same.

Then again, maybe I'm the only one who's fucked up. Maybe my parents' unconscious suffering has had its advantages. After all, they're still married and in good health, have four boys, three daughters in-law, and a half-dozen grandchildren. Hell, on top of all that, my eighty-six-year-old Reformed Dutch Calvinist grandmother is still preaching about and praying to you know whom. For the last forty years, she's been certain that she won't be around to celebrate Christmas with the family next year because the Lord will soon be taking her home to heaven.

So anyway, what I'm pissed about is that it seems I've inherited a distorted view of Man and Woman, and, in turn, a distorted view of myself. I have no idea in the world what it means to be a man, or how to relate to a woman, or how to simply be myself. I've been searching, at the very least, for the last fifteen years on a personal level, yet on a collective level it could well have been since the time of the reformation, or, better yet, since the day that Adam and Eve originated sin.

And I still say that it was all a set-up, and I'm not talking about Eve either. I'm talking about God. God needed the original sin so that He could be God, so that He could be Yahweh and shed His everlasting wrathful love over all His creation. Yeah, I know, I'll probably be struck down with some catastrophic disease for this heretical blasphemy, but what the fuck, I'm dying just the same.

December 23, 2000

It's Kelli's birthday today. I met her last September in a coffee shop in Carmel. She'd just given up her place in Big Sur and had plans of moving to Spain. A friend ran across her e-mail address a few weeks ago and forwarded it to me. We've been communing ever since. She's having a hard time finding a place in Spain, so she's in Ireland, staying with her mother in Dublin. She's beautiful: a blue-eyed blonde goddess teeming with magic. I sent her an e-mail to wish her happy birthday and to complain about not knowing what to do with my life.

December 24, 2000 - Mid Morning

Heard back from Kelli, thanking me for the happy birthday. She had a question for me: "Okay, if anything was possible, and money no object, what would you do with the rest of your life?"

My reply: "Fall for a beautiful Irish woman, chase her to Spain, and make love to her eternally!"

December 24, 2000 - Midnight

Kelli's response to my bravado: "A gentleman with patience!"

December 26, 2000

I turned forty-years-old today. I'm ready for the land of milk and honey.

January 2, 2001

There were no e-mails to answer this evening. I haven't whacked off in three weeks or so, but I did get laid on my birthday: It was Mary, an old flame who needed a little action just as I did. I don't know what my problem is these days; the drive just isn't there, not like it once was anyway.

Instead of pursuing any kind of physical love affair with a woman, I'd rather be obsessed with a benign bump on my balls that the doctor has assured me is a harmless part of my anatomy, the epididymus, where the tubes enter the testes: That's my sex life. I have a sexual disorder. I have an obsessive-compulsive relationship with the terrain of my left testicle.

I gave Mrs. Shams, my landlord, a thirty-day notice today. It feels good. I'm moving out from under the constraints of her criticism, out of the patriarchal structure that still dominates her eighty-one-year-old mind, out of what she thinks is best for me. I'm moving on to what I feel is best for me. I'm going to follow myself while she continues to follow the masses. While she continues to doubt herself and quote others, I'm going to quote myself and doubt her. She told me that too much introspection is not good for me, and I told her that maybe it was just too scary for some people. You know what, fuck her, and fuck me, too!

Moving has actually been in the works for some time. Over the past few months, on my visits to family and friends in my hometown, I have slowly been putting things into my storage unit. I had tentatively planned to leave on the first of February; now it's official.

Sheila, a physically non-intimate young woman-friend of mine, as if I had any other kind of woman-friend these days, is going to take over the studio. She broke up with her boyfriend and is fighting with her roommate. When she found out that I considered moving, she asked me if she could have the studio. I didn't think that Mrs. Shams would go for it because the old broad always talks about how she wants a man around. The token man, I suppose, makes her feel safe. That's why the rent is so cheap. Well, cheap monetarily, but after living there for a year I began to realize the rent wasn't as cheap as it first appeared; I've been paying in other ways.

I had asked the old widow what she expected of me when I moved in, figuring there must be a catch to the cheap rent; her only response was that we weren't going to be chums. That lasted for a while, but then I must have grown on her or something, because she was trying her damnedest for my 'chumship.'

Before I knew it, I, a forty-year-old man, had to sneak out of my room like a grounded teenager. For some reason, she decided that I was a wayward soul in need of her divine guidance and the wisdom that old age has bequeathed her. For the last year she's really been getting under my skin, but I've had a hard time letting go of the 'cheap rent.' Then again, maybe it's her abuse that I'm so fond of? Anyway, I presented my leave as only temporary, so that Sheila could have a place to stay, that perhaps will turn into a permanent situation as time passes and Mrs. Shams grows fond of her. If they don't hit it off, I'll still have my foot in the door in case I return. The old broad went for the grand scheme, too.

January 12, 2001

Adam and I are in Sedona, Arizona attending a seminar on creativity. It has been in the works since last June. I was sitting in the bar at the hotel having a drink with Adam and Sophia. Sophia is one of the presenters at the conference. She's a charming southern woman with a heavy Alabaman accent. She's tall and slender, with long blonde hair, blue eyes, and a beautiful smile. My guess is that she's in her early sixties, simply a lovely woman. From out of nowhere, and I don't know if this was the scotch talking or if Adam was fucking with me, but the old boy really knocked me out of my saddle.

"You know, Sophia, Malcolm's really bad when it comes to

women. I mean, he's rotten," Adam announced, and looked at me with a great big smile. "But I was worse," he added, in a proud-of- himself tone after a few moments of silence had hung in the air.

Sophia looked at me and with her southern drawl asked: "Is that right, Malcolm? Are you really bad?"

"Just a little," I answered, as I wrinkled my nose and held up my right hand, wiggling it in a so-so manner, an effort to wave off my sense of shame, not wanting to go any farther into the realm of confessing the exploits of my former life.

Who the hell did I think I was fooling? Sophia was the mother of three boys and two daughters, and on top of that... well, let's just say Sophia was wisdom incarnate. She was lecturing on *The Sacred Prostitute,* a book written by Nancy Qualls-Corbett. Sophia had me pegged ten years before my conception. She could sniff out a flighty *Puer* half a continent removed.

"I can tell you one thing though," I answered, after recovering from Adam's confession.

"What's that?" Sophia asked.

"I was having a hell of a lot more fun before I met Adam," I answered, and then we all broke into a belly laughing session.

It was the damn truth, too. I had had a hell of a lot more women wanting to work me over until this conscious making act took hold; it seems that my transformative experience has stripped the baited hook that once attracted a multitude of women, unconscious maybe, but women just the same.

I recall the days when I cared nothing for any woman's reaction to my promiscuity. If the truth was told, reveling in my wantonness probably got me laid a hell of a lot more than being one of those sensitive nice guys who could feel all of womankind's pain. My nice-guy honesty was a facade anyway, a facade that seemed to fail me more and more. I suppose that growing up demands a sacrifice, and it seems I am only now becoming aware of what exactly that sacrifice is.

For almost four years now I've been delving into my dreams with Adam, and it's had a profound impact on my life, on my whole existence. Adam is a shaman, a sage, disguised as an old man who plays tennis and wears one of those funny white hats even when he's not on the court. He's a coyote, I'm telling you, and it takes a real trickster to deal with someone like me. I've learned that not only do I dream at night, but also in my waking life as I invite the outer world to participate in the dramas that have constellated within my soul. In other words, the events that transpire and the relationships in which I engage are in a sense a movie that is produced within myself. The world is my screen, and I'm the projector.

Of the many things I have learned about myself, and the human condition in general, is that suffering is an inescapable part of life, at least if a greater consciousness is to be born, and for some reason I have chosen to cease blindly following various and sundry dogmas. Through this process, for better or worse, I'm learning to consult my inner self. By diving into the unconscious world of my dreams, waking and sleeping, I'm learning to commune with my higher, or better yet, larger self, that part of me who knows on a universal scale, the path or destiny of my true calling.

I've learned that the images of my dreams and the people whom I encounter, or dream up in my waking life, are all symbols of myself. In other words, I make people into who or what I need them to be. They are carriers of the human qualities or idiosyncrasies that I am unable to accept or recognize within myself. They are integral pieces of me that I have avoided at any cost, be it a perceived positive or negative aspect of my humanity. In my world, the events and the people in it who most annoy me are all my teachers. I'm learning that all I believed I knew is of little value, and that most, if not all, of my beliefs have robbed me of a grander existence.

Problem is I don't like what I'm learning; it's kicked the foundations out from under me. The other problem is that understanding all this doesn't make it any easier, especially when I'm caught up in some drama. It's only after time has passed; then I can look back with an objective view and have an idea of how I was shucking my shit off onto another.

It seems from what I was taught of the fairer sex in my youth, be it from my mother's lashings or her many other unconsciously dishonest ways of relating to my father and to the world around her, I now see Woman from a very distorted and skewed view. But, at forty years of age, blaming my physical mother, appealing as it sounds, would make it much easier to remain in an infantile state of helplessness, as opposed to accepting the fact that the mother who continues to haunt and rule me is an entity within.

Then there is the confusion of God and all that was bequeathed me through my Calvinist upbringing: Good old Yahweh, that wrathful God whose omniscient presence my maternal grandmother unrelentingly warned me of. The vindictive punishing God constantly watching, waiting for me to sway from the Church's puritanical doctrine, the canons of my grandmother, and that of my mother, which has for years been literally interpreted and handed down through the maternal side of my ancestral heritage. His presence looms eternal.

After forty years I am beginning to realize that Yahweh, too, is an archetypal energy within me and not a physical phenomena that looks down upon and rules the world from the throne of His celestial palace. It seems that I too possess these Yahweh aspects, judging and condemning the world and its inhabitants that don't fit into my distorted, self-righteous view of how things are supposed to be. The judge, jury, and executioner are all within me, and I have spent a good portion of my life unconsciously acting out my own wrath and other Yahweh characteristics onto others and myself. I have failed to understand that in condemning and rejecting another, I have also been condemning and rejecting myself.

Little did I know at the time that what was really going on behind all the unconscious acts of the pious do-gooders and better-than-thous of the church and clergy of my youth was a displaced energy fueled by fear. This blind following also allowed for not having to be responsible for the very lives that we had all been given. Living a pious life, according to someone else's rules, can only leave a man dead to his soul. It's impossible to have one's own religious or numinous experience when another's recipe is being followed.

Now I'm toying with the possibility that we are all vessels through which God can experience Him or Herself in different ways. As I wake to this phenomenon, I'm having a glimmer of my own God experience. To me, God is unconsciousness being made conscious through the manifestations of all creation. In other words, perhaps God needs humanity in order to experience Himself. He needs our eyes, our bodies, our feelings and experiences to know that He-She actually exists. God, without man, can only doubt His existence, yet, I, without God, have no purpose, no meaning, no reason, no need to exist.

January 16, 2001

We left Sedona yesterday. It was snowing, but the Expedition had four-wheel drive and all-terrain tires. About fifty miles west of Flagstaff the snow turned to rain. I drove all the way through the desert, over Tehachapi, and down into Bakersfield. Just north of Bakersfield, on Highway 99, we found ourselves behind a big truck. Adam had been sleeping, but he began to shift in his seat.

"What the hell's that?" he asked, a confused, sick look on his face.

"Dead cows," I answered, between my belly laughter.

"Dead cows?"

"Yeah, that's a tallow truck in front of us. They pick up the dead cows from the dairies around here and haul them to a rendering plant to make soap and stuff," I explained, as we passed the truck.

"Oh, yeah, I've heard of that, tallow," Adam answered, before he leaned back in his seat to fall asleep again.

Adam will be eighty-five on the fifth of February. He has a forty-seven-year-old wife and a nine-year-old daughter. He's one sharp cookie too, sharp enough to be onto my shit and love me through it all at the same time. Adam has packed several lifetimes into his eighty-five years of existence. Just being friends with him has changed me. He hardly ever suggests that I do anything, just listens to me and occasionally makes a subtle suggestion.

Adam knows what a rebellious little bastard I am. He knows that the only way to teach me is to let me learn myself, and that is exactly what he's been doing, providing a space big enough for me to learn in, only occasionally nudging me back to the center when I get to dancing on the periphery, in danger of falling off into the abyss. Delving into the unconscious is tricky business, and scary, too. He took me there and hung out with me until I could get comfortable out there alone. I guess you could say that Adam introduced me to myself, parts of me that I have been running away from for my entire life.

I drove another fifty miles or so and then decided to see about a room. Adam stayed in the Expedition while I ran in to negotiate. After haggling over the price, I registered and returned to park the Expedition and unload.

"What the hell is that?" Adam asked, as he stepped from the Ford.

"Cow shit," I answered, just before doubling over into another belly laughing session. The whole town reeked of it. "There're dairies all over the place around here. You're surrounded by real live shit factories," I giggled, tossing a few of our bags onto the ground.

"Good gosh, where the hell have you taken me?"

"For all we know, Adam, this might be heaven."

"Well, I'm ready to get the hell out of this heaven."

"We are, first thing in the morning."

After a reasonably early departure from cow-shit-heaven, we arrived back on the Monterey Peninsula late this afternoon. When we left this morning, we drove north to my hometown. I decided to stop by and introduce Adam to my parents. Figured it was the right thing to do since he'd been listening to me mother-fuck them for the last four years. Thanks to Adam, I'm learning to really see my parents and have a genuine relationship with them.

I recall a visit with my family last month. We all went out for dinner, my mother, father, brother Freeman and his wife Gina. After dinner we returned to my parents' home where I spent the evening. My parents still live in the same house they brought me home to when I was born. I can actually sleep in my boyhood bedroom if I so choose, but I usually end up falling asleep on a huge pillow-soft couch in the family room, as I did on this visit. My father fell asleep while lounging in his recliner and my mother was lying on another couch in the family room, a late night television show playing just as a formality. The volume was turned very low while we visited. As time passed, my mother quit talking, which is a sure sign that she's sleeping, and my father began to snore. I looked at each of them, two innocent children, sleeping peacefully, a father's snore, a mother's breath, whispering, a melody.

Having gone through drug rehab years ago, and after being introduced to the medical and psychological worlds' pathological models, I began to explore and question the history of my childhood. I found that my parents had not proven to be the faultless gods of a perfect world. I went through: *if only they hadn't done this and if only they had done that* for a few years, justifiably, as I thought then, alienating myself from them and reveling in my role as victim.

It took me a while to differentiate between my parents' humanity and the godly as well as ungodly demands I was so good at imposing upon them. It also took me a while to separate the love and good will they have for me from the inner voices of over-critical parental, social, and collective religious dogmas that I have inherited. I guess what I'm saying is that my parents aren't without fault, but I no longer expect them to be. I'm so grateful to have them; so grateful now to be able to hear their music.

Thank you Adam.

January 26, 2001

I'm waiting for Jenny. That's a whole book in itself: *Waiting for Jenny*. Why I'm waiting, I can't tell you; guess it's necessary in order for me to move on. Move on? Yes, I'm dying, or at the very least it feels as if this is happening. I met Jenny last year. We hung out for several months, but nothing more than a friendship developed between us, and when I say nothing more than a friendship, I mean no sex! Not even a goddamn kiss!

That's been my story for the last couple of years having left behind an old life that I had mastered to step into the domain of the unknown. Looking back, stepping into the unknown was really stepping back into myself and into life, but it certainly felt more like stepping into my grave as opposed to living life at its fullest.

I can't give you a logical reason why I had to leave my career and identity behind. All I can tell you is that for a few years I had been an angry, volatile man who feared death. That was reason enough for me.

Jenny, for whatever reason, never really was able to warm up to me, or at least not in my time frame. She told me she had no sex drive at this point in her life and the more I was around her, the clearer that became. She's probably having as hard a time as I am, trying to find a way to fit in and exist in this world.

The course of my relationship with Jenny is indicative of what is happening within me; my attempts to form a deeper, more meaningful relationship with Jenny have failed because I have yet to learn how to form a deeper more meaningful relationship with the Jenny within, or the feminine aspects of myself. I really don't know what the hell that means, but I think that's what my problems are about. You see, sometimes I have a hunch or a knowing of sorts about what my problems are; I just don't know how to blink my eyes and make everything better.

It's been two years since I left my old world behind. One thing happens for certain when a person runs away; it happened to me anyway. I took with me all of my projections and distorted beliefs from the institutions and people who I believed to be the cause of my discontentment. That's right, I packed them all up in my bags and hauled them right along to my new life. Problem is that they don't fit in and there's no way in hell I'm going to return them to all those assholes to whom I once paid tribute.

So, here I've sat for the last two years without anyone to shuck my shit on, not that I haven't made an honest effort to do so. While taking some classes at the community college to occupy my idle time, I found a few teachers who made good scapegoats. It didn't last for long, though.

Jenny is another person who doesn't fit into any of my old beliefs; my old mold of Woman. I was driving with her one day when she asked how I was doing. I told her that I'd gotten over being mad at her for not fucking me and decided we could still be friends. Her comeback was something like: "Oh, how wonderful! That's so grown up. And, besides, it's not my job anyway." That should have been my first clue that my old way of being had passed.

Normally, I'd have shit-canned a woman like Jenny just out of sheer principle to the men's movement, but, for some reason, my pecker's playing tricks on me. That's not exactly the truth; let me try it again. For some reason, my heart's playing tricks on me. It's actually leading me to believe that I can encounter a beautiful woman and enjoy her company without the demands of having to play hide the wiener with her, or at least having to trick her into bed.

Well, we had our moments, and Jenny's still my friend in spite of myself, and probably because she still hasn't fucked me. I learned a lot, too. In the past two years, I've had more women in my life than ever before and I've learned a lot from every one of them. Seems I've had to make some sort of a sacrifice to learn things, though. You see, I've had all these women, but none of them have been sleeping with me, and it's driving me insane, not to mention these aching balls of blue I've been forced to tote around.

You know, there's something about becoming more aware of what unconsciously runs a person. Awareness is a thief. It's robbed me of an illusion; it's robbed me of the belief that the only way a man can make love to a woman is by physically penetrating her. It's robbed me of the illusion that my main goal in life is an orgasm; my dick is no longer leading me around the way it once did. Well, it actually is, but for some reason it has decided to share its navigational duties with my heart, and now I'm being led back out into the world with a heart-on, and let me tell you, I'm not always so goddamn happy about this. At times, being a mister-nice-guy just about makes me want to puke.

It makes sense why death seems to be looming around every corner. After forty years in the desert, it feels that I am finally beginning to live my own life. I mean, living my own authentic life instead of a life ruled by dogmatism. I don't have a job, I'm not going to school and I've been living off a credit line that is close to reaching its limit. I've applied for a fifteen thousand dollar loan so that I can run off to Europe for a couple of months in hopes of reconnecting with a beautiful Irish woman who I had a single ten-minute encounter with five months ago in a coffee shop in Carmel.

Yeah, that's right, I'm living. For the first time in my life, I'm actually living and it scares the shit out of me. I just know that God's up there, peering down from his celestial throne, waiting for me to slip. Yeah, almost like he's fixin' to backhand my hotshot, little-fucker-self right smack dab back into my old world, or death: one and the same. I feel like an escaped prisoner who has just cunningly scaled the walls of hell and quietly scampered to the nearest bush to take refuge from Yahweh's wrath, hoping not to wake the almighty one as He snores away. I just know that bastard's about to come to, catch on to me and turn my scent over to a pack of thirsty bloodhounds.

I'm not going back, I tell you. There is no fucking way I'm going back to those shackles. No more ball and chain for this man. I've been serving the wrong god. I've been living in Yahweh's heaven, and I've come to believe that I'd have preferred suffering Satan's banishment as opposed to living in heaven's hell.

A liberated man has no need to justify himself. "You hear that, God? I said I have no need to justify myself... What's that? Then stop doing it? I will just as soon as you'll let me." You see, I've stopped justifying myself to the world and others... "So what's my problem then? God, you're my problem. Just turn your head and let me run. You've got all you need. Just set me free to roam and live my life, what's left of it. Go back to sleep, goddamn-it, and dream up a new world: A world where I can be free..."

January 26, 2001 - Midnight

My ass aches. My bunghole burns and my crotch is chafed from sagging into this office chair. I'm pissed; television is playing late-night sex shows. The whole flippin' world is getting laid except me. What the fuck is wrong with me? I mean... I can't even make love to this PowerBook because of my inflamed asshole. I need a new kind of sex, a new lover. I need the scent of a woman to lure me from this trance, a scent so sweet that I'll never tire of lapping up her juices. I need to breath in her image, her kiss. I need her red-hot rosy ass cheeks doing the cha-cha on my lap, my...

I'm so tired of myself, fearing death, but I'm halfway wishing... That's not true. I just don't particularly enjoy my state of being this evening.

It was nice to be with Jenny today, but after she left, I felt sad. I'm still sad and more than just a little bit lonely. It was important for me to reconnect with her. I needed to meet her from an objective place as opposed to blaming her for not understanding me, for not being what I would have liked her to be. I needed to see the real Jenny, not a Jenny that I was dreaming up. I had to honor her humanity, her creation: the miracle of her very existence.

I'm just feeling sorry for myself because I'm not in love and curled up with the woman of my dreams. I'm not sorry it wasn't Jenny; she isn't the type of woman who I can be in love with anyway. I don't feel received by her, and perhaps this has to do with me not being able to receive her or myself, but for whatever reason, we simply were unable to come together as lovers for reasons that my conscious awareness currently does not understand.

I suppose I could analyze it, try to come up with reasons why we are, or she is the way she is, to give my ego something to hang its hat on, but it would be just another failed attempt, just as all of our other encounters failed and returned us to ourselves, all futile masturbation. It's almost as if we are courting ourselves, the real reason we came together was to simply be a mirror for each other.

I phoned Sheila a few days ago and she still hasn't returned my call. I'm beginning to believe she's not going to move in here after all. It won't upset me if she doesn't, although I would like to know what's going on with her. I wouldn't mind keeping the place for the month of February, anyway. Looks as if I won't leave for Europe until the following month. I e-mailed Sophia about the seminar in Florence, Italy the end of March. She mentioned it to me while we were in Sedona. It is on the images of Mary Magdalene and exploring the feminine side of the psyche. Maybe I'll go; then try to catch up with Kelli afterwards?

January 28, 2001

It's been a long day. I packed more this morning and talked to Sheila. Says she wants to take over the apartment on the 15th. I suggested we postpone it until March 1st, and she agreed. She doesn't want the place anymore, just doesn't know how to tell me, and she doesn't want to lose her option. That's fine with me, because I'll have a place to sleep and shower when I'm in town.

Had an early afternoon coffee and lunch before heading over to Jenny's to help her move some things around her house. On the drive back to my studio, I passed Cecilia's place in Skyline Forest and decided to give her a call. I once sold advertising with Cecilia. After moving to the Peninsula and living here for eight months, I thought I needed a job and was hired to sell advertising. The job was short lived, but my friendship with Cecilia has lasted.

Cecilia was home when I phoned, so we made plans for dinner. I picked her up at seven-thirty and we went to Pablo's for Mexican food and then to Starbucks for coffee. I went through the whole routine of rebelling against the whole semantic imposition by ordering a large, in Starbucks' language a medium, white-chocolate, soy, mocha and they began to make a 'grande.' They only charged me for a medium, but I insisted on a large 'vente' not a large 'grande.' Turned out that I got the best of them this time: a 'grande' for the price of a 'vente'. Come to think of it, this may very well be my first lesson in Italian. The damn thing was cold.

I took the drink back and asked the tall, dark Jamaican attendant to steam it, but it was against policy, so they had to make a new, large, white-chocolate, soy, mocha, but first I had to get a lesson in steaming soy milk. Did you know that by steaming soymilk in excess of 140°, it burns? That's why, as a new policy, Starbucks only steams soymilk to 120°, and I was informed that in the future I need to instruct the attendant to *over* steam my soymilk by 20° but that they couldn't be responsible if it burned. After receiving this long explanation, the woman manager looked at me and asked if I understood why my 'grande,' I mean my 'vente,' or whatever the hell it was, white-chocolate, soy, mocha wasn't hot enough. I told her not really and that all I wanted was a *hot*, large, white-chocolate, soy, mocha.

Now I've got a belly full of fermenting beans boiling down below, and with every belch the remnants of a white-chocolate, soy, mocha comes bubbling up out of my nose and ears. All I wanted was a goddamn cup of coffee. It's Yahweh again; the bastard's punishing me for some unknown reason. The wind probably shifted and he caught my scent.

Why do I need this Yahweh character so badly? Why do I crave this condemnation and punishment? I need an exorcist.

I've got a bigger problem with Yahweh than I do with Satan. Satan's an asshole from the get go; I just accepted that. Perhaps they're two sides of one coin? This whole thing just never ends: coming to terms with my existence, whatever you want to call it. It is all a continuum, circular, no beginning and no end. I'm beginning to believe that I am - or humanity is - simply a vessel in which consciousness is born. We go around living our lives trying to satisfy the demands of our egos, and occasionally God, momentarily, shows Him or Herself to us in flashing glimmers of awareness while our egos are distracted, off trying to cling to another fleeting illusion.

So what's this all about anyway, life that is? I mean, what the... I don't believe that we were just put here, or created, I should say, to be slaves to life and all of the imposed dogmas of society and religion; but really, why was I born? For what purpose did I come into being other than to be a vessel through which my creator can experience life? This is really getting bizarre; all I've learned is being shit-canned. I've had to set my external physical mother free and accept that the mother who haunts me is an entity within, and now I'm poking at the possibility of having to do the same with the God of my youth.

I'm scratching around with the concept that Yahweh,

the almighty, omnipresent, omniscient, wrathful God, is all something I dreamed up. The only reason He's an asshole is because that's my only image of God. The nature of this God's haunting, omniscient omnipresence is simply my inability to escape from myself. In other words, Yahweh is all a projection; He's who I need Him to be.

It is I who can never take my eyes off myself. I need a Yahweh-God to blame in order to justify the disdainful and wrathful ways in which I see and relate to myself. I'm my own judge, jury, and executioner. I have stood in my own courtroom, before my very own bench, for most of my waking life, handing down sentence after sentence in response to my perceived and distorted view of being a rotten, good-for-nothing-sinner who will never measure up to the self-imposed dogmas to which I ascribe.

What happened to the wonder, the miracle and the awe over the simple fact that somehow I, and every other creature that has ever been born, should, for all practical purposes, never be or have been. A new image of God and of Woman, this is what I told Adam I was in need of almost four years ago. A new image of God and Woman is what I told Sophia when I met her, too. Perhaps what I needed, or need, is a new image of myself?

February 5, 2001 - Mid-Morning

It is Adam's 85th birthday today. Received an e-mail from Sophia saying there's a place for me in Florence. I messaged back and asked her to hold the space. If I get the loan I've applied for, I'm going to Europe.

Sense, why try to make any sense of it? It is what it is. I have no job, not a clue of what I'm to do with my life, and, at the same time, fear death is lurking not far behind. It will devour me if I stop moving, stop following whatever it is that I am following, and it certainly isn't sense.

Trying to make sense of any of this right now would only slow me down and allow the Grim Reaper to step closer. So what am I to do? Go to the doctor and let him find something wrong with me, or choose to love, I mean live... is there any difference? I suppose there's only a difference if I have to make some sense of it all?

February 5, 2001 - Evening

So now what? I'm good at talking, bragging to people about going to Europe, and now I'm having second thoughts because of finances. If the Bonanza sold, I'd have a fistful of money to fund my fantasy, but that would also make sense. If I waited around long enough for it to sell, it might make a little bit too much sense; enough sense to put me six feet under or in an urn that would sit on my parent's fireplace mantle. So if the airplane sells - great, and if it doesn't, well, I've already opened my big mouth. Being a man of my word and full of pride just the same, I am going to Europe. Unless, of course, I fall in love before my flight leaves.

Had my sixth Rolfing session today. It's a restructuring type of bodywork. The Rolfer goes deep into the fascia to reawaken inner muscles that have become dormant and allowed other larger muscles to take over. My seventh session is scheduled three days from now; after that, I have three more to go, but that will be after Europe, if I return that is. Oh, I'll return, but it may only be temporary. I've got to be back for Angus's wedding in early May.

My energy is being zapped, and I know why. I'm trying to step back into an old life, back to the illusion of security that living a conventional life of commerce promises to bring. In other words, I'm trying to make sense of my life again. I'm going to have a garage sale, get rid of all the old shit that's sitting in my storage unit, or at least a good portion of it. I can use the spending money, and I can use a lighter backpack. I'm also going to shit-can the damn game of solitaire that came with this computer, after a few more rounds that is.

Aha, I beat the ol' prick on the first try. Thank god, because I couldn't have stood a three-hour battle trying to snooker this machine. It's a lot like arm wrestling with God. There's no way of winning, but occasionally He or She graciously grants me a round. I suppose we all need a blessing now and then.

I feel like a wet, wrung out towel that's about to be hung out to dry. I've been shuffled from the linen closet, to the bathroom, to the washer, to the dryer, and back into the linen closet for the last forty years. My suppleness has disappeared. I don't absorb the way I did when I was a child. I feel stiff, almost as if I no longer possess the capacity to leave a woman feeling warm and caressed as they run me over their wet, naked, dripping body. Not only do I feel different to another, but to myself as well. I seem to be waiting for the day when I will be torn to pieces and asphyxiated with Lemon Pledge or drowned in a bucket of Pinesol.

Maybe this has all been one long dream. That must be it; I'm the incarnated image of another's dream. I'm fading, or whoever has been dreaming me into existence is fading, or waking up. My image must no longer be useful to my dreamer; it feels as if I no longer fit into the realm of my creator. Could it now be time to cross the River Jordan?

It all sounds good. After all, I'm tired of being dreamed up into that old useless image anyway. It was fun while it lasted, but hell, I never fit in. Not really anyway. It was all a facade, a mere justification for my existence, fueled by an unconscious fear of annihilation.

So maybe it's time to leave my forty years of wandering in the desert behind; time to quit living a life of good intentions; time to quit hiding from my mortality; time to come home, to make a home, to love, another, myself. Yes, it is time for my dreamer to dream me into a new image. I hope he, or she, dreams me into someone who is selfless, or at least not so self-absorbed. I hope to be re-imagined into a being without want or desire - with one exception - that being the need to enhance another.

I'd like to wake up and find myself: a walking, throbbing heart with the capacity to beat freely for all humanity. A heart big and strong enough to pump the blood of all God's creation; a heart brave enough to swallow up and contain all life's emptiness; a heart warm enough to melt away the necrotic wounds of past and future generations; a heart spirited enough to synchronize the pulse of the collective into a rhythm of compassion.

February 7, 2001 - Dream

I was in the mountains somewhere. Not far from a cabin. I was up on a rocky area with a child, and I looked down to my right and spotted a mountain lion and her cub not far from me, maybe fifty yards. I yelled back to someone in camp to get the gun, perhaps to my mother. I was scared because this lion had her cub, and I expected her to be protective and in the mode to attack anything that threatened. The lions walked closer and then down in front of the child and me. We never did get a gun. It was scary.

Then the lions took on a different form. They became tigers. They were growling and hissing, making huge cat noises. There were five of them. They were circling, not walking in a circle following each other, nor were they necessarily trying to surround and attack us, but they were milling, weaving in and out around us.

Then the scene shifted again to a cabin or another unfamiliar house. There was a rescue crew or animal experts who went into the home and bombed it with noise. Huge blasts made so much noise that it stunned the tigers and brought them out of the closets and anywhere else in the house they had been hiding. At first I thought they were going to shoot and kill these huge cats, but then realized they were just being tranquilized.

February 7, 2001 - Late Evening

I'm not quite sure what I have to say. Maybe it's nothing and maybe it's something. Maybe, maybe, maybe... Maybe I'll live to be a hundred and three and maybe I'll die in my sleep tonight. Maybe I'll never fall in love again, and maybe I'll find out what those five tigers were doing in my dream this morning, as well as the lioness and her cub.

Why didn't the lioness attack the child and me when we encountered her and her cub? Why did the tigers have to be tranquilized? Why was I unable to live with them? Guess it was important to bring them out of the closets, out into consciousness, but why did I have to tranquilize them? The only thing that makes sense is that having to deal with five live, hungry, hissing, moody tigers might just be too much energy to assimilate all at once.

It seems my psyche is compensating, taking care of me, allowing me to see what's been tucked away in my closets without having to engage them all at once, only to startle me into panic and retreating terror. One thing's for certain however: as of now, I certainly don't have the tiger by the tail, and it's just as well, because if I did, I might not know what to do with one of her, let alone five of these striped kitties.

I love tigers, though I've had only lion dreams before now. They're both beautiful animals. Tigers appear to be exotic, and I find this appealing. For some reason, they seem to possess a wild and volatile energy. Compared to the lion, the tiger seems a bit testier, easier to provoke. I don't know if this is true in the natural world, but I like the idea.

Time to turn in. Well, I can't let my e-mail go unchecked one last time before drifting off to never-never-land. After all, I might have a message from Kelli. I'll sleep and dream much better with her image provoked.

February 8, 2001 - 9 p.m.

Woke with a cold or allergies. I had a ten a.m. appointment for my seventh of ten Rolfing sessions. It was on the upper body, as in chest, neck, inner mouth, inner nostril, and the cranium. It was intense. Sophie actually unrolled a rubber finger-glove onto her pinky, lotioned it up, and made her way up my nostril. She'd get to a point and then have to stop, because I had to loosen up before she could go farther. She was actually able to get just below my eye, and then I began to sneeze like crazy.

The sneezing happened on both nostrils, and what was weird was that I sneezed while her finger was still lodged in my nose. It came from deep down in my chest and surprisingly it came as quite a relief. I actually started to laugh about it and couldn't really say why. It felt as if I were in an altered state of consciousness when she went in there. I felt it all, but in some way I had departed from my body as well; must have been some sort of survival mechanism.

When she was working on my legs in our last session, I was lying on my stomach. I kept retracting or wanting to hold myself a certain way, feeling as if I needed to protect myself. We spoke about this today, and I mentioned that I had this fear of dying or finding out that I had some catastrophic disease. The fear had surfaced since the onset of my Rolfing sessions. She suggested I might have been protecting an old wound; then it flashed to me: the orange HotWheel tracks on the back of my legs.

The HotWheel tracks were my toys. They were these inch-and-a-half plastic strips about two feet long, tracks that we used to race our matchbook-sized toy racecars on. I can recall Sophie's expression of disgust when I told her about it. Makes me cringe right now to think about the whole thing: Mother's rage, the welts.

That's why I was feeling so defensive. She was working on some old wounds and not just physical wounds, but soul wounds as well. It's as if my body has been living in an old, antiquated belief system, too. Can you imagine getting a good strapping from something that was once a Christmas or birthday gift and, to make it worse, from the person who gave them to you? If that doesn't confuse a kid, I don't know what the hell could.

I don't want to resurrect the resentment I carried for so many years towards my parents, my mother in particular, but it would be wrong to pretend these things never happened, that they don't have an impact on me forty years later. I mean, hell, I'm still terrified of Woman and of God. Between my puritanical upbringing in church and school and Mom literally and physically acting out Yahweh's rage on her kids, how else am I supposed to see and react to my world?

Perhaps this fear of death is real? The feelings are real, not something I made up out of the blue. My body is arrested in the past. I'm reliving an old dream. Actually it isn't old; it's just as fresh to me as it was forty years ago.

I went for a hike this afternoon at Garland Ranch in Carmel Valley. As I was climbing the trail to the fern pond, I started saying: "I'm still hanging on." At the time, I was thinking that I was hanging on to the social duties of being an upstanding citizen, as in getting another job, paying my bills and taxes, maintaining a good credit rating. You know, all the things that go along with being a shining star. I'm hanging on to this crap, but what I'm hanging onto even more is beyond an ideal. I'm hanging onto my childhood; I'm hanging onto a terror; I'm hanging onto the fear of annihilation by my own creator.

This is the disease coursing through my veins, and it will certainly consume me if I don't give it a voice. Mother; I don't want to expose her. I don't want to punish her any longer. She, too, suffered at the hands of her own mother and the dogmas of a religion. She, too, has endured the wrath of Yahweh, and I'm not going to continue by beating her, but I do have to express this. I must find my voice in order to free myself from the shackles that have bound me for all these years, the same shackles that have bound generations for centuries, and the same shackles that have kept me from loving and being loved.

No wonder I'm tired. Unknowingly, my body has been dragging around the weight of those HotWheel track welts like a little, toy, Tonka tow-truck tugging around a thirty foot Winnebago. This fear, this terror, has been calling to me, trying to get my attention, but all that I've been able to do is cringe. They've been trying to help me, trying to lead me back to myself, trying to get me to pull over and unhook that motor home, to abandon the worthless relic. They've been trying to help me see the unnecessary strain that's been on my back, my body, my spirit, my soul.

February 11, 2001 - Mid Morning

For the record, I don't hate women; I just don't know how to love them, and in much the same way that I lack a fondness for myself. I really like women and prefer their company to men, yet being a man has graced me with that ability of understanding from a masculine perspective. I guess what I'm trying to say is that I know how to be a man, act like a man, or act like how I've been taught to be a man. That part is easy, but when it comes to being around women, and I'm around a lot of them, I'm not quite sure of how to... how to... I guess what I'm trying to say, but not wanting to say, is that I'm not quite sure how to have a woman.

At this point in my life, I'm quite uncertain of how Woman thinks of me, how she views me. There're several women in my life, yet not one is my lover. Well, that's not entirely true. I guess there's still Mary. She's a nice gal, fun and all, but even then, something is dishonest or unfulfilling about the whole thing.

It seems that I was once able to fuck on an instinctual level, but, for some reason, things have changed; my heart's getting in the way. I'm certainly not in love with anyone, not consciously anyway. Perhaps my libido has turned inward, towards a relationship within myself, quite possibly with Her, the feminine aspect of myself. Well, that's all fine and dandy, but I'm still not waking up next to a warm body in the morning.

Guess that's why I left my old world behind, in order to develop a relationship with me. Perhaps now I'll be capable of having a relationship with Woman, a relationship of depth and value that I've yet to experience because of my past infidelities towards Her, and myself. Yes, by leaving that old life behind, I might well have taken my first step towards actually having such an encounter.

February 15, 2001

The loan application was denied. I e-mailed Sophia to say I couldn't make the Mary Magdalene seminar. My buddy Ryan, a manufacturer, phoned a couple days ago to see if I could help him out, so I drove to the valley and worked a trade show. It was nice, visiting with several of my old clients, people I hadn't seen for a while. Returning to that old life confirmed my decision to leave it behind, though. I'm exhausted now. Tonight, while having dinner at one of my haunts, two different people told me I looked tired.

I woke at Mary's this morning. I spent the night with her after working my last day at the show. Mary's an old flame that gets rekindled a few times a year; last time I saw her was on my birthday. After having rolled around together in a morning cha-cha-cha session, she decided to ask me what she was to do if she became pregnant. Actually, what she really wanted to know was if I wanted to know if she got pregnant, or if I just wanted her to take care of it, as in having an abortion.

Now, I wear a condom and she's on the pill, so what the fuck was that all about? I'll tell you what it was about. She just can't shut up. She's got to open her big fucking mouth and pitch her shit my way. It ruined the whole sexual experience. What was she really asking? I mean, hell, it wasn't about getting pregnant. She was somehow trying to define our relationship. We are nothing more than friends who are fucking. And now that I think about it, she's not someone with whom I care to be all that friendly. I don't trust her, probably because I don't trust myself or the aspect that she represents about myself... ah, hell, let's step beyond an analysis of the damn drama; better yet, let me tell you how I feel about the whole damn thing.

It stinks! The whole concept of even having to deal with the possibility, that is. I just can't fuck for fun anymore. And Mary's a goddamn chore anyway. She bugs the piss out of me, question after question, and I'm not even there to be present with her. I am in the physical sense, but, on a spiritual level, I've climbed into my Bonanza and flown to the freakin' moon.

My approach to sex continues to evolve. It's been taking on a whole new meaning over the last couple of years. It's as if I was lost, or a huge dimension of me has been misplaced. Seems that ever since Lauren and I went our separate ways, all I've known how to do is to fuck on a material plane, but spiritually, I've been on a hiatus. I'm telling you, I got my heart tucked away somewhere that is safe, and the problem is I forgot where I hid it.

The last woman I slept with, for whom I really had any feelings, was Jacqueline and that was short-lived. A year has passed since our brief encounter. I really liked her and had some deep feelings that I was just tapping into and wanting to express, but she spooked and ran the other way.

It was Lauren before Jacqueline, but that ended over five years ago. I felt so deeply for Lauren; I guess that's why our sex life was so fulfilling. So, with Lauren, I lost the projected connection, and with Jacqueline my hopes of resurrecting that lost experience was fleeting, but for some reason both of these women had the characteristics on which I could project my perfect image of woman. Both of these women were the carriers of an image that internally I desperately needed but physically was unable to realize.

I suppose I wanted them to serve as a compensation for what I lacked within, and now I'm beginning to see how there's really no way for me to actually have a physical woman like Jacqueline or Lauren until I come to terms with their images that reside within me, within my soul. Only after this image no longer hovers behind me as a shadow, but instead turns to meet, greet, and encounter me face to face, will she be able to give herself to me on the physical plane. Only then will I be able to accept and welcome her into my life. Sounds good anyway, but I'll believe it when I see it. I mean, I'd like to believe in all this mumbo jumbo psychological shit that I read about: you know, love yourself and all that dung, but if the truth be known, I've got about as much faith in that crap as I do religion. It's just following someone else's recipe all over again.

February 17, 2001

I'm killing myself, repeating these old patterns. This is my disease. It's Lauren's birthday today! There was something in my dream this morning about doubling a Chinese, or a double Chinese.

Mrs. Shams didn't waste time with another one of her untimely impositions. She was quick to summon me up to her lofty palace so that we could have a chat. When I answered the phone this morning, my belly started knotting up as soon as I heard her voice.

"Hello, we have something to talk about. How's your afternoon?"

"Busy, I'm meeting a friend," I answered. We didn't have anything to talk about. *She* might have, but *we* didn't. "How about now?" I suggested, wanting to take my medicine and be done with it. "I was just leaving to go for coffee. I'll meet you at the back door."

"Well, alright then," she answered in an unsatisfied tone.

A few minutes later, I was invited into her kitchen, landing in a seat at the table and feeling like a fly about to get trapped in a saucer of honey. She had just finished her morning tea and breakfast. She cleared her breakfast tray from the table and took it over to the counter next to the sink. She picked up an envelope as she rounded the corner returning to the table. She made small talk for a couple of minutes, but it was just an excuse to create the opportunity for her to shift to the item on her agenda: the power bill.

She never did ask for more rent, but she did request that my showers be kept to a minimum in time, as well as frequency. Her request bothered me a little bit, but what was to come next made me want to tell her to shove it two-feet up her old wrinkled asshole.

"Now, I'd like you to wash the windows in return."

I didn't respond, not outwardly anyway. In my mind, I was telling her that I didn't do windows or any other nit-pick household duties and that she could go fuck herself, but I didn't. Instead, I remained silent trying to make sense of what was going on. I've learned that it's safer to shut up around the old broad.

I'm telling you, that old woman's a hungry lioness disguised as a mother sheep. She explained that she only wanted a few of the windows in the front of the house washed because the exterminator had been there while I was away and had ended up spraying and spotting them. The windows were up high and out of her reach, so I gave in to her Machiavellian tendencies for just this single request, even though I don't do windows.

February 19, 2001

It feels as if I'm in a trance. I don't feel tired or ill, just distant or removed. From what I'm uncertain, possibly from an old life, an old way of being and relating to myself and to all creation. My paranoia and hypochondria has been suspended. It appears, I have accepted my death, yet at the same time I accept my life as well.

I feel very much in the moment. All panic and terror of survival has subsided. The need of people or events to adhere to the limited perception of my personally imposed divine order has also deserted me. It is as if I need nothing more than an occasional cup of coffee and one or two meals a day. My demands have become minimal. My only wish or desire of the moment is that I remain in this poetic state of nothingness, so that I can dance with the images that float into the field of my periphery and then fade away with as much grace as their prelude. Today is sacred!

February 19, 2001 - Evening

Well, it isn't feeling so sacred now. Actually it has been a day of futile toil and misdirected intentions. I'm tired of making my bed. I'm tired of having to put the laundry away as soon as I carry it through the door. I'm tired of having to have everything in order. I mean, what the fuck; who am I trying to fool, anyway? Myself, of course! Anyone else who really knows me has seen past all my in-control pretences. I'm a neurotic, chaotic mess inside and think I can escape it all by making my bed and having everything else around my apartment nicely put away in its place.

February 22, 2001

Jared is dead. Actually he isn't, but he has left a body that has suffered a physically consuming disease for the last seven years. I received a call from my Aunt Adrienne early this morning to inform me of Jared's passing. After the call, I lay back down on the couch and cuddled up in my down comforter.

Less than a month ago, I sat with Adrienne and her partner, Nolan, Jared's father, and told them how I feared getting sick, being punished for finally following myself and living my life. I was afraid of having the almighty hand of Yahweh come down and backhand me into an early grave: just as mother backhanded me across the room as a two-year-old, while I was trying to explore and learn to express my very own creative spirit.

It was quite a profound experience I had after receiving the phone call from my aunt and lying back down on the couch. I was thinking of how my more than occasional obsessive fits of hypochondria were so invalid compared to Jared's actual physical suffering and eventually being consumed by this disease. Then a shiver surged through me; it was like a shock, a current of energy buzzing through my body. When I first felt this sensation, I wanted to stop it. Then I caught myself and opened up to what wanted expression even if it meant taking me over, even if it meant that I, too, was to die. It felt as if I was suspended in air as a very powerful vibration passed through my entire body.

After the vibration ceased, I continued to think of Jared and his place in my life. An image flashed to me: a man expressing joy, his spirit having been liberated from his body. Jared is free. The real Jared - his spirit - his soul – is no longer trapped within the prison cell of his body. Jared no longer has to fight. Reflecting on the disease that his physical body suffered, it seems right that he has received a pardon from the sentence he's been serving.

Selfishly, I want Jared physically alive and with us here today, but I must confess that Jared's passing has allowed me to view death differently. I see the possibility of death actually serving us. I'm not saying that I'm ready to die and move on from this material realm, but for some reason, today, death lost the image of being a robber and thief and took on a new image. Death became the image of a mother rescuing her infant from the arms of this physically suffering material world and delivering her child into the comfort of a loving sanctuary: a place where this infant's spirit will be fed and nurtured and allowed the freedom to express the nature of its true calling.

I can't help but wonder if Jared was with me or if he actually passed through me this morning, communed with me in a way that was beyond the limited medium of words. Yes, Jared was there with me this morning. Not, *there*, as in somewhere else, but *there* as in here, in his sanctuary where the nature of his spirit can dance and sing and he can commune with his family and friends through the vibration of the spheres.

Thank you Jared. Thank you for visiting me today. Thank

you for being my teacher in all the infinite freedom you now possess, and thank you for remembering me.

February 23, 2001 - Mid Morning

In the mail today, I received a five thousand dollar increase on one of my credit cards and at a low interest rate for six months. Fuck it! I'll have the Bonanza sold in six months. I'm e-mailing Sophia to see if there's still a place for me in Florence.

Sheila ended up flaking on the whole deal. Well, not really flaking. She would have actually taken the place, but she's working things out with her roommate and has taken a new lover in Big Sur. Sheila loves it there anyway and places to live in Big Sur are hard to find, so it's just as well.

Sheila was having a hard time telling me, because she'd made such a big deal about taking over the studio. She was oscillating between making good on her word and following her heart. I finally told her I wanted to keep the studio and that put an end to her suffering. I worked out a deal with Mrs. Shams to where I could be away for a month and still pay the rent. That way I'll have a place to leave my goods while I'm off stumbling about in Europe.

Mrs. Shams doesn't like the idea of not having someone around the place, but it was the lesser of two evils. Either she lets me keep the studio, or I move out and she'll have to go through the whole process of finding a tenant who meets her standards, someone who will put up with her bullshit. Where else is she going to scrounge up a surrogate son who she can throw a good mind-fucking to every chance she gets?

I don't mind paying for the place while I'm away; it's cheap enough. I thought she was going to raise the rent when utility costs skyrocketed because of the energy crisis the state of California found itself in, but she didn't. Instead, she used it as an open-ended bargaining chip.

I must have done too good of a job on the windows. Acquiescing to her first request seems to have perpetuated her justification in calling on my services in the name of higher power bills. She's developed the habit of calling on me concerning more of her trivial needs, such as driving her down to the village to have her hair combed out, which is really no big deal either, but ever since giving way to washing the windows, her demands have begun to multiply like rabbits. I just haven't found it in me to tell the old lady to go to hell.

February 24, 2001

Received an e-mail from Sophia saying that there was still a space, but that I'd most likely have to pay an additional three hundred dollars, because I was the only man who would be attending, and the extra expense was for having my own room. I replied to Sophia's e-mail saying that the three hundred wasn't a problem. Then I e-mailed Kelli to see about a dinner-date.

February 27, 2001 - Midnight

I've been on this frickin' computer most of the day; I live a good portion of life with my head stuck in this thing! I did get one item done earlier; I booked a ticket to Zurich for the 20th of next month. Now I should know in the morning if everything took, and, if it did, I'll have my head stuck in the computer trying to figure out what to do next.

I've decided to fly to Zurich and then travel by rail through the Alps and down to Florence. When I'm finished in Florence, who knows where I'll go, besides Ireland that is.

I'm not feeling too creative lately. Perhaps I've just got to let my life take form. Chaos is becoming a greater part of my existence, a greater part of my creative process. Maybe I'm just learning how to allow the chaos, where before, it would have been too overwhelming for me to entertain. I continue to fall deeper into uncertainty and finding, in the fall, a freedom and greater truth that no longer allows me to cling to anything.

I'm now the maker of my own life. There's no one else to blame for my discontentment, my disharmony. My life is good, whatever good means. Actually, I really don't know what my life is. Good compared to what, compared to whom? My life is bad, too. Bad compared to what, compared to whom?

I was once told by a friend to pay attention to my propensity towards resentment and bitterness and the consuming role it could play in my existence, and it makes sense. My life is my life, and it doesn't need to be compared to others, because once I start comparing, the bitterness and resentment creeps in and robs me of myself.

Yes, I'm jealous of others: their lives, loves, and successes, but if I were handed another's good fortune, I'd shit on it. I know what goes along with these images or illusions, and many of these successes are paid for with the price of one's soul.

People don't give up their souls deliberately. We are often robbed of them at an early age. It's the grand design. Having been born into another space and time, I would still have inherited a psychological history: the unredeemed sins of my forefathers, and I'm not speaking solely of my birth parents. It seems that this phenomenon is just part of life. I suppose this battle will always exist: the struggle to live our own true authentic lives, as opposed to queuing up to the order of the dogmatic and conventional demands of a lost society. If we allow our integrity to be modeled by an external authority, it becomes a graven image, a dead god: the false one to whom we pray, and fall prey. Yes, that grand external authority slowly creeps its way into the marrow of our bones and feeds on us like a cancer consuming the very essence of our lives.

March 1, 2001 – Midnight

Just got my ass beaten in solitaire, again. This flippin' computer has no mercy. All in all, it's been a good day, though. I received my airline ticket in the mail and sent out my registration and check for the Florence seminar. Now all I have to do is book a rail pass and get a room for my first night in Zurich. Bills are all paid, and I'm pretty well set. Now, for the next few weeks I'll get some exercise and read some. Oh yeah, and try to learn a little of the Italian language as well. Yeah, right!

I'm excited, being the only man in a group of twenty women in Florence. The title to the seminar is: *Exploring the Images in*

Word and Art of Mary Magdalene: central to the theme is developing one's inner image of the feminine psyche.

Now, if I can't develop a new image of the feminine in a group of twenty women, I'm buying a hard hat and a jackhammer, and I'm going to take up space along the roadside where my true calling surely awaits me. With that being said, I'm turning in for the evening to see what kind of feminines I can dream up in never-never-land.

March 1, 2001 - Noon

It's Jared's memorial service this evening. I have nothing else to say. No more written words today.

March 2, 2001 - Mid-Afternoon

After waking and exercising, I showered and drove over to the Pink House for coffee. It was close to noon when I arrived. I waited for an unfamiliar car to pass before crossing the street. The driver cautiously approached as if he'd seen me and was waiting for me to cross, so I didn't. Instead, I stared ahead without making eye contact, stubbornly out-waiting the car. The car finally drove on by as I continued to stare directly towards the Pink House. I caught a glimpse of a woman holding a dog inside of the car as it passed.

A man was driving and the woman holding the dog looked a lot like Jenny, but for some reason I was slow in tying the dog Diana to Jenny. Without turning to look, I continued walking into the Pink House as the car parked in the lot where I had just parked. Once inside, I ordered coffee, and then it hit me: maybe it was Jenny? I walked to the window and looked outside to find that the car had disappeared.

It was weird, because I had thought of her earlier this morning and one of the things I was thinking about was how we never really connected. We tried, but never were quite able to come together. It's just as well we never ended up in bed. She's too weird for me. She is, but she isn't. I mean, I like her weirdness and unorthodox way of being in the world, but she drives me batty just the same.

I guess what it all boils down to is that Jenny is lost in her own dream, just as I am lost in mine. Our eccentricities didn't mesh. I never really could picture myself doing it with her anyway. As much as I wanted a woman, a lover in my life, she didn't fit into the picture I had of things.

Jake was bussing tables when I returned to my seat. Jake is in his mid-fifties. His father was a Warsaw Jew and his mother Russian. He came to America when he was four. He never married and lives in a house that he paid for years ago, and, if the truth were known, he's probably got a million bucks worth of moldy certificates of deposit buried somewhere under his home. Jake has blue eyes and graying bushy brown eyebrows that are mostly gray. His face is full. He's a big man. If a person hasn't been around Jake much, he might appear to be meaner than hell, but he's two hundred and fifty pounds of compassion. He loves kids. Hell, Jake seems to love everything. Well, everything that doesn't appear to want something from him.

He works at the Pink House a couple of days a week, but he won't take a paycheck. He doesn't give a shit about the money, and he doesn't want anyone thinking that they own him and vice versa. The only reason Jake shows up is to commune with the outside world. He shows up Fridays and Mondays for work, and all he wants is coffee, a meal, and a place to connect with people. Jake has a kind of unconventional wisdom. He has the uncanny ability to bring people back to themselves, even when the rest of the world is screaming and demanding conformity.

Lydia, one of the women working at the Pink, made a café Americano for Jake and myself to sip during our rap session. Jake and I are friends. We understand each other; we're both rebels. We found a table in the back room of the old Victorian house and started our jive.

"I saw that woman who I asked out the other day," Jake said, as he leaned back in his chair.

"Which one's that?"

"You know, that one I asked to the movies. The one that slapped me across the face with an, 'I'm busy.'"

"Oh, yeah, that one."

"Yeah, saw her in the grocery store. She acted like she didn't see me. I thought I'd at least say hello to her, but when I turned, she was gone."

Jake didn't talk about women very much. I knew he liked women, but he didn't like games, that cat-and-mouse crap.

"I mean, shit! All I did was ask her to a movie. She wouldn't even have to talk to me. I'd just go by her house to call on her, walk her to the theater, and then walk her home. I just wanted a hug. But no, she's just got to stab me in the heart with an, 'I'm busy.' What's that all about, anyway?" Jake asked, in a dejected tone.

Understandably, the rejection nagged Jake. He had been talking about this for a couple of weeks now. I felt bad for him. He's a gentleman. He's big and looks like he might be able to put the hurt to you, but he's harmless. I listened for a bit and then decided to change the subject.

"Yeah, Jake, Jared's memorial service was last night," I said.

"Oh, yeah, how was that?"

"Okay, I guess. I was the only one there from my aunt's side of the family besides her three kids."

"Say what, man?"

"Yeah, Nolan, Jared's father, is a black man, and Adrienne, my aunt, like me was raised a Dutch Calvinist. So my aunt Adrienne's kind of like the black sheep of the family," I said, smiling about the pun, waiting to see if Jake picked up on my humor.

He smiled and nodded, letting me know that he was following me.

"So anyway, when I moved here, I started visiting my aunt and Nolan."

"Yeah, I remember..." Jake started saying something, but I had already lost him.

He kept talking, but I was gone. Jenny had walked in and she was with another man. The vision I'd caught from the passing car was real. They were standing at the counter in the adjacent room and were ordering something. I ignored her and acted as if I was listening to Jake as he carried on with his story.

It wasn't like the love of my life had unexpectedly showed up with another man. Jenny and I hadn't hung out together for months, with the exception of the walk we took a few weeks ago. We had never become lovers, and I didn't particularly regret it. I mean, yeah, I wished that I had fucked her just for the pleasure of knowing that I tricked another woman into bed, but, aside from my need to conquer, I felt no regret in never having consummated anything more than a friendship with her.

It was that little boy shit again. I flashed back to the gathering after Jared's service last night. I was visiting with two of Jared's cousins, Shane and Justin, who had flown out from the East Coast for the service. I had been visiting with both of them and then Shane walked off.

"How old is Shane?" I asked Justin.

"He's twenty."

"How 'bout you?"

"I'm twenty-one."

"You the oldest?"

"Yep, Shane's fifteen months younger than me."

"I'm the oldest, too. My brother Freeman's twenty-one months younger than me and it fuckin' pisses me off, too!"

Justin looked at me oddly, with an uncertain smile.

"Well, I mean, I love my brother, but I had her all to myself until that little bastard came along and fucked things up."

Justin smiled and laughed a cautious laugh.

"Yeah, that little fucker robbed me of my mother's titty, and I've never been the same since. Fucked me up for life!"

Justin laughed an uncertain laugh again and shuffled in place. I wasn't sure if I was getting through to him, but I was damn sure getting through to myself.

Jake was still rapping to himself about some buddy of his who was married to a black girl. Rapping about how the guy had met the girl while she was a student, and he was a phys-ed teacher years ago somewhere back in New York. I looked up, and Jenny was standing in the doorway.

"I don't want to interrupt you, but will you see me before you leave?" she asked.

I nodded my head in confirmation, acting as if her interruption was untimely and turned back to Jake and the story I had previously checked out of, while Jenny and her new man went to have their coffee in another room. The kid who had been robbed of his mother's titty ran me for a bit longer, and then I remembered how unsuccessful and frustrating my efforts to connect with Jenny had been and began to pity the poor old boy who had to be banging his head on that all too familiar wall. Then I shifted back to being the tittiless older brother who was certain that she was probably giving herself to him like a newborn baby. Fuck, it was pissing me off. It's not that I wanted her; I was just pissed because someone else had her.

I kept nodding my head to Jake's story, every once in a while, catching a word or two of what he'd said and then repeating the words so that he thought I was actually listening to him. Another couple came in and caught my attention. I'd seen them both with other partners less than six months earlier. I'd actually watched the guy a few months ago drooling over some other woman out on the front porch.

Jake glanced up into a mirror on the wall behind me to follow my stare back to the drooler and his new woman who were seated across the room behind Jake.

"I've seen a lot of shit go down around here, Jake."

"I know," he said, still looking into the mirror.

"I saw them both lost in love with other people less than six months ago. I mean, that fucker was drooling all over himself right out there on the front porch!" I explained, feeling jealous of what I believed to be the guy's unconscious way of relating to women.

"I've been watching that same shit for years," Jake said, as he pulled his hat off and swept his hair back out of his eyes.

We carried on for close to another hour. I was avoiding Jenny. I didn't want to meet her newborn. I didn't give a shit who he was, anyway. A couple of women in their early twenties came in and sat down at a table next to ours. One of them was carrying a wedding magazine. Jake rapped on while the two women discussed wedding plans, the drooler, with his new love, dribbled all over himself, and Jenny sat in the other room suckling her latest baby, waiting for me to stop by to congratulate her.

Fuck her! I'd be damned if I was going to see her before I left. If she wanted to see me, she'd have to come to me. Fifteen minutes later she did.

"Okay, now I *do* want to interrupt you," she said, as she walked up to our table without her new friend.

Jake got up and went into the other room to see if any tables needed bussing.

"Close your eyes," she said, as she stood looking down at me.

I closed my eyes and then opened them, feeling a little awkward, untrusting, and self-conscious.

"Close your eyes," she repeated, as I closed them again, this time fantasizing about her kissing me, similar to how I craved for a morsel of my mother's attention while my baby brother hung from her side. "Okay, hold out your hand," she said.

I followed her directions as if I was in a hypnotic trance and feeling like a beggar all at the same time. I opened my eyes to find a wrapped package the size of a paperback book. "Shall I open it?" I asked. She nodded and then sat in a chair next to me. "I bought my ticket," I explained as I started to unwrap the package. She knew of my plans to visit Europe, but when we'd last talked it was all just exactly that, talk.

"When do you leave?"

"The twentieth; I fly to Zurich. Then I'll take a train through the Alps and on to Florence. I signed up for that Jungian seminar on the images of Mary Magdalene."

"And that's in Florence?"

"Yeah," I answered, as I finished unwrapping the book. It was from a well-known writer. It wasn't a novel, though. It was a book on how to write a book. Her gesture was kind, but I hate how-to books. I hate anything that attempts to impose another's truth upon me. It wasn't that I believed another's experience to be untrue; I just wanted to be left to have my own experience without the imposition of another.

"Thank you," I said, graciously, hiding my repulsion for the book. "I called to reserve my spot in Florence and they told me I had to pay an extra three hundred dollars because I was a man," I explained, shifting away from the gift.

"They're penalizing you because you're a man?" she asked, a confused look on her face.

"No. I'm just the only man who registered, so I have to

have my own room," I said smiling. "I called and told them no problem. I'd pay an extra three hundred dollars any time to be the only man in a group of twenty women for more than a week in Florence," I added and we both had a good laugh.

"Well, my friend's hungry, so I better get moving," she said.

"Oh, I thought you were in there having lunch all this time," I replied, and stood up.

"No, I saw you walking in earlier so we went to my house to get this for you."

"Oh, I thought you were in there eating. I didn't want to interrupt you," I said, before hugging her. It was another dull hug. Her hugs never had any depth; they were like a flimsy handshake.

"Let me know what you think of the book," she said, as she let go of our embrace.

"Okay, I'll do it," I lied, smiling, knowing that I'd never read the damn thing.

My mother used to bring us presents. That's how she assuaged her guilt. I don't think that's what Jenny was doing today, but I didn't want or need the book just the same. I just wanted to be nursed, just wanted to be wanted.

March 3, 2001

I'm feeling lonely. I almost picked up the phone to call an old girlfriend, but decided against it. I can still call her, but it doesn't seem right. I'm feeling self-pity, the why-not-me syndrome, but I know why-not-me. Why-not-me is really I-don't-want-it, because if I wanted something different, I'd have found a way to have it.

I hate my hair cut, so I'm wearing a USA Wilson golf hat, and I hate golf. I'm going to change into a pair of Levi's and an off-white cotton crew sweater, slip into my Tony Lama's, and then I'm going out to sing the blues.

I wanna not give a shit about what the rest of the world is doing. I wanna quit worrying about being "normal" or trying to conform. I wanna eat pasta tonight and not feel guilty. I wanna be able to look at my fat belly in the mirror when I step from the shower and not be ashamed. I wanna tell the whole world to go fuck themselves and still be the passionate object of their obsessions. I don't wanna be young, and I don't wanna be old. Other than that, I don't much know what else to tell you except to go fuck yourself.

March 4, 2001

Had dinner with Gerald and Gail tonight. Gerald is in his seventies and Gail is in her late twenties, maybe thirty; they've been together for a few months, and I'm damn glad about that because I thought Gerald was going to pop his cork before Gail came along. Out of fear and convenience, Gerald is still married, even though he can't stand his wife, or so he says. Anyway, it's nice that Gail has come around; now he's got someone to stare deep into his eyes and make him think he's God again.

I really like them both. Gerald and Gail that is; I hardly know Gerald's wife. They're so interested in me, with my life. Guess I'm a fascinating character to them. They're some of my biggest fans, and I've needed that, or at least my ego has. I could go into a whole long dialogue of what took place or at least what was said, but it seems pointless right now.

Well, one thing needs to be recognized and that is the beautiful brunette who seated me. I arrived before Gerald and Gail, and there was this hot, petite brunette wearing a conservatively short, black dress with a Cleopatra-style hair cut. I introduced myself to her as she seated me. I should have known it, another Jenny. I've got Jenny's running out of my ears; this is Jenny number four. So, I sat for a bit and admired Jenny IV as she attended to her duties and occasionally graced me with a smile as she returned after seating newly arriving patrons. When my friends arrived, Gerald said something about me taking Jenny to Florence. I just smiled.

Anyway, we had dinner and caught up on things. Gerald didn't care for his meal. He and Gail shared a Caesar salad and an order of Gerald's favorite: pasta la puttanesca. He complained about it being too fishy and watery, and Gail agreed. When one of the waiters came to clear our plates, Gerald expressed his disappointment. The waiter went back and told Cleopatra, and out she came to investigate the unhappiness.

After a formal apology, Jenny assured Gerald that his concern would be passed on to the owner of the restaurant, and that opened the door for Gerald to inquire of the owner's whereabouts. Jenny explained that he was spending more time with his family, and that she was running the show while Vito was home with wife and kids. Gerald asked if Vito ever came in, and Jenny said he was there every Tuesday and Thursday because she insisted on having those days off and then excused herself to attend to her duties.

"Well, I can tell you one thing."

"What's that?" Gerald asked.

"You won't see me eating here on Tuesday or Thursday," I answered, grinning my famous smart-ass grin.

"And she insists on having those particular days off," Gail added.

"Why Tuesday and Thursday, though," I deliberately asked out loud. Normally I'd have left it as a mystery but hoped to have stirred up enough curiosity in my two fans to have them make the inquiry for me.

"We'll find out in a minute," Gerald said. "I'll just ask her when she comes back," he said in a tone of justified confidence.

"Yeah, we'll just ask her!" Gail repeated following Gerald's lead.

I looked at Gail and smiled, wanting to tell her that curiosity killed the cat, but I held my tongue. "Well, if you'll excuse me, I need to go to the women's... I mean the men's room," I announced. I didn't want to be around when they did my dirty work. It would only make me look bad, and I didn't want to show my hand.

"Let us know what you find out," Gail said, as I slid out of the booth.

"You'll probably know before I do," said I, having no intention whatsoever of prying into Jenny the Fourth's personal life, especially when there was a curious cat ready to serve as the grand inquisitor.

On my way to the restroom, I spotted Jenny at the computer punching in an order or printing a patron's check. When I walked out of the bathroom, she still had her backside to me.

"Well?" Gail asked, as if I had something to report.

"I was about to ask you the same," I answered, knowing that the opportunity to find out about the habits Jenny courted on Tuesdays and Thursdays had yet to present itself to any of us.

We started making small talk while waiting for Jenny to walk past our booth. We'd talked about my upcoming trip to Europe, and about my interest in the seminar. I confessed that I hardly knew a thing about psychology.

As a social worker, Gail had a basic understanding in the field of psychology, but it was a far cry from experiential knowing. Not that I know a damn thing about it, but, unlike Gail, I don't claim to be an expert. A person can read about psychology or read the Bible, but words are just words. Experience gives birth to understanding, but reading about someone else's experience, be it in a psychological commentary, the biblical realm, or the Penthouse Forum, doesn't make the inquisitor an expert.

Gerald, on the other hand, looked lost. Now, he was a damn smart fellow, a Harvard Law graduate and, in addition to his law degree, had participated in several fine art classes at another university and was a collector of many a fine piece. If the truth were known, he had probably made more money trading art over the last twenty years than he had in his twenty-five-years as a lawyer. But, Gail was talking about the circular, and law is linear, and I've yet to find the alchemical recipe for a wedding of these two.

After attempting to explain the differences between the theories of Jung and Freud, we laymen gave up and decided to call it a night. Besides, we were really only waiting for Jenny and had grown tired.

"I guess we'll just have to leave with Jenny's Tuesday-Thursday whereabouts remaining a mystery," I said, reawaking a curiosity.

"Yeah, I guess it'll remain a mystery," Gail confirmed, while Gerald looked around to see if he could spot the little Cleopatra.

I asked one of the waiters to bring my jacket and began

for the front door, Gail a few steps behind, but Gerald lingered around our booth.

"It's just not the right time," I said.

"Yeah, come on Gerald, it's not the right time," Gail repeated, following my cue. It was almost as if I possessed some power. I didn't particularly like it, but, for some reason, I had commanded her allegiance. It wasn't that I'd cast some spell on her so much as that she, for some unknown reason, had passed her power on to me. I know it had to do with that psychology bullshit I had spread all over the dinner table. I laughed to myself, wishing to be half as smart as some people liked to believe me to be.

Jenny walked towards us as the waiter handed me my jacket. Gerald had waited it out, and it worked. Gerald walked towards her, but before he could inquire, Gail spotted Jenny and bluntly asked why she had Tuesdays and Thursdays off. She ran a medical billing service and had just started an Internet company of some sort.

That was enough information for me. I just wanted to make sure she wasn't doubling as a room mother in her kid's classroom on those days. Running the restaurant five nights a week and working two jobs during the day, didn't leave room for kids. That was just fine with me; I was damn well tired of competing for that long lost titty.

I held the door for Gerald and his curious feminine counterpart and turned to smile at Jenny one last time.

"It was nice to meet you," she said as I looked to her.

"It was a pleasure to meet you as well, Jenny," I answered in a soft shy tone, looking away.

March 5, 2001 - 7 p.m.

Dropped Mrs. Shams off at the museum this morning, then stopped by Adam's to return some clay he gave me to work with a few days earlier. I told him that I couldn't seem to create anything that I liked or found pleasing. He handed the clay back to me and mumbled something in a frustrated tone about my damn ego getting in the way. He seldom reacted as he did, just as he seldom made suggestions about the choices I made in my life. I agreed to hang on to the clay, and chatted with him a bit before making my way to the Pink House.

Teresa, the owner of the Pink House actually spoke to me and made my coffee. Her presence alone knots up my stomach, so you can imagine what it was like to have her make my coffee. Anger is usually seething from every pore of her being. Teresa's boyfriend, Rex, is in his mid-twenties, twenty years younger than she. The poor fucker's too young and too dumb to know that he could have a little hotty half mother Teresa's age. It doesn't surprise me that he's with her though. A mother can shit on a son for a lifetime and still enjoy his puppy-dog loyalty.

Teresa hasn't one bit of etiquette in the human relations department. If the Pink House didn't serve such good food and coffee, they'd have died on the vine aeons ago. I don't know of very many thriving businesses where you can stand at the counter and wait five minutes before you're even recognized and then have your order and money taken with a thankless you're-lucky-to-be-served attitude, but for some reason, I go back for more. I suppose Rex is hooked on Teresa's pot of coffee, too.

While mother Teresa put the finishing touches on my Americano, Jake and I greeted each other, only to be interrupted by Waylen, another regular at the Pink House, who was hollering at me from across the room. Jake walked off to bus a few tables, and I went over and sat with Waylen and another buddy of his who he promptly introduced me to, and whose name I promptly forgot. I'm tired of meeting people anyway. The more I hang around the Pink House the less privacy I have.

When I arrived two years ago, hardly a soul recognized me. I don't mind a little recognition upon occasion, but a greater part of me longs to be the invisible man again. I'm no longer just a bird perched on the rain gutter outside of this old Victorian where the locals gather to gossip about what, only hours earlier, they've sworn to secrecy. At this point, I could be a favored topic for all I know.

After hanging with Waylen and his buddy for a few minutes, I excused myself and went out to the bench on the front porch to read, but before I was into the second page of the book, Jake pulled up next to me and started talking about something. I surrendered to the fate I brought to myself, set the book down, and gave Jake as much attention as possible, having only been awake for an hour and a few swigs into my morning brew. He started telling me how it was growing up in New York, being Jewish and living in Brownsville.

Jake was a star football player in high school, and this helped bridge the gap when it came to racial problems. Jake was big, but in all of the stories he'd ever told me about growing up in New York, he never once mentioned having to use violence. He'd tell me about how he was always able to 'rap' his way out of a mess. He always made it a point to talk about how he would walk away from words. Most people couldn't, he said, and that was when the words turned into physical violence. "They could rap their shit all they wanted, just as long as they didn't touch me," he'd say.

Jake was deep into one of his stories when Waylen walked over to interrupt. Waylen and Jake couldn't stand each other. Waylen always complained that Jake would never shut up, and Jake had the same complaint about Waylen. Just as soon as Waylen showed up, Jake left.

"How's it going?" Waylen asked, really wanting to tell me how it was going for him.

"Not bad, man. Not bad. How about you?"

"I'm hanging," he said, in a downed tone.

"What's goin' on?" I asked in a matter of fact way that gave Waylen permission to cut to the chase.

"Danette's gone," he answered, referring to his on-again off-again girlfriend who he'd be worshipping one week and cussing the next.

"I saw you with her last week. You both seemed pretty lost in each other then."

"Yeah, we were hanging out. She moved home to her parents, though," he explained. Her parents lived a few hours south of Pacific Grove. "It's the best thing; she'll never change," he added.

"Yeah, but it still hurts," I said, to confirm his distraught state.

"Yeah it does. Hey man, I've gotta get movin'," he said,

having made the connection he needed so that he could get on with his day.

"Okay, take it easy, huh?"

"You too man. I'll see you around," he said, walking down the porch.

Waylen was about to hit the bottom step when I reached for my book, but right then Jake rounded the corner and sat down beside me. I never bothered to pick up my read. I didn't expect to get much in while I was there, but occasionally I did enjoy some solitude on the Pink House's front porch. The book was there to help me through my occasional valley of shadows, but mostly to keep me from having to converse with anyone new; it was also a blind to hide behind while I checked out the hotties.

Jake started telling me about one of the highlights of his high school football career, or about his coach's father who had a pool hall and was a bookie, and I listened the best I could. To me, Jake is wisdom. At times he'll ramble on for hours, and I listen, and most of what he says, I've heard from him countless times before, like the continuing saga of his scatter-brained friends who have moved out to the Peninsula from New York. But, within the mass of Jake's repetitions, a new nugget of wisdom always seems to emerge.

Now, whether he knows he possesses this wisdom or not, I can't tell you. All I know is that when he's handing it to me, it's real. There's no doubt about it, and I say this because I can feel it in my guts. I sit around, listening and waiting for it every time we get together, and once I receive the message, I can leave. It might take two hours, it might be ten minutes, but as soon as I receive it, I say a silent thank you to Jake and shortly after, excuse myself to go about my business.

Mother Teresa walked through the front door and down the steps to her car while Jake carried on about his silly-ass friends.

"She actually talked to me today," I said, as Teresa drove away.

"Yeah, I noticed. Right before she started dissin' me for telling you the same story I was telling someone else, earlier," Jake answered.

"Yeah, and my guts started knotting up too. You know..."

Jake nodded without saying a word, waiting for me to finish saying what I'd started to say, but already knowing what was coming. "I feel all twisted up inside whenever she's here. I mean... I'm not judging her. I'm just telling you how I feel around her. Like right now, when she pulled away, my guts started to unwind."

"Shit, man! That's how everyone feels around this place."

March 7, 2001 - 2 a.m.

All that's left to do before leaving for Florence is to purchase a rail pass, study some Italian, and pack. Other than that, I'm all but there. I leave in less than two weeks. It's really happening. I feel alive and healthy again. For the last several months it felt as if some catastrophic disease was consuming me, and maybe it was, but it seems to have subsided.

The last of my ten Rolfing sessions is this Thursday. Since I don't leave until the twentieth, I decided to finish the process before setting off on my adventure. I'm exercising, I'm feeling strong again, stronger than ever, not feeling like a whipped dog anymore. I'm feeling like a real live man again, and not some wounded, rejected little boy, the displaced firstborn.

I've never really felt this way. I've been living as the victim; I thought that I had stepped beyond it, but it's very subtle. I was very much aware of how the "why me?" ran me - that became conscious to me some time ago - but it's this "why-not-me?" that had to be flushed out from behind the rocks. This is one of the demons that has had me by the short hairs ever since losing mother to Freeman.

I'm going to tell you about Sheila, how I set her off when she called the other night. I'll admit it here, but probably never to her face, that I was out of line with my flippant remark about her not being able to wait for her current lover to get back from his three week vacation. I should have kept my damn mouth shut even if it is the truth.

I was teasing her about growing tired of her man's absence and taking another lover, which is a damn good possibility, knowing Sheila, and it isn't a problem for me. Well, it is a little bit of a problem, because if she *did* take another lover, it wouldn't be me. Sheila isn't interested in me that way. She'll go out with other men my age, but it's the other guys who manage to get into her pants, or rather I should say, she allows into her pants. It's that whole titty-thing again.

Casey, her current man, took off on a three-week fling to Cuba with another woman, a trip planned long before Sheila and he had become intimate. Sheila had been seeing this other guy for close to a year, and when the excitement of whatever they shared together petered out, she dumped him, and within a couple of weeks took up with this Casey. They'd been flirting with each other for several months, anyway. So you might say it had been in the works.

I've known Sheila for a year and a half, met her while she was working at Tillies, a restaurant that caters to the locals. She was just breaking up with her then current boyfriend: the guy who she left for the next guy who she left for the guy who just left for Cuba, and that's the simple story. I guess I could tell you about a few of her short-lived affairs, but they were nothing more than that, not that they were any different than her long-lived affairs, both served the same purpose: dressing for an open wound.

I'm something else for Sheila, and I'm still not quite certain what it is, but I'm something different for her, and maybe that's all I'll ever need to understand. As much as I hate to admit it, my flippant remark about her not lasting three weeks was fueled more by a jealous why-not-me, than a simple jousting among friends. If I was a woman, I'd have probably gotten away with it, but I'm a man, and even a whore doesn't want to be called a whore by a man. If a woman calls another woman a whore, it can be taken as a jealous compliment, but if a man calls her a whore, it becomes character assassination, and I've done just this.

She called the other evening from a restaurant down in Big Sur where she was having drinks and appetizers with one of her girlfriends.

"Hey Malcolm, what's up?" Sheila asked, greeting me in her normal cheerful, upbeat fashion.

"Hey Sheila, what's going on?" I asked, expecting her phone

call. We had talked a few hours earlier, her hinting about me driving down the coast to join her for dinner. Sheila can't stand being alone.

"I'm still with Chelsea, we've only had one appetizer," she explained, which meant that she'd probably had a few glasses of wine and wasn't finished hanging out.

"That's cool. Why don't you girls catch up on things," I suggested. The evening was stormy, and a drive to Big Sur was less than inviting, especially to court a woman who has no intention of taking me to bed.

"Yeah, I'm burnt. Think I'll hang out here for a while and then call it a night," Sheila answered.

"Sounds good to me."

"But I did want to call, you know. I'd expect a call from you just the same," she hinted.

"Okay, that sounds good to me. I'm not up for the drive anyway," I answered, truthfully. "That way if you run into something good you can take him home to keep you warm tonight," I teased.

"I met these two guys last night who are staying at the monastery," Sheila answered excitedly. Not being her lover, yet a close friend, allowed Sheila the space to open up to me about her escapades. I had started it all several months earlier when I began bragging about my past exploits with women. Over time, Sheila began to trust me and told me her personal history. Her bravado seemed more of a confession, whereas my bragging was a way of compensating for the inferiority I felt because she hadn't chosen me to be her lover.

I wouldn't go to bed with her anyway; I know her too well. I really like her; actually, I love her. I love Sheila, because she's me. I have the same gashing wound, and God knows I've tried to heal it in countless ways, many of the remedies similar to Sheila's. Now, with that being said, I was still jealous. There was still that pissed off little boy in me who had lost his mother's titty to his younger brother thirty-eight years earlier.

"Sheila, you'll never last three weeks," I said in response to her enthusiasm about the guys she met from the monastery. It happened; the voice of that pissed off little two-year-old had finally slipped past the persona of maturity, slipped out from behind the rock where years ago I had stashed him away, and out plopped his truth.

"Don't even be saying that!" Sheila snapped back. I knew it struck a nerve because of her reaction. I didn't mean to hurt her intentionally, but intention or no intention, my words had penetrated through to that tender spot.

"I was just teasing!"

"You'd better be just teasing," she said, still in a dejected tone. "I can last three weeks. You want to bet?"

"How much?" I asked, buying time, knowing that I had to choose my words wisely.

"Hundred bucks," rolled off her tongue in a split second. Sheila was fast and especially when she came to defend her character.

"No way!" I answered.

"That's right because you don't have a hundred to lose," she announced righteously.

I didn't respond, knowing that it was time to acquiesce.

"Okay then," Sheila said, indicating that she had corrected any misgivings and that we were moving on to a new topic. It seemed I had escaped any stings from the hive I'd just kicked. "Well, I work tomorrow night if you want to drive down for dinner," she added.

"I might. Let's see what it's like tomorrow," I answered.

Something has changed for me. I'm tired of just being a friend who stands by while she gets all the action: I've been satisfying her emotional needs, while her physical needs are met by another, where there are no emotional ties. I know that's what she's doing, because I've done the same for years. I'll still be her friend. I'll always be her friend, but my attention is shifting elsewhere.

Sheila's had her way with me and I've let her. I'm glad I did. For some reason she needed a man like me in her life; perhaps someday she'll have a man with whom she can share herself emotionally as well as physically, and perhaps I'll be able to share something similar with a woman, too.

Gerald phoned the following day, so I never did make it down to Sheila's; I didn't even bother calling. She called again yesterday. She has school in the evening and often tries to connect with me before her class. I was in the shower when she phoned, so I returned the call after drying off. I told her that Adam was playing tennis until one or two and that I planned to meet up with him after his match, otherwise, I was free.

I went quite deep into some dream images with Adam that day and was lost in the process when his wife knocked on the door, startling me back to the waking realm. Sometimes our communion has a way of bringing time and space to a screeching halt.

I was still considerably fragmented when I left Adam's house, but this happened quite often. I've actually grown accustomed to living life this way in spite of my ego's retaliatory fits of trying to drag me back to the conventional life through bouts of self-doubt and fear-driven paranoia. I've been dying for well over the last year, and not without a whole lot of kicking and screaming, but dying just the same.

In my mind, I have suffered a variety of catastrophic illnesses, which I was certain would take me to my grave within a very short time. Funny thing is, the short time catches up to me, and I'm still not dead, then I have to dream up a whole new catastrophe in order to keep my obsessive compulsive mind fixed upon thinking that it has some sort of control while my soul reorients. I'd be awfully ashamed if the whole process had been video taped. I'd be the innocent fool running around like a headless chicken, but in reality only suffering from a hangnail.

Anyway, back to Sheila. I had just pulled away from Adam's when about a half a block from his house I caught a glimpse of Sheila's Honda. She used to work around the corner from Adam's, and I had once shown her his place. Normally I'd have hidden the fact that I was delving into my dreams but, for some reason, I'm proud to be associated with Adam. It actually makes me feel a bit noble. I've clouded it up with nobility anyway, but if the truth be told, not finding Adam would probably have left me dead or in prison for killing some poor soul who was the object of one of my many misdirected impositions.

I was on a one-way street, so I pulled over. Sheila pulled up and parked behind me. She reached over to unlock the passenger side door.

"Hey Sheila," I said, trying to sound upbeat like she

always did, even if I was still floating around in my archetypal heaven.

"Hey Malcolm! Did you get my message?" she asked in a cheerful tone, but something wasn't right.

"No," I answered, shaking my head.

"I lost my little gold book, so I called your house because I couldn't remember your mobile number."

"Well, what was the message?" I asked, looking down to the passenger's side floorboard that was cluttered with trash and several empty water bottles.

"I was going to Tillies to hang out and have a coffee or something."

"How about Morgan's instead?"

"Sounds good. I'll follow you."

"Okay," I said, nodding and looking down at the floorboard again. "Hey, Sheila, Why don't you clean some of this shit out of your car?" I suggested while closing the door.

"You know what, maybe I like that shit!" she yelled out of the driver's side window as I walked towards my Expedition. I knew she was still pissed, or at least hurt. Her eyes had revealed her emotions in spite of her feigned smile.

There were a couple of open parking places in front of the French Bakery, so I parked and Sheila took the space directly behind mine.

"Hey there Mr. Clean. Mr. Everything has to be perfect," she said, as she stepped onto the sidewalk.

I gave her a great big hug, kissed her on the forehead, and then picked her up and spun around half a spin before setting her down. I still had a penance to pay for my flippant remark on the phone the other night, as well as for not bothering to show up or call her the following evening.

"Want to go in here?" I asked, eying the pastries as we passed the bakery.

"No, come on!" she demanded.

I felt like a kid, sitting in the cart in a checkout line, getting his knuckles rapped by his mother when he was just inches away from snagging the object of his desire. We kept on to Morgan's, which was just a short block from our parking places.

After getting our drinks, we sat at a table outside. I still felt fragmented, and edgy. I had yet to get myself glued back together from my time with Adam, but that wasn't the only source of my discontentment.

"So how was it at Adam's?"

"Okay, I'm not all here yet, though," I explained.

"What happened?" Sheila asked, wanting to have something to talk about.

"I'm not quite sure yet," I explained, telling the truth, but even if I was aware of what was going on right then, I doubt that I'd have spoken of it. What often happened in the time we shared was sacred. I didn't mind talking about it later, after its impact had subsided, but while I was in the middle of things, I found it important to treat my process with silent respect. I had learned that if I didn't, I could very well be robbing myself of something.

I started telling her about my conversation with Shane and Justin, Jared's two cousins who had flown out from the East Coast for Jared's memorial service. Told her about how Justin's younger brother Shane had walked off, and I started telling Justin about how I loved Freeman, but hated the little fucker too, because I was never the same after he had come along and robbed me of my birthright.

"That's not right!" Sheila started.

"Well, I didn't..."

"You shouldn't be angry at him for that. It's not his fault."

"I'm not angry at him..."

"Yes you are!" Sheila interrupted again. "I can hear it in your voice. I can see it."

"Sheila, you're prejudging me. You didn't let me finish telling you the story."

"Okay. Okay," she said, in a tone that told me she'd already made up her mind.

"You're pissed at me."

"No, I'm not," she quickly snapped.

"Yes, you are."

"I am not," she insisted, defensively.

"You can be mad at me if you want. It's alright with me."

"I'm not, but I know I can."

I took in a breath and sat back in silence.

"What was it that you said? I can't last?"

"I don't know exactly how I said it, but anyway..."

"You know I just don't give it up to anyone."

"Sheila, my remark wasn't a judgment of your character."

"I know, you were clear about that in your e-mail," she said, but she didn't know. Sensing her reaction to my remark the other evening, I had sent her a message saying that I was sorry if I had hurt her feelings, and that I wasn't attacking her character, but to Sheila, the message was just words.

"I don't see you as a slut," I said, risking having more of her anger sent my way. I didn't see her as a slut, either, even if that jealous little two year-old in me did get a nice jab in the other evening. I would never trust her enough to be her lover, but I didn't view her as a slut. I didn't trust her, because I didn't trust myself. I know what lengths a person will go to in order to find some relief for that insatiable longing to be loved, to feel complete.

"Well, you know how sensitive I am about that."

"It's not my fault Sheila. I wasn't judging you. You might very well meet another guy today and take him home. You know that, too, and even if you do, I don't think any less of you. It might be the best thing that'll ever happen to you. I mean, who the hell am I to say it's wrong?" I reasoned, as I caught Sheila eyeing a young, good looking cop who had walked into the courtyard where we were sitting.

"I think that's the cop I met one night at a party. He's a motorcycle cop," she said, thinking out loud.

"It's not my fault, Sheila!"

"I can't help the way I am," she said, as she stood up and followed the cop to get one last look before he rode away. Then she walked back to our table with a lustful grin on her face.

"Sheila, it's not my fault!"

March 7, 2001 - Late Afternoon

I was just looking over the correspondence that Kelli and I have exchanged over the last few months. I never dreamed it would come to over sixty pages worth of whatever I should call it. Perhaps I should be ashamed of such foolishness? I'm at a coffee house on Ocean Street in downtown Santa Cruz. All the tables inside are occupied, so I'm sitting outside in a really nice garden patio.

It's a gorgeous day. I was awake until three this morning and woke around nine, but there isn't a bit of fatigue. I'm in love today and haven't a woman in my life. Well, I have women, but I'm not talking about women; I'm talking about life. I'm in love with life today and at peace. I woke up feeling this way, and let me tell you, it's been one hell of a long time.

So, I'm in love with life again, and it tastes so sweet, like that little sliver of meat between those thin, outer two bones of a roasted chicken wing. That same Sunday afternoon chicken wing that my grandmother would pull from the oven to let me sample before the rest of the world was called into the dining room for dinner. Ah, and that angel food cake with the different colored specks baked into it, and the powdered sugar glaze frosting that was drizzled over this sweet piece of... and when I was a seventh grader, on our way home after the last-day-of-school picnic, riding together in the back of my father's camper, a 1963 white Chevy pickup truck, kissing the prettiest of the eighth-grade girls who had just graduated goodbye... and when I was seventeen-years-old, at the drive-in theater with my high school sweetheart, the first time I ever... and that first swig of whiskey; only a true alchy could saver a whiskey like I did that very first time. And Lauren, the love of my life; I could find no part of this woman that I didn't want to gobble up, devour. I could have lapped up her juices for the rest of my life, the only sustenance I would ever need. Making love to her was like sucking that last sliver of meat from between those two bones.

March 8, 2001 - Midnight

Sheila phoned this morning. She stayed in town with one of her girlfriends last night and wanted to meet before heading back to Big Sur. I caught up with her an hour later at Whole Foods. I had a Rolfing session scheduled at noon across from the market.

Sheila came buzzing into Whole Foods like a whirlwind. She was running late. She'd been at Target loading up on plants to take home to her garden. I hugged her and then like a dust devil she spun off into the market to get something to eat; I sat back down in the wooden booth and sipped my coffee. I was gone; it takes me a long time to wake up, forty years to be exact. Minutes later Sheila returned with a plate from the deli with a vegetable stack and a California Roll from the in-house sushi chef. So there we sat: the Turtle and the Hare.

"Okay, I met this woman in Macy's yesterday. I want you to meet her," Sheila announced, loud enough to let the blonde, who was sitting in the both just behind me, in on our conversation.

I didn't answer. I knew better. I'd been hanging around little miss Aphrodite long enough to know when to shut up. Well, most of the time that is, and this was one of the times I mastered the silence.

"I really liked her. You know, you can tell when you meet someone. You can just feel it," Sheila explained, while mixing wasabi and soy sauce together for her California Roll.

"I'm not all here yet, Sheila," I announced, just to make some noise and at the same time saving myself from having to take the bait.

"Come on. It's almost noon," she said, bouncing around in her seat and slicing into her veggie stack. "Want some?"

"For breakfast?" I asked, slowly turning sideways in the booth and pulling my left knee up to my chest.

"They're just veggies. They're good for you... so, anyway, I set Carmen up with Jess, our head chef," she announced, all proud of herself. Carmen was the girlfriend with whom she had just spent the night.

"I bet you did," I said, with a slight grin, beginning to see what was fueling her desire to find me a woman. Her motivation was two-fold. First, she'd bagged one deal earlier that morning, having set up Carmen and Jess, and now she was going for a double. The second reason is that she knows I leave in less than two weeks and she wants to make sure I have a reason to come home.

"Her name's Diana. I got her phone number. She said to

call," Sheila went on, flipping Diana's business card across the table to me.

"What's her story?"

"Was married for twenty-four years and divorced. I met her in the petite section at Macy's. She's a dirty blonde."

"Sounds like my kind of woman," I teased.

"Shut up, Malcolm. She's cool."

"Why me? I mean, what makes you think she's a match for me?"

"Because she's a neat person who needs to meet someone, and you're a neat guy who needs to meet someone," Sheila answered all cheery-like, sidestepping my question.

"She lived in Big Sur for awhile, but now she's in Pacific Grove. She has some kind of an art studio somewhere. She told me to come by to check it out some time."

"So you know her from Big Sur?"

"No, but she remembered me. She saw me with Casey."

Casey was a player. He was close to my age, maybe a few years younger and was doing what I was doing a few years ago: fucking everything in sight, and loving every minute of it. "I told her that I was just hanging out with him, but that I know how he is. You know, how he is with women," Sheila explained trying to remind me of an earlier conversation we'd had.

I didn't answer. Sheila and Casey were playing each other. Sheila knew she was playing with fire; she was fire, too. It was just a matter of time before one of them got burnt. I knew not to say anything, even if Sheila wanted a response from me. She liked knowing that I was standing by with a life preserver to pitch her way if the waters got too treacherous.

The blonde who was sitting behind me got up and walked out. "Now that's what I like," I said, my eyes following the blonde to her car.

"Great! She probably thinks you were with me."

"No, she doesn't. She could hear you. It doesn't matter anyway. I think she's married."

"Well, that's off limits then."

"I was just showing you what I like."

"Okay, I gotcha," Sheila winked.

"So, what's the scoop on Diana," I asked, not wanting to

play it down as much as I had been while the blonde was sitting behind me.

"Well, she's been seeing this guy, and the sex is good, but there's still something wrong. That's when I told her about you, about how much I like hanging out with you. Not that we're having sex or anything, but, you know."

"No, I don't know," I answered, feeling more confused. All I need is another woman to befriend, to help meet her emotional needs while some other guy pours the meat to her. Fuck that! I'm tired of being mister understanding: here, let me help you get a new image man, so you can run off and find the love of your life.

"So you gonna call her?"

"No."

"Why not?"

"You think I'm just gonna call some woman I don't know out of the blue? Hell, I don't even know what she looks like."

"How about if we all meet for coffee next week?"

"Maybe."

"When?"

Damn was she hot on bagging number two. "I gotta go Sheila. I'll call you later."

"Why don't you come down for dinner tonight?"

"I might. I'll phone you this afternoon."

* * * * *

I returned to the studio and showered after my Rolfing session, before driving over to the Cornucopia deli at the mouth of Carmel Valley for Lunch. I ordered a turkey sandwich on a Franchese roll with lettuce, avocado, cucumber, tomato, jack cheese, light mayo, and grain mustard. A new employee was working behind the sandwich bar, a young man in his early twenties. He was nervous. I wanted to say something to put him at ease, a vote of confidence of some sort, but I decided to keep my mouth shut and let the fellow do his job.

It was a beautiful job indeed, but he forgot the cheese, so I asked him about it, and he added the cheese, but it had shaken him up some, forgetting something that is. So then right at the last moment, with the cheese on and everything else in place, he went to fold the two sandwich halves together, but he got shaky and flopped it. That beautiful creation that he had just built came toppling down like an old building in an earthquake. He did fine right up to the last minute, then he got nervous, his hands started trembling, and he lost it all right there on the spot. He tried to recover, starting to stuff back what had fallen out from between the two slices of bread, but I finally had to speak up.

"Stop! You were doing just fine until you second-guessed yourself. Start over. Use the same stuff, but restack it all."

He did so and cut a fresh avocado to use as filler, kind of like mortar to piece together a wall that had previously come crumbling down. He got it that time. I thanked him, and again told him that he was doing fine until he second-guessed himself and that was when everything fell apart.

* * * * *

Sheila phoned around four. She wanted to have dinner at Deetjens. I drove to Big Sur a few hours later, parked, and walked to her door to find her ready to go. I entered the gate ahead of Sheila, making my way towards the Expedition. Normally, I'd have opened the gate to let her go ahead of me, you know, the polite ladies-first thing, but I wasn't feeling all that polite. I continued to walk towards the driver's side door.

"Aren't you going to get the door?" Sheila asked, almost as if she was thinking out loud. Without answering, I retraced my steps to the passenger's side and opened her door. "Don't stop getting the door," she said, as I closed it before returning to my side of the Expedition. She was quick as a deer picking up a new scent, sniffing my lack of attentiveness.

Dinner was fine. I let Sheila order, as I usually did. She liked to be in control and she liked to eat off my plate. She could never decide on one dish for herself, so, instead of waiting two hours for her bifurcated state to settle, it was a lot easier to let her order for both of us.

"Angus phoned today," I said, starting the dinner conversation after we had placed our order.

"Angus your brother?"

"Yeah, he asked me to be his best man!"

"That's nice."

"I'm so honored. I'm twelve years older than he is. I mean, I used to change his diapers," I said, holding back a tear.

"Oh, how sweet," Sheila replied, as I drifted off into a dream I'd had a few months earlier. I was standing in the middle of a stream and there was a bride and groom on opposite sides of the river. I was somehow a mediator in the river bridging the connection between the betrothed, like I was helping them to exchange something, maybe a bouquet.

"So, what day are we going to meet Diana for coffee?"

"Sheila, I'm not looking for another woman to hang out with. I've got plenty..."

"I was thinking about her being your lover."

"She has a lover."

"No she doesn't," Sheila quickly answered. "She did, but I don't think that other thing is happening any more," she added, back peddling from what she'd told me earlier in the day.

"She did this morning."

"She used to."

"That's not what I heard this morning," I repeated.

"Well, everyone has a side salad. Even you do."

"No I don't."

"What about what's her name?"

"That's not a side salad. It happened a few times, but it's not happening anymore."

"No chance?" Sheila questioned, trying to draw me out from behind my defiance.

"None."

"Well, I don't care what you say. Everyone has a side salad."

"No, they don't. Some people don't hop from one thing to the next. Some people can hang alone and deal. I'm not interested in someone who's got something else going on," I answered, holding my ground.

"She doesn't."

"She does, too. If she's got this guy..."

"But that's just sex."

"Yeah, and if that's how she's relating to a man, I don't want any part of her. What would I just be? Besides, I've already got a woman."

"No you don't."

"Sheila, I don't need to be fixed up. Something's happening inside of me. In fact, it already has; my outside world will take care of itself as my inside world evolves."

Something has changed. I'm not the same man that I was when I first met Sheila, and whatever it is, it's coming out in our relationship. After dinner, I drove back to her cabin.

"You want to come in?" Sheila asked. "You can kick here tonight if you like."

"No, I'm going."

"There's nothing here for you, so you're leaving," she said, as she stepped out of the Expedition.

"I just feel like going home," I answered, making my way around the front of truck to walk her to the door.

"For what?"

"I don't know."

"Yes, you do."

"No, I don't," I answered, as we hugged goodbye.

"Will I see you before you leave?" she asked, as I walked back for the Expedition.

"Yeah, probably so," I answered, walking around to the back of the Ford. I started to take a piss while she was still standing at her door. "My friend Devin called today," I hollered. "He's getting married, too."

March 9, 2001 - Mid Afternoon

I set myself up for it all, but I'd still like to choke the old bitch. When I got home from Big Sur last night there was a note on my door from my Mrs. Shams, asking me to leave out the pipe that she wanted hung in the doorway of the heating room, just outside of my studio door. She has a whole house upstairs to hang the goddamn thing in, but, no, she wants it hung downstairs next to my room.

It was half-inch, galvanized pipe, threaded on the ends

so that it could be screwed into flanges that bolted at the top, on opposite sides of a doorway. Her husband had put the contraption together for her more than twenty years ago, and I say this because he's been dead for twenty years.

We'd been getting along because she didn't want anything from me. Then a few days ago, she called asking me to meet her downstairs because she wanted to talk. I left my room just as she was descending the stairway, pipe in hand.

Like I said, it was just a few days ago, but impatience got the best of her, so she enlisted the help of some man from her Friday morning yoga class. The note said nothing about her man Friday being a yogi, but that's where she rounds up help and the companionship of others who are made to feel sorry for her. She wanted the pipe hung to do stretching exercises; a yoga thing I guess?

It was late last night when I returned from Big Sur, so I didn't bother going back to get the pipe out of the back of the Expedition, didn't feel like traipsing through the garden in the black of night, trying to find my way to the garage. Hell, I might have stumbled upon a serpent, or some other evil deity. Mrs. Shams has become nothing but a royal pain in the ass over the last year, I'm telling you.

The first year in the apartment she left me alone, but for some reason she's taken on this sense of entitlement, like I owe her or something. It started with my volunteering to do things. I didn't mind helping out occasionally, but when someone starts expecting something from me... well, then helping takes on a whole new meaning, and this is exactly what's happened.

As I said, I set myself up. She banged on my door at nine this morning. I heard her walk down the stairs and back up after she had discovered that the pipe wasn't lying out for her. A few minutes later, I heard her walking down the stairs again. At first a gentle tap, but, when I didn't answer, it grew into a full-fledged rumble. I got up, put on my hat and sweat pants, and without a shirt, swung open the door.

"Malcolm, where's the pipe?" she asked in her excited, high-pitched elevated-tone, head bobbing around on her shoulders.

"It's in my truck!" I answered in a disgusted tone, acting as if I'd just been woken up from a deep sleep, which in some ways I had, but it had been a slow arousal, not one of those startling heart-somersaulting-in-your-throat awakenings. I was more pissed than startled. Actually, I was enraged.

"In your truck?"

"Yes, and I told you that I'd take care of it!" I bellowed out, before slamming the door in her face. I could hear her mumbling to the guy upstairs about the pipe being locked inside the Expedition.

I turned around and noticed that the message light on the answering machine was flashing. Not wanting to be disturbed before my time, I turn the ringer and the volume off at night before I go to bed. It was the ol' Mockingbird. "Malcolm, Malcolm, I'm going to have to wake you up." She had tried calling after she came downstairs the first time.

"God-damn-it," I screamed, loud enough for the old bag to hear. She's become one of those recurring nightmares that just won't go away. I have nurtured this critical mother for long enough. I have endured her disparaging evaluations and attacks on me for the last time. It's time to leave; if I don't, I'll probably go to prison for assaulting the old bitch. I'm done doing time in the old folks home, this old folks home anyway.

I checked my e-mail as the rage continued to course through my veins. There was some Christian message from one of my religious friends; not wanting to be rescued from my indignation, I deleted it after reading the first line. I got into the shower and screamed and cussed as if I was singing some heavy metal rock and roll song. It felt good. I'd been too nice for too long. Some people can receive a gift without expecting another; others can't.

I drove to Pacific Grove for a coffee at the Pink House. A couple of miles before arriving, an old blue-hair turned the corner on a red light; pulled right out in front of me. Then she puttered along up to the next red light, and sat there after it turned green until I laid on the horn. Her head bobbled a bit and then she putted on ahead of me at fifteen miles an hour. I finally got tired of her, and took a quick left and then a right hoping to parallel her on a street. I relaxed into my drive, only having to stop for some old man who was wearing those dark shades they give you at the eye doctors after having your pupils dilated. As I waited for the ol' boy to shuffle by on the crosswalk, the old blue-hair came around the corner and turned directly in front of me, just as the blind man stepped from the crosswalk up onto the sidewalk.

I laughed, still pissed off, but recognizing the humor in the inevitability of my morning's fate. I picked up the car phone and dialed my buddy Lewis.

"Hey man, what's going on?" I asked, in our normal way of greeting one another.

"Not much, man. How 'bout you?" he asked, waiting for me to reveal the purpose of my call.

"She's at it again. Can you come over and help haul my couch and a few things back to my storage?"

"Yeah, what about your armoire and bed?"

"I think I can get the armoire into the back of my Expedition. The bed stays. I'm done sleeping in that mother-fucker!"

"I bet you are."

"When can you come?"

"Wednesday or Thursday," he answered. "That way no one has to know about it," he added, 'no one' meaning his wife or boss.

"That'll work out okay," I replied, really wanting to haul the things out right then and there. "I'm out of here the following Sunday anyway."

"Yeah, and that way you can stay longer in Europe if you decide to."

"As long as I'm back for my little brother's wedding in May."

"Yeah, but you can turn around and go back after the wedding. Who knows, you may never go back to Carmel."

"Well, one thing's for certain..."

"You're not going back to that old bitch's place," Lewis said, finishing my thought. We'd been friends long enough to know what one was going to say before the other had a chance to say it. "Besides, you might just fall in love with some beautiful European woman and live happily ever after."

"Yeah, and if not, the worst thing that can happen is my leaving that dungeon."

It was all happening for a purpose. I think that's why I didn't go after the pipe when I got home last night and found her note. Lewis was right; I'm not coming back to her place. There's really only one thing that I *have* to do: be back for Angus's wedding. And that isn't really a *have-to*; it's a *want-to*, an honor!

March 9, 2001 - 11:00 p.m.

Mrs. Shams is getting on my nerves, and for the last time. But, what about that obligated little boy who, in spite of his rebellious nature, still wants to please her, still doesn't want to disappoint mama. The only mother I've got left to defy is within me! Fuck! I can't stand this inner drama any longer! If she weren't gnawing away in my guts, she wouldn't be bugging me in the drama of my waking dream as well.

I know why some kids kill their mothers: their image of mother never takes a subordinate position in their soul and neither does their undeveloped infantile ego. Both forces are constellated and the divine drama takes over the individual's life. He or she might live to be a hundred and two, but if something doesn't shift and allow these two deities to subordinate to the Self, the higher Self, life is lost to this drama, this very same drama that has been reeling off in me time and time again for the past forty years. I'm telling you, saying goodbye to that old bitch is more difficult than ripping that belt out of my mother's hands for the last time when I was twelve years old.

Just because a person knows something doesn't necessarily make it any easier to live with it. When an archetype is activated, it's activated. It doesn't matter if you're Sigmund Freud or Carl Jung; when a person is caught in the throes of a constellated archetypal possession, it overtakes him. It's all energy; something wanting to happen beyond our capability to understand: an unbridled energy that can leave an ego ass-busted and bruised on the trail, elbows on knees and head in hands, trying to figure out what or who spooked the horse.

Are falling in love and murder the product of the same authority? I'm tired of beating this same old drum. I'm leaving this place, and I'm leaving it for good. For forty years I've been a little boy. For forty years I've been trying to court my mother, and for forty years I've been rejecting myself. Yes, it began at the hand of my physical mother at the beginning of my life, but when does a boy leave that shit behind?

When does a boy become his own man? After he has exploited the lot of physical Woman? After conquering the commercial world? After he has amassed wealth? After he has lived up to and exorcized the defined dogmas of all social and religious orders? After he has completely sold out every last drop of his blood to an authority other than himself? How many fucking dragons does he have to slay? How many times does he have to tell mother goodbye? I don't know. I don't fucking know. All that I can tell you is that I'm tired. I'm tired of this battle. I'm tired of the aches and pains my body suffers as it goes through this amalgamation. I'm damn tired! Eleven more days of this winter! Eleven more fucking days! Eleven more days before the flowers begin to bloom. Eleven long days!

March 10, 2001 - 12:30 a.m.

Alright, now it is just *ten* more fucking days! It's Ramos's birthday today. He is a grade school pal of mine. We're not even buddies anymore; haven't seen or heard from him in years. Drifted apart in high school, but for some reason I just can't forget his birthday. I think that's why I'm so fucked up. Not because of Ramos, but because of the type of memory I've been bequeathed. In many ways my memory serves me, and in just as many ways it haunts me.

I'm twisted. I finished my tenth Rolfing session thirty-six hours ago. It has really opened me. I'm gushing with anger; it has always been with me, but it seems to have gained much more strength than in the past. It's coursing through me, a ball of energy. Mrs. Shams pounding on my door after only a few hours of sleep really set me off. I've yet to recover, even if more than twelve hours have gone by. I feel like a bear prematurely awakened from hibernation. I want to chew her up and spit her out.

I've already gone to bed about three times tonight. I could use my punching bag right now. I could use a lot of things right

now. I could use some rest for starters, but it isn't coming to me
for some reason. This energy; it's building like a head of steam.

March 10, 2001 - Noon

She caught me when I was backing out of the garage.
Thought I'd snuck out without her knowing, but all of a sudden,
just like a wart that won't go away, she's standing next to the
driver's side door waving her arms, that fucking Medusa! So I
rolled down the window.

"I'm going to have to scold you," she said in a righteous
tone, shaking her right index finger at me. Give me a fucking
break! I'm a forty-year-old man, and I've got this eighty-year-
old, eighty-five pound, blue-haired old lady fixing to give me a
scolding. The next thing I knew she'd have me wearing a flea
collar.

I huffed and I puffed and held up my left hand, pointed my
index finger back at her and said in a forceful voice, "I'll be out
by the end of the month. It's time for me to leave."

"Oh, let's not be that way," she said in a startled tone. She
looked as if she was going to melt, just like the wicked witch of
the west did after she was dowsed with a bucket of water.

"Like I said, I'll be out by the end of the month. It is time
for me to leave."

"Oh, you're making me feel very badly," she said, and then
dropped her head in shame and hurried back in through the
front door she'd left open when she came out to give me a
scolding.

March 11, 2001 - Midnight

Mrs. Shams might have been one hell of a wife, but she was
one fucked up mother. She would also have been the mother-
in-law from hell. Pity the poor woman who married her son,
pity her son, and pity... well, I've been putting up with her shit
as if I was married to her daughter, or like a daughter in-law,
and I was neither. The only thing keeping me here has been the

cheap rent. That's bullshit! The only thing keeping me here has been my short-looped psyche; I've been caught up in my very own hell. I'm a lot like a kitten, too young to know I've been chasing my own tail and having too much fun doing it to care. Well, after forty years, this kitty cat's now a roaring, raging tiger ready to gobble up and shit out anyone or anything that tries to drag me back to that lie.

It's a silly drama. Behind it all she's just lonely and wants communion. I get so frustrated with the old lady, though; she's such a critical old bitch. I'll move into storage what little is left in this studio before I leave on the 20th.

Mrs. Shams has been a grand teacher, and I'm grateful to her. Our ongoing drama over the last year has enlightened me. I told Adam that I needed a new image of God and of Woman four years ago. I didn't know why I said it. It wasn't a logical knowing; I just knew that it was true because the words came from a place of truth, from somewhere deep within me. Things don't come to me overnight. I'm still trying to flush out these old ghosts, still trying to make peace with these demons, the dark-sides of these gods and goddesses.

It's taken me a few years to realize that I have been carrying on the tradition that was passed down to me from my primary relationship with Woman. I physically ripped the belt out of her hand when I was twelve years old and thought I'd thrown it away, only to discover that I turned it on myself, picking up where my mother, her mother, and her mother's mother left off.

It's timely for me to be going to this seminar in Florence, exploring these, new to me, images of the feminine. Images, which I hope will allow me to view Her as a companion as opposed to an adversary, images that will allow me to receive Her without the unconscious fear of being annihilated, images that will open me to Her love.

* * * * *

Dear Mrs. Shams,
I want to thank you for providing me with the opportunity to live here for the last two years. You have given me a

sanctuary for a much-needed time of rest and recuperation.

I want you to understand that I am leaving for my sake, and not because of anything you have said or done. I am a forty-year-old man, and it is simply time for me to be the man of my own home once again.

I'd like to apologize for hurting your feelings. I believe that you have always had my best interests at heart, and I am grateful to you for all that you've done for me.

* * * * *

Lie, lie, lie; it's all a fucking lie! Fuck her! But she's still a human being, and I have no right to leave this place without showing her some respect, honoring her existence, her humanity, as well as her inhumanity. That's why I wrote her this letter, this lie, and I'll tell her another lie. I'll give it to her in the morning; I'll leave it on her doorstep.

March 14, 2001 - 2 a.m.

I'm in love; I can feel it. I haven't a woman in my life, but I'm in love. I can feel it right now while listening to music; other times it's a scent, a sunny day, or a sunset; sometimes a smile, and sometimes when I'm screaming bloody murder inside, wanting to kill something, or myself. Rage itself isn't such a bad thing. It's the action, or reaction that it provokes in a man that gets him, but just having a good old-fashioned passionate fit of rage can be something to be in love with, too.

Sheila was all hot and bothered about getting Diana and me hooked up, and for that very same reason, I wasn't. Sheila's been trying to set me up with older women ever since we met. She'll go out with guys my age all day long, but for some reason she sees me differently. She sees me as an old man or something. I mean, it's fine that she isn't attracted to me like she is these other guys, but what bugs me is that she's always trying to hook me up with someone's grandmother. Hell, some of them could pass for my mother.

Sheila bounced into Whole Foods the other morning like

she'd just downed a can of octane booster, all set on getting me and this mother-of-three hooked up. Well, I've been through enough set-ups that I don't count on shit. As a matter of fact, I don't go for set-ups, not unless I've had a sneak preview of what I might be getting into. Once an assessment has been made, we can get down to considering the possibility for me to tolerate the cackling. Mind you, it can't be just any type of cackling; the tone has to be right, no screeching birds. I don't like birds.

Don't get me wrong, real birds are okay, wild birds, birds that fly free: blackbirds, sparrows, finches, seagulls from a distance, and pelicans, doves... hell, I like real birds, just don't like women who are birds and some of them really remind me of such. Anyway, I never did find out if Diana was a bird. Sheila went to hang out with her a few days after they'd met, and her desire to unite us dwindled. Sheila was like that. She loved people; saw the good in everyone. I, on the other hand, have been engendered with the blood of half a Calvinist Dutchman: you can smell the critical judgment on my breath from a mile away.

I was still kind of entertaining the possibility of meeting this woman until Sheila started telling me how her middle boy was twenty-five or twenty-six, and that meant the oldest boy was at least two years older than the middle kid. Okay, so let's keep it conservative and say that the oldest was twenty-seven. Eighteen, if she was that young when she'd had number one, it would put her at forty-five at the youngest. Now, if we put her at twenty and placed him at twenty-eight, well, that's forty-eight, maybe even forty-nine. Sheila can chase forty-year-old men like me around all day long, she and that hot and hard twenty-five-year-old body of hers, but for some goddamn reason, I'm only good for sag-assed women who are twice Sheila's age.

I know what's going on. She can't have me, but neither can anyone else. Sheila knows that I won't mess with these older women anymore than the guys she sees. She won't set me up with any of her younger friends because she runs the risk of me hooking up with one of them. It's safe to act as if she will set me up with these older single mothers because she knows I'll never go for it. Sheila has her cake and she's eating it too. There's just one thing that's about to get in her way. I'm taking my forty-year-old buns out of her display case; I'm finding myself a new bakery. Hell, this Diana gal she was trying to hook me up with had been in a religious cult of some sort. It took Sheila three days to come clean on that one...

March 14, 2001 - Mid-Afternoon

Well, it worked. Mrs. Shams called to thank me for the nice letter. I'd have probably considered keeping the place if she could have left me alone, but 'ifs' don't count, and I'm out of there.

Her call today was to thank me and to test if I was going to stay for the month of April, which I had originally planned so I'd have a place to return to after Europe, but when things started getting testy the other day, I used that as an opportunity to make my exit. It was way overdue anyway. In her call today she said she had been spoiled having me as a tenant, and I thanked her. She's sad to see me go, and for more than one reason.

Yeah, I'm a symbol of security for her, as in the masculine figure that stands over and protects her household, but, on a deeper and unconscious level, I am the boy she can ridicule and find fault with. It's like she needs me there, a wayward soul desperately in need of her divine guidance. I'm not saying that I don't need the feminine image as a guide; I just don't need that old bird.

Anyway, I want to write about how relaxed I'm feeling here in Santa Cruz. I moved a few more things up here to my cousin Nate's garage. After unloading, I pulled into Coffeetopia for a hot cup of Italian roast. It's a beautiful sunny day, so I took a seat out here to soak up some rays and watch the pretty women come and go as they bring their children to the dojo next door for Karate lessons. If I hung out here long enough, I could probably turn myself into a husband and a stepfather. Good thing I leave for Europe in less than a week.

So, I'm soaking up the sun, and feeling relaxed, which is rare for me. I feel this way because I'm leaving my dungeon and the tyrannical rule of the wicked witch upstairs. I know that she'd have shoved me into an oven or some huge boiling caldron to stew my ass long ago if she'd had a chance, but she didn't. She came close a time or two, but it never happened. That's what the call was about this morning, to thank me for the nice sweet letter and to try, one last time, to entice me into her kitchen. I'm finished there; I've officially received my degree in the study of her kind, and believe me, I've earned it.

I now have an education in how to break out of the dungeon of a tyrannical, all-consuming mother; I hope. Imagine being a forty-year-old man who was told he lacked confidence and academics. Imagine a forty-year-old man who had to sneak out of his apartment attempting to avoid another one of her interrogations. Fuck! I'm getting pissed off all over again just thinking about it.

Anyway, I feel relaxed sitting out here in the sun, breathing in all the beautiful mothers as they come and go while I sip my coffee, knowing that I am done sleeping in that bed at Mrs. Shams's, knowing that the next bed I'll probably be sleeping in will be in one of these mother's castles, the very same castle that her ex-husband is still stroking the payments on. It all sounds good to me, her stroking me, and her ex stroking the bills. I know I'll get that titty back someday. I know there's justice out there just waiting to be served.

I'm no different than any other man, my suffering or anything else for that matter. We all suffer, and it starts at the very moment we're birthed out into this great big cosmic drama. I've come to the conclusion that the source of our suffering has not been purposefully inflicted, but rather is an innocent byproduct of naïveté. A naïveté generated by a naïve creator and handed down for generations since the beginning of time, fueled by a rebellious rage incited at the time of one's expulsion from their very personal Garden of Eden.

Yeah, forty years ago I was kicked out of paradise, and ever since that cord was severed, I've been cussing and screaming and wanting a pound of flesh for what my mother did to me. I love hating and despising her just like I've loved hating and despising the wicked witch upstairs. Imagine that, a man hating and despising his mother for actually giving birth to him. Any woman who has been with me during this first half of my life never stood a chance. I fucking hated her long before I ever knew her, long before I ever fell in love with her. I've despised her since the beginning of time, and I've been despising myself for aeons as well.

Anyway, I was just trying to explain how relaxed I am today, sitting outside here soaking up the Santa Cruz sun, checking out the pretty mother's who are bringing their kids to karate practice, and sipping a sweet Italian brew. "God, thanks for making so many beautiful women, and thanks for not knowing what you were doing when you set this grand design into motion, and thanks for not swatting my pissin'-and-moanin', ungrateful, poor-ass self with that great big fly swatter of yours, this poor self who is just now catching a glimpse of the divine and finding an appreciation for this gift of life I've been given."

March 16, 2001 - 11 p.m.

Spent a good part of the day with relatives. I leave soon and it felt right to return to my roots, to visit my family before embarking on this new journey. It feels as if death is looming. Perhaps I've returned to say goodbye. Actually, it feels as if I've been saying goodbye for some time now. Perhaps I'm already dead, a ghost, and this is all a formality, all these goodbyes...

Leaving the Nest...

March 20, 2001 - 8:30 p.m.

It was a long stretch down the runway before the MD-11 lifted off the ground. A few years have passed since I was last a passenger on an airliner. I've flown myself in N1MC, and now She's about to be sold, or might already be, and I just don't know it yet. Two days ago, I received a call from a WWII veteran who was looking for a V-tailed Bonanza just like 1MC. I left it in the hands of my attorney, as well as other things of importance, while I'm out of the country.

I flew myself around the States for years, but I'd be damned if I was going to be one of those adventuresome types who added tip tanks to the wings and additional fuel tanks to the baggage compartment of a four-place single engine airplane just to say I'd flown myself across the Atlantic.

Besides, I don't need to fly myself anymore. 1MC was my symbol of freedom, a symbol that no longer serves me. I now have my freedom. I'm no longer the prisoner of the past, or if I am still a captive of my personal history, I don't know it.

My chest was tight as we barreled down the runway. It's been tight for the last couple of weeks. If it was tight before that, I was too numb to know. I was clinging to so much history that, unknowingly, I could probably have suffered a coronary, but things change.

It's been two years since I left my old career behind, and after having completed most of my general education at the community college, I've grown bored. The counselor at the college said I had to take algebra as a prerequisite to statistics in order for her to *give* me a degree. I told her to forget it. Then she asked me what I was going to do without that piece of paper. I told her that I was going to walk out the door and go live my life, and that is exactly what I did. Hell, I'm forty years old; I'm done jumping through hoops. Who the hell does she think she is anyway: *give* me a degree?

I've hardly met any single women on the Peninsula, none that interest me or none whom I interest. Most of the ones I've met are ten years my senior at the very least. There were too many old ladies hitting on me, and not enough younger women to reel me out of my spiraled funk. I don't know what I'm to do with my life, but I know it won't be done in Carmel-by-the-Sea.

So, I have a tight chest, and it scares me a bit, but not living scares me a hell of a lot more than dying does. It wasn't that way a month ago. Paranoia ran me with hypochondriacal fits, but, after Jared died, things changed. Jared's passing has changed me. He showed me that dying might not be so bad after all.

Jared's father, Nolan, and my Aunt Adrienne were my ride to the airport. I arrived at their home in San Jose a few nights ago. The Expedition will be parked at their place while I'm away.

I'm on Swiss Air flight 109 direct from San Francisco to Zurich, a twelve-hour flight. On the way to the airport I recall telling Nolan and Adrienne how I felt like a teenage boy leaving home for the first time, and in a lot of ways that is just what I am. When I left home the first time, as a teenager, I was drunk and drugged and had no idea of how I felt. I guess that's why, after twenty years have passed, I have to do it all over again. I suppose I'm fortunate to get a second chance.

March 21, 2001 - Late Evening - Zurich

Arrived in Zurich around five this afternoon. It was and still is overcast and cold, not freezing, but cold. Enough people spoke English to point me in the right direction. I found an ATM machine in the airport and got some Swiss Francs. Then I was able to buy a ticket for the train that took me to the main station in the city center.

My hotel was supposedly just a few blocks from the main station, so I set off with my carry-on slung over my shoulder, tugging both wheeled suitcases, and hoping to stumble accidentally into Hotel Montana with the least bit of effort, and it worked. That's one thing I haven't lost over the years: my intuition. Within fifteen minutes I was checked into my room.

On foot, I returned to the train station to reserve my seat on tomorrow's train to Florence.

Oh, the women. Now that's a whole other story in itself. They are beautiful, and they are everywhere, blondes, brunettes, and all very European, and some very delectable dishes at that. They were crawling around the main station like ants in a bag of sugar. While standing in line to make my reservation, a young blonde woman in her early twenties asked me something in German.

"English only," I responded. That was the end of that, I thought, but it wasn't.

"You are American?" she asked.

"Yes," I nodded.

"I lived in Wisconsin for a year as an exchange student," she said in a friendly tone.

"When were you there?" I asked, trying to figure out her age.

"1998."

"My sister in-law is from Wisconsin," I answered, still trying to do the math.

She smiled and then motioned me to move on, as it was my turn to step up to the counter. For a moment I thought that my destiny had been fulfilled, but after making my reservation, I found no evidence of the little hotty. It was just as well, because I have to be in Florence tomorrow. Although, I must admit, the fantasy of taking her home to make babies was fluttering its way throughout my body.

After confirming my seat reservation for an early morning departure, I walked over to a vendor and purchased a sausage, roll, and bottled water. Munching the tasty bratwurst, I stood around watching the local drunks get drunker, while all the pretty girls strolled by.

Shortly after my snack, I returned to Hotel Montana, requested an early wake-up call, and then soaked in a hot bath. Bet I stay here. Bet I find a new home here and stay.

* * * * *

What follows consists of the dreams (that have been italicized) and the unconscious, uninhibited reactions I had toward them in an unconscious and semi-unconscious trance-like state during my one night stay in Zurich. They are unedited, as all the dreams that I record are unedited. They have been typed word for word as I recorded the content into my tape recorder, with the exception of what you find in brackets; these are notes of what came to mind while I was typing the raw material into the computer:

March 22, 2001 - Dreams - Zurich

I'm at Adam's, and something is going on in the background... *this Traci [from the Avanti center years ago, the outpatient facility* *that I attended when I quit drinking and drugging] and maybe* *Frances, maybe not. More like I felt her presence.*

Oh, Elaine [Elaine doesn't want to be called Elaine any longer, *she wants a new identity, wants to be called Elsa. She also got rid* *of her old clothes and bought a whole new wardrobe], and maybe* *another person, and it's like I'm elected to do something. Can't* *remember exactly what it is, but anyway I'm angry with Adam.* *[I'm angry with him about becoming conscious; angry at myself, the* *Adam in me who won't let me lie to myself any longer.]*

Adam says something. It is like I've been selected to speak and/ *or to do something, and I... yeah, the anger starts to come out. It is* *almost like I start to justify it, or I want to tell the story, but I stop.* *Adam said, yeah, well... it's like he, Adam, doesn't want to go into* *the drama of the thing. Elaine looks a little bit perplexed, trying to* *figure it out.*

Anyway, I wake from the dream and now I'm getting the feeling *of Kyla, a girl [woman] who agitates me, and I don't know if I see* *her image, not so much her image, but feel her presence. Ah, the* *agitation I feel is her: Kyla's presence is coming up for me right* *now.*

Just remembered how one time Kyla said that Adam was like *a mother, he just mothered us through all of this stuff. God, she* *bugs the piss out of me. It is her negativity, her thinking, and all* *her questions. She thinks she's knows everything all the time and* *is better than. Ooh, yeah, she is just like that fucking Mrs. Shams.* *Just because they know something they think they're better than or they know more than. It's like their way is the only way. There is no other way.*

This has something to do with my uniqueness and my not being able to honor that. I always want to compare myself to others. This has something to do with my not being able to accept my uniqueness, my individuality, my individuation, not being able to value what I have to bring, having no right to exist.

This has something to do with how I don't value myself. I'm not valuing what I have to bring to the world. Has something to do with not being understood. Has something to do with my having to explain myself. They always want to know... but why? Well, why? Well, why? And me having to justify it. Oh, wow, Mrs. Shams, I'm thinking about her questions, her trying to figure me out, and Kyla, her questions, and her trying to figure me out.

I remember I woke up feeling warm, and I'm still feeling very warm, and I have a little bit of low back pain, but most of it is radiating down to my left [right] calf and into the right ball of my foot, a deep pain in there.

I was drifting off and it was like something about leaving the physical bodies behind, those words came to me, and this image of a plastic wedge or something like... I was pushing it with my right hand. The thought came to me that I am dead, and I just haven't... I'm dead, but I'm still here doing things. It's like I haven't moved on, yet. Also has something to do with atrophy. Like how some of my leg... the soreness or the pain... its atrophy because of not using it enough or compensating for it in some way.

Right leg, down the toe, and up into the calf. I was worried that there might be a tumor in there, and I believe that's what it is probably... ah, it doesn't matter what I believe that bump or that fatty cyst is. It's all tied together because there is something that... compensation, or something that my body has worn itself into, a routine of some sort, a belief of some sort. It is tied or timed into my psyche. It is tied into my victimhood, a belief of my victimhood, or not so much my victimhood, but my belief of my victimhood.

Something to do with my doubt, my self-doubt, the doubting of myself, of not believing in myself... not believing that Woman can really be attracted to me. It is that doubt. It is about the way I view myself, the wounded way of seeing myself.

Stagnation. Down in my right leg. It is all a stagnation that holds shit. That's where it is all being carried. The limp, the lymph, hum, it is all a stagnated pond of shit down there, a belief that doesn't serve me, a belief that has kept me a wounded little boy, a belief that keeps me relating to myself as wounded and not enough. This is the part that wants to keep comparing myself outside of me, by other's standards, and none of them by my own [standards]. That is why Kyla, Mrs. Shams, piss me off sometimes: because they want to compare me to something. They want my standards to be somebody else's. I believe they do anyway.

Okay, so that's what that pain is about: the limp is a part of me that doesn't want to change. That wounded part of my soul that wants me to believe that I'm shit, that I'm not enough, that whatever I am is not enough. It's that beaten part of me that wants to stay beaten! Instead of rising above it. So, whenever I have the pain, I can honor and welcome it instead of trying to get rid of it, give it a voice, write about it.

It all has to do with the funk that I've been in since Jacqueline, that "why-not-me" thing. The finding fault, that spiral shaming "why-not-me" thing, that spiraling disbelief in myself, that core disbelief in myself, my soul, a core disbelief, the non-valuing of myself, of who I am, of the core of who I am.

It has something to do with me identifying so much with my wounding that I haven't been able to see who I am. I haven't been able to see beyond the wounds. I haven't been able to be seen. I haven't been able to see myself or be seen because of how I view myself. I haven't been allowed -< laugh>- I haven't let others see me. How others view me - or how I believe they view me - is distorted. I believe they see me as wounded or incomplete because I believe myself to be wounded and incomplete, so I'd just as soon that they see me that way as well, wow! That's why Mrs. Shams bugs me so much. That's why Kyla bugs me so much.

For some reason, in the dream, Adam sees me as incomplete, or, the Adam part of me sees me as incomplete. Better yet, I see myself as incomplete, and I can't stand that part of me, either. Wow, whoa, okay, basically it boils down to the belief of how could anybody love a piece of shit like me? A tainted: a wounded, tainted piece of shit like me because underneath the facade, and everything else, is the wounded little boy - that is a belief - and he is there, but he doesn't have to run me anymore. Ah, that's why I left home, Mrs. Shams. I set out on my own as a teenager now, for the first time.

Image of Sophie [my Rolfer] arriving here in Europe, and it was like the massage or the Rolfing... she walks in, like she will help me get better with this leg thing, this wound. The people who are waiting for her [two women] tell her no, your responsibility is to yourself. Your responsibility is to your self. You can't make somebody else better. Your responsibility is to your self. These two women were waiting for her.

The responsibility is to your self - as I write this, the image of the two nuns from my August 97 dream comes to me.

I know why I'm madder than hell at Adam in the dream, too. It's because I'm going deeper into myself – coming into more awareness. My ego is mad at Adam, or the Adam in me, taking me there. My ego wants to remain naïve, wants to remain wounded: wants to remain in that old belief system, wow! Wants me to remain there with it [me] too. That is just exactly how my body has its own belief system. It's there in my bones, in my flesh, therein... wow!

Something about no longer having to define and externalize the justification of my value and worth to somebody else or to myself. This has something to do with not having to compensate for who I am anymore [or who I think I am]; it has something to do with not having to live a life of compensation. This compensating thing - that means I don't have to prove my worth to myself any longer. So I no longer have to prove it to Woman, either, and I don't have to relate to myself that way - from a place of trying to find value, at the core of who I am. Perhaps what it amounts to is that I can love and allow myself to be loved. It's about loving that core part of who I am, instead of compensating for what I think I am not or what I think I lack, or for how I view myself, as incomplete.

This is the part that has been hidden. This is the part that shrank when the beatings started to come. This is the part that went into hiding, to protect itself, to keep me alive - my body and my spirit. This is the part that hid in order to continue living, so that I could continue to live. If this part had been beaten out of me, I'd be dead. Yeah, it's that hidden life spirit that has been pounded away.

That's the nugget, that kernel, the core of who I am that has never been allowed, never been permitted to express itself for fear of being squashed, annihilated.

It has to do with accepting my uniqueness and not trying to be somebody else or have somebody else give an external definition. It's about loving my own uniqueness and in turn allowing it to be loved. It's about erasing those beatings, about taking away what was done to me, and giving birth, life, to the unique core part of who I am: recognizing it, nurturing it, and allowing it to bloom. Ah, that's why I left Mrs. Shams, so that I could do that. Yes, okay, okay, I can do that. I just left Mrs. Shams on the outside because I was doing it on the inside or had already done it on the inside. Wow, okay, good. No wonder that rage is there. No fucking wonder that rage was - is - boiling down inside of there - inside of here.

That's why I fell in love with Lauren. She saw that in me, saw my uniqueness and mirrored it back to me, and I fell in love with her. Oh my goodness, no wonder it hurts so much to be away from her, away from myself.

An image: I'm in the train station and all of these old people are walking by. I've opened up this gate, and I'm letting them pass. They're old people. They are pushing carts with luggage and stuff. It's like they have been waiting for years. It's like, it's not just me; it's generations before me that haven't been allowed to move out into their own until now, but now can. Oh, wow, I'm not just opening the gate for myself: I'm opening the gate for the collective or for the universal things that are to happen along the line of my heritage. It is going back, wow, all these people are moving out into themselves now - past, present, and future generations.

Image of myself walking into the train station, and I walk through these doors - leaving this part of me behind - a boy. It's that "why-not-me" part of me. I'm waving. I walk through the doors. I turn around. I wave and say goodbye. It wasn't me; it was a false me. It was a part of me that I took on to survive, that I don't need anymore. It's time to say goodbye to the little guy. I no longer need to cling to these false pieces of me. Yeah, it's time to let them go. I just keep walking, turn around, nod my head, and then a crowd of people come walking by. Then suddenly, he's gone.

I don't need to apologize on this trip for being an American and only speaking English. I don't have to compensate for what I believe the rest of the world sees as arrogant. I don't have to take that upon myself. I can just be myself, speak English and value and respect people, and, in turn, be valued and respected. Wow, I don't have to compensate. I no longer have to apologize for being me.

From now on I'm the only one who exploits my own energy; no one else exploits it. I'm the one, who gets to exploit it, and I can do it consciously, but nobody else can: not in the business world, not in the relationship world, not in any world.

It was all a false identity that I believed in, that I was living and now this little boy in me has vaporized or gone away, a false god, an old image that I worshiped, a false god, an image that no longer serves me.

Now a new image of a little being, inside of me, a golden little being who is encased in my body, who is my power, who is the real king of who I am, who is the real authority of who I am. Oh, it's this golden... radiant golden being that I'm carrying within me. Yes, my true inner authority.

Now I know why I've been having the drinking and drugging dreams, and the people in my dreams, how I... it's why I drank. That hidden part of me wasn't allowed, a loud. I was drinking away a wound, but I was also... it was also not allowing me to be who I was [or am]. That's what the drinking and drugging did - gave me the freedom to feel... it gave me permission to feel free, to be myself. That's what the drinking and drugging did for me, gave me the freedom to live extemporaneously, to move from within, to be my own authority, to be the author of my own life.

That's why I drank. It gave me permission to be myself. That is why my Tonys, my boots, are so important to me: they are me. I'm walking in my own boots, not someone else's. The first dream I ever worked on with Adam, I was a boot being pushed around in a wheel chair. Now that I think of it, by an old client who is still a prisoner of his inheritance.

The notes I took yesterday about the wounding to my balls, or the belief, my concerns, worries, my obsession with them. It is a symbol of doubting myself: doubting my own creative energy, my own seed.

Realizing now that I don't want a young woman stuck in a girl's psychology to fuck me from an unconscious place. I want a woman to make love to me from a conscious place, and I want to *make love to a woman from this conscious place. Not from a place that has a need to be filled, or a wound healed, or something else healed or filled. It needs to come from a place of giving and not of need, a place of sharing, of coming together, of bringing our selves, our whole selves there, our entire selves and giving, or sharing. I no longer want to fuck unconsciously. This is why my love or sex life has gone to hell for the last couple of years, because I can no longer lie to myself in this manner. This is why I'm pissed at Adam.*

The French woman came and sat by me in the airport in San Francisco before our flight left... she spoke to me in French and I was unable to respond. Then I saw her again at the baggage claim in Zurich. I ended up with her on the train from the airport to the main train station and how she hadn't bought a ticket and was standing in the passageway between cars. All of a sudden she was able to speak English to me and explained that she wanted to be between cars. She hadn't purchased a ticket. When the conductor caught her without a ticket, she, in another language used the excuse of having to help me. She told him she was helping me. She didn't think I knew what she was saying or how she was using me as an excuse.

Dream: Tom and Jerry in my hotel room in Zurich [Jerry is a real religious fundamentalist, and Tom is about as heathen as they come.] In the dream, a young man and his girlfriend are working in my room. She works in the hotel and he [the boyfriend] is there; she just came to change the bed. I tell them that they can hang out, and I tell Jerry and Tom that they can hang out. I have to take a shower because I woke up late. I didn't hear the answer, or I didn't hear the wake up call, and I said something, and she thought it was sexist or derogatory, but it wasn't. Tom kept throwing things at me, teasing, like trying to get me to quit doing it [flirting with the girl], but I wasn't being sexist, I wasn't even trying to initiate anything.

Then I showed Tom the books, my book on the computer. I was opening it up and he wanted to know what I was doing with them. Oh, he told me how he was bringing his daughter into his business. I told him I'm not doing anything, I'm just writing them right now [or righting them right now]. I just fired up the computer, and the young couple got up and they wanted to see what I had done, and I woke up.

In the dream it was almost like the girl made one bed so she didn't have to make... two? So I wouldn't be sleeping in both beds. I would be sleeping in just one bed and she wouldn't have to make it, make the other one.

March 22, 2001

Restless night, little sleep, but great dreams; I'm busting full of energy. Slept from ten-thirty to twelve-thirty and then from three to four. Got up before the five o'clock wake up call I'd requested. Checked out and had breakfast from six to six-thirty, then walked to the train station, boarded the train, and now I'm en route to Firenze. This train is exceptional, riding first-class; I wish the plane ride yesterday had been as enjoyable and as comfortable. I'm on the Cisalpino, and these seats are better than I've ever dreamed.

We're traveling through the Alps. They're phenomenal. I'm actually doing it, not just talking about it. And, I'm doing it on my own, with my own resources, and on nobody's clock. This is my trip and mine alone.

The rails cut through some extremely steep ravines and then through tunnels that have been bored through the mountains. It's pitch black for minutes, and then a sudden quickening out into the dramatic Alpine realm. Old barns are scattered about the landscape, some possibly cisterns. Water gushes down the steep slopes in natural chute-like canals that the snow runoff has created. They're like mini-rivers that run straight down hill.

I'm sure that it's quite cold here, yet I picture myself wintering over in a chalet, or even one of these alpine farmhouses, like the one we just passed as we wind our way south at over 150 miles per hour. We zipped through a village called Wassen, and I took a snap shot of a church tower. The mountains rise above the village like a huge grizzly bear shadowing its prey. A dream, this has to be a dream.

Back into a tunnel, this passage, lasting for what seems to be several minutes, has robbed me of any sense of space and time. Sounds as if another train roars by in the opposite direction, but it's too dark to confirm my suspicion. Just popped out of the tunnel. Everything is blanketed in the white of snow. I flash on Hans Castorp in Mann's *Magic Mountain*.

An old Swiss couple is sitting across the aisle from me. They remind me of farmer friends back home, people who seem simple and appear to live uncomplicated lives, but I know better. These people have endured a lifetime of harsh summers and winters, their livelihoods at the mercy of Mother Nature and unpredictable markets. They are people with soul, people who live close to the earth, people who won't sell out for a buck, people I am proud to know.

* * * * *

Three and a half hours have passed since the train left Zurich. My feet and ankles are swelling. I could sense the discomfort on the flight over from the States yesterday, but it is becoming more evident. I'll be glad to arrive in Florence. We're at the halfway point, just crossing the border from Switzerland into Italy.

We've stopped to let the Italian crew take over the train. The Italian customs officers got on the train and are making asses of themselves, flexing their muscles as they randomly question passengers and check passports. The feel of the ride up to this point has changed.

The Italians seem a bit testier about checking to make sure everyone is a ticket holder. The Swiss had one person checking tickets, but the Italian crew check passes in groups of two, if not three men sometimes. It's like a whirlwind of chaos hijacked the train at the border.

A woman seated across the aisle from me is catching some flack because of the type of ticket she possesses. It appears she's being fined or at the very least has to come up with an additional fee. She's nicely dressed, a woman in her fifties. She doesn't appear to be a scam artist. She doesn't seem happy about the whole event but paid just the same. I made eye contact with her, caught her looking my way and she quickly shifted her glance. Maybe she's a con after all?

Things certainly have changed though, and again I find myself in a new world. I'd heard that Swiss trains run as smoothly as Swiss timepieces, and my experience has validated this, but the Italian trains are a completely different story. I'm counting on their food to compensate for the chaos. We just stopped to dump the customs agents.

* * * * *

We've arrived in Milan. I don't have to change trains, just a scheduled ten-minute stop to let some passengers off and to let others on, but ten minutes has come and gone and we're still not moving. Staring out of my window, over to the empty loading platform and down to the rail itself, there are several pigeons, the filthy things. Discarded by passengers before boarding their trains, there are clusters of cigarette butts piled several inches high between the platform and the rail. It's a good place for pigeons.

Now, after a twenty-minute stop, we're finally beginning to move. I've been on the train for four and a half hours. Announcements in English stopped after crossing the Swiss border. Now the fucking train is stopping again. I'm getting frustrated; perhaps it is best to do in Milan as the Milanese do?

An American couple boarded the train in Milan with bags big enough to hold half the state of Texas. The woman is wearing a red, Northface ski jacket. She's a brown-eyed brunette, about five-eight, with the current trendy almost-shoulder-length shag haircut. She's in her mid to late twenties, soon to be considered bottom heavy.

The guy's wearing wire rimmed glasses, a little freckly, and oozes preppiness. He's wearing a faded pair of 501 Levis and a gray sweatshirt embroidered with the words U.C. Berkeley Haas School of Business. His hair is cut short, almost military like, but this little fucker isn't military. Well, maybe he is, but it's the military branch of his family heritage. I can't imagine that this preppy little faggot has ever even taken a shit on his own schedule.

The wife has fallen asleep, her head leaning against the window, a pout on her face, the same kind of pout my ex-wife would wear when she was trying to get her way, which was all the time. Papa's boy is reading some book about civilization in the Middle Ages while his wife pouts away in worlds unknown. They are probably on their honeymoon, and when it's over they'll return to the order of their ancestors, make babies, her ass will grow big and wide, and he'll take up golf, joining the same country club his father and grandfather joined at the same stage of their lives to pretend that they are happy and fulfilled.

He won't divorce her because he has a little dick and knows that any other woman would take one look at him and laugh his happy ass right out of his hand-me-down heaven. The pouter won't divorce him because of the kids and because she'll be holding on to her husband, who will be holding on to his father, who's still holding on to the ninety-five year old grandfather who is unwilling to give up the ghost and leave the business for them all to piss away. Go pops, if you can't haunt 'em dead, haunt 'em by staying alive.

It's a dirty shame. I see two dead souls who have sold out to a stillborn's honor. I see nothing but an aborted life in that woman's pout. I'm nauseous, nauseated...

Maybe their lives are, and will be nothing like what I'm imagining. Maybe it's just me. Maybe she swallows, and they're happier than hell. Maybe he doesn't even like a good old-fashioned blowjob. What do I know?

That's horseshit; I'm still willing to wager a thousand that says he has a little dick and she doesn't swallow, doesn't come anywhere close to it. Am I bitter? I don't know, maybe more like enlightened. Yeah, that's it; I'm an enlightened cynic, that's what I am.

The asshole behind little dick is something else, too. He's part of another husband and wife team. He's sitting there, dickin' with his wife's mobile phone. Ten minutes ago, he received a call. She answered, and, acting like a secretary monitoring his calls, asked for a name before handing him the phone. The request seemed more to satisfy her curiosity than anything else. They're British; proper fucks in their fifties. She probably does swallow, but only when she wants something or when she's doing her lover for lunch.

Her phone's ringing again. She just went through the whole call-screening routine before handing Leroi the phone. We just passed into a tunnel and the call was dropped, but this goofball must think that shouting "Hello" three hundred times at the top of his voice will resurrect his caller from the dead.

Alright, I know I'm being an impatient judgmental asshole; I'll stop. Besides, the pace has picked up, and once again we're tooling through the countryside at high-speed, so I guess it's only proper for me to leave the greasy-haired bastards alone for a while.

I can't help it. Leroi's gettin' a scolding from his wife for not listening to her instructions on how to use the mobile phone when he was trying to return the dropped call. Now he's finally gotten through to the other party; it's a call related to the stock market taking a dump.

So here I sit, en route to Firenze, Leroi shouting out the perils of the stock market to the whole world, his wife scolding him and telling him to keep it down, while little dick tries to scrub a soiled spot out of his faded blue jeans that should have been shit-canned years ago and his wife pouts away, still lost in space.

* * * * *

Finally arrived: ah, Firenze. It's two-ten in the afternoon, right on time. The Italian chaos does have its own order. Being in Zurich taught me about myself, or at least a part of my heritage, its demand for punctuality, its rigidity. This train ride today has helped me to become aware of my own ambiguous nature.

March 22, 2001 - Midnight

After leaving the main station - Santa Maria Novella - and dragging my bags around several blocks in what was beginning to seem like a futile attempt, I somehow landed at the doorstep of Hotel Albion and was greeted by a thin, short woman in her twenties with blue eyes and mid-length, straight, light-brown hair.

"You must be Malcolm," she announced in a Florentine accent, as I dragged my bags inside through the double doors.

"You got it," I smiled. Of all the men in the world, how did she know that I'd be Malcolm?

"I've been waiting to meet you," she announced. "You are brave. Do you know that you are the only man who is attending this seminar?"

"No, but that doesn't surprise me," I lied with a smile. This was my karma. I couldn't stand women. I loved them, but hated them just the same. In my old life, almost everything was of the patriarchal good-old-boy world, but ever since leaving all that behind, women have been falling out of the woodwork and into my world. I'm not getting laid, but I've got women coming out of my ears.

I was shown to my room and then complained. It was dark, and only had two windows that started at the base of the floor and rose up about eighteen inches. I would literally have to get down on my knees if I wanted to look outside. Then I was shown another room, but it was worse, so I told them that I'd take the original room. Then I went in search of a bank teller machine so that I could get some of the local currency. Florence was bustling right along, full of life.

When I returned, they had another room for me to look at. It was on the third floor. It was a lot of stairs but a good source of exercise while away from home. After settling into the new room, I walked over to the window, opened it, and then swung open the shutters to take in the new view, listen to the city's clamor, and breathe in a bit of Firenze along with the fumes of the countless motor scooters that zipped through the city streets.

I'm telling you, there are motor scooters everywhere, lining the streets like a Hell's Angels convention. The window of my room faces the River Arno, which is about a hundred yards from Hotel Albion. Between the river and the hotel is a heavily traveled road that splits off in three directions directly in front of my room. In other words, it's a highly traveled road with cars and motorbikes passing by in a continuous state of frenzy.

I tried to take a nap, but the noise was too much. It was either the slow puttering backfire of a decelerating two-stroke engine or the winding acceleration of the same scooter after having slowed to take a corner. It reminded me of the damn gardener who used to show up early on Tuesday morning to do the neighbor's yard when I was living in my studio in Carmel. That goddamn backpack blower would whine constantly for an hour on Tuesday mornings, but this is going to be much worse. I pulled out a pair of foam earplugs from my overnight kit and slept soundly from five 'til nine.

I had what was, to me, a late dinner, but, by Italian standards, the evening was in its prime. I dined at a restaurant half a block from the hotel: the Monstrino, something about a monster. I had spinach gnocchi sautéed in butter and sage. It was a so-so meal, but the cappuccino and the grandmother's cream cake that followed my original experience did indeed leave a very fine taste in my mouth. I guess that's why I'm here, to redeem original experiences for new ones, to re-image the lifeless inner idols that no longer serve me.

I returned to the hotel after dinner and learned that the woman who had greeted me by name earlier was Sara. Her parents, Susanna and Massimo, own the hotel, and Sara and her younger sister, Swana, work there. It's a family affair. Sara is twenty-five, and Swana a couple of years younger. The two girls have been in the States before, four days in New York and an extended trip to California where they have friends who have been hotel clientele for over twenty years.

Oh, I almost forgot to mention Rufus, the family dog. He's a Pekinese, whose backside has been completely shaved, having undergone back surgery two days ago. Rufus could no longer walk with his hind legs and the family was going to put him to sleep, but, at the last minute, opted for the Veterinarian to perform experimental surgery on Rufus's spine, and it worked. So, Rufus is still with us, walking around grunting as if he hasn't a care in the world. He's on pain medication though, and the family is concerned with the addiction he's developing for the chicken they have to wrap his pain-pills in to get him to swallow the dope.

Susanna walked up while Sara was telling me about Rufus. "Our kids, Malcolm, when they are sick, we give them an aspirin, but when Rufus isn't well, we immediately rush him to the doctor," Susanna joked, as she leaned down and rubbed Rufus' head. "Isn't that right, Rufus?"

Sara looked down at her mother carrying on over Rufus and

smiled. She didn't seem one bit jealous of her mother's love for another.

March 23, 2001 - Dream - Florence

I was going home, somewhere... a frame to a chair, a metal frame, the kind that a cloth sets down into and forms a seat. The kind of chair I once fell through and busted my ass at Turner's house. Some kids see me and they yell at me to get my attention. I'm in a really good mood, so I go over there to see what's going on. They're playing like they're on a TV show. One is going at me: "hey mister, hey mister." He's reaching up. He's a little kid, a little blonde haired kid, and I grab and touch his head, rub his hair and stuff. Feels like parts of his head are missing. He's just lump headed, that's what it was; he was kind of a lumpy headed kid. There was a blonde girl on the ground in the backyard, too. She knew me from somewhere else. She had just seen me earlier in the dream, from where I can't remember. She was all excited about something. Oh, yeah, she ended up being with her boyfriend. Telling him all about it, about why she was excited for me. I remember the kids in the backyard pretending like they were on TV, trying to get me to play. They were doing the Today Show.

March 23, 2001 - 2 p.m.

I'm sitting in the bar or lounge area of Hotel Albion. Breakfast is served every morning in the dining room. After breakfast, I walked back up to my room to get a sweater. I passed two young men in the hallway, one of them smoking a cigarette and carrying a bucket of paint, the other man carrying a ladder. After washing the remnants of breakfast from my face, I slipped on a sweater and left my room.

The scent of fresh paint oozed from the room next door. I couldn't decide which odor was the most offensive, the cigarette smoke, the fumes from the motor scooters, or the paint. The paint would dry, and probably by the time I got back from my walk, but the smoke and fumes seem to be an integral part of this Florentine atmosphere.

After walking down from my room, Sara asked me to follow her into the dining room to introduce me to four of the women who were participants of the seminar. Three of the women had just finished getting their PhD's in psychology. The fourth woman was a sister of one of the psychologists. I guessed all these women to be in their fifties, but estimating age has become troublesome for me over the last few years.

I started to become aware of this a few years earlier. Working around the house one weekend, yard work and stuff, I had loaded some things into the back of my truck. Instead of stepping out of the truck-bed like a grown man, I jumped over the side thinking I was still a teenager. I went about my business as if nothing had happened, because I didn't think anything had. Then later that night, after a hot shower, I sat down on the couch, and that wasn't bad either, but getting up was quite another story. It took me about three months to recuperate from that little lie I tried to tell myself.

About a year later, I was having a bit of a relapse. It was low back pain, but it also felt like I'd been kicked in the nuts, so I phoned to see my physician, and they had me come in the following day.

Dr. Carver was a short, thin Jewish man in his sixties. He loved to tell me that I was too fat when I went in for my annual physical. He'd tell me that I needed to lose twenty pounds, and I'd tell him that was bullshit. He'd tell me ten pounds then, and that he'd see me next year if I didn't need to see him before. This visit was one where I needed to see him before.

"Mr. Clay, what can I do for you?" Dr. Carver asked.

"I want you to check my nuts."

"What are your symptoms?"

"Feels like I've been kicked in the right one. My lower right back and my balls hurt. It's probably my back, but just in case, I want my nuts checked."

"Alright, lets have a look... huh, smooth, no bumps, no abnormalities."

"That's what I figured, but I don't like taking chances."

"Always best to check when in doubt," he answered, as he reached for a medical reference book. "Lets see here, yep, L-4 or L-5, radial pain. It's a nerve irritation from your L-4 or L-5 vertebrae in your low back. See this diagram."

"Yeah, I know what the problem is," I answered without looking at his reference book.

"What's that?"

"New girlfriend."

"What the hell has that got to do with L-4 and L-5?"

I looked him dead in the eye and grinned. "I've got a seventeen-year-old's hard-on attached to my thirty-seven-year-old body. She's hotter than hell, Doc. My dick's keeping up with her. It's the rest of my body that's falling apart."

"Put her on top," he said, shaking his head.

"What?"

"You're straining your goddamn back. From now on she goes on top. Now get the hell out of here."

So anyway, that's when I first began to realize that I wasn't as young as I wanted to believe I was. That's when I also started to notice that a lot of women who were close to my age appeared to look much older than I looked, or so I thought.

The first question asked by one of the four women was if I was a psychologist. The second question came from another of the four; she wanted to know if I had signed up for this seminar when I learned that I would be the only man attending. The answer to both questions was, of course: no. Then they wanted to know what I did for a living; so I told them that I was a tractor salesman. That was fun, watching their reaction, watching them dangle in that silent void.

One psychologist, the same one that asked me if I was there because I was the only man, just knew that I was there to find a bride.

"Are you a marrier?" She bluntly asked me.

"A what?"

"A marrier; are you looking for a wife?"

"I tried it once, and it cured me of the desire to ever step off into that fantasy again," I said defensively.

"Oh, I thought that maybe you were a marrier like my brother in-law. He just married for the seventh time."

This particular shrink was going to be an interesting study. She was already trying to tack a label on me. I had suspected that this might happen; I just hadn't expected it to happen quite so soon.

After that whirlwind introduction, I set out on a solitary walk. On my way out the door, I passed a slender, gray-haired gentleman who was entering the hotel. I nodded and smiled at him and he did the same in return.

I got lost on the walk, just exactly as I had planned. It took over two hours before I found my way back to Hotel Albion. In Florence, getting lost is easy to do, but I didn't mind it. I liked stumbling into the unexpected treasures that life has a way of handing out when we least expect it. Perhaps my wanting one of these unexpected treasures to appear this morning is what kept this from happening.

When I arrived yesterday, I was very much in a dream-like state. I had hardly slept for two days, much of it because of excitement and not wanting to miss the plane and train, but now I'd arrived and enjoyed a fair night's sleep. The walk was more to get a feel for Firenze, about getting my bearings. It will take a few more days to get really oriented, but this walk was to get the initial shock behind me.

On my return, I stepped into the lobby of Hotel Albion and noticed the same gray-haired gentleman who I had passed on my way out. He was sitting on a bench that had been tucked against the wall next to the front desk. The bench was directly in line with the front door. We smiled and nodded, again mirroring each other. To my right was the staircase that would have taken me to my room, but I walked to my left, past the front desk and into the bar area.

There were five tables in this lounge area and a small bar that served espresso drinks, teas, and liquor. A table stood in one corner of the room between the bar and a large, draped, full-length window that ran from floor to ceiling. I took that seat. I sat there yesterday for a few minutes and liked how it felt. It served as a good observation platform for what was happening inside the hotel as well as outside.

I'm glad I asked for another room. The original room that had been assigned to me was just above the bar and across the hall, from where I could hear an argument of some sort. The quarreling went on for several minutes, until finally a young woman came stomping down the steps, walked into the lobby, picked up Rufus, and stormed out through the front door. It had to be Swana. I had yet to meet her, but it had to be her. She was about Sara's height and blue-eyed, but a little heavier. Swana's hair was lighter, redder, shorter and wavier, and cut in a shag. She was definitely feistier than Sara, or at least wore her feistiness for the world to see.

A discussion continued upstairs, but the voices had become muffled, and a few minutes later, Massimo, the father walked down the steps followed by Susanna. Massimo went outside, and Susanna slipped behind the front desk and started visiting with Sara about what appeared to be business affairs. I pulled the curtain back and looked across the street to the park and spotted Massimo and Swana facing each other in discussion, Rufus now in Massimo's arms. Massimo seemed upset, and my guess was that it was more about his fiery daughter's reaction than it was about Rufus. One thing was certain, though, with a wife and two daughters, Massimo was outnumbered.

So Hotel Albion has its own little dramas just like those acted out all over the world. The slender, gray-haired man walked up to the bar carrying a tray with a variety of clean cups and dishes. He took them behind the bar and put them away. He must be the grandfather. I looked outside again; father, daughter, and Rufus had disappeared. I watched the old man walk back into the lobby as Massimo came in through the double doors. Massi said something in Italian to the old man; the grandfather took the words in but didn't respond.

It looked as if Swana had prevailed, but not until after reconciling with her father. In my few brief encounters and observations, Massimo appears to be a kind and compassionate man, but very much a man with his own way and style of doing things. He appears to be in excellent health. He's slender with light-reddish brown hair that's combed back but has the habit of falling forward, so he occasionally has to comb it back with his fingers. He's wearing a long-sleeved shirt and cotton pants with suspenders to hold them up. He has a thin beard, and the same blue eyes as Sara and Swana.

The women in his life might outnumber Massi, but he hasn't been emasculated. The other thing I like about Massimo is that he has no need to prove his masculinity; he simply carries it within and lives it out in his daily life. It's like he allows himself to be vulnerable towards his life, his family, and the relationship that he's engaging; yet fear appears to have no influence on his exposure. It's as if he has stepped beyond the fear and into himself.

I love this corner chair, getting soaked up into the woodwork, so that I can soak in the eternal divine dramas that are being acted out in the temporal waking world. I also love to watch the pretty girls go by, and I like almost as much, but not quite, the heads of the men that these women turn. Ah, the bouncing ponytails, wafting their scent, leaving a fragrant trail of their longed for essence in the imagination of their on-looking masculine counterparts.

So the rest of the family, Sara, Susanna, Massimo, and the grandfather, gathered around the front desk while Swana and Rufus were out frolicking through Firenze in search of chicken chunks to satisfy Rufus' newly developed habit. After a short discussion, Sara went upstairs to the room where Swana and her parents had earlier held the first round of negotiations, and Grandfather walked back into the kitchen, probably to see if there were any clean dishes for him to put away.

This family doesn't work here; they live here, and they don't seem too concerned about having to hide their personal lives from their guests. They don't go out of their way to impose upon their patrons, but they don't hide just the same. Their conversations have been in Italian, so I have yet to understand a single word, but emotions and expressions are universal.

I took another look outside. The painters were on their lunch break, sitting in their small, white Fiat pickup truck that was parked across the street from the hotel, in front of a phone booth. They were eating, smoking, and sharing a laugh or two. They were also sharing the sights and smells of the pretty feminines that wandered up to make phone calls.

Sara returned downstairs with a backpack and two bags from an earlier shopping spree. She started saying something to her father, it almost sounded heated, but as I looked on, it was about some business detail, possibly a reservation or a reference to the books. It wasn't heated or disrespectful; Sara was just being direct and clear in her communication. Massimo made a quick phone call, his conversation almost as clear and direct as Sara had just been with him. He then pulled a thin attaché case and a helmet out from behind the front desk. I don't know why it surprised me that Massi had a motor scooter. I could hear my physician's voice: "From now on, put her on top, and get the hell out of here."

March 23, 2001 - 11 p.m.

I was sitting in the corner of the lounge area, in my favorite seat, awaiting the welcome reception that wasn't scheduled to take place for another couple of hours. A woman arrived to check-in, an American, fifty something. She was tall, with brown hair that had auburn highlights. A large-framed woman, she wasn't overweight, but not a petite type either. She had a cane and walked with a limp. Susanna checked her in and showed her to her room, which had to be accessed through the bar area. It was on the ground floor, and I think the room had been assigned to her so she wouldn't have to use the stairs. On her way back from showing the new arrival to her room, Susanna stopped to check on me.

"Malcolm, can I get you anything: a cappuccino?"

"Nothing, thank you for offering, though," I answered, setting the pen down in my notebook.

"You are welcome," Susanna answered. Her reply was sincere; it wasn't feigned or a formality. She really was able to hear and receive my thank you, had taken it in, and responded genuinely. How refreshing. I smiled and nodded to her as I sat back and took a deep breath. "Malcolm, no working here. You relax," Susanna courteously reprimanded, as if she had been assigned the duty of caring for my soul.

"I haven't worked for over two years," I reassured her.

"So you are, how they say, retired," Susanna said, nodding, raising her lower lip over her upper lip as if she was trying to contemplate how a man of my age could be retired.

"Yeah, I guess you could call it that," I confirmed. "But I must go back to work one of these days," I added, to appease my own inner sense of duty.

"Of course," she answered, as if to support my knowing what was right for me.

"So, don't worry, I'm not working," I reassured her, as she nodded in agreement and then started to back away from my corner to return to her duties.

I thought about work. Work was something a person did for money or for some other type of compensation, possibly in service to an obligation. I wasn't working; I was having fun. I was there for me, strictly in service to myself, and it felt good.

The woman who had just checked-in walked out of her room and up to the bar.

"Hello," I said, greeting her and letting her know that I was a fellow American.

"Hello there," she said, looking down at me from the bar.

"Are you here for the seminar?" I asked.

"I certainly am."

"Me, too. I'm Malcolm."

"I'm Abilene," she said, as Susanna arrived to serve her.

Abilene ordered tea and a large bottle of water, paid for it and asked if she could join me. I welcomed her company. She took the big bottle of water to her room and then returned for a sit.

I had an image of Abilene's father. A shrewd, tough old southern man who had built an empire from scratch, and all of this because of Abilene's name and the way she carried herself. My guess was that she had no brothers, possibly an only child, but that was just a guess. She had green eyes, and in them I could see strength and compassion dancing, intertwined.

"I've had a heck of a day getting here," Abilene announced as she sat back and took a sip of her tea.

"Did you fly directly from the States today?"

"Yes, and I missed my connection in Paris. I should never have waited for that wheelchair."

"You have back problems?"

"Multiple Sclerosis," she answered, as if she had a common cold.

"Where' you from, Abilene?"

"Birmingham, and you?"

"California."

"Are you an psychologist?"

"No, just a burnt-out tractor salesman trying to run away from an old identity. How 'bout you?"

"I'm a psychiatrist, but don't know much about Mary Magdalene. Tell me, though, how does a tractor salesman end up at a psychological seminar in Florence, Italy to explore the feminine aspect of the psyche?"

"That's a damn good question. I met Sophia out in Sedona in January, and I fell in love with her," I answered. "I went to the seminar to hear another lecturer, but his bedside manner left much to be desired. Sophia, on the other hand, I found to be more than a delightful woman."

"I met Sophia when I was asked by the Episcopal Church to welcome and show a woman, who was both an Episcopalian priest and a Jungian psychologist, around the Birmingham area. Sophia had been asked to do the same and that's how we became friends."

"How lucky you both are," I answered.

"She's been trying to get me over to one of these seminars, but my health just hasn't permitted me to do so in the past. I'm getting around pretty well right now, so I figured it was time to take advantage of my good fortune."

Abilene and I visited for a while longer. Abilene had been married and, after having two children, her husband had decided that marriage wasn't fun anymore, so she raised the children on her own. After talking for a bit longer, Abilene decided to turn in to freshen up before the welcoming reception, and I followed suit.

* * * * *

In the lobby, on my way to the dining room to attend the welcoming reception, I had the pleasure of meeting Maria Theresa, Sophia's colleague. Maria Theresa is quite a lovely woman who is in her early sixties. The only way I can really describe her is that she's one classy woman, exuding elegance and grace. She's a native of Northern Italy, but also keeps an apartment in Florence. She has a great deal of knowledge about the history and culture of the area. Maria Theresa's mother was a Florentine. She's well acquainted with the works of many famous artists that are housed in the museums of Firenze.

Maria Theresa is to serve as our guide, first in reviewing slides and photos before actually going out to view the images, and then guiding us through the city and to the actual paintings and frescos themselves. I suppose you could say that Maria Theresa is to be our modern day Beatrice.

The welcoming get-acquainted hour was interesting. In the center of the dining room was a table overflowing with wine, cheese, and several other tasty Italian specialties, all in finger food form. Around the perimeter of the room were chairs that formed the shape of a horseshoe around three sides of the table. I walked in and sat down at the bottom of the horseshoe and didn't say a thing, knowing that my silence would more than likely be short-lived.

A woman was sitting two seats to my left. I acknowledged her with a "hello" as I sat down. She was in her mid-forties with shoulder-length sandy-colored hair. She was attractive, one of the most petite among the women. She didn't exactly ignore me, but was slow to acknowledge my presence.

"And who are you?" she finally asked.

"I am me," I answered, a bit put off by her form of introduction.

"I thought this was a woman's seminar," she said, still failing to formally introduce herself.

"You know, I wasn't aware of that," I answered.

"I'm Kerri," she finally volunteered. I guess she sensed my reservation towards her initial approach.

"It is a pleasure to meet you Kerri. I'm Malcolm," I answered, and just then two other women entered the room and walked directly over to me, one of them saying, "You must be Malcolm," in a heavy southern accent, extending her hand. "I'm Christina and this is Julia." They were attractive women, both blondes, Christina mid to late forties, my guess, and Julia a couple of years ahead of her.

"It's very nice to meet you both..." and that is how it went for about the next hour. I didn't have the opportunity to meet every woman individually before we took our seats and formally introduced ourselves, but I had met most of them and was certain that the opportunity to meet the few remaining women one-on-one would soon present itself.

Towards the end of the gathering, Sophia walked up to one of the women attendees standing a few feet in front of me. While speaking with this woman, Sophia slyly pitched an apple up in the air for me to catch. I quickly snagged the fruit, and we both smiled.

The formal gathering adjourned and Sophia asked me to join her in the bar where I was to have the pleasure of not only her company, but several of the other women as well. We gathered around my favorite table.

In addition to Christina and Julia, Carrie, a different Carrie, also joined the festivities. She was a surgical nurse, who had suffered a heart attack less than a year before. I guessed her to be in her early fifties, a strawberry-blonde with freckles and wire-rimmed glasses. She seemed a bit nervous, on the edgy side. She was a writer working on a book about the Mysteries of the Villa of Pompeii.

Another woman, Bianca, who had arrived late and walked in at the tail end of the reception, joined us as well. Bianca was eccentrically dressed in a leather biker-type suit. She also wore a bandana over her long dark hair. She had olive skin, probably an Italian woman, mysterious. Bianca was short but in excellent physical shape, a dancer from New York. She was about the same age as Carrie, the nurse, but her presence was more youthful. In addition to her youthful appearance, Bianca had a quiet, serious side. She appeared to be fatigued from her travels, yet she joined us in spite of her weariness.

Christina brought up the subject of pomegranates and somehow we got onto the subject of peeling them.

"Oh, you don't have to peel them," I explained. "They burst open when they're ripe."

"Really?"

"Oh, yeah, they're grown in California."

"And they just burst open when they are ripe?" Christina asked with a childlike wonderment.

"Well, maybe they're ripe before they burst open, but when we used to steal them from the neighbor's trees, we always picked the ones that had already burst open," I explained.

"Ah, the forbidden fruit," Sophia quipped, nodding with a big smile, and savoring the metaphor.

"I never thought of it that way, but you're right," I answered, having to rethink the whole image of one of my youthful follies.

It felt as if the women were all watching me, trying to figure me out, or, at the very least, figure out why the hell I was there.

"Maybe you're the one who will be writing the book," Bianca said, giving me a serious look. It was the first thing she had said. The rest of the time she had been listening, gleaning all that was taking place, taking it all in.

"You know, now that's not a bad idea at all," I answered, grinning as if I'd just stolen another pomegranate.

March 24, 2001 - Dream

Near my grandparents' house, the home of my paternal grandparents. Going around there to park, do something like paperwork. Some guy comes by on a motorcycle or two guys. They pull in front of me, run a stop sign. I flip them off and they see it and they come back around and want to have a confrontation. They are split up though, and I turn down some side street and avoid them.

Then I finally get back to the house that I was returning to. I think it was Turner's or Aunt Hannah's house, Turner's house or somewhere. Had almost the feel of Manteca. Yeah, it has a feel of... oh, I was thinking about getting a job in that dream, and I remember I was thinking about going back to Harter's. Has the feel of Harter's in it, too. Possibly being jealous of Harter's like I was jealous of Staton's, both past employers.

Anyway, I avoided them; the two guys who were trying to track me down for flipping them off. I couldn't find the alley to my grandparents' house. That's right, I was going to park back in there because I thought it would give me some energy.

That is also the alley of a house in another dream from not long ago, a house that needed a roof. It's also the alley where I met my grandfather when my brother Freeman was about to get married, and again when he was about to become a father. I was saying how crazy he was and my grandfather said not to worry, it was giving him something to live for, giving him meaning.

Oh, wow, that house that needed a roof had been torn down in this dream. There was no house there. That's right, it was a vacant lot, or it seemed to be vacant. I just knew it was like... when I was on the road. It was the alley, the back, it was a road one over, and as I drove by, I could see that it was a vacant lot now.

Anyway, I thought that I had avoided these two guys who I had given the finger, and I was driving... wow, in my high school pickup truck, my golden Chevy step-side pickup. I went in the house, and I came out. I start to go out, and I look and see a sweater and a few other things sprawled all over the truck's hood. I look and it's the two guys. They said: "You know what we want." I said: "Look it, alright man, I did it, just... I'm sorry. I flipped you off, big deal, I'm sorry."

That wasn't good enough; they still wanted to beat my ass. An apology just wasn't good enough, and they still wanted a piece of me. It was almost like I was there to... I don't know... I woke feeling weak, like I was going to be... like I was going to die, or I was... they were going to kill me. That's how I woke. Just feeling weak. When I walk the stairs I huff and puff. I get so tired... seems like I get tired so easy. Wow, maybe I am tired. I'm worried about my heart.

Another Dream. I was at another hotel with a woman, another woman. With one woman, and somehow Kelli spotted me there, and I had been awaiting a package. Kelli came up to me and said: "Let me know if the package comes in." And I said: "Oh, I will." And she goes and gets into your-her car.

The other woman was there, and I said goodbye to her, and I hugged her, and I must have... ah... ah... and she said: "You're really liking this aren't you?" Or, "you're really into this" or "digging this. You are really there." It was something like that and I said: "Yeah." And she kind of held me that time a lot longer than she normally does and it was almost like she did this so that Kelli could see it, like to make her jealous, and we separated, and I was waiting for a package to come in that some... for some reason, my grandmother was in the background of the package that was coming into her house.

Before that was another part of the dream, or another dream. I was at the ocean, and I was supposed to have met Leroy somewhere, and I had missed him or something. Caught up with him there at the ocean, and I walked down to this... it was for some birthday celebration, and I walked down to this cliff... no this rock on the cliff by the ocean, and I yell: "Hey, Leroy, come over here." It was about throwing a party, and he ran over there, and he was coming down the hill to go to the rock that I was standing out on, but somehow he ran out over the cliff and fell over, fell into the water and almost hit this tree that was across it, but didn't. Some other guy on the shore dove out to try to rescue him, but Leroy came up out of the water, and he was... I don't think he needed rescuing, but this other guy went in after him anyway.

March 24, 2001 - 10 p.m.

This morning we gathered in the upper room, above the bar, opposite the room that I was to have originally, in the same room where Swana and her father had their discussion yesterday, before they adjourned to the park across the street. It was a long narrow room with a low, rounded ceiling; it reminded me of a cylinder that had been cut in half lengthwise. In the back of the room was a stained glass window in the form of a half circle that took up almost the entire wall.

Again, the chairs were set up in a horseshoe format and, again, I sat at the heel of the shoe, directly in front of the stained glass window, with my back to it. The women attendees sat on both sides of me and then along the walls up towards the front of the room, while Sophia and Maria Theresa sat at the open end of the horseshoe. Maria Theresa and Sophia shared the responsibilities of hosting the seminar; Sophia lectured, and Maria Theresa presented images first in slides before guiding us through the city to see the real thing.

Sophia did most of the lecturing based on Nancy Qualls-Corbett's lectures on Mary Magdalene, with references on the written word from the first four gospels of the New Testament Bible, as well as Gnostic scriptures taken from the Nag Hammadi library, and several other books with references to Mary Magdalene and her relationship to Jesus Christ, quite possibly their secret marriage.

In addition to others, Sophia also referenced a book written by Margaret Starbird: *The Woman with the Alabaster Jar*. I had stumbled upon this particular book and read it before arriving at the seminar. The book discusses legends of Mary Magdalene fleeing after Christ's Crucifixion, quite possibly carrying his child. She sought refuge first in Alexandria where she gave birth to this child, a daughter named Sarah. She continued the journey with Sarah as well as Martha and Lazarus, crossing the Mediterranean Sea in a small boat, eventually arriving on the southern shores of France at a small fishing village now called Les Saintes Maries de la Mer, not far from Sainte Baume where she lived out the rest of her life in seclusion, still despairing over the loss of her lover.

Another version of the myth is that Joseph of Arimathea, a friend of Jesus, was the protector of the Holy Grail, the Grail being Mary Magdalene. Joseph of Arimathea was responsible for assisting Mary and her unborn child to escape to safety, Mary Magdalene being the chalice that contained, Sarah, the royal blood of Christ himself. To this day there is a gypsy celebration held in the later part of April to celebrate Saint Sarah, also known as Sara Kali, or the Black Queen.

Now, being a tractor peddler without any formal, let alone scholarly, education, I can't substantiate if one bit of this is true, any more than I can prove the validity of the Bible, or anything else for that matter, and thank God that I don't have to. It doesn't matter if it is literally true or not. To me, all that matters is the metaphor: if the symbolism rings a bell whose tone resonates deep down in my bones, into my soul, if the symbolism speaks my truth, my inner knowing, I couldn't give a damn if it came to me from a comic strip in the Sunday funnies.

Sophia's talk was based on Nancy Qualls-Corbett's lecture: *Images of the Magdalena - Controversy and Confusion*. Sophia discussed some of the myths that had been attached to Mary Magdalene including her being portrayed as the penitent whore who Christ supposedly had healed by casting out seven demons.

We also discussed how Mary Magdalene might have come from Magdala, a port town known for silks and dried fish, a town where Mary might have acquired the reputation of being a whore, even though she might not have been a prostitute at all. Maybe she was a prostitute and maybe she wasn't; maybe on an archetypal or psychological level we've transformed Mary Magdalene into the image that we need her to be on a collective level?

Sophia also discussed how Mary Magdalene, being the woman at the foot of the cross in the crucifixion paintings, was a metaphor of being near the heart.

Obviously Mary Magdalene held a very high position with Christ that has not only been given to us in Biblical passages, but in images as well. The Bible speaks of how Mary Magdalene was the first person Christ revealed himself to after his resurrection. Not only are we able to read this, but also see the image in the countless *Nolo Me Tangere* - the Don't-Touch-Me paintings.

After about a two-hour lecture, Maria Theresa presented slides of Mary Magdalene that we would be viewing in person over the next few days, as well as other works of art from the Pitti Palace. Then we left on foot for the Pitti and had lunch along the way.

March 25, 2001

Sophia talked on Nancy Qualls-Corbett's lecture: *Revisioning the Image*, and Maria Theresa presented slides of the work of Fra Beato Angelico from the San Marco Convent. At 3:00 we were scheduled to meet outside the convent.

We discussed how Mary Magdalene was a symbol of not only sin, but also of redemption. In a sense, Mary Magdalene redeems Eve: just as there was a split between the masculine and feminine in the Old Testament when Adam and Eve fell from grace, so there is a reconciliation of the masculine and feminine as Christ accepts Mary Magdalene as a repentant sinner. Thus the masculine and feminine images are reunited.

We also discussed Gnosticism and its befriending Christianity: how salvation was derived from having secret knowledge; gnosis meaning knowledge, a mystical inner knowledge based on one's own experience as opposed to trying to recreate an experience based on another's recipe. Not to say that the Gnostics had it all figured out, either, as they were often extremists whose desire was to overcome the material with the spiritual and, in so doing, cut away at the core of their very own physical existence.

At three in the afternoon, we met outside the San Marco Convent and entered. Of all the works there, it was Fra Beato Angelico's *Nolo Me Tangere* fresco in the first cell of the convent that reached out to me. Certain painters, believed to be orthodox, were in fact allied with the heretics who were in opposition to the patriarchal Church's denial of the feminine.

The Church had a vested interest in protecting their image of a celibate savior who was beyond what may be considered the sins of the flesh. These certain heretical artists would paint symbols into their works to convey their own beliefs and secret knowledge and yet spare themselves the wrath of the Church's inquisition.

In Fra Angelico's *Nolo Me Tangere*, there are three red Xs painted into the landscape of grass and flowers that Mary Magdalene's hand points to. These red Xs are believed by some to be a secret symbol of a hidden truth, suggesting that Christ indeed had a wife or lover.

It was interesting to have first read of this, and then to experience this fresco in the raw with my very own eyes. In a way, it brought me back in time, yet also brought time forward; if these symbols secretly revealed a truth at the time of the Renaissance, it seems that they also reveal a gnosis in our present day of denial, or I should say, in my present-day denial of the feminine. Symbols are universal, eternal, and even if the material replicas of these images are destroyed, they live on and come back to us, if not again in the material, then at the very least ethereally, as images within our dreams, our souls, or worse yet, acted out in neurotic suffering.

* * * * *

I'm having a nice time in Firenze, following along with the group of women. The food as well as the landscape is magnificent, even if I don't know where I am. It damn sure... well, I... hell,

I'm just some ol' country boy who somehow stumbled into this whole mess. I mean, yeah, I signed up for the trip and all, but I was naïve as they come about Florence. I had no idea that it was the birthplace of the Renaissance, let alone have much knowledge what the Renaissance really even was. To me, the Renaissance was a bunch of goofball Americans with identity crisis, dressed up in this goddamn goofy garb, carrying around a turkey drumstick in one hand and a beer stein in the other as they gathered on weekends to play grab-ass and make complete idiots of themselves.

Anyway, here I am, right in the middle of the Renaissance wonderland, the real McCoy, that is, and it's nothing like those goofy bastards back in the States portray it to be. So, I suppose you might say that I've already re-imaged one thing.

I wonder how Kelli is doing. She's in Palestine, working on some sort of commission. Think I'll send her an e-mail when I find an Internet café.

March 26, 2001

Sophia's discussion was based on Nancy Qualls-Corbett's lecture: *To Make Her a Man*. Marie Theresa presented some historical and artistic aspects of Florence, and then a walking tour of Florence, with lunch on the way.

Sophia discussed a passage from the Gospel of Thomas in the *Nag Hammadi Library*: Simon Peter was complaining to Jesus about Mary Magdalene, and Christ's response was that he, himself, would lead her so that he could make her a male.

I suppose that from a feminist viewpoint this sounds quite chauvinistic. Yet, by stepping around the battle of the sexes and deeper into the symbolism of this text, this passage has the power to return a woman to a lost part of herself: her masculine image or inner counterpart. And it can have a reciprocal effect in returning a man to a lost part of himself: his feminine image or inner counterpart.

Sophia also mentioned something in reference to another one of the Gnostic Gospels, something about Jesus kissing Mary Magdalene on the lips.

March 26, 2001 - 4 p.m.

It was more of a playful afternoon today. On our way to lunch we stopped in a Basilica (Ognissanti, where Botticelli is buried) to see a fresco of the Last Supper, but at that time of day, the part of the church with the fresco was closed to the public. We walked on, and I ended up having lunch with Carrie, the nurse who was writing the book on the Mysteries of the Villa of Pompeii. I very much enjoyed her companionship. We exchanged some of our personal histories and, after lunch, caught up with more of our group who were wandering around the Ponte Vecchio. We then explored aimlessly for a couple of hours before returning to Hotel Albion to rest and clean up before driving to the country for a Tuscan dinner.

In the countryside, Susanna and Massimo have a villa: Le Boscarecce, open for business from spring through fall. They plan to open for spring business next week and have offered to prepare a Tuscan style dinner for our entire group before the official opening. Swana is to be our Chef. She has attended culinary school specializing in dishes from the region.

March 26, 2001 - Dinner in Tuscany

We were shuttled out to the country in the hotel's van and another family car, and Maria Theresa drove as well. It was a forty-five minute drive from Firenze. The countryside was breathtaking: green, rolling hills, farmhouses, orchards, vineyards, fields of Fava beans, and high clouds floating, slow-dancing across the blue sky. We arrived in time to sit outside and breathe in a spectacular sunset before the call for dinner.

Swana prepared the meal, and the rest of the family served it, with the exception of Sara, who remained at Hotel Albion to watch over the other guests. Our meal consisted of an Asparagus Risotto, Pasta Carbonara, veal, and pear pie with pine nuts. With her culinary expertise and the support of her family, Swana prepared an exquisite meal.

I sat across the table from Victoria, a psychologist from Birmingham. She was on her second marriage, and from the way she spoke of her husband, it was a happy and solid affair. Victoria was high energy: she woke up every morning and ran for a few miles before the lectures. She also appeared to be a woman with nothing to hide. She seemed to live and speak her truth; it just rolled out of her uninhibitedly.

I can't remember how our conversation started, but before I knew it, she was telling me how her twenty-something-year-old daughter used to live in Florence but was now back in the States all involved with some guy who was totally up in his head.

"I sent her a postcard today," Victoria said in a matter of fact tone.

"How nice."

"Yeah, it's a picture of five guys leaning over the brick wall along the Arno with their butts sticking up in the air. We'll see if that brings her back to her feeling function," Victoria said, in a confident that-ought-to-work tone.

Hell, I couldn't help falling in love with Victoria right then and there. I began to tell her some things about myself, about my life and how it had eventually led me to Florence. I told her the story of Mrs. Shams and how leaving there was like being a teenager leaving home for the first time. How I was a numb drunk when I actually left home for the first time years ago, and that this was like my second chance to feel and go through all that I had once avoided.

Victoria spoke of her marriage, about being on her own after her divorce, and how eventually she met her second husband and what a great thing they had together. He was actually flying to Paris to meet Victoria the following week.

I then told her about Adam, and how I had to learn that my problem wasn't with my birth mother or any other human being out in the world as much as it was the mother within who continued to abuse and victimize me.

"It's amazing what happens when I am able to take back the projections that I spin off onto others. Just by recognizing and withdrawing the blame, it creates a space for others to return to themselves. My mother phoned me about a month ago and started to tell me about her fear that my brother Freeman was close to beating his oldest teenage boy. I just shut up and listened, and the next thing I knew, my mother's very words were: 'I'd be in jail for what I did to you kids.'"

"Oh, my gosh, how beautiful," Victoria answered.

"That erased it all. I mean, it didn't matter if she had ever beaten me or not. What's so amazing is that I never once asked her for this confession. I just kept looking within myself, learning to love my parents for the human beings they are instead of the gods I wanted them to be," I told Victoria as I held back tears.

We continued our visit over dinner, touching on a few lighter topics and pretty soon one of the women asked about my age. "Forty," I told them, and soon learned that in addition to being the only man in the group, I was also the youngest, to boot, and I liked it.

After dinner, having been surrounded by so much feminine energy and feeling the need to withdraw into a space of my own, I retreated to the corner near the door. The women were gathered in different clusters, clucking away excitedly, and I know I'll probably catch hell for calling it clucking, but it was clucking to me just the same.

So anyway, there was a lot of clucking going on until one of the clusters began to sing: *I don't Know How to Love Him* from the movie *Jesus Christ Superstar*. Then several of the other women joined in. How sweet it was. I stood there in the corner, breathing this all in. It was an honor to have been allowed into their sanctuary, but at the same time, I asked myself: "How in the fuck, of all places in the world, did you end up here?"

I had been a passenger in the van on the way out to the country, but rode back with Maria Theresa. I sat in the front and Rachel rode in the backseat. Not far into the drive I started to nod off. I dozed and woke up embarrassed, making a remark about my falling asleep.

"Yes, and with a woman driver," Maria Theresa quickly responded.

"You got that right," I said. "I used to drive fifty-thousand miles a year. I cringe whenever I'm the passenger. I'm always the one behind the wheel."

"My how things have changed," Rachel commented from the backseat.

"Yes they have. I'm a pilot and fly my own airplane, too. A couple of years ago I met my friend Jillian who at the time was in the process of getting her instrument rating. I flew with her as a passenger and a spotter pilot when she was doing cross-country work, before she went for her check ride. Now let me tell you, letting a woman take over the controls of an airplane that I was flying in was one big step."

"I have pilots in my family," Rachel said.

"I'm selling my plane," I answered.

"Why?" Rachel asked.

"Have you read Marie Louis von Franz's, *The Problem of the Puer Aeternus?*" I asked. This is an analytical evaluation of Saint-Exupéry's *The Little Prince*. Saint-Exupéry was piloting himself when he died in a plane crash. It is von Franz's theory that he was a *Puer Aeternus,* meaning eternal child, and that he was unable to step from a boy's psychology into a man's psychology. She believed that a *Puer* who is unable to make this inner transition is often cut down in life by some sort of tragedy: like a man in the throes of a midlife crisis who dies in his sports car, or flies his airplane into a mountainside.

"Yes, I have, but..." Rachel started to reply.

"I flew to Oregon to go fishing the day JFK junior went down. I checked into my room at the hotel and turned on the television before they had even confirmed that it was JFK for certain. As soon as I heard it, I knew what had happened. He was only a month older than me; he'd lost his mother not long ago and his marriage was a bit shaky. He was approaching midlife. He couldn't step into the next stage, and it got him, and what's even sadder is that he took two beautiful women with him. Talk about the ultimate denial of the feminine."

"But, Malcolm, if you're aware of this..." Rachel began to say.

"I know, but my guts said to sell it anyway," I defended. "Besides, I don't need the plane anymore. It was once my symbol of freedom..."

"And now you have that freedom," Rachel answered.

"You've got that right. This *Puer* has landed."

March 27, 2001

The discussion led by Sophia was based on Nancy Qualls-Corbett's lecture: *Why we need a Penitent Whore*. Maria Theresa presented slides from the Uffizi Museum and then we were to meet at the Uffizi, the gathering point outside the Piazza della Signoria, under the statue of David.

In today's lecture, Sophia suggested that we need the Penitent Whore archetype in order to restore our relationship with God. So now the question comes to me, how have I been a whore? How have I sold myself, compromised myself? How have I been led away from myself? I've certainly been guilty of buying into conventional, social, and religious dogmas at the expense of compromising my inner knowing, my integrity, myself. So by compromising, I am at odds with God and with myself, huh?

So if Yahweh is a voice from within, then when I prostitute myself, I become a victim of Yahweh, I become the victim of myself. I'd like to believe that the imposed standards I am not living up to are from an external dogma, but damn. The source might well be inherited, yet I'm a grown man, and what I've inherited, I've allowed to run me. I've claimed it, taken it in, and allowed it to run me. I'm living the unlived lives of generations gone by instead of living *my* life, *my* truth.

Yes, I'm forty years old, yet with the emotional attitude of a child at times, still responding as a child does to a parent, still being led by the hand, the heart, the innocent heart of a child as opposed to the mature heart of a man. I am the victim of my very own hand, my own doing. Perhaps I need the whore within me to be redeemed, to become reconciled with Mother, Father, God... perhaps I need the penitent whore to become reconciled with all the inherited entities within myself, and in turn to become reconciled with all humanity?

Sophia spoke of how viewing another's sexuality or emotion is really a projection of myself onto external physical woman. In other words, I'm usually projecting my own promiscuous nature off onto woman. Again, am I seeing another, or am I seeing myself? The whore or saint isn't out there; She's in here, within the recesses of my soul.

Sophia spoke of how the love goddess is missing from the Christian myth, that the Christian myth has no Aphrodite. Mary Magdalene is an archetypal image that has gone underground, into hiding, repressed into the shadow lands of my own psyche as well as the shadow of the collective unconscious. Yet, I'm beginning to see how I need her redemptive image to become reconciled within myself.

All my past loves and addictions have been unconscious attempts at an inner reconciliation - vain attempts, but attempts just the same. No wonder I can no longer fuck unconsciously, from a primitive place. I have been blind to the spiritual side of this communion with woman, with myself.

Mary Magdalene might have been dumped off into shadow land, but she continues to exist and influence me in spite of my best efforts. Until I bow to Her, I'll continue to whore myself out for personal gain, blindly selling out. Love and power, exclusive entities that don't mix.

So, this is all fine and dandy, but how do I maintain my masculinity, my virility, and at the same time integrate Eros, Mary Magdalene, the feminine?

March 27, 2001 - 4 p.m.

We went to the Uffizi gallery, first meeting at the designated gathering point outside the Piazza della Signoria under the statue of David, under David's penis, as some of the women suggested. I'm about fed up with galleries. Art is great, and the Botticelli's in the Uffizi: The Birth of Venus, La Primavera... they're all masterpieces, far beyond what my words can describe, as is this great city far beyond description, but I can only take in so many images of Mary Magdalene and Mother Mary.

For the moment, I'm more interested in the here and now, creating my own art, my own life. I'm still game to look at the images in the symbolic sense and investigate their deeper meaning, but to be herded like cattle through a bunch of exhibits has about as much appeal to me as does an inflamed hemorrhoid.

I'm a little tired of the whole process. I want to fish for a while. I want to make love for a while. I want to quit thinking about how things will be, once I've got it all figured out, once I've integrated the feminine. I want to cruise, live outside of myself for a while. I want to swirl a worm along the bottom of a riverbed, teasing a trout.

It's time to be kind to myself for a change, kind to myself in a different way. I know the time I've taken has been an act of kindness, but it's time to be kind to myself in a different way. I'm just uncertain of how to do this. Maybe it is simply time for me to travel, time to quit analyzing everything to the tiniest degree, and instead start living?

I'm sitting in the bar here at the Albion, at my favorite table, and this character has come back in. I saw him at the train station the other day, and I've seen him here a few times. He's short, maybe five-six, about fifty, with short gray hair. His nose is pushed back into his face, kind of piggish looking, and he is wearing some sort of wire-rimmed spectacles with thick lenses.

I asked Sara about him. I thought he was some guy who hung out at the train station trying to drum up business for Hotel Albion, but Sara says that he's a teacher from Milan. He's married and has two children. Sara says he's crazy.

Today he's wearing a pair of canary yellow jeans. He brought three Japanese boys with him into the bar. Massimo is at the bar. Yellow Jeans and Massi are speaking in Italian. Massi offers to make the boys a cappuccino, and Yellow translates Massimo's invitation. Yellow must be teaching these boys to speak Italian. At first the boys decline, but then Yellow gets them to accept. After making the cappuccinos, Massimo and Yellow shoot the shit for a bit, but now Yellow's ready to run. Yellow starts to walk out saying: "grazie, grazie." He tells the boys to say "grazie." They all say "grazie," and giggle, and now they're following Yellow out through the door.

An older, white haired woman just came into the lobby of the Hotel, possibly the grandmother of Sara and Swana. I wonder if they ever get bored here in Firenze, wonder if it ever becomes mundane, becomes their prison?

Living in Florence must have its advantages. It has to be one hell of a lifestyle, but I can't help question the family's untiring commitment to service. I left an old life behind, having grown tired of being in service to others. Guess it was really about being in service to myself, to my bank account, to the illusion of security my ego demanded, but it somehow lost being of service to my soul. For some reason, I still doubt my capacity to ever again find contentment.

Something has changed for me today. I'm not sure what it is, but I sense a new freedom, a new life. Do I really need to learn how to integrate the feminine; or do I have Her? Perhaps I just need to learn how to love Her, welcome Her existence and influence in my life?

March 27, 2001 - 10 p.m.

Had dinner on the other side of the Arno, on via Santo Spirito, a place where Victoria and her husband ate last year. There were seven of us: Abilene, Rita, Carrie, Kerri, Victoria, Bianca, and myself. We sat at a long table with one end pushed up against the wall. I sat at the head of the table, with Carrie the nurse on my left and Kerri the minister on my right.

As soon as we were seated, Victoria excitedly ordered two big bottles of vino for our table. Having been there before, she acted as host. I loved Victoria's energy, but she talked non-stop this evening. She, or something, was getting on my nerves. I think being the only man in the group is starting to wear on me a bit. I'm starting to feel as if I am the masculine ambassador, here just to keep things in balance, like: "Hey, us men aren't so bad." I was the problem, more than Victoria.

We toasted, the ladies with a glass of red wine and me with mineral water. Then one of the women suggested that we break bread, tearing a piece from a full loaf, saying what we were thankful for, and passing it on. I hated doing shit like that; I really did. It's not that I didn't want to be there; I just wanted to eat and not make such a big deal of things. When the loaf reached me, I tore a piece and thanked them for receiving me so warmly into their group as I reflected back to last night and all of them singing: *I Don't Know How to Love Him*. Most of these women knew that their relationships with men in the waking world were a reflection of loving themselves, their inner masculine counterpart.

I had rigatoni with a salad, again an exceptional meal. We all had dessert, and I got a kick out of Kerri the minister asking for roach clips so that she could dip her bite-sized biscotti dipping-cookies into the Vinsante wine that was served along with them.

We broke up into smaller groups after dinner. Some took taxis; others walked in one direction, while Kerri the minister, Bianca, and myself returned to the Hotel Albion.

"Are you sure you're only forty?" Kerri asked.

"Yeah, I'm forty. Why would I lie about that?"

"You just seem a lot older at forty than I did."

"Believe me, forty was a hard one for me. So I'd like to savor it a bit; forty-one will be here soon enough. But if it makes you feel better, you can say you're younger than I am."

"No, that's quite all right. I remember when I turned forty. It was about the time in my life when I had to accept that my body was what it was. That there was no going back."

I didn't comment on that one. I knew better. Bianca was walking a few steps behind us, listening to our conversation. "You think forty was an adjustment, try fifty."

I didn't comment on that either.

"We usually have a ritual that the youngest person has to go through at these gatherings," Kerri volunteered. "That's why I was really asking…"

And now, I've retreated to my room. The motorinos are still whizzin' their way through the streets below, and the exhaust fumes continue to creep in through the cracks and crevices of Hotel Albion.

I already have the feminine, have what I've been searching for all along. I'm just having a hard time loving her, or me, that part of me. So, how do I stay a man and love her? How do I get to keep my genitalia and still make love to a physical woman?

I'm beginning to see that the wounded women, or the way I view women as being wounded, is really a projection of my inner feminine, of myself, onto physical woman. I'm also realizing that the dark women in my life are also a projection of the dark feminine, of the whore within me that wants to use and exploit others through seduction and power. So how do I

love without exploiting, without being exploited?
Kelli, I wonder how she is, where she is, what she's doing?

March 28, 2001

In today's seminar Maria Theresa introduced the group to the highlights of San Miniato Church before traveling to Piazza Michelangelo with its wondrous view of the city. At three in the afternoon, a discussion led by Sophia based on Nancy Qualls-Corbett's lecture: *Despairing Love.*

March 28, 2001 - 11 a.m.

The group went to San Miniato Church up on a hill that overlooks Firenze. I planned on going, but ran out of cash. I sought out two different teller machines; both of them failed repeatedly to link up with my bank, a computer glitch of some sort. After being denied at the second machine, I took it as a sign to leave the group and go it alone.

So here I sit in my corner seat after all the women have gone to see the cathedral on the hill near Piazza Michelangelo. It's just as well. I've seen a lot, been around a lot of *hers*. I need a break from it all. I need a break from having a schedule; I'm not used to living by one.

I plan to wander off into the city somewhere and fall into Florentine life. I have no expectations, yet, I'm quite certain that something magical will present itself. I have been mistaken twice now for being a local, once in Ognissanti, the Church of All Saints, a block from Hotel Albion, where we went to see a Last Supper fresco. It was an older Italian woman who was carrying on about something, probably some religious experience she had just had. She never gave me a chance to say a word, so I didn't and she kept on speaking to me in Italian. I didn't understand a thing she said, just kept smiling, listening with an occasional nod. Then she finally left seeming satisfied that she had been heard and understood.

The second time I was mistaken for a Florentine was when

I was returning to Hotel Albion after having been rejected by the bank teller machine. It was some guy in a delivery truck. He spotted me walking down the sidewalk and got out of his double-parked vehicle to ask me directions in Italian. "Only English," I confessed, passing on the rejection that the teller machine had just spit out to me. He nodded courteously, as I continued my walk to the Albion.

A local, huh? Perhaps I should become one? I have no idea what I am going to do with my life. I have no home to return to; perhaps these coincidences are an invitation? Then again maybe they're nothing more than a simple coincidence?

I've been feeling uptight for some time now, even before leaving on the trip, but something else is stirring in me and it isn't an irritation that I packed and brought along from the States. It seems to have been initiated here in Florence, quite possibly from the contents of the seminar, and perhaps from feeling guarded. I'm trying to give allegiance to all the voices that are calling out from within, demanding my loyalty. It's crazy making, like Kafka's Secret Raven, the mad bird that flaps around in the mind. It doesn't help me to know why I'm haunted by this source, but knowing that Kafka had that flapping Raven makes my insanity more bearable, or at least not so lonely.

I'm going up to my room for a few minutes and then I'm going for a walk. I'm going to breathe, and I'm going to let Her, my Beatrice, guide me into life.

March 28, 2001 - 2:30 p.m.

When I was walking along earlier today, close to the main train station, I stepped in a pile of dog shit that some un-obligated pet owner left behind; thanks a lot, Beatrice. The streets are laden with dog turds. Perhaps it's a reflection of a carefree lifestyle where people don't mind feasting amongst their excrement?

I walked into the train station and out the opposite side. There some man asked me to sign something to help prevent AIDS. How could someone's signature prevent AIDS? What were they going to do, slip a condom over the pen that I was to use? Not trusting the solicitation, I ignored him and walked on. I crossed a busy street, walked behind a bus terminal, and then faded into a less traveled area of the city. After zigzagging through the side streets, I found a park and sat on a bench.

There are lots of pretty girls here in Firenze, many of them buzzing around on their very own motor scooters. I love how their hair hangs out from under their helmets, flapping around as they zip through the city. Driving a motor scooter doesn't seem to keep them from dressing themselves in fine clothing, nor does it make them less attractive, if anything maybe more inviting. I'm hungry.

I found an operable teller machine shortly after leaving the hotel and managed to get two hundred thousand lire. I guess maybe Beatrice was looking out for me after all, even if she did let me step into that pile of dog shit. My body asked for food, but my intuition asked me to wait, so I sat on that park bench waiting for an angel to appear, or some other divine encounter.

Maybe it was just a simple person whom I was awaiting, or one of the swallows that were floating around the park, riding the currents of invisible sine waves? Perhaps it was just a simple breeze that I was to meet, or even myself? That's it; I went to this park to meet myself: Piazza dell' Indipendenza. Girls, there were lots of pretty girls, everywhere.

My reaction to the city's propensity towards allowing their dogs to shit randomly on the sidewalks without cleaning up after the pets would have been less hostile if I hadn't stepped into that creamy green turd. My ass was beginning to ache, and I was getting the shakes. I had to get a bite to eat, so I walked down the street into the market area and found a slice of pizza with prosciutto and artichokes. After wolfing that down, I bought a cone of pistachio gelato. That was enough to get my energy level up and helped me out of my bad mood. I started to make my way back to Hotel Albion and grabbed a sandwich at another day bar along the way.

Sophia was in the Lobby when I walked into the Hotel and asked if I would like to join her for lunch. I hesitated, having just stuffed my face, but then decided to accompany her. We walked a couple of blocks and found a place called the Propheta, one of Sophia's favorites. I ended up eating again. We had some freshly grilled vegetables as an antipasto, and, for a main course, asparagus with butter and some freshly grated cheese. I don't know if it was grilled, steamed, or what, but I have never had asparagus that tasted that good. They were fresh and fully cooked, but when I bit into them, they were warm, almost meat-like; they had too much substance to be a vegetable.

Sophia and I were visiting and she mentioned about being kissed by an angel. I told her about how I most certainly had been at times throughout my life. She asked me if I could give her an example.

"I checked myself into a rehab at the age of twenty-five, and I've been sober ever since. One of my good friends died five years ago. It finally caught up to him. Why him and not me? The angel," I confirmed.

I learned that Sophia and her husband had been at the tail end of raising their fifth child, who was in her last year of high school, when she returned to school. She'd had a moment while cooking for just herself and her husband when she realized that things would soon be different when there were no longer children to care for. She said that they didn't have any small pots to cook with, so they sold their home and the three of them left for Zurich.

"You mentioned how much you enjoyed Zurich," Sophia said.

"I was only there for one night, but I loved it. I felt as if I could live there."

"Ever think of studying there?" Sophia asked.

"I don't even have an associates' degree," I answered, knowing that, at minimum, I'd have to have a master's degree to even be considered for the higher learning that Sophia had in mind. "There's a lot of school between me and a piece of paper," I added.

"Yes, but that can be done."

"I don't know Sophia. That's an awful lot of work," I defended.

"If you aren't careful that same angel who kissed you, just might turn around and kick you in the ass," Sophia suggested, with a loving smile.

I picked up the tab. It was 90,000 lire, twice what I expected it to be, but I paid without questioning the waiter. I didn't want to look like a cheap ass in front of Sophia, especially with it being one of her favorite places.

March 28, 2001 - Mid-Afternoon

In the lecture based on Nancy Qualls-Corbett's *Despairing Love*, Sophia spoke of how when one is in love, there is a feeling of completion, or wholeness, but that only love, not romance, encompasses elation and despair.

The crucifixion causes Mary to lose Jesus the man but not the spirit of Christ or transcendent love. Mary Magdalene weeping in the garden is symbolic of her wanting to stay in the past and remain a child, ruled by the unconscious powers of the patriarchy, her inner patriarchy and her relationship to her primary image of man. In other words, for her to remain a victim.

In the written word as well as in the *Nolo Me Tangere* paintings, the don't touch me paintings, Mary Magdalene is being told not to cling to Jesus, not to hold on to a dead image. Not clinging to an image forces one back upon one's self. Mary had to let go of old beliefs and fantasies: a letting go of ego needs, demands, and wishes. Clinging to a past image prohibits our coming to a new perception of love, which calls for a surrender of ego to the soul.

When Christ tells Mary to tell others that he has arisen, as a new image, he is acknowledging his belief in Mary Magdalene; acknowledging the birth of consciousness, the birth of a new image within herself. By not clinging, Mary Magdalene was able to become conscious. Despairing love is a loss of the sense of self, but despairing love returns us to ourselves, to our suffering. Without suffering, without sacrificing our ego needs, we remain in an adolescent state that is dependent on an old dead image and we are unable to access our own truth, or gnosis.

Sophia spoke of how serial relationships are just a reinforcement of a need for proof of one's being loved; seeking outside of ourselves because of the lack of relationship, lack of love for ourselves: our internal masculine and feminine counterparts. Instead of loving our own images, we project them out onto others and once they fail us in our need for them to be more than human, we seek the god-like image in yet another, who, in their humanity, will once again fail what is really an inner calling for communion.

Sophia spoke of how we steel ourselves when in despair, we become cold, icy, and by doing so close ourselves off to experiencing the divine. This really hit home, because with the exception of only a few women who have been my lovers, I have closed myself off, only allowing our sexual encounters to be a physical act, lacking any form of spiritual communion. This is why most of my sexual encounters have failed in what I had hoped to achieve: satisfying a deeper longing. I might have been eating three square meals a day, but still finding myself to be malnourished.

Sophia spoke about how that which is transcendent doesn't belong to man and how we seek human relationship in order to escape the relationship with the transcendent. When love is defined by the ego, we become forsaken by others: we become the victim. Surrendering of the ego or of an old belief allows for transcendent love to be realized. It doesn't rely on another's love for us: it comes from within.

Sophia spoke of how allowing our self-worth to be defined by others leaves us still clinging, still unconscious. Being bound to something that is dead makes it impossible to experience the transcendent love within. She also talked of how transcendent love is hard to comprehend. We have no real images of this, but perhaps the Mary Magdalene myth is a personification of man or woman on this path.

March 28, 2001 - 11 p.m.

I'm feeling a rage, well, maybe not a rage, but I am feeling an enormous amount of energy pumping through me. Perhaps it's my environment, all these women, this feminine energy that's beginning to get on my nerves, or perhaps it's something else?

I'm tired of talking about the inner feminine, mine or anyone else's for that matter. I want to be connecting with an outer woman, and I want to be making love to her as well. This is all wonderful information that I've been receiving, validating and enlightening, but something's still missing. I sent an e-mail, but I've yet to hear back from Kelli.

This rage is about not being received, about being unable to receive myself. I've got a ball of energy pumping through me. I'm a walking hard-on, a forty-year-old erection; I'm the raging eternal phallus wanting to explode. That's it; I'm looking to penetrate a heart, a woman, a soul. God, damn you!

March 29, 2001 - Dream

A dream that I can't remember, but this is what I recorded sometime last night. That rage last night or that emotion that is in me, that energy, what was in me then is still in me when I wake. It's across my back, trapped in here. There's a rage, an emotion, an unexpressed energy of some sort... fury looking for an outlet, wanting to go somewhere, wanting to be received.

My flow of sexual energy is not being allowed or honored. It is getting short-circuited somewhere, or it is getting... yeah, shoved down, repressed, and remains unexpressed.

Repressed somehow because of how I relate to my inner feminine, my inner Her. I am not allowing Her to receive me. I'm viewing Her as wounded or something. I'm viewing Her as someone who doesn't enjoy sex, who doesn't enjoy me, doesn't want me. I experience Her that way.

March 29, 2001

The morning topic discussed by Sophia was based on Nancy Qualls-Corbett's lecture: *Marriage of the Magdalene*. Marie Theresa presented slides of the Opera del Duomo, the Bargello museums, and the Accademia. We were scheduled to meet at 3:00 outside the Opera del Duomo.

At the lecture, we discussed the marriage of Jesus Christ and

Mary Magdalene as a symbolic marriage of the masculine and feminine. We also discussed the meaning of heresy, it being a belief opposed to religious doctrines or a common belief.

We discussed the yearning for the Sacred Marriage and the need to unite the two archetypal images of Jesus Christ and Mary Magdalene, as well as their sacred marriage within our own souls.

The discussion included the birth of the Divine Child as a result of this Sacred Marriage. Sophia mentioned that Sarah in Hebrew means queen or princess. The celebration of Sara Kali, the Black Queen, is held every year at the end of May in the village of Saintes Maries de la Mer in Southern France.

After the lecture, still in the sanctuary of the upper room, things got interesting. Julia had a tape of the sound track for *Jesus Christ Superstar*, and they started playing *I Don't Know How to Love Him*. Bianca, the dancer from New York, began a dance and, soon after, several of the women joined her. They had scarves and they twirled and danced uninhibitedly. One woman tried to coax me into the dance, but I remained in my seat.

I was amazed, yet afraid, and not of any one woman in particular, but more of the spirit that hovered within the upper room. I was afraid that if I were to join in the dance, I might well be torn to pieces in the rage of a Dionysian ritual gone astray.

I was honored to be there in the sanctuary, experiencing the celebration first hand. I felt privileged to be included and even invited to participate in the dance with all these beautiful women. But at the same time, it scared the living, loving shit out of me. I feared being annihilated by Her, the feminine.

The women then gathered in a circle, arm in arm. Again I was invited to join them. So there I was with twenty women, arm in arm, humming, singing *I Don't Know How to Love Him*, and me not knowing how to love Her, Him, my Self. Then, silently, I began to ask: *What in the hell are you doing here? I mean really, Malcolm, what the fuck are you doing? How for heaven's sake did you get here? How have all the events in your life, everything that has ever transpired up to this point in time, lead you to this, these women, this dance, this dream?*

March 29, 2001 - 10 p.m.

At three this afternoon we met outside the Opera del Duomo Museum. The highlight was Donatello's sculpture of the despairing Mary Magdalene and she truly was something, so emaciated, skin and bones. How Donatello captured the pain and suffering in her face and in her eyes, I will never know. It's certainly beyond words.

I had a wonderful dinner of Beefsteak Florentine at Buca Mario this evening with several of the women. It's the second to the last night that this particular cut of meat can legally be served. Prepared using a sliced through T-bone exposing the interior, it is believed that the Mad Cow disease may be carried within the marrow of the bone. After tomorrow night, Beefsteak Florentine will never be the same.

On the way back to Hotel Albion, walking arm in arm with Sophia, she asked me a lovely question: "Malcolm, tell me, and this is strictly for research purposes, have you ever had a lap dance?"

I started laughing before I could answer and then pulled myself together. "Of course I've had a lap dance."

"What's it like?"

"It's nothing. I used to take clients back east to the tractor factories and our nightly entertainment was at the strip clubs. I had to go just to make sure my guys didn't get into trouble, you know," I explained with a big grin.

"Hum, I see," Sophia nodded and smiled.

"The younger guys always liked buying me a lap dance. They got a big kick out of it. It's nothing though. The last thing I'm interested in is a naked woman dancing and rubbing herself all over me and not being able to lay a finger on her. Hell, I want the real thing."

March 29, 2001 - Midnight

I'm restless, can't sleep. I am... I want to say pissed, but it doesn't seem quite the right way to describe myself. Something is boiling in me, energy of some sort that so far hasn't been able to find expression. It might be a desire, or it could be something much more than simple lust. It seems I have something that needs to be exchanged; some sort of intercourse needs or wants to happen. Intercourse is the right word here, too. I feel the need to penetrate and fertilize something. I want to impregnate, to become a father.

It feels right that I become a father, a creator, to share my seed with a woman whom I love, to bring forth a new her and a new me, a coming together in order to manifest and realize the divine. Up to this point on this excursion of mine, this is the most profound awakening I've had. The need or desire to become a father. It seems that I am now willing to sacrifice my ego and fear to this calling.

March 30, 2001

The day's schedule was for a meeting from 9 -11 for an open discussion. Our afternoon was free, and at 7:30 there was to be a banquet on the top floor of Hotel Beacci-Tornabuoni.

March 30, 2001 - 3:30 p.m.

It is all over with the exception of dinner this evening. Yeah, that's it: the last super. Then, hopefully, I'll awake, or, better yet, arise, in a few days, from the dead. I feel achy today. It's all the walking, the food, the bed; it's all right.

Yes, it is all right. I've done a lot of walking, and I've taken in a vast amount of new images. My body still has to adapt to all of this. I'm ready to leave. I'm ready to go north possibly. I'd like to meet up with Kelli if heaven allows.

My time here has been enlightening, and will certainly continue to shine upon me. Closing today was interesting. One of the women got off onto asking what is *man* doing for *his* soul. That's all it took to shift the sacredness of what had been taking place into a goddamn three-ring-circus. It became a faultfinding mission of external man, instead of dealing with her inner masculine image; a modern day witch hunt, but of the opposite sex. Things always end up getting dumped on someone or something other than the responsible source.

Then, one of the women who had just recently hung the label of a PhD from the brim of her hat, started bragging about her being happily married for nearly forty years and that it was still a great thing. She was trying to show the rest of us how psychologically evolved she was.

"What men need to do is nurture the feminine into their lives, and this includes you Malcolm..." the happily married PhD commanded.

It scares me whenever anyone thinks they know what someone else needs. Just as soon as she suggested what I needed, I shut down. I went into this whole thing about: *who in the fuck do you think you are to even consider the possibility of knowing what I need.* I started to boil inside. How could she, or any other person, know what I, or any man, needs? What we need is to be a universe unto ourselves removed from this kind of thinking. This know-it-all shrink is possessed, I tell you.

Well, that started the volley and we completely lost sight of our purpose. Finally, I had to speak up.

"You know, this bothers me. I'm getting really uncomfortable with this 'what is *man* doing for *his* soul' stuff and the whole idea of knowing what is best for any man. I've been pretty quiet for the last several days, but something is happening here today that hasn't happened so far during this seminar. Maybe men *are* doing something for their souls. I see every one of you women through my eyes, through the filter of my own experiences, and what I'm seeing, and who I'm making you into, probably has little to do with who all of you really are. Perhaps right now you, in turn, are making man into who you need him to be, as well. Maybe we men are afraid to express ourselves. There have been an awful lot of angry women running around for the last thirty years who have been fighting mad about what they've been cheated out of. Maybe we've learned to shut down because we have been repeatedly shut down. It seems to me, we get shut down just as soon as we start to express ourselves because the person we are confronting with our need for expression always interrupts with her own preconceived ideals. What man needs is to not be condemned..."

"Yeah, but Malcolm..." the know-it-all shrink interrupted.

"Hold on," Sophia said. "I don't think Malcolm was finished."

"Granted, for generations women have suffered immensely under the patriarchy, but I can't help but ask myself, aren't men also suffering from the patriarchal? I don't know, I thought that we came here to explore images in order to gain a better understanding of how they related to us and how we relate to ourselves. But, right now it seems to me that the source of our suffering is getting shoved off onto an image that doesn't really deserve this sort of scapegoating. Maybe men and women aren't so different. Maybe the battle isn't between the sexes in the outer world. Maybe the battle has to do with the divisions within our own souls. Maybe, when we are all able to meet, commune, and give a voice to these bastardized infants who long ago were dumped at the orphanage of our own shadow-land... well, maybe we'll be able to put a stop to this gender battle that is being waged in the waking world. I am not sure, but it seems to me that when we are fighting someone else, we are really doing battle with a part of ourselves."

One of the three PhD's whom Sara had introduced to me at breakfast on the first day of the seminar, who had been sitting with Know-it-all, spoke up and said something about how much we all suffer when we are separated by gender. I was glad that she did; she was the only one of those three psychologists who seemed glued together. Then Know-it-all tried to get the last word in, but Sophia announced that the seminar had come to a close.

I was building a head of steam; actually, it had been building for several days, if not years. My speech wasn't directed at everyone, because not every woman there was putting man in the wrong. But a few of the women there were, and their efforts, conscious or unconscious, tainted the sacredness of what had been taking place.

I don't know if I was heard, and I can't say that it really mattered. If nothing else, I needed to hear myself. I didn't speak up to change anyone; I spoke up for my soul, so I didn't have to carry that shit around in silence any longer. I needed to give voice to what had been brewing in me, quite possibly, an unspoken universal voice that needed to be expressed by people throughout the world.

I'm angry; I'm tired of being a man trying to live up to the standards of the women's movement. I'm tired of being made wrong and viewed as primitive, less evolved, less enlightened, a less-than-feminine human being. The women's movement was very necessary, but it has gone to an extreme and now needs to come back to the middle ground: a place where man and woman, or the masculine and the feminine can meet and unite. It's time to bury the hatchet. Maybe I had to speak up so that I could bury the hatchet between the battles that rage within myself? I'm deathly in need of allowing myself to be a man, my own man, the man I was created to be.

Lack of conscious understanding scares me. Especially when it comes from a so-called know-it-all psychologist who doesn't have a clue of the psychological complexes that still possess her. Today, it became very clear to me that there are some pretty incompetent professionals out in the world of psychology, as most certainly there are in other professions as well. Just the same, there are some damn competent psychologists who have gone into those dark places within themselves and have reconciled with and reclaimed their illegitimate castoffs. It's becoming ever clearer to me that it isn't what we know that runs us; it's what we don't know.

Needless to say, Know-it-all had struck a nerve. I can't stand anyone who thinks they have all the answers. My work is to nurture the feminine, which I understood her to mean that she'd have my nuts on a platter just as soon as the lights went out.

That dingbat has been trying to figure me out, put me in the wrong, and label me ever since our very first meeting. Who in the fuck does she think she is: God Almighty Herself? How does any one person, any person at all, have the nerve to think they know what is right for another human being?

I've spent enough time with Adam to know that the only true answers to our questions and our doubts come from within, where there are no dogmas, no rules or molds to bind me. Adam said yes to me long before I was ever able to say yes to myself. He's been a mirror, reflecting the images that I've been projecting onto him back to myself. What and who I see in him, I already possess.

Know-it-all and one of her counterparts have been trying to shoot holes into metaphors since the beginning of this seminar and they've been doing so because it scares them. They're afraid of their own shadow, afraid of the confrontation with themselves!

Christina phoned my room about an hour after we had adjourned. She wanted to talk about what had taken place during the closing ceremony. I told her that I was on my way out to wash some clothes and invited her to walk with me.

"What was that all about earlier today?" Christina asked, as we started our walk.

"All that I can tell you, Christina, is that there are a few certain individuals here that haven't got a clue as to what's going on."

"What was that?" Christina asked again.

"Remember the first day I mentioned that I'd suffered at the hand of my mother's rage?"

"Yes," Christina confirmed.

"Well, after that first lecture, I walked across the street for a cappuccino and she was there. She asked how many kids were in my family, and I told her four boys, and her flippant response was: 'Well no wonder your mother beat you.'"

"My gosh. She couldn't see you," Christina said, as we stepped inside the laundromat. "That must have been terrible," she added, as I looked over the token machine trying to make sense of the instructions. "How did you respond?"

"There was nothing to be said to a remark like that. Oh, then her counterpart who was with her started asking where my father was when my mother was beating me. She got real defensive, telling me that my father was just as much to blame and that I needed to do my father work. I immediately told them that I had spent years doing my mother and father work and that I am more interested in loving them for the human beings they are and enjoying our lives together."

"What did they say to that?"

"That shut 'em down. That's just like a goddamn know-it-all shrink. They become therapists and heave their own shit onto others so they don't have to look at themselves. All I can tell you is that they're both dangerous..."

We talked about things for a while, and Christina helped me carry some clothes to a dryer before she set off into Firenze for an early afternoon walkabout.

After Christina left, I began to think about Know-it-all psycho-shrinks Number-one and Number-two. Number-one, the same crazy bitch that was trying to label me a 'marrier,' thought my mother was justified in acting out her rage, and Number-two thought it was my father's fault. Number-two actually cornered me about two days into the seminar, and I must admit she is nothing near the mess that Number-one is, but what caught my attention was that she wanted to know what I thought about the whole Jungian theory.

I remember telling Number-two that I really like Jungians, but that I certainly didn't think they had all the answers, nor did I limit myself to approaching life so narrowly as to throw all else away. To me, Jung was a man and Jungian is a term. I had no intention of getting locked into becoming solely identified with a word or a concept as if it were my religion. She was so caught up in the right or wrong of it that it kept her from experiencing the Jungian approach for what it might have to offer.

I thought about Mrs. Shams, thought about the whole assertiveness and confrontation thing that people had been taught over the last couple of decades. It was bullshit, and often did more harm than good. All I need is to have a voice and the choice to use it; just having the choice to speak is as powerful as actually speaking. Not speaking is only a thief if one's voice can't be found due to a lack of choice. Communication often takes place in silence rather than with words.

I returned from my clothes-washing excursion around two, and after an unsuccessful attempt at an afternoon nap, decided to take up residence at the bar in Hotel Albion. Abilene was there, and I joined her for an afternoon tea. Abilene, like many of the other attendees, departs tomorrow morning and was concerned about getting to the airport for her early morning flight out. Abilene is traveling alone and, having missed her connection in Paris on her way into Florence, didn't want to get caught up in a mess like that again, especially with her inability to move about at a normal pace (whatever normal is). And speaking of normal, right then, Number-one and Number-two walked in together and said something about having to catch an early flight out in the morning. I suggested that Abilene share a cab with them. They worked out the details right then and there, putting Abilene at ease.

After deciding on the following morning's departure time, Number-two excused herself, but Number-one invited herself to join Abilene and me. As much as she bugged me, I figured the least her idiotic naïveté could do was entertain me, so I indulged her and stuck around for the court jester's act. She started babbling on about how she and her husband traveled with her brother in-law and his wife.

"Is this the Marrier?" I asked to draw her in.

"No, this is his other brother," she answered, and went on to tell about some boring outing they had taken. Her next topic shifted to one of her daughters, Molly, the oldest, who was thirty-one, divorced, and without a child. "She has a man in her life but doesn't want to be married to him. She says he's not father-material," Number-one justified.

"Is your youngest daughter married?" I asked, already having a good idea that she wasn't; I was right.

Abilene sat listening without comment.

Number-one carried on about her two daughters, kept harping about how Molly wanted to have a child, but that this guy she was with wasn't father-material. "I told her she was crazy to get married just for the sake of having a child. Hell, she doesn't need a man to have a baby. I told her that I'd take her to the sperm bank," Number-one rambled on recklessly.

Having returned from her walk, Christina came into the bar, overhearing the tail-end of Number-one's rhetoric. She looked at me with a not-this-shit-again look, and I nodded, grinned, and winked in affirmation. She smiled in amazement and went up to her room.

"There's this one guy who's a friend of the family. He'd be great sperm, but both the girls say that he's boring. I don't see what's so boring about him, and he'd make for beautiful babies," Number-one babbled.

By her comments, I could now see that it wasn't just me she had been trying to slap a label on; it was all of us sperms. Her daughters didn't need a man, just sperm. For forty years she had been married to the same eunuch; God save the queen. I wonder where her husband's dried and shriveled-up old scrotum is hanging; probably in the garage, dangling from an old rusty nail that has been partially driven into the cross of a couple of intersecting two-by-fours. Forty years of that horseshit told me that he was either fucking gay or fucking his secretary.

"How about you, Malcolm; do you date women?" Number-one asked.

"That's all I date."

"Do you live with them?"

"I lived with my ex-wife before we married."

"I get the feeling that you've really been burned," Number-one said.

I get the feeling that you've never been properly fucked, I wanted to say, but instead answered: "Oh, I'd hate to take it to that dimension. After all, I asked her to marry me, and it was me who ended it."

"My thirty-year-old son has recently fallen in love, and I know he's in love because he told me he's willing to give up the motorcycle, his most prized possession, for this girl," Abilene said, with a smile and a gleam in her eyes. "He had his heart broken a while back. Less than a year ago he told me he'd given up on love; now he's met his soul mate."

"I fell in love after getting divorced," I said, thinking about her son's loss. "Now that one stung," I added, waiting for Number-one to step in and tear my confession to pieces.

"So that's why you don't live with a woman," she promptly responded.

"No, I don't live with a woman, because I haven't found a woman that I care to live with."

"Well, I'm glad I have girls. I'd pick girls over boys any day."

"Why's that?" Abilene asked.

"Because boys always end up going with the in-laws," Number-one answered.

"What do you mean?" I asked.

"They move away. They go with the girl's family," she said, as she jiggled her head.

"Not in my family," I answered. "There's four of us boys and that hasn't happened," I explained, shooting holes in her hot air balloon. It probably wouldn't be the case with her son-in-laws, either, if she ever gets any. Number-one reminded me of this woman I once dated; she was a suicidal psychologist who had all the answers and the lingo down pat but didn't understand a single word she was preaching. She thought she could save the whole world but was missing one thing: the ability to save herself. Who do you suppose she called on to deliver her from evil in her time of despairing need? That's right: some old fucked-up tractor salesman.

Abilene and Number-one both excused themselves. We had been sitting in the middle of the bar and the seat in the corner was free. Not long after I had moved to my perch, Victoria walked in. As usual, she had to be speeding along at a hundred-miles-an-hour. I liked her energy. I liked her, all of her. By golly, if Victoria had been my shrink, I'd have fallen in love with her and forgotten about my mother years ago.

"Hi Victoria," I said, as she walked in. Victoria and Abilene were rooming together, so Victoria had to walk through the bar to get to her room.

"Hi Malcolm," she said in her sweet southern way. She had a handful of bags and kept her stride going towards her room. After dropping off her goods, she came back to the bar for a visit.

"Whew! What a day," Victoria said, as she sat down in the seat opposite me.

"Had to get that last-minute-shopping in, now didn't you?" I teased.

"You got that right. Now, I've got to go buy an extra suitcase to get this stuff home."

"I believe it," I said, smiling. "You know, Victoria, I really like you. It feels good to be around you."

"I really like you too, Malcolm."

"Victoria, you got something. You got it inside of you. I mean, I can tell that you really love man, and that tells me a lot about you, who you are and what's going on inside of you."

"I do have something, and I'm grateful for it," she answered in a humble tone. Victoria wasn't one bit arrogant. What she had, she had earned. She'd been through a few things to get to where she was, and she had the courage to go into those dark places to retrieve herself. Her previous marriage and divorce had a profound affect on who she'd become, but it hadn't overtaken her like it did some people.

Victoria had somehow risen above the situation and made a new life for herself, a rewarding life at that. Victoria didn't paint her husband as a God, but she loved the man. I could tell by how she spoke of him, how she looked forward to meeting him in Paris the next day, how she referred to him by his name and not 'my husband' and by the warmth I could feel coming from her when she spoke of him, by the sparkle in her eye. Victoria knew how to love him, the Him in her, and the him who was her husband. I love women who love men, who are capable, who know how.

"Victoria, thank you."

"For what?"

"For the work you're doing. You know how to meet people. I mean, you know how to see past the mask and see them for who they really are and you say yes to them. So thank you, because when you do that you're doing it for the entire world," I explained, as tears crept into the corners of my eyes. I meant every damn word I said, too. People like Victoria do change the world, and I'm not making Victoria into a saint at the expense of Number-one.

Victoria didn't talk a bunch of psycho-babble-bullshit; she was simply being herself and saying yes to life and to the people she encountered. She didn't have time to slap on labels, trying to find fault or the wrongness in herself or others. Victoria was too busy living and in the process having a huge effect on the people who came into her life.

"Well, thank you for saying that. I want you to know that you are welcome at our home anytime. I think Alan and you would really hit it off."

"Thank you, Victoria."

"I mean that now, too. I'm not just saying it."

"I just might surprise you one of these days," I told her.

"Okay, now I've gotta go after a bag."

"Victoria, there's a place right around the corner. Go out the door and turn right. Then turn right at the next corner, and left at the following corner. You'll find a shop full of reasonably priced luggage about halfway down that street."

"Now, how did you know that?"

"I do get around, you know," I answered, with a wink.

"I just bet you do, too," she said, in that sweet southern drawl and wearing a grin of knowing to match her inflection.

I also had the privilege of meeting with Kerri the minister after Victoria went chasing a bag. I thanked her for her ministry, for bringing consciousness into the world of religion. She was able to look beyond the literal and towards the metaphor. She too had an effect on the people who came into her life.

March 30, 2001 - 11:30 p.m.

The last super was at the Hotel Beacci-Tornabuoni, a fine restaurant on the top floor. There was a patio area where we could take in a rooftop view of Firenze. It was colder this evening than it has been, so most of us walked out on the patio to have a look, but then returned to a reception room where we were served aperitifs and a little doughy pastry that was hot out of the oven and lightly salted. After socializing for a bit, we were called to dinner.

The tables in the dining room had been set up in a square as opposed to the horseshoe shaped seating arrangements we had in the upper room of Hotel Albion. I was the last to be seated, and couldn't fit my legs under the table. Christina asked me to sit with her, but my seat was where two tables came together and a narrow table had been squeezed between them to make enough room for our entire party. There was simply no way that I could sit through dinner and enjoy myself.

There was a seat across from where I sat, so I went to sit there and found it to be the same. The seat was between Maria Theresa and Kerri the minister, and I finally complained out loud. I told them that I had been well behaved and very quiet all week, but that I just couldn't live with the seat that had been left for me. Kerri traded places with me; I finally fit in. I ended up sitting between Kerri and Lillian, Natalie's crazy mother.

Natalie was a therapist from South Carolina. She was in her early forties. I never asked her age, but when I announced my age that evening in the countryside, Natalie complained because she just knew that she was the youngest.

It was another grand dinner. For the second night in a row it was Beefsteak Florentine along with several other fine Italian dishes. The dinner was quiet with the exception of small talk amongst us. There were no special announcements; our only agenda was to gather together one last time to break bread.

Lillian was nice and meant well, but she got on my nerves. She talked without giving any thought to what poured out of her mouth. In the upper room, earlier in the week, before the lecture started, Lillian was talking about some man who bored the hell out of her and how she'd like to stick a red-hot poker up his ass, but didn't even think that could move him. Tonight she was talking about stabbing a knife into someone's heart. Kerri was talking to Maria Theresa, and Natalie, who was sitting on the other side of Lillian, was talking to the woman next to her, so it left me with Lillian.

I was already about womaned out, and in a considerable trance, but Lillian would be damned to leave me be. She kept rattling shit off while I tried to ignore her. I didn't want to be rude; I just wanted to be quiet, just left alone, but the more I wanted quiet, the less of it I got.

"Have you heard about that book on silence?" Lillian asked, while I tried to meditate.

"No," I answered. "Have you?"

"Well, I've heard about it from Natalie, but I haven't actually read it. I'm introverted. I talk too much."

I didn't know how to respond to such an ambiguous declaration. "Where did you say your son lives?" I asked, having finally figured a way to respond.

"New Jersey."

"Do you visit him often?" I asked. Lillian's husband had recently passed away, within a year's time.

"Only when I'm invited, which isn't that often. You know,

they're busy. They have their lives. You know, my husband hated pantyhose."

"Then why did he wear them?"

"Oh, now that was quick," Lillian said, as Natalie stopped talking to her neighbor and looked at me with a big grin. Actually, we all had a big laugh.

"What did he hate about them?" I finally asked.

"You'll just have to use your imagination on that one," Lillian answered smugly.

I smiled and remained silent, but after a few minutes Lillian had to break the spell.

"I don't listen to my intuitive."

"What do you mean?" I asked.

"Let's just say that I have a habit of saying things without thinking, and I end up stepping in a lot of doodoo."

I nodded and smiled.

All Fools Day, plus a few more...

April 1, 2001 - 9 p.m.

I woke around ten yesterday, showered, had breakfast in the dining room with Christina and Julia, and then joined Sophia in the bar at the corner table. During the last supper, Maria Theresa mentioned that she'd given Sophia some information on Saintes Maries de la Mer. I asked Sophia about it, and she said it was in her room.

"Do you need it right now?"

"No, but I'd like to have it before you leave."

"I'm going up to pack in a while. Stop by my room and I'll have it for you."

"Sounds good."

An hour later, I received the brochures from Sophia and was off to the train station to see about booking a seat to the south of France. Arles was west of Marseilles and looked like it might only be a half-hour bus ride to Saintes Maries de la Mer. A train left at midnight, and the next departed at one-thirty the following afternoon. I had reserved the room at Hotel Albion for the night. I didn't book a seat, because I didn't know if I could get out of my room reservation.

When I returned, Sophia, Christina, and Julia were standing in the lobby waiting for a taxi to take them to the airport.

"Well, have you decided on a destination?" Julia asked.

"Yes, I'm going to the south of France."

"When?"

"Well, if I can get out of having to rent my room this evening, I'll take the midnight train tonight. If I can't, I'll go tomorrow at one-thirty," I explained, loud enough to drop a bug in Susanna's ear. She was working the front desk.

"You'll just go with the flow," Julia said.

"I'll try," I answered.

The taxi arrived, and I helped the three women carry their bags out. I hugged them, said goodbye, and then walked back into the hotel. Susanna was behind the front counter, so I went up to her to discuss my plans.

"Susanna, are you fully booked here at the hotel tonight?"

"Yes, we are."

"Do you think you can sell my room?"

"Maybe, but you have to let me know right away."

"Okay, sell it if you can. I'm almost all packed and ready to go. You can put my bags in storage if you rent the room."

"Okay, Malcolm, we will try."

"If you don't, I'll stay the night and leave on the afternoon train tomorrow."

I went up to my room to finish packing. Ten minutes later I was back down stairs. Susanna had left, and Sara had taken her place at the front desk.

"Hello Sara," I said, stepping off the last step into the lobby.

"Hello Malcolm," she replied, looking up from her book.

"What are you reading, Sara?"

"I'm studying German."

"For your German guests?"

"No, for my visit to Germany."

"When will that be?"

"Oh, I'm not sure."

"Where did your mother go?"

"I gave her and my father the afternoon off."

"Did she tell you to try to sell my room?"

"Yes, she certainly did…"

Sara went on about some writer who she enjoyed reading, an author who was unfamiliar to me. Then she started talking about the crazy schoolteacher, Yellow Pants, when some young American kid who had been staying at the hotel walked up to the desk to ask Sara a question. After the American kid walked away, Sara told me that he was a crazy one, too, that he was only seventeen years old, and that his grandfather had sent him to live in Florence. The kid was from the south and Sara made fun of the way he talked.

"When he talks it sounds like he's eating something."

"I thought he was a friend of the family. I see him eating with you sometimes."

"We have all kinds of people who come to eat with us," Sara explained. "All the crazies. This one tall black guy who sells things on the street comes in almost everyday to see us." Sara's family gathered mid-afternoon and late evenings for dinner in the dining room, and they often had guests, such as Yellow Pants and the American kid. They only served breakfast to the hotel guests. Other than that, the dining room was for family meals or to host a gathering like the welcoming reception we had on our arrival.

Instead of sitting in my favorite corner, I sat at a table in the bar that allowed me to continue visiting with Sara over the next couple of hours, in between phone calls and other front desk duties that demanded her attention.

Around seven-thirty, I walked across the street to a pizzeria and had some pasta. I was finishing the last few bites of my meal when Olivia and Antonia walked into the dining room; I invited them to sit with me. Of all the women at the conference, I had gotten to know Olivia and Antonia the least.

They were sisters, and Olivia was one of three women who had recently received her doctorate. Olivia was the woman who was able to hear what I was saying at the closing when Number-one had climbed on her high horse announcing what men needed to do to incorporate the feminine into their lives. Olivia briefly brought up the topic again, saying something about how her colleague had gotten carried away the day before.

When I returned from dinner, Susanna and Massimo were back from their afternoon get-away. Massi was in the bar visiting with some friends who had come to Florence to buy some goods at an auction. Susanna was behind the front desk.

"Hello," I said, in my usual friendly tone.

"Hello, Malcolm. We have sold your room," Susanna announced in an accommodating tone.

"Wonderful."

"Now, we've put your bags away, so you better make arrangements for what you will do next," Susanna instructed with a warm smile.

"My train leaves at midnight, so I'm just going to hang out here for another hour or two." It was only nine o'clock.

"That will be fine. Make yourself comfortable, Malcolm,"

she said, motioning for me to have a seat. "Can we get you a cappuccino or something?"

"Yes, a cappuccino will be fine."

After making my drink, Susanna sat down with Massimo and another couple, joining in the discussion they were having in Italian. The phone rang and Massimo stepped behind the front desk to answer the call. I decided that it might be a good time to pay my bill, so I walked to the counter.

"Massimo, I guess I should give you some money," I said, after he finished the call.

"Money, okay," he said, reaching for an old cardboard box and shuffling through a batch of folders until he settled on a certain one. He studied it for a minute, as I looked the ledger over from upside down. "One extra night?" he asked, referring to my first night; I had arrived a day early for the seminar.

"Yes, and I had two waters and one orange drink from the mini-bar."

"And some drinks here from the bar," he said, as he was looking over my charges. "That's it?"

"Yes, that's it," I answered.

Massimo closed his eyes and acted as if he was calculating the charges in his mind. "How about two hundred seventy thousand," he said, opening his eyes and looking at me.

"Sounds good," I answered, handing him my MasterCard.

I didn't believe he added up my charges, which didn't bother me one bit. Actually, I probably came out ahead, and I liked doing business that way. There was nothing stiff about it. Besides that, I had managed to get out of having to pay for an extra night's stay.

At eleven-thirty, I asked to have my bags brought down. Nick, one of the employees, brought them to the lobby, and I tipped him twenty thousand lire for lugging my goods up and down the stairs, from room to room when I had first arrived, as well as for helping out on my departure. Nick carried my bags out the front door and parked them on the sidewalk. We shook hands, and then off I went, wheeling my two rolling bags over the cobblestone sidewalk toward the train station. I arrived fifteen minutes later, having successfully dodged several stray dog turds.

There were no first class cars from Firenze to Pisa. From Pisa I was to take a train to Nice, where I would change trains one last time before arriving in Arles. I boarded one of the train's front cars and took a seat in the back of the car, facing the rear. Three drunk, teenage boys boarded my car; one of them was exceptionally hammered. They sat down, but it was short lived as the really drunk one started wandering about from car to car.

Outside on the boarding platform were two hot young blonde girls who were no more than twenty, possibly younger. They were being hounded by two, dark-haired, slick-looking Italian men who were at least ten years their senior. Eventually the girls boarded the train, and one of the blondes stepped into the compartment directly behind the section I had boarded; her greasy pet followed her onboard. From my seat facing the rear of the car, I could see through the windowed door into the compartment where the first blonde had taken a seat. The other girl was standing in the entryway, in the stairwell of the car, visiting with the other pooch.

The guy who had followed the first girl into the car tried to sneak a kiss, but she pulled away. He didn't give up, though, from the disgusted look on the young woman's face, it was evident that the greaser's efforts were only making things worse. The two girls had bitten off more than they could chew; their salvation appeared to be our impending departure.

The train soon began to pull out of the station, leaving the two slugs at the loading dock. It was an uneventful ride with the exception of the drunk boy stumbling in and out of the cars. His two buddies, who hadn't lost all of their faculties, were close behind in an attempt to watch over the lost soul. The drunken kid finally settled into the entryway of our car, went down onto his knees, and started puking into the stairwell. Watching this kid reminded me of myself twenty-some years ago. I remembered having more than my share of days similar to this fellow's.

I stepped over the puke-ridden stairwell and out onto the loading platform of the Pisa train station. Pisa wasn't so inviting, especially at two in the morning. There were a lot of drunks sleeping in the depot. I didn't feel so safe. While walking about the station trying to get oriented, I spotted the two little hotties who had rid themselves of the slimy slugs at the depot in Firenze. Their parents were waiting for each of them; I had guessed the girls to be older than they were, either that, or my senses were right about it not being all that safe at the Pisa station.

I asked a couple of young men a question, but they couldn't speak English. I leaned against the railing across from loading platform number one, trying to figure out how to get to rail platform number five where the train for Nice would soon be arriving. I finally spotted some stairs and lugged all of my bags down them.

I followed the tunneled walkway to gate five and stood there trying to catch my breath before having to carry all my goods back up the steps. I looked back down the tunnel that had led me to my resting place and noticed five young women approaching. They smiled as they approached the stairs, but didn't stop to take a breather. Ah, youth. I'm not an old man yet, but I'm no longer seventeen, either.

"Are you going to Nice," I asked, hoping that they could respond to me in English.

"Yes," answered one of the women in a French accent. "Are you an American?"

I nodded and then followed all five of them up the steps and out onto the platform.

"Where are you from?" another one of them asked with a sweet and friendly smile.

"California. How about you?"

"My sister and I are from Spain," she answered, pointing to her sister.

"My friend and I are from France," answered the girl who had first responded to me at the bottom of the stairs.

"And I am from Argentina," answered the fifth girl.

"What is your name?" asked one of the Spanish sisters, smiling with a flirty sparkle in her eye.

"Mal."

"Mal," the sisters repeated in unison with their Spanish accent, and giggling. "Mel Gibson," the first sister added.

"I wish. It's Malcolm," I answered smiling, envying his

success. Let me tell you, they were some real cuties, those two Spanish girls.

The French girl who had responded to my initial query about going to Nice walked up and started speaking to me about her desire to visit the States. I asked her about Southern France and she said that it was beautiful, but that she was partial because she was from Avignon, a town just north of my destination in Arles.

When the train arrived we learned that it consisted of only sleeper cars. All of us boarded the same car. The sleepers were made up of cabins that housed six people; unfortunately they were mostly full or partially filled with sleeping bodies, which meant I wasn't going to find myself cuddled up with all five of the girls.

It was difficult to see through the cabin windows of the sleepers and we were unaware that we were supposed to open the doors to look inside in order to help ourselves to any available seats. Finally the accommodating French woman took charge, opening and closing the cabins until she found seats for all five of the women and me; the girl from Argentina joined me in the same cabin.

Things got quieter once inside of the sleeper. It wasn't a comfortable ride. The seats didn't recline; they had these cup-like headrests that kept my head from rolling side to side but, other than that, it was like sleeping while sitting upright in a chair. The train made occasional stops, gaining and losing passengers intermittently. A ways into our journey, a couple who had been occupying the sleeper departed and, shortly afterwards, a thin woman with long kinky reddish-brown hair stepped into our cabin and sat down next to me. I ignored her and tried to return to my restless sleep.

The woman who sat down next to me began talking to a man who was sitting directly across from us, but I was able to drown out most of their conversation with the foam earplugs I carried. My sleeping was still intermittent, the sleeper cramped and ridiculously uncomfortable. Eventually the man who was carrying on the conversation with the kinky haired woman sitting next to me got off the train, and I was able to stretch my legs out a little farther, but my sleep was close to an end.

We were still in Italy, having just left Genoa, when a huge red fireball began to rise out of the Mediterranean. It was really something. I'd seen plenty of sunrises, but never one as brilliant as this one. It seemed to hover there in that red state of rapture for hours.

"That sunrise is something else," I said, to the woman sitting next to me with the kinky hair.

"Yes," she answered in a soft tone. She had her index finger on her bottom lip, and looked straight into my eyes, as if she was trying to read me. "My English is not good," she added, after I met her gaze for several seconds.

"Where are you from?"

"Rome," she answered, dropping her finger from her lip, but continuing her gaze.

"And where are you going?"

"Paris. And you?"

"Arles."

"American?" she asked, continuing to study me.

I nodded. "Have you been to America?"

"No, but I would like to see San Francisco someday."

"Yes, it is very nice there. What's in Paris?" I asked, figuring it was a man.

"I'm a dancer. I'm going to Paris to dance."

"How nice," I smiled and nodded, our eyes continuing to meet.

"The Butoh dance."

"The muto dance?" I asked.

"Butoh," she answered, putting more emphasis on the B.

"Butoh, huh?"

"Yes, it is a Japanese dance," she explained, still speaking in a soft tone. She seemed spacey, trance-like. "I missed my train in Firenze."

"Was your train late?"

"No, I don't know. I just missed it and now everything is confused."

"Yes," I answered and nodded. I wanted to say you mean everything is all fucked up, but for some reason I believed her lost and chaotic state to have an order in spite of how it appeared.

"I would have arrived in Paris soon, but now it will be twelve hours, but I must do this."

"It is your passion," I said, looking over at the young woman from Argentina to find her sleeping, and then looking back at the dancer.

She nodded and continued to study me.

As we visited, I reached into my pocket to retrieve a business card. I wrote my e-mail address and scratched out my Carmel phone number, which had recently been disconnected, but left the mobile number that I've had for well over fifteen years. "Here, now you have a friend in California you can call upon once you have arrived," I said, handing her the card.

"Thank you," she replied, gracefully accepting my gift and looking at it. "Malcolm," she said, continuing to study the card. I'd have thought her to be on some sort of drug by the tone of her voice and her long stares, but she had been awake and talking to the other man in our cabin for the last couple of hours, so I ruled out downers, because she'd have fallen asleep long ago and she was acting too spacey to be hyped up.

"Do you have an e-mail address?" I asked.

"Yes, she answered, and I handed her my pen and a credit card receipt for her to write the address on.

After putting down her information, she returned the pen and receipt. "Andreanna," I said, extending my hand.

"Yes, Andreanna," she answered, taking my hand.

"Well, it is a pleasure to meet you, Andreanna," I said, receiving a great big beaming smile from her. "And your e-mail name is Bezzaebea?"

"Yes," she nodded.

"How did you pick that name?"

"My friends call me that, because I get... I don't know how you say it in English."

In a guess, I held my finger up and slowly spiraled it down through the air.

"Yes, you know."

"I know," I nodded.

"And it is not because my boyfriend left me for another woman."

"It is much bigger than that," I confirmed.

"Yes, yesterday, I was sick with a fever. I was crazy, but I had to leave Rome. I got on the train, and now the fever is gone."

"You listened to yourself."

"Yes," she whispered.

"Andreanna, you are not crazy."

"No?"

"No way."

"Sweet Malcolm," she said softly, beaming another smile.

Our communion seemed to make the train ride pass by more rapidly, but when I looked outside, the red ball of fire was still hovering low on the horizon. It was almost as if the sun had had a late night and was having trouble rising to its duty. I began to wonder if it was me who was in the trance, or maybe I was asleep in my room at the Hotel Albion and this was all a dream.

It was close to ten in the morning when we arrived in Nice. Andreanna was carrying one small bag, so she offered to help me with my luggage, and I let her wheel my smaller suitcase into the terminal. Once in the terminal we looked at the board to see about the timeliness of our connecting trains and learned that Andreanna's train to Paris had been cancelled: a rail workers strike that had been an on-again off-again thing for the last few months.

"Let's check on a rental car," I suggested, as she tried to come to terms with her dilemma.

"A car?"

"Yes, why not drive?"

"I think it will cost too much."

"Well, let's at least check on it. Come on," I said, leaving the train station and walking out to the road to see if there was a car rental agency close by. I considered shit-canning my Arles trip and driving to Paris with her. I wasn't all that attracted to her, but I was also trying to listen to the moment. I thought that maybe we had come together for more than just our brief encounter on board the train; she could possibly have been my next guide, pointing me in the direction of destiny's calling.

Andreanna flagged a taxi driver down and asked him how long it would take to drive to Paris and learned that it was close to a twelve-hour drive. He suggested that she get to the airport and catch a plane; she started juggling that possibility around in her head along with the rental car idea.

"Maybe we should just wait here for a bit and see what feels right for you," I suggested.

"Yes, I think you are right," she answered.

"Maybe you are not supposed to go to Paris."

"What do you mean?"

"I mean, you missed your first train. You are still traveling a day later trying to get there, and now your other train has been cancelled. Maybe it is too hard. Maybe you aren't supposed to be going."

"I don't know," she answered, still trying to take in what I had suggested. "When does your train leave?" she asked.

"Thirty minutes," I answered.

"Let's go inside. I will wait with you while I think about what I can do."

We were standing in the middle of the station, in front of the gates where people were passing in and out, having just arrived or preparing for their departures. Andreanna decided to inquire about reserving a seat on a later train, and I waited in the middle of the lobby with my bags. While standing there, someone called out my name. I turned to find one of the sisters from Spain batting her sparkling eyes and beaming a smile that seemed to be saying you-wish-you-could as she walked by. I smiled and said hello. She was right; I-wished-I-could. I'd have dropped everything to run off with that sparkling-eyed Spanish beauty. She was walking toward the other four girls who had assembled around a phone booth. While I was watching them, Andreanna walked back up to me.

"Well?"

"I can take a train later and will arrive tomorrow morning," she explained, still with the same look of bewilderment she had taken with her to the ticketing window.

"Did you reserve it?"

"No, but I think I will."

"Okay, well, I think I should go then," I said, reaching in my small bag to find the phone number of the hotel in Arles where Sara had e-mailed requesting a reservation for my arrival this afternoon. Once I found the phone number, I scribbled it on a receipt and handed it to her. "This is where I'm staying in Arles. Call me if you need anything."

She thanked me, and we spontaneously hugged and kissed each other's cheeks before going our separate ways. I wasn't certain what I'd do if Andreanna phoned later. I had e-mailed Kelli before leaving Florence and invited her to join me in Arles. I didn't think Kelli would accept my invitation, as she hardly knew me aside from our brief ten-minute meeting at the coffee shop in Carmel and the rhetoric of all my e-mails, which, for all she knew, could be as fictional as the rest of life's illusions.

It didn't appear that it would have taken much arm-twisting to get Andreanna to accompany me to Arles, but my heart wasn't really in it. Sure, it would have been nice to have a little fling, but, then again, it wouldn't. Sometimes just knowing that it could happen was enough. Besides, I was tired of leaving my heart out in the waiting room, while I dragged my instinctual desires into the massage parlor.

The train from Nice to Arles was a TGV train, which meant that it had a first-class section and that it was fast. I had lost all of my young sweet feminine guides, but I was riding in style. I boarded the train, but felt a little uneasy because I didn't see the town of Arles on the route board. It did say Marseilles, so I was pretty sure that it was the right train. I attempted to ask an older French couple who were seated across the aisle from me if the train stopped in Arles, but they didn't speak any English, or acted as if they didn't. I was tired, so I decide to go where the damn train would take me. The worst that could happen was that I'd end up staying in another unknown destination in Provence.

I felt disheveled. The first class seat eased some of the ache in my back that I'd acquired in the cabin from Pisa to Nice, but the train had a cold feel. There were people all around me, but not once did I make eye contact with a single soul. I focused my attention out of the window, into the countryside. Flowers were in spring bloom, the colors brilliant. The lavender had the most stunning effect, yet the entire landscape of yellows, reds, oranges, and green grasses dispersed throughout the rolling countryside as we zoomed from village to village was breathtaking. It was one great big magnificent bouquet.

Two and a half hours later I stumbled off the TGV at the Arles station and began my unsuccessful search for a cash machine. Sara had e-mailed to the reception of the Hotel Constantine requesting a room. The reservation was never confirmed, but I decided to pursue it anyway. I asked a few people at the train station if they could direct me to the hotel or a cash machine, only to find shaking heads and shrugging shoulders.

If I had been successful in accessing some of the local currency and in sidestepping my conservative and stubborn nature, I might have hired a cab, but I had no luck, so I walked and came upon an area where a carnival with kiddy rides had been set up. Across the street from the carnival, I spotted a map of the city and walked to it. I tried to make some sense of it but only felt overwhelmed.

There was a woman at a payphone on the corner, and, when she finished her call, I asked her for some help. She was a German woman who spoke some English and was working on a cruise ship that traveled the Rhone River. They were docked in Arles for the day, and she was unfamiliar with the area. I thanked her and walked on aimlessly, dragging my luggage behind me, alternating my grasp on the handle between my two hands every five minutes or so; I felt like a gloveless pencil pusher who had been forced upon the task of hoeing Johnson Grass in a hundred acre cotton field.

There was a definite Muslim influence in Arles, people who had crossed over from Northern Africa - my guess, but it was just a guess. I'm just as lousy in geography as I am in algebra. I asked an Algerian or Moroccan man who was sitting on a park bench outside of the Roman coliseum if he could direct me to a bank, but he didn't understand me.

After another thirty minutes of bouncing my luggage over the cobblestone streets and up and down curbs, I found a cash machine at the post office. A few blocks later, after acquiring some of the local currency, I happened upon a visitor's center with a lovely young woman of Moroccan or Algerian descent. She spoke English; I could have kissed her. Her English was not only fluent, but contained a sweet sounding accent to boot, and I needed it all. She phoned Hotel Constantine for me and made certain that they had a room and pointed me in the hotel's direction which was another ten minute walk from the visitor's center. Her smile and fluency in my mother tongue eased a building tension.

Walking to the hotel, I heard a crash and looked out into the street to find that a motor scooter had just run into a small pickup truck that was turning across traffic. The driver of the truck got out to check on the scooter driver. Several others who had witnessed the accident gathered around to see the fate of the motorcyclist. The driver of the truck seemed to be at fault. It appeared he had turned in front of the cyclist, so I was quite surprised to see the motorcyclist stand up, walk over to his scooter, start it, and quickly zoom away as if he was trying to escape the scene of a crime. The bystanders, as did I, looked on in disbelief. Maybe the motor scooter had run the stoplight; I can't tell you for certain what happened. It's even possible that the cyclist was in the country illegally.

With the collision drama over, I walked on and within five minutes found Hotel Constantine. A blue-eyed Husky dog was the first to greet me as I dragged my bags through the hotel door into the small reception area.

"Hello, do you speak English?" I asked a thin blonde thirty-something-year-old woman.

"A little," she answered in a heavy French accent.

"A woman just called to reserve a room for me," I explained, reaching down to pet the Husky who was waiting for my attention.

"Ah, yes, Mr. Clay."

"What's his name?"

"Herod."

"And yours?"

"Elizabeth."

"Nice to meet you Elizabeth."

She made some comment on how I pronounced Eliza-beth, but I didn't think much of it, and then she offered to help carry my bags up to my room without my signing or registering for my stay. I let her take the small suitcase and followed her up the stairs with my other two bags. I asked Elizabeth if there was an Internet café in town. She didn't know of one, but said that she'd check with her husband to see if I could use their computer. I thanked her, and then she returned to her duties downstairs.

I set my bags up on a shelf and noticed that the wheel on the big suitcase had actually been torn off. It didn't surprise me with all the cobblestone sidewalks and curbs it had been hurdling since leaving California. The room was papered in yellow with a green and blue floral pattern and had a few small van Gogh prints hanging on the walls. The cloister oozed Provence; it was warm and comfortable.

After a shower, I walked down and asked for dinner recommendations. Elizabeth suggested several locations, and I settled on a place called Chez GiGi, only a ten-minute walk from the hotel. It was owned and operated by a Canadian woman. There was a cute, petite, brunette waitress setting tables for the evening trade.

"English?" I tested.

"Some," the brunette answered.

"I'd like a table for one," I said, admiring the beautiful young woman.

Before the brunette could answer, the woman who owned the place walked into the dining room. "It will be another forty-five minutes before we are ready to serve."

"Put me down on the list, and I'll return in forty-five minutes," I answered.

I walked around the narrow streets between the two and three-story stone buildings. I tried to remember my way back to Chez GiGi's but got lost. I stopped in a small candy shop and bought an ice-cream cone and wandered on. I found several other restaurants, all of them still preparing for a later opening.

Providence led me back to Chez GiGi's. Warmly welcomed by both the waitress and the owner, I was seated immediately and served an appetizer of olives and crunchy, bite-size, Japanese rice crackers with a soy glaze.

Craving fish, I ordered salmon as my main entrée and a bottle of gassed water. Since it was Sunday, they didn't have an extensive menu, so my salmon came with fries, and a grilled tomato. It was an excellent meal. I needed something different, too. All the Italian food was beginning to get to me. I wasn't sure if it was the food in Italy I was having a hard time digesting or if it was the horseshit that Number-one had been dishing onto my plate. Actually, it was Number-one.

After a very long journey, I returned to Hotel Constantine to turn in for the night, and for the previous evening as well.

April 2, 2001 - Mid-Afternoon

I'm sitting on a stone wall, on the west side of Arles, along the Rhone River. I slept for more than twelve hours, waking up at ten-thirty; a much needed rest. After showering, I walked down to the front desk, uncertain of what my day might bring. Elizabeth's husband was on duty, and I asked him about Internet access. He offered the use of his personal computer and led me to their bedroom, asking me to pay no attention to the mess.

There were two messages from Kelli, one in response to an old message that I had sent her. It was about her having to be evacuated from Gaza because of missile attacks. Kelli's an artist and has been commissioned, with a group of others, by a Palestinian firm to put together some type of handbook for their employees. She's made several trips to the Middle East for this project. Her second message was in response to the e-mail I sent her just before leaving Florence. It was about meeting her in Ireland and about having to get her own place soon. She's been staying with her mother for the last few months.

Kelli left Big Sur six months ago after having lived there for several years. She moved just a few days after I had met her at a coffee house-Internet café where she came to check her e-mail. She had plans of chasing the sun to Spain and finding a studio where she could paint. I was really taken by her and did a little snooping around with my Big Sur connections. Three months after meeting Kelli, Sarina, my Big Sur source, came through with Kelli's e-mail address, and that was the beginning of our correspondence.

Kelli had gone to the Esalen Institute in Big Sur with the intention of it being a short stay and the short stay stretched to several years. She was born in Boston to parents who were both Irish citizens. As a child, she had lived in several European countries because of her father's work as an international businessman. I think she was around twelve when the family returned to Ireland.

I remember seeing Kelli for the first time when she walked into the Internet café in Carmel on that early September day. She was a tall, thin blonde with blue eyes, and I have always been a sucker for tall, thin, blonde, blue-eyed women. We made eye contact almost immediately after she walked into the café. I was sitting in a seat, right in front of the desk where the on-line computers were kept, reading a history book for a class I was enrolled in at the community college. I might just as well have shit-canned the book at the first sign of Kelli; I was gone just as soon as I spotted her. It was as if a thirty-five-year-old Miss Universe had walked into the room and actually noticed me.

Kelli was having trouble getting on-line, so, being the gentleman I am, I volunteered my expert technical services by jiggling a few wires and praying sixty-nine hail Mary's. The computer never came around, thank Mary, and it gave me the opportunity to speak to Kelli. That's when I found that she would soon be leaving the States. I gave her my business card and suggested that we meet for coffee before her departure, and her response was: "Maybe I'll see you here again," and I had a pretty good idea what that meant.

I returned to the café the next day, a note in hand with my e-mail address, wishing Kelli well and asking her to keep me posted as to how she faired in Spain. I entrusted the note to the girl who worked at the counter and asked her to pass it on to my new goddess.

There aren't many women I'm willing to make an ass out of myself over, but of the few I've ever met, Kelli is one of them, and it's more than her physical beauty. It was how she carried herself. It was something that came through her and had to do with her presence, her spirit. I recall telling her how I'd left my old world of selling tractors a few years earlier, after reading James Joyce's *The Portrait of an Artist as a Young Man*. As I told her how this book had helped me to realize that I wasn't creating anything in my life, her blue-eyes were locked on as she listened intently. Our conversation was brief, not more than ten minutes, but I felt as if I was actually being heard and received.

It felt like what I had to say mattered.

I didn't forget about Kelli, but I'd given up on ever hearing from her as weeks passed. Three months later, when I received Sarina's call with Kelli's e-mail address, my hope was resurrected. It was as if the stone had been rolled away on the original Easter Sunday. Kelli's response to my e-mail was like Mary Magdalene herself meeting the risen lord for the first time after the crucifixion, an incarnated *Nolo Me Tangere*, with the exception of our gender roles being reversed, I of course being the penitent whore. Separated by an ocean between two continents, I couldn't touch her, but, with modern day technology, I had been granted the opportunity of communing with her in Spirit.

After responding to Kelli's e-mail, I walked out into Arles with the intention of finding a coffee. Across the street and down a couple of blocks from the hotel, I walked into a place and ordered a cappuccino, figuring it to be a universal drink. The woman responded with a "no cappuccino" and in French gave me two options to choose from, neither of which I understood. I stood there trying to decide how to respond to her. I didn't like her tone, her curtness and seeming impatience with me. I looked up at her and, without saying a word, turned and walked out of the place. I was going to spend my time and money where it was welcomed.

I wandered to the east edge of town and found a pâtissière across the street. There was a plate of freshly prepared sugar coated bonbons next to the cash register with a hand written sign that read three francs. I held up two fingers, and the old woman behind the counter shook her head and held up three fingers. She thought I was trying to bargain with her. I shrugged my shoulders, nodded, and handed the woman a fifty-franc bill that had Saint-Exupéry's Little Prince embossed into it, as well as the image Saint-Exupéry drew of a Boa constrictor who has swallowed an elephant.

In the story, adults mistook the first drawing for a hat so Saint-Exupéry drew a second picture that reveals the inside view of the Boa constrictor along with the elephant that has been swallowed. Saint-Exupéry used the first drawing as a test of true understanding and if the people he tested it on couldn't see beyond the hat to the Boa, he would then lower himself to talk about things that greatly pleased adults or so-called sensible people...

The woman bagged my bonbons and exchanged the fifty-franc note for a handful of change. Walking out, I spotted a bottle of water in a cooler and returned to the register a second time. I held out the handful of change the woman had just given me, letting her take what I owed. She laughed as she picked through the coins. I was uncertain if she was laughing at my naïve ignorance or my trusting her. The bonbons were heavenly regardless of what inspired her chuckle. I only wanted two bonbons, but she had bagged three and for that I was glad. Lack of communication served me that time.

Arles is a very old city. It has a Roman coliseum, a relic from an era gone by, as one of its highlights to draw tourists. The coliseum was on the east side of the town. The Rhone River served as a natural border to the west of Arles. I continued my walk around the perimeter of the city, walking north, along the outer wall of the coliseum. I always seem to be drawn to the outer-edge when things in the center carry a chaotic, unconsciously driven tone. It's important to find refuge in a quiet place, allows me to reorient and come back to myself, at least when I'm new to an area. I prefer a little foreplay, dancing around the periphery before diving off into the heart of darkness.

I followed the road northbound until it curved west following the perimeter of the town. It was the same path I'd taken yesterday in search of a cash machine and Hotel Constantine. I was approaching the area where the carnival had been whirling about a day earlier. A little boy, two or three years old, walked out of an establishment waving a baguette in the air as if it was a sword, and then the little knight started banging his breadstick on the sidewalk. He noticed me approaching and stood to greet me in his native tongue. All I had to offer in response was a smile. He repeated himself as he handed me his sword. I held out my hand to receive the token, but teasingly, he quickly withdrew his offer, and then walked back into the café, swinging the baguette in the air while speaking his piece.

I continued on to the end of the block, finding no other cafés that looked inviting. I returned to where the little boy had been carrying on, hoping to get my morning cup of coffee. The place was called Café Vincent, named after van Gogh who had spent time living in Arles. The town liked naming streets and businesses after famous people like van Gogh, Victor Hugo, President Wilson, and other famous people with whom I'm naively unfamiliar.

I sat at a table outside of Café Vincent and stumbled my way through the menu. A wind came up, blowing dust all about and adding to my already unstable condition; I moved inside. Café Vincent's walls were painted yellow and from them hung several prints of framed van Gogh images.

I had no problem getting my coffee at Café Vincent; it even came with a dark chocolate wafer that I immediately dissolved in the hot coffee. I also ordered a couple of crepes. The waitress had a hard time understanding me, but at least she tried, and it was her effort that made me feel welcomed.

While eating, I noticed that a table on the other side of the room had been set and some sort of baked pasta dish had been placed in its center. Shortly after noticing the set table, a man came out of the kitchen with a pan in his hand and started scooping either a lamb or beef dish onto the plates.

Next, a little boy, younger than the one who had been wielding the baguette, anxiously approached the table. The man who was dishing out the meat motioned the toddler to take a certain seat. Then a woman walked into the room and helped the little one up onto his chair. The little baguette thief stepped onto the scene and took the seat next to his younger counterpart; almost immediately the two of them began a boyish jostle. The older boy pawned some of his meat off onto the smaller boy's plate when the little one turned away, but the little guy's mother was in the process of cutting his meal into bite-size pieces, and was quick to return to the baguette thief what he had been trying to pass off.

My waitress ended up being one of the partners of the two couples, the mother of one of the two little boys who were breaking bread together. My guess is that the young boys were perhaps cousins. I watched the two families interact, enjoying the rivalries that came up between the two youngsters at the dinner table. I flashed back to my youth, to kicking one of my younger brothers in the shin under the table for no justifiable reason other than to see if I could get away with it.

The parents refereed the matches that arose between the youngsters, occasionally glancing over to my table to see how I was reacting to the little ones' discontentment. They seemed so patient and understanding of the youngsters' fieriness, almost as if they were proud of their progenies' dispositions, and well they should have been.

I liked being at Café Vincent. I wasn't interested in the architecture or the history of Arles. I was much more interested in making and enjoying my own history. I wasn't even sure if I'd make it to Saintes Maries de la Mer. I was much more drawn to things like the two little boys who were getting away with as much as they could. Then again, maybe they weren't getting away with something; maybe they were just being true to themselves.

I know it takes time to acclimate to unfamiliar surroundings, but the general feeling of being unwelcome still upset me. The difficulty of my arrival yesterday and my first encounter this morning while trying to get coffee threw me off kilter. Thank goodness my experience at Café Vincent had a redeeming quality for the Eve-like wrongness of this morning's original sin.

I have actually considered saying fuck off to all these Frenchy bastards and catching a flight right here and now to Dublin, but I'll wait a day or two to see if it might be an over sensitivity on my part. Then, if I find this to be the source of my unsettledness, I'll blast the hell out of Provence, never again to return.

I might be here for a reason. One could be that I need to get an objective view of the States and what my life has been up to this point in time. I might also need to gain a perspective view of all that I've taken in during my stay in Florence. And perhaps there's also a reason beyond my limited ego's current state of comprehension.

I left Café Vincent and walked to the Rhone River, only a couple of hundred feet west of the café. The carnival crew had torn down the rides and was camping along the Rhone. A caged trailer was filled with live tigers; that was a bit surreal. Two small cruise ships were docked along the eastside of the river with people lounging on the deck, sunbathing: it looked inviting. I thought about returning home to California, buying a boat, and living on it for the summer, maybe even longer. I walked south along the river and came across a couple sitting on the sidewalk, backs leaning against the wall of stone, swigging orange soda from a two-liter bottle.

The woman said something in French, and I responded with: "English only." She quickly and smoothly converted her speech to English, asking if I could spare some change. They looked strung out on drugs or booze. I guess drugs and booze are one and the same. I fished out two ten-franc pieces and handed them to the woman. I never gave beggars the time of day, let alone money. Normally, I would have turned my head and pretended they didn't exist, but, for some reason, I acted, or reacted, out of character. Being where very few people understood me, or cared to admit it, has changed me some.

The drunks were me, my inner couple, an unseen part of myself that once ruled over me. They reminded me of my failed marriage, the ex-wife and myself. We weren't strung out on drugs, but we were strung out on the individual histories that had formed us. Both of us, unknowingly, had carried forward those old images, those old dead deities, into our marriage. Neither of us could really see the other, let alone ourselves. We worshiped an idol, strung out on a belief of how married people should act, a dogma, or dogmas that had robbed us of creating a belief, or better yet, a knowing of our own.

I'm settling in a bit, or my stomach is anyway. The food was magnificent in Florence, but I over-did it. The Italian cuisine might not have been the sole source of my indigestion; it might have been a combination of the food and all the foreign feminines. Being the only man in that group, my cup and plate had been overflowing. At least there had been a variety. The women were very much like different dishes: some exquisite, leaving a heavenly taste dancing first on my tongue and then wiggling her way down deep into my soul, some were like a nice fulfilling meal that could ease me into a peaceful nap, and a couple of them were like gagging on sour milk.

A few hundred yards after passing the forlorn couple, I decided to sit up on the same wall that they'd been leaning against and take in some sun. Five cops rode by on bicycles, three men and two women, they didn't see the drunks huddled up against the wall, or they didn't care. An old woman and her yellow Labrador retriever passed in front of me. My brother, Freeman, once had a yellow Lab. I thought about Freeman, about his life, and about how he lives it. He has designed his life to serve him instead of him serving it. Freeman's a gunsmith. He's probably at home, out in his shop, repairing some hunter's deer rifle or shotgun so that his client can go out and hunt down who knows what kind of critter to take home and mount on his wall. His kids will be getting home from school soon, and he'll be there to greet them.

The idea of marriage and a family once seemed a lifelong prison sentence. Now it appears to be one of life's finest desserts; one that I have failed to taste and savor. In my youth, I recall my parents embracing in the kitchen once when my father came home for lunch, they may have even exchanged a kiss. But I can only remember their displays of affection and warmth for each other in my early years; it disappeared somewhere around the time I turned eight or nine.

That's what scares me about marriage, the thought of having a partner for life. I'm afraid of the mundane staleness that can creep in. I'm afraid of love turning into bitterness, into resentment after the naïve romantic illusions have vaporized and after the projections of god and goddess become estranged images and return to the archetypal world for future generations to worship and fall prey to.

My brother Luther is probably teaching class right now. He has been married for close to five years. He and his wife both have their doctorates in comparative literature and teach at a private college on the east coast.

Angus, my soon to be married youngest brother, is probably at home sleeping after working a twelve-hour shift; he's an emergency room nurse and works at night. I'm twelve years older than Angus. I once changed his diapers; in a month I'll have the honor of standing next to him while he and his bride exchange wedding vows.

I am the oldest of four boys, and the only single one. Maybe I'll return to California, build a cabin somewhere in the Sierras, marry a new bride, and have children who will come home to greet me and happily interrupt what I'm doing, to remind me who I am. I'll be graced to see myself in their faces, their smiles, their tears, their demands for my attention... They'll remind me of what's really important in life.

It is a sunny day here in Arles. There's a light breeze. It feels good to have the sun penetrate me, soaking into body and soul. This is the life: just sitting here, letting it all come to me, breathing it in, tasting it, swallowing it, and at the same time being consumed by it. I want nothing but this moment, to savor the sweetness of this dream. I'm tired of finding fault with myself, others, life... it isn't about working or about waiting; life's about living.

A group of teenagers smoking cigarettes and babbling in French are walking by as I sit perched on this stonewall. It seems that smokers by far outnumber non-smokers in Europe, and the cars are all compacts, or at least compact by my standards. Some of the lasting images that I have collected so far on this excursion are the small cars, cigarettes, motor scooters, and those sparkling-eyed Spanish sisters whom I met yesterday at the train station in Pisa. I wish...

April 2, 2001 - 10 p.m.

This evening I fell into a funk and have decided that I don't like France. It feels like I have to apologize everywhere I go, for being an American or, worse yet, for even existing. Perhaps this is how I've lived my entire life, apologizing for my humanity, for having been born. Maybe it isn't France, and, instead, me, trying to fit into life, my feelings of being inferior, misunderstood, unacceptable, and the rest of those old ghosts that have kept me shackled.

Fitting in doesn't sound good; climbing out of that old mold sounds far more appealing. I don't exactly want to die; it's more like I want to live. Many of my maybes, my doubts, have been my truth, an ignored truth. I recall the words of a friend of mine when he heard of this trip I am now living. He said something about how I'd be able to live anywhere after having made my journey. I feel alone and disconnected here, yet it isn't so much different than when I'm home, wherever home is.

I purchased a phone calling card and left a message on Kelli's answering machine saying that I'd probably be in Dublin towards the end of the week. I look forward to seeing her again. I have a hunch that our coming together this time will somehow reorient both of us, and if not Kelli, it will certainly help me. One way or the other I'll be able to get on with my life, with or without her. It isn't that I need anything to happen; my travels so far have proven to be more valuable than I could have imagined. Leaving California has helped me to step out of that life-long dream I've been stuck in.

This voice keeps telling me that I should be out on the town doing something productive, like trying to meet women and getting laid. This voice likes to accuse me of not fully living my life; it likes to confuse me, create doubt and lead me away from myself. "Go eat. Don't even think about taking a nap. You're in Europe, you fool, and you're letting it all slip away..."

The funk threw me into an obsession about my health, or lack of it, and my lost youth. But I caught myself and did with the obsession what I had done with the accusing voice: I gave it permission to exist, and then put it to bed just as a parent would do for a tired child who had stayed up well beyond his bedtime. If I wanted to be a hermit, I was damn well going to be a hermit, and the hell with those illegitimate voices that wouldn't grant me permission to be my own person.

I don't need the French to like me. I don't need to talk to a damn one of the nose-in-the-air bastards, or anyone else for that matter. I'm jerking myself off! This is about bowing to a dead image of myself: a misunderstood outcast.

My neck was stiff before leaving the States, but it grew stiffer on the train ride from Florence to Arles. It's about not turning to look back. I remembered telling Andreanna about how she couldn't go back; she could return to Rome, but not as the person she was when she had left. Something had shifted within her; whether she returned to Rome or not, she could never again be the person who she once believed herself to be. Andreanna couldn't return to that old image, she couldn't serve a dead idol; she had to live in service to herself, to her life in the present moment of its unfolding. And me... well, perhaps I dreamed Andreanna up, just to hear myself speak these very words.

I have a joyful anticipation about meeting Kelli again, yet I also want to run home to mama. The truth is, I'm more nervous than I care to admit. Well, fuck! How many crazy idiots meet a woman for ten minutes in a coffee shop and end up chasing her from California to Ireland without even knowing if a kiss awaits him? I'm entitled to my nervousness. I've already begun showing my ass, and I'm on the verge of exposing even more. I'm baring myself, becoming vulnerable, but trying to convince myself that I am not worried about the outcome of our coming together. I long to live life exposed to vulnerability, abandoning the need of my efforts to bear fruit or to protect an old wound. I want to open myself to the potentials, to a life I once believed impossible. Am I shedding my previous loyalty to these dead gods?

Sophia said I reminded her of Parsifal, the innocent fool, stepping off into life, onto that unknown train, without a plan, without an understanding, without knowing what was to become of me. I wonder what it was like, Mary Magdalene and Sarah's passage in that small vessel across the Mediterranean to Saint Maries de la Mer.

I became restless and was on my way through the door to go and eat, or perhaps to phone my friend Lewis back in the States. I locked the door behind me and started walking toward the steps, but turned around and returned to my room. I wanted to escape myself, the solitude that I normally boast about needing and enjoying. There I was, back in my room, alone, pen in hand, celebrating myself, my loneliness or at least my aloneness.

The word atonement came to me. I don't know why, but occasionally words, like images, just pop into my mind for no apparent reason, and when they do, I play with them like a cat might play with a string of yarn. At-one-ment with myself; is there really anything else I need? Is this it? Is this the meaning of my life, to learn to be and stay with myself? Maybe, and then again, maybe not. Time will tell.

I entertained the thought of letting go of attachments, letting go of having to manage and manipulate my life, simply accepting and welcoming its unraveling to be complete unto itself. Why did van Gogh kill himself? Was he unable to contain all the energy that moved through him? His body could quite possibly have been a 110-watt circuit that was connected to 220, or, better yet, a 440-watt source. He might have tapped into an archetypal vein that seized him just as a stray electrical wire can do to a seemingly innocent victim who happens through the wrong place at the wrong time.

Dancing around in the archetypal realm demands a huge tariff and it seems that this tax is levied at the expense of one's own body. It is consciousness, or better yet, unconscious content being converted to consciousness, and, in this exchange process, a good deal of energy has passed through me over the last few years, leaving me like a drained battery in need of rejuvenation. That's it; I've been dipping into the underworld and converting the high voltage down to a more manageable current. I flashed on my dream with the lion and her cub, how they turned into the five tigers, invaded my home and had to be sedated.

What I made of the dream at the time was that I had tapped into a huge power source, too much for me to handle all at once, so the tigers or energy had to be contained, not killed; just subdued. Now that time has passed, it's becoming clear to me that this energy was too powerful for me, for my body, to convert into consciousness in one fell swoop. The revelation of this dream: a reflection of my soul's huge act of kindness, its abounding grace.

A higher knowing, something much larger than my limited ego, regulates my psyche. It knows how unkind and impatient I am with myself, and I have been graced with this dream to reveal what I contain, and, at the same time, it is compensating for my inability to handle this surge of energy in one fell swoop. My ego lacks a reverence and respect and would take on all five tigers at once, but something wiser knows that I can't handle it, that it could cause me to go mad, to go van Gogh.

I had to eat before I went berserk. I walked to a McDonalds two blocks from Hotel Constantine. The McDonald hamburgers in Arles aren't prejudiced: they give the same heartburn in France as in the States. I walked around Arles for a while, window shopping and thinking about purchasing a new bag to replace the limping one. After finding nothing, I returned to the hotel.

My room sounds like a cesspool. When the toilet from the room above flushes, I wait for the juices to burst through the walls. It sounds like they're dumping their excrement right into my chambers. There are motor scooters, but not as many as in Florence. Occasionally, a reckless soul zips around the streets on his high-pitched whining motocross bike. It sounds as if the driver is making a mad dash for the finish line. Perhaps this maniac has just robbed a bank or committed some other heinous crime?

April 3, 2001 - Dream

Dream of being, or returning to Scott's dealership in Ripon and going inside. Scott's dealership is Scott Equipment Company - I was a good friend of Sheldon, the man who owned the company. I ended up purchasing his airplane N1MC from Rena, Sheldon's wife, a few years after Sheldon passed away. N1MC was one of Sheldon's cherished possessions. It was a family owned and operated business. Nikki is Sheldon and Rena's oldest daughter. I was also born in Ripon. Nikki was working at the bar and she... one of the rooms before you walk in... Nikki is offering to make a drink for all the people around there, and I say: "Yeah, I'll have one," and I end up getting it to go.

I remember going inside, into different rooms, there were different layers, and it reminded me... I was at the dealership of Scott Equipment Company, but it reminded me of Europe, these European buildings that I'm going into and then it seemed that I got it to go and it ended being like a lunch in a basket. I don't remember if I went farther into the room or not, but I do remember going out, being outside, like in front of the dealership and Vince, a farmer friend of mine who I went to high school with was there, and I asked or he asked... we were talking about something?

I said something about her, Rena, buying my membership into Triple A. He started laughing and saying, teasing about being in that business now, selling, asking what was I selling now? I remember telling him that I wasn't selling anything. Then I asked how things were going for him; he had ended up filing for bankruptcy. And I wasn't selling anything. Vince is a forty-year-old man who still lives with his parents. His mother waits on him hand and foot! There was a photo of Sheldon Scott, a black and white, an older one, in one of the rooms before you went into the inner room where Nikki was at the bar.

I went back to sleep and into the same dream, fighting with her... Rena's mechanics... actually working for them again, the Scott's - fighting for her with them or just having it out. They were upset and there was a new sign. Actually, I'm upset there is a new sign. There is a realtor and some other cheap brokerage thing tied to their business, and I go on, carrying on about what a cheap fucked up mess it is, ranting and raving. It's edgy, and the other mechanics are upset, and we just start having a meeting. There is some other guy there who used to work for Case; it's a round circle meeting. We were just getting it out there, and we almost have a fight.

They want to know how badly I fucked her when I bought the airplane, and I ended up telling them what I paid for it. I just threw it out there and leveled with them, and then I thought: why am I doing this? Why am I justifying myself; for sleeping with her, for screwing her, we agreed on our deal? Something about how I view myself, of taking advantage of women, as if they are helpless and don't have their own voice. This is an illusion or a belief I have. Why do I even have to do this? Then I... well, why not? I'll just throw it out there and let them deal with it as they will.

One of them went to the couch and sat down. It was my black couch in this big shop. It was like a tractor shop, but it was an old airport hangar out by Crows Landing, near Gustine, 40 to 50 miles west or southwest of Ripon, farming communities. I wanted to hit that guy who fell on the couch. I wanted to hit him or kick the shit out of him, and I went over there to do it, but I didn't. Instead, I fell on him and his buddy came over and it was almost like we were gonna cry. I said, man, you guys are good guys, you don't do... you don't... you're not like this. It was almost like I brushed one of the guy's hair back, like he was a little boy who was upset. They were fighting because they were upset, because they wanted to fight. Yeah, there was anger and stuff.

They had stuff to air out. They thought I had been dishonest and deceived Mrs. Scott. I remember the guy who used to work for Case, the guy mediating didn't like my ranting and raving about the sign, *my saying what a piece of shit it was and how chintzy it looked and on and on… it was a three part sign, like at the top was SEC, the next was another guy, and the next was another guy. It was like they were all tied together, like some cheap old auction thing. It was like SEC had sold out.*

I remember telling them that I gave her 70, but I offered her 60 and she said she wanted… was asking 75. I offered her 60 and ended up giving her 70 for it. I said something about it needing a paint job.

Another dream, this one about Jenny and how she almost made love to me, she wanted to, but she just wasn't quite there. She couldn't settle down enough to let it happen. She wanted to, but she was still spooked in some way. Then I remembered that she was seeing another guy, but she was entertaining being my lover, turning her energy toward me, but it was still a chaotic energy and she hadn't quite been able to channel it into making love to me, but it was just a matter of letting her find her rhythm, letting her chaos come together.

April 3, 2001

I had intentions of waking up earlier this morning, but again, like yesterday, woke after ten. I showered and went down to the bakery for some more bonbons. My next stop was to be Café Vincent for coffee, but they were closed. I continued my walk around the corner, down to the train station, and stood in line. When it was my turn at the reservation counter, I asked if they spoke English and ended up having to let people go ahead of me until the only English speaking clerk became available. I made a reservation to Paris on the TGV that departs at seven, tomorrow morning. Not wanting to book a flight and run the risk of missing it because of the unpredictability of the train strikes, I decided to buy my plane ticket to Dublin once I arrive at the airport.

My next stop was at the bus depot, just across the street from the train station. A bus would be departing within the hour for Saintes Maries de la Mer. There was a pay phone on the corner, so I walked to it, attempted to phone Kelli and was surprised to get through to her. I explained that I had a reserved seat on the TGV to Paris, but wasn't sure when I'd get to Dublin because I hadn't yet booked a flight. She suggested that I phone her mobile once I knew more. We chatted a bit longer and, after saying goodbye, I walked over to wait for the bus.

The ride from Arles was supposed to be just shy of an hour, and I was to pay the tariff directly to the bus driver, another opportunity to be shunned because of the language barrier. I suppose this is good for me in some way, just haven't figured that out.

Now that I'd figured a way to get there, I was looking forward to Saintes Maries de la Mer. My curiosity had somehow returned to me; going there gave me a bit of purpose and reason for being in a place that I would have otherwise fled long ago because of feeling so unwelcome.

My neck was still stiff, but it had improved considerably from the previous day. Two young women walked up to the depot, and I heard them say something about Saints Maries de la Mer, so it looked like I might have a little company on my ride to the sea. One of them was cute, but the other one had lots of pimples, so I figured she didn't like sex or wasn't getting any, but, then again, I loved sex and wasn't getting any, and you couldn't have found a pimple on my ass with a twenty power magnifying glass.

By one o'clock the bus was boarded and we were en route for Saintes Maries de la Mer, which was forty kilometers south of Arles, located in the Rhone delta between the Mediterranean Sea and the Camargue, a national wetlands reserve. From Arles, the bus drove through town picking up more passengers. We then crossed over the Rhone River to a western part of Arles that, up to then, I'd been unaware of, and then motored south through the countryside, occasionally making stops to let passengers off or to take new riders on.

Spring flowers were in bloom and the bus drove past vineyards, wheat, and rice fields. I spotted John Deere tractors tilling the ground. The tractors were the larger American versions that were built in the States as opposed to the smaller European manufactured models that are scattered throughout Europe.

The area had a definite feel of the frontier. The marshy

wetlands reminded me of California and the San Joaquin River Delta area, but the fields were smaller; they appeared to be twenty and forty acre plots. A white breed of horses and horned black cattle were the predominate animals of husbandry. The marshlands were full of flamingos and several other waterfowl species.

Saintes Maries de la Mer was a small port town with farming influence; it was fun to see an occasional tractor wheeling through the village streets. The town did, however, appear to be moving towards tourism. Construction was going on almost everywhere I turned, but it wasn't new construction: it was remodeling. Most of the buildings were painted white and had red tile roofs.

I got off the bus and wandered about, walking past the local trade until I arrived at the church. Instead of going right in, I decided to walk farther south until I came to a bullfighting arena that was on the beach. Just to the left of the arena was a tourist office. I went in and received a small bit of printed information. Then I took a path to the east that paralleled the beach. I'd heard about the topless beaches in Southern France, but the only topless female I found was a woman nursing her child.

After walking east for a few hundred yards, I turned back to the arena hoping to find a bathroom. There were facilities, but they wanted money to use it, so I continued walking west until I came to the harbor. There were several docked boats, mostly pleasure vessels. There was also a harbor cruise offered for a fee; I passed.

I walked north, across from the harbor, and looked out into the wetlands of the Camargue. I'd never been to Saintes Maries de la Mer, but if it hadn't been for the flamingos and the white houses with red tile roofs, it felt as if I'd spent a good part of my life living in that untamed frontier.

I continued north along the Camargue until I came to a road that led eastward back to the town center. The narrow street was lined with small residences, many with rent, lease, or for sale signs in the windows. I made my way back to the center by using the church's Romanesque bell-tower as a navigational landmark.

Gypsy women stood outside of the church. One tried to pin something on me, a small trinket of some sort, but I pulled away. She babbled something in French and the only word I could make out was Sara. They were beggars. I didn't trust them. I was afraid of being pick-pocketed. They kept repeating their rhetoric, and finally I said: "English." That stopped them, they couldn't speak English, couldn't beg in English. How nice; the language barrier finally paid off.

I entered the Church and took in the art and architecture and then stepped down into a sanctuary, a crypt where there was a statue of Sara Kali. In honor of the feminine, and all that I had learned in Florence, I dropped a coin into the statue of the Black Sara; she actually spoke some recorded words as the coin dropped into the hidden change bucket. I thought about the gypsy woman who was trying to pin something on me as I had approached the church. I wasn't superstitious, but for some reason believed Sara would bring me luck or grant an unspoken, unconscious wish that I harbored.

I paid ten Francs and climbed to the top of the church, winding up this narrow, spiral, stone staircase. I stepped out onto the roof, still below the bell tower that was to the east, and was able to get an astounding aerial view of the town and the surrounding area. After taking a few photos, I descended the spiral staircase and popped out through some side door of the church. It felt as if I had made my way through a secret passage and that I was now somewhere I wasn't supposed to be. The gypsy women were still running their hustle; I snuck away as they went over to a crowd of people who were approaching the church. I felt invisible.

The roads into the city center had been closed to all forms of traffic except pedestrian. The streets were lined with businesses. There were ice cream and candy vendors, clothing stores, souvenir shops, and street cafés everywhere. I had trouble choosing a place to eat because there were so many restaurants.

I was hungry and a bit overwhelmed, but finally settled down in a café. After using the toilet, I picked a table outside on the sidewalk that was covered by an awning. I watched the foot traffic. Across the way there was a man on a ladder with a hammer and chisel, chipping out and exposing a hidden fracture in the plaster wall like a surgeon cutting into flesh, exposing a cancer, and preparing its proper removal to provide a healthy platform for the patient's full recovery.

Had I been paying attention, I wouldn't have picked this particular restaurant. There were at least a dozen, noisy, teenage boys sitting a few tables behind me, and then several other smaller groups of them scattered about the patio. My seat was situated between several of their tables and their youthful camaraderie was overpowering. They weren't bad kids, just noisy and obnoxious; at least they weren't having a food fight.

Pointing to a visual menu, I ordered a plate of sausages and French fries that looked rather inviting. I had given up watching my diet. Two years ago Dr. Carver told me my cholesterol was high and that he wanted me back in three months to test it again; I never returned.

After a lengthy wait, my lunch arrived. There were two different types of sausage, neither of them looked like the illustration on the menu. I cut into what looked like a French poodle turd; it tasted better than it looked. It was a bit spicy, but dry. I sliced another piece and found a hair. I motioned to the waiter and pointed to the hair, unable to use words to express my complaint. He looked at me dumbfounded, and I pointed to the hair again and motioned for him to take my plate away.

Again, I waited for my lunch, sitting in the middle of all the noisy boys, watching the man across the street chisel the plaster. I also took in much of the pedestrian traffic, occasionally fixing my stare on one of the many beautiful women. There was a stray German shepherd, a fine specimen of the breed, wandering in and out of the different cafés, looking for a snack, only to be shooed away like a pesky fly. The variety of dogs on leashes was outstanding, and all of them purebreds. It was apparent that the French took dog ownership seriously. In all, I spotted several breeds, a French-German shepherd, a Weimaraner, a Bichon Frise, a Silky, a Yorkshire terrier, a Weiner dog, and even a Jack Russell terrier.

The waiter eventually returned with my plate and the same piece of sausage that I had cut into when I found the hair; it had fresh fries though, and there was no evidence of the hair. I pushed the cut sausage to the side, and ate the other links and fries, no tip for this waiter.

After lunch, I found a place to get an ice cream to ease the indigestion that the greasy sausage would soon provide. I paid twice for the ice cream compared to what the sign said, or what I thought it said. I didn't care. I just handed the girl a French bill and trusted them to give me the correct change. I didn't want to care. I didn't want to know if I was getting fucked, and that's what probably kept me from beating the shit out of the cocky bastards and ending up in one of their stinking jails.

It was after four when I decided to return from Saintes Maries to Arles. The bus was scheduled to pick up at five. The stop was only a five-minute walk from the village, but I'd seen enough.

An Englishman stood waiting for the bus. He was getting impatient. He had some kind of an electronic portable pocket watch and a monocular. He kept pulling his electronic toy from his front pant pocket to check the time and then he'd step out into the road looking through his one-eyed binocular. The bus came up behind him when he was still out in the road staring off into the horizon. Life's funny that way; while waiting for what we believe is in front of us, it often sneaks up from behind and bites us in the butt.

The pimple faced girl and her kinda cute friend were on the bus back to Arles. It was a warm ride. Several school children rode the bus out into the country. The driver pulled up at the children's stop where their mothers where awaiting the arrival of their offspring. When the driver opened the door, he teased the children and talked to their mothers as they left the bus. The rest of the drive, I watched the tractors working the fields, and thought about returning to Chez GiGi's for dinner.

I walked along the Rhone from the bus station back to Hotel Constantine. It was nine in the morning in California. Leaving in the morning, I had several minutes left to burn on my long distance calling card that was only good for calls from France, so I decided to phone a few friends. I called Adam first and caught him at home. He thought that something might be wrong because I was calling. I assured him that I was fine. Told him I was thinking of him and just wanted to say hello and make sure that all was well back in the States.

My next call was to Lewis. I made contact with him on his mobile phone. His home had been up for sale for some time now, and it had finally been sold. We bullshitted some, and I told him about all the hot looking Italian and French women that I'd come across so far on the trip. He asked if I'd slept with any of them. Then I told him about Andreanna, assuring him that I could have had her if I wanted, mostly to make it sound good to Lewis and to reassure myself that my balls were still dangling down there where they belonged and that I hadn't left them behind in some foreign country or in the hands of Number-one.

After visiting with Lewis, I began to pack for my early morning departure on the TGV to Paris, where hopefully I'll catch a flight to Dublin. While shuffling through my receipts, mentally trying to keep track of my expenditures, I heard a crash and looked out of my window to spot a car that had rear-ended another while trying to merge onto the northbound freeway. I closed the window, and felt the same relief as when turning off the volume of a mindless chattering talk show where the guests brawl and duke it out over some newly exposed incestuous family affair.

I took a shit. My turds had changed from a greasy, mushy, dark green Florentine influence to hard round brown Frenchy tootsie rolls. It seems that the constitutional trend of my feces geographically follows that of the dog turds left lying on the sidewalks, as well as the attitudes of the countrymen.

I had a late dinner at Chez GiGi. They were packed, so I had to sit at the opposite end of a table where three men were having dinner. I ignored them; I wasn't into befriending another just to be snubbed again. The young brunette waitress remembered me from dining there two evenings earlier. She couldn't have been more than twenty, but she was gorgeous. It was her eyes, her smile, but more than anything it was her naïveté. She didn't seem a bit afraid of me. It was apparent that up to this point in her life she had been spared man's betrayal.

I had lamb with potatoes and vegetables, and a large bottle of carbonated mineral water.

"Would you like some mootard?" the young brunette asked,

after she had set my order down in front of me. She spoke in broken English, and often had to ask the owner of the restaurant to translate for her.

"Mootard?" I asked, completely clueless of what she was offering me.

"Yes, don't you know what mootard is?"

"Oh, mustard. No thank you," I smiled, and nodded my head, relieved that I had figured out what she was trying to convey, more for the sake of not looking like an idiot to the young sweet French girl as opposed to missing the influence of *mootard* on my lamb.

The meal was great, but I felt cramped sitting next to strangers; it wasn't a French thing, though. I easily feel cramped. It's important for me to have my space no matter where I am.

April 4, 2001

Woke up without any dreams, at least none that I can recall. I'm on the train en route to Paris; perhaps this is all a dream. My taxi was on time. It arrived at six o'clock sharp, but the driver screwed me on the tariff. It was 5,500 francs, but he charged me 6,700 francs because of my luggage and never even bothered to help with my bags. I gave him 8,000 francs and told him to keep the change. I had saved that much walking around that goddamn city the day I arrived and was grateful for not having to tote my flat-tired luggage back through hell again this morning.

I'll ride first class on the TGV, but won't even spring for a cab ride across town once the train has delivered me to my destination. I'd rather beat myself to death in defiance and wear a wheel off a hundred dollar suitcase than spring for a ten-dollar cab ride. Being cooped up in that overnight train from Florence to Arles had produced a prodigious vigor in me that day, so I probably wouldn't have hired a cab when I arrived anyway. Besides, I had no French currency at the time... ah hell, it doesn't much matter anyway, that sun set four days ago.

The last time I checked my e-mail was the morning after I arrived in Arles. I never found an Internet café and didn't want to impose on the innkeepers at Hotel Constantine. They had been quite accommodating, in spite of my negative attitude towards the general French population. Yesterday, the innkeeper booked my taxi in advance for the early morning departure. He actually got up to see me off this morning, making sure that my taxi arrived on time. He was really a fine fellow, as was his wife Elizabeth, and Herod the Husky wasn't such a bad creature either.

The TGV arrived on time, and I slid into the comfort of my first class seat for the three-and-a-half-hour ride to Paris. Avignon was the first stop; it smelled like an outhouse. Once we pulled into the train station, the odor died down, so I assumed that we must have passed their sewage plant on the outskirts of town.

I'm ready to be rid of France; it stinks! Fuck these Frenchies, even if I did have a superb meal last night. Besides, it was actually prepared by a Canadian. The train is full of coughers and nose blowers who just add to my agitation. I know of one country where I'll never live, let alone pay another visit, or should I be careful with my hasty prediction?

I wonder what my odds of catching a flight to Dublin are this afternoon. I'm always trying to calculate fictitious statistics; it's so fruitless. The woman across the aisle has started another one of her coughing fits. She needs a cough drop. Hell, she needs to be at home. She's infecting the whole flippin' railcar with what she's hacking up.

I wonder what Lauren's doing? Of all the women in my life up to this point, she has probably had the greatest impact on me. The sting's gone; embarrassment has replaced my feeling of loss, at least for the moment. My stomach is growling. I'm hungry. I ate a lot yesterday. Besides coffee, my first meal is usually lunch, sometimes not until one or two. Maybe I'm just hungry for what I had, or wanted to have with Lauren.

The embarrassment has to do with my insecurity, or my then insecurity. Now the bastard next to me has started sneezing. It has to be all the cologne that these fucking Frenchies douche with. I wondered if it's still there, the insecurity, lying dormant inside of me? I finally got off a sneeze of my own to match the rest of my fellow infirmants.

I was so needy when I was with Lauren, but I'm beginning to see the need is less of a problem than I once believed it to be. Maybe there's something right in loving and in needing to be loved. What's so wrong with being tied to another? Tied, wow, now that's an interesting word. Maybe it's the word that I'm hung up on, or the image of being tied, bound and constricted. Communion sounds better. What's so wrong with communing with one another?

As much as I long for a mate, a companion, I also see it as a weakness, a dependency of sorts. It's another one of the many pop psychology fallacies that I've fallen for. You have to love yourself before you can love another. Now just what exactly does that mean? I can't tell you, but behind this modern day myth that I've been clinging to, there's a frightened man longing for connection and communion with another human being, a woman, a lover. Psychology might say this is really a longing for a connection and communion with one's Self, and that's all fine and dandy, but where does my outer life fit into this grand philosophy?

I suppose that Lauren and I were only meant to have a passing love affair. I, or something in me, as well as Lauren, knew it, too. That's why we didn't last. It was some damn good sex, though. Quite possibly the best I've ever had. It was nice to let go into her with that wild abandon. That's what made it so good. I didn't dive in with my dick first, the way I have with most of the women in my life; my heart led me to her sacred chamber.

It'll be nice to lead with my heart again, and this time with my neediness exposed instead of being a hidden villain. This time my abandonment will be different. It'll be a conscious abandonment... yeah, right!

This train is one fast mother. We've been zigzagging across the Rhone River Valley. The landscape turns greener the farther north we advance. There are wheat fields with eight to ten inches of stalk growth, fruit trees are blossoming with white, pink, and purple flowers.

A mobile phone just rang behind me. A woman answered. "Merci, merci..." she shouts.

Merci, merci, my ass; merci for nothing you bunch of rude

bastards. I'm beginning to enjoy my righteous indignation. I'm beginning to take pleasure in my disdain for the whole bunch of these finicky poodles. There's a nuclear power plant with four cooling towers letting off steam. My suffering, man's suffering, humanity's suffering; is it created by a battle opposing the manifestation of consciousness?

April 4, 2001 - 2:45 p.m.

I've made it to Paris and booked a flight. Now I'm waiting for the airplane. After arriving on the TGV, I stumbled through the train station, down to the metro and took it out to Charles De Gaulle airport. At an information booth, I found out that Aerlingus was my best bet for getting a flight to Dublin. The Aerlingus ticketing counter was closed for lunch, so I wandered around and checked on flights with a few other carriers, not finding anything.

Once the ticketing agent returned, I purchased a round trip ticket for 210,000 francs, the equivalent of nearly three hundred US dollars. The flight is to leave in less than two hours, and the return flight is booked for Monday, the day after Easter, which gives me almost two weeks to explore Ireland. The ticket has a rebooking fee of forty-five US dollars in the event that I want to leave earlier, or stay longer.

I had hoped to get a less expensive flight, but I wasn't in much of a bargaining position, nor was I in the mood. It felt good just to buy the ticket without weighing my pocket book. If this trip was about saving money or making sense, I wouldn't be here in the first place. As unwelcome as I feel, I'd have probably given a thousand dollars for a glass of cold water while sizzling away in this hell.

On checking my bags, I learned that my flight would be delayed twenty minutes. What do I care? How can I care; I don't have to spend another night in this country. I don't want to care either, not about running a little behind schedule anyway. Maybe the plane's tardiness will save my life in some unknown fashion.

If I'm going to care about anything, it has to be worth

caring about, and that little honey at the Aerlingus counter who checked me in most certainly appears to be something or someone whom I could learn to care about. I'll never know, though, not unless I get a job with Aerlingus, and even if I do, they couldn't get me to work here in Gay Paree.

Once in the departure area, I phoned Kelli and left a message on her voice mail informing her of my arrival. It's going to be nice to see her, I hope. Even if it isn't, it will damn sure be good to be back in an English speaking country.

There are plenty of redheads gathering around the boarding gate. I'm sitting in the non-smoking section of the pre-boarding area. A couple and a teenage girl were standing in line at the Aerlingus counter when I first purchased the ticket. Looks like they'll be on my flight. The woman's a nervous sort, the kind of person whose anxiety invites and creates more problems than necessary. They've had problems; missed an earlier flight. The woman appears to be Irish, and I think the man and teenage girl are from a north European country like Sweden, Denmark or Norway. I don't know this for certain, but their language sounds as if they might be Scandinavian. The man stinks of body odor.

What in the hell am I doing here? After only a brief meeting with Kelli in California, tracking her down on the Internet and corresponding for several months, we're finally going to meet face to face again. I'm nervous, yet excited. Coursing through my veins is a sense of freedom and abandonment that for years has been lost: quite possibly misplaced when I was tying on my last good bender, well over fifteen years ago. That's it: I feel a bit drunk, and all without having had a single pop.

The time has come to board the plane, but there's no plane to board. Now they're announcing that the flight has been delayed for another thirty minutes. Aerlingus isn't getting off to the best start with their new client. My carefree attitude is quickly disappearing; their belatedness is beginning to agitate me. I just thought about feminine energy, which was a subject discussed at the Mary Magdalene seminar. Sophia spoke of how it appeared to the masculine as uncontrollable or uncontainable, and how often it was discarded instead of embraced. Is this what's pumping through me right now?

An Indian man and his fat wife, dressed in the traditional silky gown with a ruby-like stone glued to her forehead, have taken a seat in the non-smoking section not far to my right. The woman just let out a screaming fart, raising her a few inches off the seat. I'm looking at her right now, about to gag. She's staring off into space as if nothing has happened. Her husband just lit a cigarette. The voice on the loud speaker keeps repeating that the terminal is a non-smoking area, but the guy just ignores it and keeps puffing away. Between the two of them they might just blow this place up. France can have them both; they deserve each other.

The nervous woman accompanying the man with the teenage girl just sat down to my left. The man stepped over to the smoking section to have a cigarette. I don't get it. An announcement keeps sounding; saying that this is a non-smoking terminal, yet there's a designated smoking section.

It's the nervous woman who has the body odor, not the man; good gosh! Maybe it's both of them, but it's certainly the woman who's spreading her scent right now. She's up again, taking her stink over to the Aerlingus counter to ask about the flight. They said something to reassure her and now she's walking away. Now she's pacing, taking her coat off and then putting it back on. I can imagine what it must smell like over there.

Five minutes have passed, and Nervous is at the desk to find out what happened. They're beginning to get irritated with this stinky broad. Now they are telling her to take a seat and to quit bothering them.

The plane has just now pulled into the gate, at the time of its scheduled departure. It'll be at least forty-five minutes to an hour before we're airborne and that's if air traffic control cooperates, and I have yet to find much cooperation with these Frenchies.

There's a restless energy looming around the terminal. At the station, one gate from where we are to board, a phone keeps ringing, but no one's there to answer the call. It rang thirty times before the caller gave up.

Several of the passengers waiting to board the flight are hovering around the boarding tunnel door, standing in the way of the deplaning passengers. They're already airborne in their minds; it's just their bodies that have yet to be lifted off the ground. Is this what dying is like? They're dead, I'm dead, and this is all a fucking French nightmare. This is hell! No, there is no hell; there's only France. I've died and been sent to France. "Fuck you Yahweh! What's that? You said I chose France. Yeah, well, fuck you anyway!"

A pissed off American man has just deplaned and is rushing to the desk, thinking he's missed his connection. He's changed his tune now that they've reassured him that his connecting flight is running late as well. The American is sitting down in the non-smoking section, where the farting Queen of Sheba and her clueless smoking husband once sat.

Now the rushing American is dipping into his carry-on and spreading his goods out over four seats, kind of like he's staking out his territorial claim. He can have that fart-ridden real estate. He's got the headphones he stole from the plane, a computer, and a Bible-thumper's religious novel of some sort. It's the kind of book where the author projects his dark-side and his own capacity for evil out into the world of ghosts and spirits that are taking over and controlling the general population of the world. I've got to piss.

I just left the bathroom, standing in the smoking section, close to the boarding gate. I'm toying with the illusion that standing here might make things move along faster. Churchy is still sitting in the non-smoking area sorting through his goods, his panic has left him, but it continues to swirl around this terminal. Another man is trying to sooth his one-year-old crying daughter with a stuffed Garfield cat. The phone at the next gate is ringing again, and goes unanswered. I was about to walk over to answer the goddamn thing, to tell them that no one the fuck is home, but an Aerlingus employee stepped over and finally answered the call.

Now I'm looking directly in front of me, back into the smoking section of the non-smoking terminal. I've spotted a narrow-headed, dark-haired Frenchy who is staring at me. He has a finely trimmed goatee, and is dressed all in black: shoes, socks, pants, shirt, even his overcoat is black. He's a perfect match for the incarnation of a Satan-like character from Churchy's religious novel. This dark soul is probably about to take over the captain's body, highjack our plane and fly us straight to hell, back to Arles. Then again, maybe we're already in hell and this dark character has been sent to deliver us from evil? I guess the authors of these religious novels deal with their dark-sides much like I do; I just shovel my shit off onto the French. "Fuck you, Yahweh! You've had me for the first half of my life, the second half is mine!"

I've boarded the plane and am buckled in. The captain has just announced that our take-off time is in thirty minutes. Once airborne, the flight to Dublin will take ninety minutes. I can hear the little girl crying, but I can't tell if she's in the front or rear of the plane, which is a good sign for my not being haunted by the little one's discontentment for the next couple of hours; I can hardly handle my own.

I bet these goddamn Frenchies have things stacked in their favor, and all Air France planes are running according to schedule. At least I have an aisle seat, and in an emergency row exit. I have more legroom than on my flight over from the States.

People are sneezing all over the plane, just like this morning's train ride. Only divine intervention can keep me from catching something. Most of the passengers are reading magazines and newspapers written in English: what a relief.

We're taxiing out towards the runway. Four or five Air France jets have just departed ahead of us. Now we've taxied onto the runway, and we're rolling, and now... we have departed.

Au revoir, you friendly mother-fuckers! Leaving San Francisco felt like it had opened up the arteries of my heart; leaving Paris feels like the greatest bowel movement I have ever had. I promised Lewis to do one thing before I left France, but I failed to make good on my word: I forgot to shit in one of their bidets.

To Be or Not to Be...

April 4, 2001 - 10 p.m.

I've made it to Dublin; I can breathe. It feels good here. It was crisp outside when I left the airport terminal, twelve degrees Celsius. It was mostly sunny. The way clouds floated over, it appeared that a storm had recently dissipated.

I looked around the airport to see if I could spot Kelli. I didn't expect to see her on such short notice, but in the event she had received my message, I didn't want to overlook her. Yeah, right: like I could have if I wanted to. I was worried that I wouldn't recognize her; you know how when you first meet someone, then when you see them again, sometimes they change. She was so beautiful, though. Hell, she was more than beautiful, and I usually don't lose the image of such a stunning woman, yet our original encounter was so brief that some doubt remains.

There was an Irish Tourist Board office in the airport where I hoped to be pointed in the right direction. They were able to reserve a room for me in the city center, at the Royal Dublin Hotel on O'Connell Street.

After booking the room, I found a bank teller machine in the airport. Not having a clue of what the exchange rate was, and not caring, I bought two hundred Irish Pounds. I was also told that the airport was several miles from the city center, so I decided on a cab. There was bus service to Dublin, but I was done lugging my bags around, trying to kill myself. I paid the extra ten pounds for delivery right to the front door of the Royal Dublin.

I walked out of the airport and directly to the curb where a taxi had just departed, another cab slid into its freshly vacated spot. The driver was a short, bald, pudgy fellow who I guessed to be in his late fifties or early sixties.

"Can you get me to the Royal Dublin?" I asked, as he got out of his car.

"Sure can," he answered in a heavy Irish brogue, stepping around to open the trunk for my bags.

"Damn, it feels good here," I said, sitting in the front seat next to the driver.

"Where'd you come from?"

"France, and you know what..."

"Oh, those fuckers. I've heard all about 'em," he interrupted, and it was the most welcomed interruption I'd had in some time. I loved the way 'fucker' rolled off of his tongue, like he was singing a melody. I knew I had come home.

"I was in Paris ten years ago and had a pretty nice time, but those bastards down in the south of France can go fuck themselves."

"I've never been there, and from what I've heard, I never will," he answered.

"The countryside was beautiful, but goddamn, whenever I tried to ask someone a question in English you'd have thought I'd been trying to fuck their wife or daughter."

"Have you ever been to Portugal?" the cabby asked with a chuckle.

"Never have, but I grew up in the States around a bunch of Portuguese. Pretty fine people."

"I haven't been their either, but I hear nothing but good about them," he confirmed.

Fifteen pounds later, I was standing on the sidewalk in front of the Royal Dublin Hotel and shortly after that I was checked into my room. I tried Kelli's mobile phone from the hotel room but couldn't get through. I was unfamiliar with the phone system and hadn't dialed enough nines, ones, or zeros. Somehow, I managed to get through to her mother's home and left a message on the answering machine. Maybe I'll hear from her, and maybe I won't. I hope so, but I'm also entertaining the possibility that her image has simply lured me to Ireland for something completely different than what I have in mind. Whatever my reason for being here, I've arrived. Now all I have to do is pay attention, things are sure to reveal themselves.

Something has already changed for me though. It began when I lifted off the runway in Paris and was completed by the time we touched down in Dublin. I don't even remember landing; all that I remember is speaking to the lovely Irish lass who was giving me a brief overview of Dublin City.

I found an Internet café on O'Connell Street, two blocks west of the Royal Dublin; a stone's throw from the River Liffey. I had a few e-mails, one from Kelli that had just been sent. She had returned from a day trip to Wexford. Since it was late, she suggested that we meet the following morning. I sent her my phone number at the Royal Dublin with a message to phone me in the morning with the time and location of our meeting.

April 5, 2001 - Dream

It was like I was in Oregon, a small town just across the California border. I was meeting Kelli there. I was staying at a small hotel or motel. We finally meet up, and we were sitting and talking about... what... I don't know? She was a friend of the people who owned the hotel. She went into the other room and then somehow we were talking to each other over the phone. I teased her about something having to do with one of her hundred men, and she defensively told me that she had had only two lovers in her life. "I know, I know, I'm messing with you. I can see how easy it will be to set you off or push your buttons," I teased.

I remember thinking or comparing the town in the dream to a town where I once stayed in Oregon while selling my first airplane. I got stuck there for a weekend because of some business formalities - a title search that had failed to arrive on Friday, so I had to wait it out until Monday. It was a small town with a small town feel, a place where I would easily get bored. I remember thinking in the dream that I might live there for a short while, but it wouldn't last. I would grow tired of it, of its simplicity, like growing tired of fucking, just to be fucking.

April 5, 2001 - 7 p.m.

I phoned Kelli at nine this morning; her mother answered. She asked me to hold and then returned saying that she'd called to Kelli from outside of her room, but she hadn't answered.

She said that she had been traveling the day before and was probably still sleeping. Kelli's mother apologized for the cold rainy weather, and I assured her that it was out of her hands and that there was no need for her apology. I gave her the number of the Royal Dublin, and she said she'd have Kelli phone when she was up.

I showered, went down for breakfast, and returned to my room to see if the message light on the phone was blinking; it wasn't. I didn't want to seem pushy, mostly because I despised pushy people myself. Instead of phoning, I walked down to the Internet café and checked my e-mail. There was a message from Kelli saying that she had attempted to phone me three times, but that the hotel had no record of my registration. In her note, she suggested we meet at two in the afternoon at Bewley's on Grafton Street. She'd have her mobile phone with her in case we couldn't find each other.

On my way back to the Royal Dublin, I stepped into a phone store on O'Connell Street and, after getting straightened out on the dialing formalities, placed a call to Kelli's mobile, finally getting through to her. She gave me directions to Bewley's on Grafton Street.

"If you get there before I do, have a coffee and take a seat. Keep your eyes open for an old gray hag with missing teeth," Kelli teased.

"Yeah, right! I'll see you at two."

I returned to the Royal Dublin and complained about not getting my phone calls, but no one seemed to know a thing about it. I went up to my room and tried to think of something to do while waiting for two o'clock to come around. I decided to set out for Bewley's. I didn't want to be late, and locating our meeting place was certain to relax me a bit.

I walked south on O'Connell, crossed the River Liffey and came upon Trinity College. I asked a pedestrian the way to Grafton Street. She pointed south and told me one block. Grafton was bustling. Things seemed to change south of the Liffey. The buildings and shops were cleaner, and much more refined. Grafton Street was only open to pedestrians, packed full of Dubliners.

It didn't take long to find Bewley's. I was an hour early but went inside anyway. An older woman was directing the foot traffic as they entered the restaurant, alerting the patrons that they could find service upstairs as well as on the ground level.

"I'm supposed to meet a lady friend of mine here around two. I'd like to find a seat so I can see her when she comes in through the door."

"I'm sure that you could share that booth over there," she suggested, pointing to a booth that was occupied by an older gentleman.

"Oh, I don't want to disturb him. I've only seen her once several months ago and then only for a few minutes. I'm a little worried I won't recognize her."

"I'm sure you'll recognize her. You just think you won't, but she'll come back to you just like that when you see her again," the woman responded, attempting to put me at ease.

"You're probably right," I answered, grateful for her encouragement.

I stayed on the lower level, went through the cafeteria line and ordered coffee.

"Black or white?" the attendant asked.

"Black," I answered, not knowing the difference but not wanting to appear ignorant.

After paying for the coffee, I found an empty seat towards the back of Bewley's and sat down. I had forgotten to take a spoon to stir in some sugar and had returned to the front of the restaurant looking for the silverware when I spotted an empty corner booth by the front entrance. I hurried back for my coffee, and returned to the booth, skipping the spoon and sugar for fear of losing my new perch.

It was a one sided booth, a bench against the wall and two loose chairs on the opposite side; I sat on the bench. A man in his thirties walked over with his coffee and sat down in one of the chairs. I asked him to explain the difference between a black and a white coffee. In a spooked and guarded fashion, he said something about steamed milk and then stood up and moved to another table that had just been vacated but not yet bused. You'd have thought I had a gun at his head.

A short, thin, brunette woman in her twenties with wire rim glasses and a pointy nose was the next to take Spooky's seat. She was conservatively dressed with the exception of her leather snakeskin-looking jacket.

"Can you tell…" I caught myself interrupting, as she was about to take a drink of her coffee. "Excuse me."

"No, it's okay."

"I just wanted to know the difference between a black and a white coffee."

"Yes, a white coffee is half steamed milk."

"Thank you," I replied nodding, and then left her to enjoy her break in peace.

I began to take in Bewley's architecture to pass the time. It was an old building with modern influences. From my seat, I could see up to the railing that encompassed the second floor and then on up to the ceiling; it was so high it gave the place a hall-like atmosphere. The rooms were trimmed in a dark reddish-brown wood. The tables and chairs were wood stained in a shade similar to the trim. The tabletops were marble. Some of the walls were painted brick red, while others were painted orange with strands of green like an almost ripe orange. A few of the walls had geometric shapes painted on them. Most of the artwork was modern impressionism. There was an eclectic feel to Bewley's. History had been made in this building, but it was still alive and making more history for future generations to forget.

The woman in the snakeskin jacket left without our acknowledging each other. Shortly after her departure, a petite woman in her fifties took her seat. She wore a pink scarf over her auburn red hair. She was an elegant woman, wearing gray woolen slacks, a black overcoat, and pinkish-red wool gloves. She had a European look, but no Irish features. There was a darkness to her, a sullenness; she had possibly come from Eastern Europe, maybe the Balkans.

The woman was spooning a white cream-looking dessert from a small bowl when a middle-eastern girl wearing jeans, black boots, and a red wool sweater came and sat down next to the older woman. The girl was in her early twenties. They didn't appear to be related, but there was some sort of relationship between them. The older woman could possibly have been the girl's English teacher, or perhaps a dance instructor. It was almost two o'clock, and I was growing more nervous about our impending encounter.

The older woman stood up and walked back into the food line, soon reappearing with another dessert bowl full of the same treat. I was curious; it looked like a sweet cream dessert that I had in Florence.

"It's not cream, it's yogurt," she said, as she caught me looking at her. It was as if she had read my mind.

"You certainly knew exactly what I was thinking," I answered smiling, and then left her to enjoy her yogurt.

There was a wooden pillar that partially hid me from view, but Kelli spotted me almost as soon as she entered Bewley's. I stood up as she walked to my table, and then we embraced for the first time.

"What would you like to drink?" I asked nervously.

"Let me get you something," Kelli offered.

"I've already had a coffee. Here, sit down. What would you like?"

"A coffee would be fine," Kelli answered.

"Black or white?"

"Black."

"I'll be right back," I said nervously, and then walked off.

Kelli was beautiful, so much more than I remembered. I shouldn't have doubted myself. I hadn't flown all the way to Ireland for anything less. She had hooked me back in the States at that fateful moment in Carmel and had been playing me, reeling me in on-line over the last few months. Her face was hypnotic. Those magical blue eyes seemed to be other worlds calling out for me to come and explore. The way her head turned ever so slightly to the side when she smiled, the way she walked, the way she carried herself... She was nothing but elegance, an incarnate goddess.

Kelli found an empty table while I was shagging her coffee. While standing in line to settle up with the cashier, I watched her move my jacket. Then she came to guide me back to our new seats.

"How are you?" she asked.

"I'm fine, now that I'm out of France."

"Oh, that's right. I was thinking about moving there, too."

"Well, I'm sure a beautiful woman like you will have no trouble," I said, fidgeting in my seat, wondering how I appeared to her. I was afraid that she'd judge my disdain for the French and find it a complete turn off. I didn't want her to think I had the capacity to hate someone or something so passionately.

"Or I might find it worse than you did."

"Maybe, but I doubt it. I think a lot was the language barrier, and my being a bit oversensitive. Are you hungry? Can I get you something to eat?" I offered. I was having a hard time paying attention, getting lost in her eyes.

"No, but I feel like I should be getting something for *you*."

"Oh, don't worry about me. I've had lunch and too much coffee already."

"So you're coffeed out?" Kelli said, with a beaming smile. She seemed so carefree compared to my serious nature.

"Wow, you *are* real," I said, gazing at her. "I can't believe how nervous I am."

"Are you sure I can't get you something?"

"Yeah, a shot of whiskey would be nice," I teased, having previously mentioned in an e-mail that I didn't drink.

"How about an Irish coffee or don't you drink at all?"

"An Irish coffee sounds great, but I don't drink anything with alcohol. You know, sometimes I think I probably could, but then I think what for? It's already robbed me of a whole bunch of life. I don't really wanna give it another chance of doing the same thing all over again."

"Good," she answered, smiled, and turned her head ever so slightly.

After Kelli finished her coffee, I suggested we go for a walk, and she agreed. We left Bewley's, coming out on Grafton Street.

"Where would you like to go?" she asked.

"I haven't a clue. I'll follow your lead."

"Trinity College is this way. We can walk through there for starters," Kelli suggested.

"Sounds good," I answered. I'd have followed her around the block for the rest of my life. All she had to do was smile. Hell, she didn't even have to smile.

We went through the gates and onto the grounds of Trinity.

After walking across the campus, we made our way to a museum that Kelli was familiar with. It was windy and sprinkling off and on. I was holding my umbrella over Kelli when a gust of wind came along and flipped the damn thing inside out; she burst into laughter.

"I've been waiting for that to happen. It happens to me all the time," she said, her laughter turning to a giggle.

"Yeah, I bet you have," I laughed. "So where are all these damn Leprechauns you Irish folks are always bragging about?"

"All that I can tell you is that if you see one, don't blink," Kelli giggled again.

In the museum we looked at several old Celtic artifacts, tools and carvings: particularly, a wooden canoe-like boat that had been carved from a huge tree trunk. We even came across some Sheela na Gigs, but they were rather odd looking images. They looked like old hags squatting and baring their genitalia, appearing much too old to be symbols of fertility. Kelli mentioned that, at one time, people in the latter stages of their lives still had a place in society and were valued; unlike the way our culture dealt with and treated old people today.

"Everyone has something to offer, it's just a matter of our opening up to this. Instead of putting people away in old folks home, why not let them care for the children?"

"Yes, and they learn from the children, too, an innocence that can be useful as they approach the end of their own lives."

We walked out of the museum, and I suggested that we get some water. Kelli spotted a pub.

"Why don't you find a seat, and I'll get our drinks," Kelli suggested. I located a seat and settled in. During our break, I became familiar with some of Kelli's family: her parents and younger brother. I also talked about my family, and then we continued our walk. We stopped at another museum that was full of stuffed animals, and I teased her about dragging me into the damn animal morgue. We had another good laugh over that.

Our next stop was an art museum where we went to look for Magdalenes. We didn't find anything of the sort, but while looking for Her, we came across a dark abstract painting with a streak of light emanating from its center; it caught me up. I fell into the painting, and Kelli wandered off. When I came to, she was gone. I walked about the museum for ten minutes until we finally found each other.

"If you could bring one painting home from here, which one would it be?" Kelli asked, as we walked down the steps back into the waking world.

"The dark one with the light. It's the only one that moved me," I answered without hesitation.

We walked on and stepped into a small café for tea. This time I asked Kelli to get a seat, and I went up to the counter to order.

"Two hot teas, please," I said, not knowing that hot tea is all that's served in Ireland.

"Tea for two," the woman at the register announced for the help behind her to get started on. "Have a seat and we'll bring it out for you."

Tea for two; I liked how that sounded. I sat across from Kelli, and, shortly after falling back into her heaven, our order was delivered.

"I never knew there was a certain way that tea had to be brewed until I had a sit with my eighty-year-old landlord last year. She was so picky about making sure we got boiling water."

"Oh, yes, some people even have to stir it a certain direction after it has steeped," Kelli explained, as she poured some cream into her empty cup and then attempted to pour some for me.

"I'm not sure if I want any yet," I announced.

"Oh, okay," she said, taken aback as she set the cream down. "Guess I deserved that one."

"I might want some, I'm just not sure yet," I replied, wishing that I had allowed her to serve me. I was afraid I might have come across in a tone that was offensive, putting her on guard. I was trying so hard to impress her and to be myself all at the same time. I had left the selling world behind, but I was still selling. I've been selling myself from the cradle, and will probably do so all the way to the grave.

Kelli poured my tea, and I sat back without rebelling. I have a habit of not being able to accept offers or suggestions from people, not spontaneously anyway. I think it stems from the paranoia of becoming indebted. If, after some time has passed, it feels right, I am occasionally able to receive another's offer of generosity, but it has to feel right before I can accept.

Kelli mentioned that she soon needed to be going. We had spent close to four hours together, but it seemed like minutes. She was staying with her mother in Blackrock, a suburb south of Dublin. She'd taken the bus into town to meet me, and, in turn, had to catch the bus back to Blackrock. I walked her to Grafton Street.

"I hope I can take you to dinner while I'm here in Dublin," I said, not wanting to be pushy, but testing her response.

"Maybe Saturday evening?"

"That sounds good. I have to find a place to stay because the Royal Dublin is booked this weekend."

"You might check out Dun Laoghaire. It is south of Blackrock. My father lives there. I can walk there in twenty minutes. I wish I had a place of my own to offer, I'd put you up."

"Thank you, but I wouldn't impose on you that way," I answered, wishing to be curled up with her in bed right then and there, but knowing that my fantasy was far from becoming a reality at that point in our relationship.

She smiled and we continued our walk.

"My bus stop is right across the way," she said, as we walked up to the corner across the street from Trinity College. She stopped and turned to hug me goodbye. "I guess we can keep in touch by e-mail until you find a place to stay," Kelli suggested after we embraced.

"That sounds good. I'll probably go check out Dun Laoghaire tomorrow. Come on, I'll wait with you for the bus."

"I think you just want another hug," Kelli teased as she stepped out to cross the street.

"Thanks for the idea," I answered, a step behind her. "I'm pretty sneaky, but I hadn't thought about that."

"My grandmother used to keep a coat and hat nearby that she'd pick up before answering the door. If it was someone she wanted to see, she'd say she was just getting home and to come on in. If it was someone she didn't want to see, she'd tell them she was just on her way out the door."

"I'll bet that's hereditary, too," I teased.

I got another hug in as Kelli's bus arrived. Then I skipped across the River Liffey, all of the way back to the Royal Dublin, stopping at an Internet café to send Kelli a thank you note for taking the time to meet with me today.

Damn she's a beauty. I don't know what to do. All I know is that I don't want to fuck this deal up. Maybe we'll never come together again... or maybe we're just getting started? I don't know, and I don't want to have to control the outcome. Well, I do want to control the outcome, but I know better. If I grasp at her, there will be nothing on which to cling.

Now I'm sitting in my room at the Royal Dublin. Outside my window, from west to east, clouds float over, swirling, dancing to a silent tune, beckoning to my heart, to open, to sing once again.

April 6, 2001 - 11 p.m.

After breakfast, I checked with the front desk at the Royal Dublin and found that a few rooms had opened up because of a one-day strike by Aerlingus. I extended my stay for another day and walked down O'Connell Street, stopping to check my e-mail. There was no response to the thank you I sent Kelli last night, but someone had sent me a good joke, so I forwarded a copy hoping she might respond to the humor as opposed to my thank you that had a 'please respond to my neediness, so I don't feel so insecure' attached to it.

I crossed the Liffey on my way to a church that had been converted to a tourist center a block north of Trinity College; Kelli pointed it out to me yesterday. On the steps of the tourist center a young woman with an infant sat on the sidewalk, begging for change. I walked by, trying to ignore her without offering anything. I thought of how tough it must be to bow in submission, lowering oneself to the feet of humanity and begging for her child's next meal.

The tourist center was full of people and I didn't feel like waiting in line, although I was able to get some rental car rates from an agency that had a booth inside the converted church. I paged through a few travel guides but decided to leave without purchasing any of them, figuring I could do just as well, if not better, on my own.

I left the tourist center, walking to the bus stop near Trinity where Kelli had caught the bus the day before. It was the number seven bus; the same bus that would take me to Dun Laoghaire, a few towns south of Blackrock. On my way down the steps of the tourist center, I reached into my pocket and found a few pounds for the mother and child.

The bus arrived in less than two minutes. The tariff was one pound fifteen. I dropped one pound twenty into the machine and received my ticket and a five pence coupon that could be redeemed at one of the main bus stations, which I'd never do. I climbed to the top deck and took a seat towards the rear of the bus; I've always wanted to ride on the top of a double-decker.

At the next stop, a man in his sixties, neatly dressed in suit and tie, boarded the bus and took a seat across the aisle from me. He was nervous, fidgeting in his seat and obsessively signing the cross over his chest. The ride was rough. The driver took off like he was in a race and then came to a screeching halt twenty-feet from the next stop as if he'd fallen asleep at the wheel and woke up at the last second. But I don't think the driver was the cause for the Hail Mary's parting the lips of the poor ol' soul sitting across the aisle.

It took forty minutes to get to Dun Laoghaire. I got off in front of a mall, walked inside to have a look and ended up in a store that sold luggage. I didn't buy anything but was still thinking about replacing the suitcase with the worn off wheel. The lady who worked there was nice. I asked her if she knew where I might find a decent bed and breakfast house, and, like the Delphic oracle, she pointed me in a few different directions.

I left the mall and walked a few blocks into the residential area and found a few B&B's, but they were all booked. I continued my search on foot for some time, still unsuccessfully. I finally went down to the port of Dun Laoghaire and found another tourist center. The woman on duty did a computer search for a B&B in the area, but all were booked for the next week. Next weekend is Easter and many people have reserved these places in advance for the entire week.

"Do you have a car?" the woman asked.

"No, but I was thinking of renting one."

"Well, if you do, you'll have an easier time finding a room in the country," she advised.

"How much is a car?"

"For how long?"

"A week, maybe."

"For a week or longer it comes to twenty-five pounds a day."

"Do I have to take it from here, or can I pick it up in downtown Dublin when I check out of my room tomorrow?"

"You can pick it up downtown tomorrow if you like."

"I'll do that then. Can you reserve it for me?"

"I'll need a credit card and some information."

"Not a problem," I said, handing her my MasterCard. I'd be mobile and maybe Kelli would accompany me, show me around Ireland. I wanted to drive off with her for good, take her back to California and make a home.

I've had women scare me off, and I've scared a few off myself. I wasn't sure what to do or how to handle the situation. I was torn between pursuing her or hanging loose, but leaning more towards the pursuit. I was impatient, having a hard time allowing fate to unfold. I like to remind others that to allow often means to suffer, so I tried to follow my own advice and suffer through the ambiguity.

I was becoming tunnel-visioned, thinking I had to have Kelli respond to me a certain way and all in my time frame; it was locking me out of my life and all its possibilities. I was also feeling pressure to take in as much of Ireland as was possible within the next ten days. I wanted Kelli to be my travel partner, but I wasn't exactly sure if I should ask her to join me. I didn't want to push her, but my time was limited. Fuck it! I'll ask her. I'll be damned if I'm going to dangle in fear and leave Ireland a voiceless coward.

I checked my e-mail after returning from Dun Laoghaire, but still no response from Kelli. I sent her another message, telling her that I hadn't been able to find a place to stay in Dun Laoghaire. I had extended my stay for one more evening at the Royal Dublin and had reserved a car for hire beginning tomorrow morning for the next week. My message went on to say that I was looking for a travel partner and asked if she was just getting home or if she was just leaving. She checked her e-mail quite often, so her lack of response was beginning to bother me.

It began to rain in Dublin, not a heavy rain, more of a drizzle, an on-again off-again thing, mostly clouds and wind. The weather's ambivalence was aggravating. I could see the sun shinning through an opening; it was almost heavenly, ascension-like. It reminded me of the painting that so impressed me in the museum yesterday.

I'm going to have to risk it again, step out of the safe place that I've been hanging in for the last couple of years. I left an old, dead image that no longer served me and plunged into the unknown without a new god, or better yet, goddess. It's now time to step back into life, step into the person that I am becoming, yet I'm tortured by an old fear: I have no proof that I can do this, and I'm afraid to fall back into worshipping that old dead idol. It's purgatory, goddamn it! I'm afraid of retreating into my old hell, and I'm afraid of taking that final step into heaven. "Fuck you Yahweh! I know you're the one throwing the kink into this whole mess."

* * * * *

At nine this evening, I walked back to the Internet café. There was still no response to my prior queries. If I don't hear from her in the morning, I'll set off on my own. Hell, I've always been on my own and always will be, even if someone else is with me. We're all alone; just as soon as the umbilical cord is cut, we become responsible. We might not be able to walk over to that titty whenever we're in want, but we can raise enough hell to get it brought to us.

So, how can I make enough noise now? Am I being punished for past infidelities, for not honoring and respecting Her presence in my life for so many years? I'm not an old man yet, not in my eyes anyway, so what's my problem, or do I even have a problem? I'm a pretty sharp guy, but maybe women don't want a sharp guy. Maybe woman just wants man to bring home the bacon and father a child or two so that she can fulfill her motherly calling. Sure doesn't make it sound all that much fun to be a man.

I've given up along the line somewhere. I've given up too easily, haven't fought the good fight, haven't fought hard enough for a woman, a real woman, or for myself, and then again, maybe I'm full of shit. I haven't made enough noise. One thing seems apparent... fuck it, if it doesn't work with Kelli, I'm throwing my arms up for good, moving to a cabin up in the high Sierras and becoming a recluse. I'll burn wood all winter long, and go flippin' mad in a snow storm. Some nature freak on a cross-country ski trek will find my naked Popsicle-ass frozen stiff with one hand on the door handle, a log under the other arm.

What's my life all about anyway? Why can't I be normal, just simple? I long to drink beer, watch football, and forget my mother's birthday, but for some godforsaken reason I haven't been dealt this hand.

With or without Kelli, I'm going to wake up in the morning - God willing - pick up the rental car, and set off into the Irish countryside, me and Her, Her and me, one and the same, Sophia, Mary Magdalene...

I've forgotten all the good days I've had before this one. Just because today has turned into a shitter doesn't mean everything has gone to hell. The world isn't coming to an end; it's just the loss of yet another illusion. I have no need to search for something outside of myself in order to fill the void.

Who am I shittin'? Hell, I'm missing something. I mean, if I'm so fulfilled, why the hell am I here?

"You're searching for the magical Her. You know, the Holy Grail."

"Fuck you Yahweh! Who asked you anyway?"

April 7, 2001 - Dream

I was going to work. Oh, no, I wasn't going to work. I was messing with a car dealership, acting like I was going to buy a car. I was bored, and I went in to work. I went in to work them. I went in to deal with them, and they were in Ripon, and I lied to them, telling them I was going to work for such and such a place and they wanted to know my affiliation because of how this company would be buying cars for all of their salesmen. I said: "No, I'm buying it alone. I'm self-employed." Their salesmen were all in there and it was like the scuttlebutt was that I was going back to work and da-dada-dada...

Then Vince came into the dealership to see me. Dusty did too, and I don't know who else? Somebody did, they interrupted my looking at any vehicles. So, anyway, it turned into a bullshit session, and I never did get to talk about vehicles, and it was like these people all thought I was going back to work, to the machinery business, but I wasn't. The other guy might have been Jeremy Collins, but it was Vince and Dusty for sure.

Then, at the end of the dream, Hal and Cole were in the dealership... oh, and I remember that: "No, I've been off a couple of years." He said: "How long ago did you go to work for them, like twenty-five years ago today?" And I said... I looked at my watch to see the date. I said: "You know, it's been almost twenty years close to the date."

Then Von Philips appeared in the dream. He was going on about how they had the American flag flying out in front of Staton Equipment Company (Freedom? Or maybe loyalty), but Cole was selling stuff and Hal was selling stuff and somebody else and somebody else, but tonight we were talking about how the new salesmen weren't selling anything and how they had an American flag out in front of the place, and then I woke up.

I remember I was going to keep in touch with Vinny (Vince). Vinny was selling some aluminum or some stuff that went down in the ditches to save money from water... kept water from percolating back into the ground. He had seen me there and had stopped just to say hi, but in another dream I was trying to go fishing or camping. I was driving to Alaska and back, and, on my way back, I was going to stop at Roger's (Roger from Redding or Anderson), my fishing guide... for him out there too... At Roger's up in Anderson to go fishing, and I remember following him up or down some stairs. They were asking about Okie, and he said something about he had died back in August. I remember asking him about his wife too, and she was about the same.

Yeah, I remember I was going to get a boat and start being a fishing guide like Roger.

April 7, 2001 - Midnight

At nine-fifteen this morning, I had yet to hear from Kelli. I'd been growing a beard since leaving Florence, and now was vacillating back and forth, trying to decide about shaving it off or leaving it to grow. The beard is a goatee, and it really changes my appearance, makes me look older, tougher, and less approachable. I kept the beard. I have to get back to accepting what the universe is giving to me, instead of demanding certain conditions be met in order to constitute my happiness. The rest of the day turned out to be crazy, one of the craziest days in my life.

When I phoned Kelli this morning, her mother told me she was bathing and to call back in half-an-hour; so I did, but the line was busy. The next time I phoned, the answering machine picked up. I tried Kelli's mobile and got her voice mail. I left a message saying I felt as if I was making a pest of myself, and asked her to e-mail if she wanted to get together, and, if not, I understood and wished her the best. Then I walked across the street from the Royal Dublin and signed for my rental car.

The car was actually parked in the underground parking lot of the Royal Dublin. This made it easy to load my bags, all I had to do was take the elevator to the basement and walk fifty feet to the car. The little buggy was bright red, brand-new with less than twenty miles on it. It was a five-speed and, as all cars in Ireland, drove from the right-hand side. The roads, of course, were also the opposite of the States; the flow of traffic was from the left-hand side of the road. I loaded the bags and then went up to settle my bill.

The concierge asked where I was off to and I told him I didn't know.

"Wicklow," the young man was quick to suggest. "When you exit the garage make a quick left, and then a right. It'll bring you out to O'Connell Street right here in front of the hotel. Cross over the Liffey and keep driving until you get to the N11 and that'll get you to Wicklow."

"Wicklow it is then..."

I made it to Wicklow without having a wreck or running anyone over, but it took a lot of concentration, as if I needed another source of disorientation. In two weeks time, I've been to four different countries with three of them speaking foreign languages, and all with different currencies, not to mention my ignorance of their cultural practices.

Wicklow is a small quiet town on the coast south of Dun Laoghaire. I pulled into the first empty parking space I could find and set out walking. It was windy, cloudy, and cold, but it wasn't raining. I tried to find an Internet café. I was confused; I hadn't taken Kelli to be a person who would brush me off by ignoring me. She appeared to be a woman of integrity. It also didn't make sense for her to entertain our on-line relationship for so long just to suddenly lose interest.

Of the few businesses in Wicklow, most were closed for lunch. I was walking around a neighborhood and happened upon a woman on her way home. I asked if she knew where I might be able to get on-line and learned that there was no local Internet café.

"My daughter has some device that she uses to get her e-mail on the television. You can come with me and try it if you like."

"Thank you, but I don't want to impose," I answered, feeling taken back that a woman would actually invite some strange man into her home for such a trivial thing.

"It's no trouble. I'm just down a few houses," the woman encouraged.

I took her up on the offer and followed her home. I couldn't get the damn television device to work, so I thanked the gracious woman and walked back out into the cold. I was fighting things, having a hard time letting go of not coming together again with Kelli. I'd usually just say *fuck it* and walk away, but something kept me from doing what I usually did.

After lunch, I drove farther south, hoping that time and distance would relieve my disappointment. She was beautiful, single, and seemed to possess the qualities that made for a wonderful partner. My guts were churning; they felt like a wrung out towel. I hadn't exactly fallen in love with her, but I had fallen in love with the possibility of falling in love with her. I had high hopes of making Kelli into that magical woman.

The drive south along the coast finally brought me to Wexford, two hours from Wicklow. Wexford was a much bigger city than Wicklow. It was a harbor town. I figured it would be no problem finding an Internet café, so I parked in a lot on the outskirts of town and started walking towards the city center. Half a block later, I spotted a computer store and walked in.

"Can you tell me where I can get on-line here in town?"

"Right back there," the proprietor answered, pointing to a computer and a young girl who was about twelve-years-old. "Hey kid, this man needs to use the computer," he shouted. "I can hardly pry her away from the damn thing," he said, rolling his eyes.

Kelli had finally replied. She said that she was very much looking forward to having dinner with me and to phone her at five. It was four-thirty.

"How much do I owe you?" I asked, after having used the computer for less than five minutes.

"Don't worry about it. You did me a favor getting this kid of mine off that damn thing," he answered, looking at his daughter who had joined him at the front of the store. "What part of the States you from?"

"California."

"Oh, I love it there," he said, and then went on to name all the places he had visited on his past visits to California. "Are you on holiday?"

"Yeah, I guess you could call it that."

"What do you do?" he asked.

"I used to sell tractors, but I burned out on it and quit two years ago."

"How you getting by?"

"Well, I sold a lot of tractors."

"So you're retired."

"Kind of, I guess, but I don't like that word."

"Well, it sounds like you've done alright for yourself,

anyway."

"I'm not exactly rich, but I'm not poor either... one of these days I have to get another job."

"Selling's a hard life, isn't it?" the man asked.

"It's phony. I don't mean you are, the job is. You've got to put on a different mask for every person who comes through your door."

"You're telling me. I'm tired," the proprietor said, looking at me with a worn out expression.

"I know."

"So, where you headed?" he asked, changing the subject.

"Well, right now I've got to find a pay phone. You see, I met this beautiful Irish woman in the States several months ago, and I came to find her and bring her back home."

"I see," he said, his eyes lighting up.

"She's beautiful. I caught up with her the other day, but I've had a hard time getting back together with her again. That's why I wanted to check my e-mail. There was a message that said to call her at five."

"Use the phone here to call if you like," he volunteered.

"You sure?"

"Hell, yeah, go ahead."

"I'll pay you."

"I don't want your money, but if I come to the States again I damn well better get treated the same way."

"If you come to the States, you let me know," I said as I reached into my wallet and handed him a card.

The owner of the computer shop had a young man working for him who was standing behind the counter listening to our conversation. The young fellow handed me the phone receiver, and I gave him a card with Kelli's phone number so that he could dial. I overheard the shopkeeper's daughter teasing her father about not having a girlfriend when the young man dialed Kelli's mobile.

"Kelli."

"Malcolm, hi."

"I just got your e-mail."

"Where are you?" she asked.

"Wexford, but I'll be back there by seven," I answered. "I'm in a computer store, so I have to make the call short because I'm calling from their business line."

"Okay, I'll meet you at the coffee place in Blackrock."

"What's the name of it?"

"I don't know, but it's in the city center. You can't miss it," she answered as the store's second line started ringing.

"Okay, I'll see you at seven. Oh, bring your mobile phone in case I get lost."

"I will."

I handed the phone receiver back across the counter to the young man and thanked the storeowner. He told me that I better be on my way if I had a date for seven in Blackrock. I hurried off to the red rental car, and started hauling ass back towards Dublin. I had gone from being a broken-hearted fool to an excited kindergartener that had just gotten out of class and was running home to his mother.

I spotted a B&B in Ashford, which I estimated to be about thirty minutes from Blackrock. It was an en suite room, which meant that it had its own bathroom. I paid the twenty-eight pounds, carried my bags in and showered quickly to rinse off the sticky crap that had been oozing from me for the last couple of days. It was six-thirty before I was back on the N11, heading for Blackrock.

It was seven-twenty when I arrived in Blackrock, twenty minutes late. There were two coffee shops. One was closed and the other was just closing. Kelli wasn't at either of them, not inside or out. I walked up and down the street looking into the pubs and restaurants hoping to spot her but didn't. I called her mobile number, but her voice mail answered. She either had it turned off or the phone wasn't picking up a signal; I guess it didn't matter why. My next call was to her mother's house, but the answering machine picked up there, too.

I hung around outside of the coffee house, occasionally telling a few different people my problem: that I was to meet her in the middle of Blackrock and asked if I might be at the wrong spot, but no one knew of any other coffee houses in Blackrock. Then I phoned Kelli's mobile again, this time leaving a message saying that I was standing across the street from the coffee house in front of a pub called the Wicked Wolf, and that

I'd be hanging around there so that she could find me in the event that she received my message. I then called her mother's house and left a similar message.

At eight o'clock, I began walking up and down the street, looking into the pubs and restaurants again. I spotted a blonde woman walking toward Café Java, but was too far away to be certain if it was Kelli. My heart began to calm, actually it changed from a despairing excitement to one of relief for what I believed was soon to be a fulfilled anticipation. It wasn't her.

I was confused. If she didn't want to have dinner with me, why did she respond to my e-mail and then to my phone call just a few hours earlier? I had a growing concern for her well-being. Why didn't she answer her mobile phone? She said she'd have it with her. There was a market on the corner, so I walked inside to buy a bottle of water. On my way out, one of the clerks, a man in his early twenties was sweeping the doorway.

"Are there any other coffee houses besides Insomnia or Café Java here in Blackrock?"

"I don't think..."

"Man, I was supposed to meet this woman friend of mine here in the city center of Blackrock at a coffee house at seven tonight. I got here at seven-twenty and there is no sign of her. I just wonder if I'm missing something?"

"Ah, you were late, huh?" he asked, with that never-keep-a-beautiful-woman-waiting look.

"I know, but fuck... I have her mobile number. She just doesn't have a way of calling me back. Can I use your phone here for a call back number?"

He hesitated for a minute. "I'm not supposed to, but okay," he answered, and then gave me the store's number.

"Thanks a lot, man. Listen, I'll be walking right around here if she phones," I said, beginning to feel like a played fool. "Her name's Kelli."

"Alright, man," he said, with a look of compassion, as if he'd been through this scene a time or two himself.

I walked back to the Café Java and crossed the street to the phone booth in front of the Wicked Wolf. I phoned her mobile and left a message saying that she could call me at the store and left the number. I also said that I'd wait until nine, and if I didn't hear from her by then, I'd return to my room at the B&B. I left her the number there as well, in the event that she cared to get a message to me later.

While pacing about frantically, several thoughts and feelings passed through me. Maybe she had an emergency and was unable to contact me? I thought about her brother, whose wife had just left him and taken his child out of the country. Kelli had spoken of how distraught and withdrawn he had become. I hoped that nothing had happened to him, or that he hadn't done something irreversible.

Then I went from the sublime to the ridiculous: perhaps this was a test that Kelli had staged, so that she could watch me the entire evening from a vantage point, laughing herself silly the whole time. Then again, maybe she had grown impatient with my tardiness, turned off her phone and left, just to punish or teach me a lesson, and if that's the case, then to hell with her. I've had enough kooks in my life.

It was approaching nine. I walked back towards the market to check one last time to see if she had phoned. My emotions had calmed, no longer oscillating between joy and despair. I began to laugh, and it wasn't a laugh to try to convince myself that things were other than what they were. I was laughing because I was finally able to step back and listen to the universal theme that was looming. I had gone from disappointment, to elation, to devastation, and then finally to a laughing respect for what was taking place.

I realized that there was a grander theme behind it all. It was far beyond just she and I coming together, or better yet, our not coming together. It was much more than just about the two of us; a universal theme of separation was taking place. For whatever reason it might be, Kelli and I weren't supposed to have dinner this evening.

I looked inside and the clerk shook his head no. I smiled and nodded, then looked up into the night. A full moon was rising, coming and going from behind the passing clouds. I thought about the Leprechauns, the Irish magic; was there ever really a Kelli or has she been an illusion? Maybe she's me, my double, or better yet, I'm dead, died in a car wreck speeding back from Wexford, and it's really me who didn't show up for dinner. Maybe I'm in a nut house somewhere, on a lithium high. Maybe I'm a senile, ninety-year-old man, curled up like a fetus, sucking my thumb. Maybe I have a brain tumor. I don't know. I just don't fucking know.

All I know is that I'll soon be wrapped up into yet another great big mess if I keep doubting myself and ignoring the signs that continue to present themselves.

When leaving the B&B in Ashford earlier this evening, I reset the trip odometer. That way, I'd know the exact mileage back to the B&B. I didn't want to miss the turn on my way home in the dark. When I arrived at Blackrock, the trip odometer read 20.3 miles, so it should have read 40.6 when I returned to Ashford this evening. It read 48 miles; I blinked.

April 8, 2001 - 2 p.m.

Woke up this morning with my guts in a knot, showered, shaved off my beard and then went into the dining room for breakfast. The gentleman who owns the house asked if I wanted the traditional Irish breakfast, and I said "sure" not knowing what to expect. Shortly after my request, I was served bacon and eggs along with toast, juice, and tea. Hell, I hardly ever have more than a cup of coffee in the morning. I can tell you one thing for certain: the bacon in Ireland doesn't have all that fat marbled in between the meat like back in the States.

After breakfast, I drove north on the N11 back towards Dublin, stopping in Bray, another coastal village just south of Dun Laoghaire. I stopped at a gas station for some mints and was told that there was an arcade in town with an Internet café.

At twelve thirty, I still had not received word from Kelli. She hadn't called the B&B, she didn't answer her phone at home or her mobile, nor had she e-mailed anything. I was about out of patience. I sent her an e-mail saying that I was concerned, confused, and that I'd phone her at five this evening.

This whole thing has turned into quite a ride. I'm clinging to a hope, a desire, and the tighter I grip, the farther it moves from me. I'll call at five, and if she doesn't answer, I'm cutting bait. Her computer, mobile phone, and her mother's answering machine aren't all on the blink. Maybe she has a girlfriend?

After leaving Bray, I drove twenty minutes north to Blackrock. I went into the Insomnia coffee house and ordered a triple Americano. All of the seats inside were full, so I got my drink to go and returned to the rental car. Now I'm sitting in this car, sipping the coffee, and looking around the town center where I was pacing about last night. Today, I feel different. Despair isn't running me, although my curiosity of what has happened with Kelli is still swatting at me like a playful kitten. Kelli's a Leprechaun, disguised in the costume of a beautiful middle-aged woman. I really am on a chase - of my own tail, or is it tale?

At least I've had the privilege of spitting in the River Liffey. I also have the quarantines for the foot and mouth epidemic to blame for not seeing all the sights that one day I'll be asked about. I wonder why it's so important to go places and see things? My family and friends suggested that I go to all of these places and see everything they've ever heard or read about, but that doesn't appeal to me. I'd rather just wander about and fall through the next door that opens.

Heavy raindrops have started to pound the roof of this rental car. I don't even know the make of the automobile, just know that everything in it is backwards. Fortunately, I've only found myself on the wrong side of the road twice so far, and for only seconds. Over the last few days, I have been spending as much money at pay phones and Internet cafes as I have on food. I was going to say as much as food and lodging but that would be a lie, just like the lie I'm telling myself about Kelli, and the other lies I've told myself before. If she hadn't appeared to be so god-awfully-beautiful when I met her again in Bewley's last Friday, I'd be off chasing all the other Irish goods over the Celtic countryside. But no, Kelli had to grow twice as beautiful since our first encounter.

There's a three-story brick building across the street from where I'm sitting. It has weeds growing out of the chimney and other places where the brickwork is cracked and has allowed a stray seed to take refuge. I wonder where my next home will be, probably somewhere in the States. I'm going to drive to the airport north of Dublin. Maybe I can rent a mobile phone. It'll be nice to have while traveling the countryside.

April 8, 2001 - 11:45 p.m.

I drove out of Blackrock and followed the road signs to the M50. The M50 is the expressway that runs from the bay north of Dublin to the bay south of Dublin, forming a half circle. It's the major artery from which all the highways spin off, the most northern highway is the N1 heading north along the coast, the most southern highway, N11 runs south of Dublin along the coast. Dublin is like a heart, or a half-heart, in which the main artery is the M50, and the N1 through N11, are the veins that carry the life force to other vital organs of Ireland.

I took the N1 exit off the M50 and drove to the airport. There wasn't a place to rent a phone, although I was told that I could probably purchase one in downtown Dublin for twenty or thirty pounds at one of the many local phone stores. I bought a candy bar and sat down in the airport, watching the herds of people coming and going, and then left, uncertain of my next destination. I ended up driving north, considering a drive to Belfast, but stopped in Swords, the first town north of the airport on the N1.

I parked and walked into a video rental store where, by chance, a phone company had rented space to a retail mobile phone outlet. The cheapest phone was twenty-nine pounds, but it called for five Bewley's token-like coupons in order to receive the discounted price. I managed to talk the clerk into letting me have the deal without the tokens, but by the time I got out of there, it cost me forty-four pounds, because I purchased a charger that plugged into the car's cigarette lighter.

I returned to my car and plugged the phone charger into the lighter receptacle. Remaining parked, I dialed Kelli's number.

"Hello," a woman's voice answered, but the reception was terrible.

"Hello, Kelli," I said, surprised that she answered and still uncertain if it was actually her that I had reached.

"Who..." was all I heard before the call was dropped.

I hit the redial button to check the number, thinking that I might have misdialed, but I hadn't. Great, I had fallen for a beauty with a multiple personality disorder. Defiantly, I phoned again, but her voice mail answered.

"Hello Kelli, this is Malcolm again. I have a mobile number where you can now reach me. This is my last call. I'll leave it up to you to contact me if you care to. My number is 086-328-4518."

While I was on the phone, a SUV pulled up next to me and double-parked. A kid swung the back door open banging it into the side of my new rental car. It happened so fast that it still hadn't registered, but when the kid returned after dropping off the video, he did it again, and I was ready for him. I hopped out of my car and the kid's mother rolled down the window to apologize.

"I'm sorry, he's just a kid."

"This is a rental car. I've got to pay for any damage that happens to it, you know!" I answered in an angry and defiant tone.

"He's just a child, nothing happened," she said, as the husband started to drive off.

I pulled an ink pen from my pocket and wrote their license plate number onto the palm of my hand, and for some reason, they stopped. Her response was pissing me off. I wasn't pissed at the kid; I was pissed about her blaming it on the kid, as if that brought morality to damaging someone else's property. The husband came storming out like he was going to whip some ass and came up to me as I was inspecting the side of the car for damage. We both looked it over and couldn't find any chips. Then he mumbled something and walked back to the SUV. The wife was standing outside observing from a distance, and motioning her husband to write down my license plate number. He just mumbled again and climbed behind the wheel, his wife following his cue.

The kid who sold me the mobile phone suggested that I pay a visit to Galway, so instead of driving north to Belfast, I took the N1 back onto the M50. Galway city was directly across from Dublin on the opposite side of the island, about 200 kilometers west, at the end of the N6 artery. I missed the N6 exit and wound up in a residential area, a relatively new housing development that had a strip mall with a grocery store, fish-and-chips, dry cleaner, and a few other businesses to support and be supported by the locals. The neighborhood looked new, but showed signs of premature deterioration. It almost appeared as if the people living in the homes didn't quite know how to manage their good fortune.

I parked. In the fish-and-chips I looked over the menu and decided to order some cod. It took several minutes to prepare the meal, and I was entertained by a red-faced, drunk, middle-aged man who was apologizing to the help for his inebriated condition and teasing two little girls who were no older than five and seven. The little girls were waiting for their food order. The jolly ol' boy seemed harmless, but I kept my distance, careful not to make eye contact and engage him.

I settled up at the cashier for my cod, and walked over to the grocery store to buy some bottled water. On my way out of the market, the man who either owned or ran the place asked how I was doing.

"Pretty good, but I'm a bit lost," I explained.

"Where you headed?" he asked.

"Galway City."

"Yeah, you are a bit lost, I'd say," he said grinning.

"I've got a map, but..."

"Come on," he said, walking me to the door. "I'll show you how to get out of here."

The good fellow reminded me of my cousin, Mitchell, who owns a couple of markets back in the States. Mitchell grew up in the grocery business. His parents, my Aunt Hannah and Uncle Luke, have a store in a small community as well, and they do a lot more than just sell groceries. Their real job is to serve the community by cashing checks, good ones and bad, carrying people until payday, and delivering to people who can't get around; all this in addition to listening to peoples' woes and giving directions to lost souls such as myself.

"Okay, see here," he said, pointing to the map I'd just retrieved from the car. "You'll drive out of here to the first roundabout and go left. Then at the first signal go left, then go straight through the next three roundabouts and that will put you right on the M50 and you can only go north on the fifty from there."

I repeated the directions out loud without looking at the map, instead, forming a mental picture to use while I drove. After confirming my recitation, the man asked, "Are you on holiday?"

"Yeah, I sure am."

"Where've you been?"

"Italy, France, and now here," I answered. "And fuck the French," I added, and then apologized for my outburst.

"No, no, that's okay, it's okay if that's how you feel," he said, supporting my expression.

"I really like it here, though. I met this one Irish woman in the States right before she moved back here and that's kind of why I'm here. I met her the other day, and she said she wished she had a place to put me up."

"That's how people are around here," he said, proud of the Irish's reputation for hospitality.

"Yeah, well, then I was supposed to have dinner with her last night. We spoke on the phone and set a time and place just two hours before we were to meet. She never showed up, and now she doesn't answer my calls to let me know what happened."

"Yeah, well, you can find a little of that around here, too," he rebutted, offering me a cigarette.

"No thanks. I just wish she'd..."

"Tell you to fuck off."

"Yeah, then I'd get on with it all. I mean, what's so hard about that?"

"It's just how some people are," he answered, as he exhaled a puff of smoke.

"I guess so. Okay, then it's a left, another left, and then straight through three roundabouts until I get to the fifty."

"You got it."

"Alright, I better hit the road. Thanks, huh?"

"No problem, you know," he answered with a nod, happy to have been able to assist.

I backed out of the parking space and he was already busy visiting with a local. They both waved to me as I drove off. I smiled and returned the gesture.

Passing the houses on my way out of the neighborhood, I was again moved by the rundown look the new homes had. The coarseness of the place reminded me of neighborhoods back in the States, built as a result of a booming economy. It allowed people to live well beyond the means of their past. It was like the people were making more money than they'd ever made before, and in turn were living a new lifestyle, but their psyches had yet to catch up with their material good fortune.

There's a roughness about the Irish, a crudeness, an edge, yet it's very human. I'm not sure if they're still numb, or if it's a sharpness, but odd it is. Unlike with the grocer, there's a distant look in the eyes of many of the people; it isn't that they're unwelcoming or cold; it's just that they have to be reached somehow, drawn out of their trance-like state before any real communion can take place. Asking a question is all it takes to draw them out of the trance; then I almost always receive a kind response, unlike those goddamn Frenchies. Behind the edgy exterior is compassion; the Irish remind me of the farmers I used to do business with. If I had been raised in their environment, I probably wouldn't see the people the way I do. I wouldn't be so aware or sensitive to it, because I'd be a part of it.

The whole thing with Kelli, the mixed messages have spun and confused me. I understand what it's like to be torn between two allegiances. Maybe that's what's happening on some grand sort of scale for Kelli. Then again, maybe she is a multiple personality, and She - the moon, shifted Kelli into another one of her identities. She's damn beautiful, but not the woman for me. As if there really is a woman for me.

There's an incongruity with Kelli, and it scares me. I have the habit of falling into these patterns with women. She isn't as subtle as the last woman I was seeing, and at least it hasn't taken me ten months to figure things out. I've gone through depression, elation, devastation, and then laughing acceptance of the whole thing not unfolding in my favor, and all in a rather speedy fashion. I'm able to step back into myself, or at least I'm starting to step back into myself. I'm still clinging to her image but getting closer to saying fuck it.

Maybe that's why I'm here, to get the Irish edge: that "fuck off," that the guy at the grocery store spoke about. Yeah, that's it; maybe I've come here to find my "fuck off!"

I stopped at a B&B at eight-thirty this evening on the eastern edge of a town called Loughrea, fifteen miles east of Galway City. It is a newer house, and my room is on the second floor with a huge picture window facing south out into the countryside. It's an en suite unit with a queen-size bed and a huge bathroom. It's a master bedroom suite, the nicest place I've stayed since leaving the States.

The two and a half hour drive from Dublin to Loughrea was nice, but fatiguing. The drive wasn't so tiring; it was the forty-eight hours preceding it that took their toll. Purchasing the mobile phone was probably a waste economically, but it freed me emotionally, or saved me from waiting around hoping to hear from Kelli. Now she can't say that she has no way of contacting me. It feels liberating to throw my hands up in the air and drive away from such a gorgeous woman. Who am I bullshitting? I've walked away from dozens of beautiful women. That's my tale.

April 9, 2001 - 10 p.m.

After a good night's sleep, I woke to a magnificent view of the Irish countryside from my bedroom window. Rays of sunlight were shining through a mostly cloudy sky adding to the dramatics of the rolling green fields, separated by stone walls.

I told the woman at the B&B I'd take the room for another night because I had slept so well. I think leaving Dublin and the drama behind helped. Being inland away from the coast also made a difference. I drove into Loughrea to a laundry and dropped off my dirty clothes.

I had packed two sweaters that I had yet to wear. One sweater was a gift from an old love, a young woman whom I had walked to the car to say goodbye after having her over for the weekend, just minutes before meeting Kelli for the first time. I forget where I bought the other sweater, but it wasn't a gift.

I asked the woman at the laundry if she could find a home for the two garments, and she assured me she could, but only after she'd first cleaned them, of course. There were other articles of clothing that I had considered discarding, but that was all I was willing to relinquish for the time being. After dropping off the laundry, I drove west to Galway.

Galway City is nowhere near the size of Dublin, yet it has all the amenities. It's a college town. I parked close to the city center and walked around to get a feel of the place. I went into a mall, figuring that I could find a cup of coffee. There were a couple of cute girls working in a store, and as an excuse to check them out, I went in and asked where I could find an Internet café. They pointed me in the right direction, across the street from the mall.

I had two messages. One was from Sheila; it said something about her missing my cute cheeks. I replied by telling her that she had never seen my cheeks. We had a friendship; a friendship that sex would have fucked up long ago, and we both knew it. We were too much alike; it was safer for us to have sex with people who needed little if any emotional investment; having to open our hearts and become vulnerable had been too costly for us in the past.

The other message was from Kelli, saying she was so sorry for not making dinner, but that she was really, really sick, and became nauseated whenever she moved. She asked me to forgive her and said she'd call me when she had arisen from the dead; like Lazarus, she said. I didn't respond.

Instead, I wrote to Adam. I had sent him a message the same day I met Kelli at Bewley's telling him that she was beautiful, even more than I had remembered. This time I wrote that she was beautiful, but borderline and bi-polar at the very least, and possibly even a multiple personality.

After signing off the Internet, I found a place in the mall called Café Kylemore and stood in line to order coffee.

"What would you like?" the girl from behind the counter asked.

"I'd like an Americano."

The girl made a funny face, as if I was speaking a foreign language. To her, maybe I was.

"Don't you know what an Americano is?"

"No, I don't."

"Oh, well, it's on your menu there," I said, pointing to the board behind her. Another woman employee who was a few years older than the girl overheard our conversation and came to explain to the inexperienced barista.

After paying ninety pence more than the advertised price for the Americano, but not wanting to argue, I found a seat in the smoky café.

I was pleased to receive a message from Kelli, even if it was a fucked up deal. For some reason, getting the message helped me to feel like a human again, a respectable being. Her lack of response had caused me to question the reality of my very existence. She might have been sick, but a courteous call to the grocery or the B&B was more than warranted, especially since we had spoken just a couple of hours before our intended meeting. How sick could a person get in such a short time?

I was returning from the oscillating trip, bifurcating between love and punishment that an original sin had initiated. Kelli's behavior two nights earlier had resurrected this old ghost. Her actions had revived that same mistrust I carried for women and their unpredictability. The situation was turning Kelli into a human being as opposed to a goddess. It was high time that I woke from that happily-ever-after-fantasyland dream.

If I hear from Kelli again and she wants to get together, I'll give her a chance, but if she confirms my suspicion a second time, I'll drop out of her world in the twinkling of an eye. She's damn beautiful, though, on the outside anyway, but the prospect of being her lover is quickly diminishing.

It's as if I had entrusted her with a responsibility, which I must now take back because she was neither ready nor able to bear this mystery. Perhaps it's wrong to expect so much of her. Giving this vital part of myself to a woman, expecting her to hold on to something so mysterious, is like waiting for my mother to pick me up from the playground after school to go for an ice cream cone, when I know damn well she wouldn't be off work until midnight. It takes two willing individuals to come together, a willing man and an equally willing woman.

I looked over at an older Irishman in his late sixties; he was spooning up a bowl of soup. When I went through the line for coffee, I noticed the daily special on the board had potato soup chalked onto it. I thought about the great famine of the middle eighteen hundreds along with other periods of depression and poverty that past generations had suffered.

From the old man spooning potato soup, I turned to look out into the modern day shopping mall to watch the current Irish population wandering around. Like a virus, people scurried about, consuming goods with the resources that their expanding economy has bequeathed them. It was as if they'd just found a healthy potato crop to infect. I love potato soup; the only time I can fault it, is if it's been burnt.

The lunch rush was thinning out along with the cigarette smoke. This Kelli-thing was serving me in some fashion: bringing her down from the pedestal I had her dancing on, making her a human being, making her real. Now, if we do have a relationship, it'll be real: no more Mr. Nice-guy, no more pretences.

Maybe she's depressed and trying to escape despair instead of facing it head on: avoiding descent into the perceived destructive element that could ultimately reward her with a new life? Maybe I can reach her, and maybe I can't; I don't know. Why am I even making it my job? I'm angry and tired of fucking around, tired of doubting myself. Hell, I'm not a kid anymore. I've suffered my initiation into manhood. Problem is, I've forgotten what I earned; misplaced the bankbook, so to say, and forgotten all the previous deposits I made, but now I've found it and discovered that the interest has grown into a small fortune over the many lost years.

I walked over to the counter and ordered a Coca Cola, American style with lots of ice, and then returned to a different seat along the wall of Café Kylemore. It was a padded bench seat that my bony ass instantly fell in love with, although it was smokier than where I had previously been seated. Three teenage girls sat down at the table next to me, lit up, and started gossiping about the dramas in each of their lives.

As they chattered and spewed smoke, I realized that once again I had been searching for the ethereal in the corporeal. Much of my life has been busy finding and pursuing physical woman, and then leaving her high and dry once my illusion of her divinity has been dashed. Yes, I came to Ireland in search of a Leprechaun, the disappearing She-God. The same illusive image I'd chased in the States for the last forty years.

Sitting in the café for a couple of hours, I suddenly realized what a wonderful gift I had received. It might never have happened if it hadn't been for my meeting Kelli and chasing her all the way back to her homeland. Things don't ever really die for good; they just come back in different forms.

Now ready to respond to Kelli's e-mail, I returned to the Internet café, signed on, and composed the following letter:

Dear Kelli,

I'm sorry to hear that you are not feeling well. As a fellow human being, I don't feel it is my place to grant forgiveness, although it is in my capacity to love and accept you, which includes your being ill.

I am relieved to have received your message. I was concerned about you. I must admit that when I met you in September, and, again last week, I was drawn to your physical beauty as well as a feeling from within, but after not meeting you Saturday and not hearing from you, I became disillusioned and thank heavens for that, because now you've become a real human being to me.

Kelli, please feel free to phone; I'd love to hear from you. My mobile number is 086-328-4518, but think about the following before you call: I've been writing to you for a few months now and have shared much about myself without learning much about you, and I trust that this has been the right thing for you, but it is no longer right for me.

I want to meet Kelli. I want to know what moves you. I want to know about the light and the dark, your joys and your sorrows. I want to know about your fears and your dreams. I want to connect with you, really connect with you on a heartfelt level and that is the only way I want to connect with you, because for me there is no other way.

I am here to see you! I am sorry if this scares you in anyway, but my intentions are honorable and are not meant to provoke fear or hurt you in any way.

There, I've said it. Call me crazy if you will, but it is my truth. Crazy as it may seem, it is all I have to offer you, that and my love. I wish you the best and a speedy recovery from what ails you. I trust that you will follow yourself and do what is right for you, for your soul...

I had a raging hard-on that was leaking to beat hell when I finished the letter. A subtle anxiety coupled with excitement danced within as I stroked the send button on the computer, wondering what would become of my efforts. Love was simmering inside of me. For the last few days certain songs on the radio brought tears to my eyes and at other times laughter. Sometimes music fills one with hope, an anticipation of what's soon to be coming around again.

Sending the letter also renewed a lost sense of power. I felt like a man in charge of his life, willing to say and do what needs to be said and done for the great potential of his destiny to be realized. Power has nothing to do with money or material possessions, or the illusion of power that material possessions bring.

My relationship to money has changed. I know how to make money; I've already proven that to myself. My goals have surpassed the need to accumulate material wealth. Money will take care of itself. I'm tired of spending my energy worrying about what is to become of me economically, while worries rob me of life. My goals have shifted to a woman, and fully incorporating her into my life.

I took off on a stroll west of the mall and discovered a completely different side of Galway City. It was still commercial with businesses lining the streets, but there was richness to it. The shops and buildings had character, they had color; it reminded me of Carmel, but the city with its age, its history and architecture overshadowed Carmel like a moon eclipse. There was also youth bustling up and down the streets of Galway, a youth that Carmel lacks.

I found a used bookstore and located two John Cooper Powys books to bring home to Adam. I flirted with the woman clerk who rang up my purchase. I asked her how she was doing and drew her from her daydream; a smile lit her up from within. She seemed shocked that I had actually noticed her and cared enough to ask how she was doing. She thanked me four times. It felt good to have flustered her, to watch her fumble my purchase into a bag.

We exchanged smiles, and I went over to another table, acting as if I was looking at another book, but really just hanging out to watch her, to see if she'd continue to respond to me. Another clerk walked up, and her allegiance shifted, yet her unspoken response helped me to regain a lost confidence.

It was close to six when I decided on a restaurant for dinner. It was a modern restaurant in an old building that had recently been remodeled. I noticed an asparagus-prawn stir-fry special that was posted in the window and decided to give it a try. After entering, I walked across the hardwood floors into a lounge area. A crescent-shaped bar separated the lounge from the kitchen. To the right of the bar area was a dining room where I was promptly seated.

There were high ceilings, cinnamon in color, and the walls were painted yellow. Some New Age teardrop looking lamps dangled from the ceiling. A cinnamon-colored padded bench ran the perimeter of the walls for seating on one side and wooden chairs with padded brown seat covers were on the opposite sides of the tables. Part of the way up, below the yellow paint, the walls were finished in wood similar in color to the floors. The doorways were arched. Easy listening rock music was playing in the background, not too loud, but not too soft. It reminded me of the music I'd be listening to at home or while I was driving about in my Expedition. It was a warm and welcoming atmosphere.

I ordered clam and mussel chowder and an asparagus-prawn stir-fry, but the establishment was out of both items that had originally drawn me through the door. Lured in by yet another illusion; life's funny that way. I settled on the seafood pasta. It was a fettuccini noodle, but they had a different name for it. The pasta was served with seafood in a light cream herb sauce, along with salad and garlic bread. It was excellent. I left out the dessert because of several slices of homemade bread I ate as an appetizer before my meal had arrived. The bread was hearty, a coarse, brown, grainy texture; I spread the butter on thick and fell in love.

I ordered an Americano after dinner and topped it off with

a spoonful of brown sugar and a short shot of cream. It was a memorable dinner for sure. A dinner I shared alone, feeling complete within myself. I've spent a good portion of my life eating dinner alone, but very few of them have left me feeling nourished in spirit. This evening, it was almost as if I had the love of my life sitting across the table from me in that empty chair. Life ripens with my recognition of its impermanence. I was so much alive, savoring every bite of food, every new breath of air. Living in the ecstasy of the moment was something quite unfamiliar to me. I clung to no past or future; I clung to nothing. In the past, this feeling of being at peace had only come to me in an occasional fleeting burst, like a falling star: here one second, gone the next.

Driving back to my room in Loughrea, I thought about the possible reasons why Kelli's marriage or old love affairs had ended. Maybe they couldn't stand her depressions, if depression was really even the problem? Maybe her partner just couldn't be there, to walk with her through the fire? Maybe what Kelli carries brought her lovers too close to their own hidden source of suffering? Then again, maybe it was all in reverse. Maybe it was Kelli who had done the deserting, who couldn't walk through the fires. Who knows? Certainly not me.

I've just showered and climbed into this comfortable bed that gave me last night's restful sleep. Earlier, I anticipated another good night's rest, but something is stirring and won't let me fall into a new dream. There's some detective show on television. It is based on the prosecution of a mother who has abused her daughter, and the case against the mother is being built on the history of the abuse that the mother suffered as a child.

This goddamn television show is stereotyping people who have suffered childhood abuse in any form. It's almost like giving people permission, or better yet, expecting people to follow suit to their pedagogy. It's self-perpetuating, forcing people into a system of belief that encourages them to fall into a pattern of being both victimized and victimizer.

The show pisses me off because it pathologizes and perpetuates a perceived illness; a form of labeling designed to create a psychological model as a basis for comparison and evaluation of so many suffering people. Where are the television productions that show the path to health and applaud those who overcome the traumas and abuses they've suffered? It happens, you know; people do step out of their hells and into new lives. Where in the hell are the television shows that project these positive images?

If psychology, television, the media would start modeling a new image, people could start living a new reality, but no, they continue to perpetuate victimhood, and we remain stuck in this unfulfilling dream, or better yet, nightmare, stuck in an old psychology, clinging to an old image and worshipping another dead God, another idol that no longer serves humanity.

April 10, 2001 - Dream

Playing pool. First it's pool or maybe it wasn't... maybe it was... oh, wow, it was a video game where you have to shoot something, but I thought it was ping-pong, too. The woman I was playing against suddenly became my partner, against these other two people. I remember the animosity we had toward each other, my new woman partner and me. Then we had to come together, had to be on the same team, and I said something about it being a marriage made in heaven. When I said this in the dream, I was teasing, yet in the dream I was well aware of the soulful symbolism. I had an awareness of the coniunctio: a psychological awareness, while still in the dream. I said: "Oh, a marriage made in heaven," almost a bit sarcastic or joking, a nervous joking. There is a little kid in the dream who is clinging to me. He comes and will hurt me and then goes away. Like he pinches me or does this or that just wanting some form of attention, for what I didn't know, but I'm going back to sleep, to see if I can keep dreaming to find out about this kid.

April 10, 2001 - 11 p.m.

It's been another long day. I had breakfast and settled my bill at the B&B, before driving to Loughrea to pick up my laundry. It only cost ten pounds, but I gave her twelve.

"Where you off too?" asked the woman who owned the laundry.

"I'm not sure, over to the coast and then south of Galway I think," I explained as a young woman, who I guessed to be her daughter, came out of the back room and stood next to her mother behind the counter.

"You might want to take in the cliffs of Moher," the older woman suggested.

"Yeah, I saw that on the map," I answered.

"You have a map, do you?"

"In my car."

"Bring it here. I'll show you the best route," the woman offered, as the daughter looked on.

"I'll be right back," I answered, carrying my clean laundry to the car and returning with the map.

"Okay, let's see where we are here," the mother said, unfolding the map. She located Loughrea and began to point out a route. The daughter had been quietly looking on, but, after her mother had made her suggestion, the daughter stepped in with her two pence: a shortcut. There's nothing more confusing than to get two different sets of directions to the same place.

The mother and daughter started arguing about which was the better route, and I just grew more confused. Finally the daughter walked into the back room, while the mother carried on with me. A few minutes later the daughter returned with a map that was much more detailed than the one the rental car agency had provided.

"Okay, you see this spot right here?" The daughter asked, drawing a circle on the N6. The mother finally gave up and let the daughter take over.

"Yes."

"Okay, it doesn't show a road there, but there is one. There's a train crossing, and once you pass over it, there'll be a road that takes off to your left. There'll be a school on that road; that's how you'll know if you made the right turn."

"I turn right?" I asked confused.

"No, look here," the daughter said, drawing my attention back to the map. "You turn left just after you pass the tracks, and then you'll drive by a school and that's how you'll know if you made the right turn," the daughter explained, as the mother looked on wanting to say something, but holding her tongue.

"Okay, I got you now."

"Then stay on that road until..." the girl went on. It seemed that she needed to give me directions worse than I needed them, but I listened just the same, more to let her be heard than to hear.

"You can have this," the girl said, offering me the map.

The mother got one last jab in, saying something about living there her whole life, which had been a lot longer than her daughter, and that she ought to know what she was talking about. I thanked them and set off on my way, following the daughter's route. It probably didn't save me any time, but the girl seemed so insistent on my taking this drive, that I decided to value her word. I turned left just after the train crossing and spotted the school, so I knew I was on the right road.

New homes were being built all over the countryside of rolling hills. It was beautiful, but the outer world didn't match my inner landscape. I should have been feeling content and fulfilled in such a magnificent place, but all I felt was gnawing emptiness, a disconnection. Again, that moment of being at peace with myself, like I'd had at dinner last night, had fled.

Birth came to my mind, being born into an unknown world. In a sense, that's exactly what's going on, too, and I don't quite know what to do with my freedom. It's overwhelming, probably like it was four decades ago when my mother actually did give birth to me. I feel so much that I don't quite know what to do with it all. This seems to be an endless theme in life: death and rebirth.

There was a road sign for the Kinvarra turn-off. I made the turn and kept driving as the daughter had suggested. An old dump truck had rolled over on its side on a dirt road that most likely led back to a farmhouse. I've felt this same desolation many times before, like when I flew Adam to Yachats, Oregon. We flew to Eugene and then rented a car to drive to Yachats. I dropped Adam off and then took off on my own, driving along the northern Oregon coast for three days while Adam visited with friends and played tennis.

When I was twenty-three I moved in with my Grandmother.

I began selling farm machinery when I was twenty and became quite successful. I was living on my own, but was discontented, and also in the process of negotiating a job with my competitors. I moved in with my grandmother and, within a few months, took the new job. Not long after that I started the process of sobering up. I had taken the job and left my hometown on a career move, but unconsciously my soul was leading me away from my environment so that I could objectively see myself: so I could chose to live.

For the next fourteen years, I enjoyed a successful career. I had a short-lived marriage that lasted two years: no children. Shortly after my marriage fell apart, the Lauren thing happened. That's when discontent really began to creep back in. I was still licking my wounds from the Lauren thing, feeling sorry for myself, and a bit burnt out from work so I visited some friends on the Monterey Peninsula. I looked up at the mountains and breathed in a big breath when it hit me: I had lived my entire life in the San Joaquin Valley and I wasn't going to live forever; I wanted something different. I bought a newspaper and that same day rented a studio in Carmel for the month of January.

Adam and I became friends that January, but, at the end of the month, I gave up my studio and returned to my job and identity, but my heart was no longer in it. A few months later, I was reading Joyce's *Dubliners* and *The Portrait of an Artist as a Young Man*. That's when I phoned Adam and told him how I'd spent my whole life selling but wasn't creating anything, told him that something was missing. The next thing I knew, we were exploring my dreams.

Six months latter, I rented out my Valley home, moved most of my possessions into storage, and myself in with my grandmother for the second time in my life. I kept my job, and rented a studio in Carmel. I continued my work in the San Joaquin Valley, staying with my grandmother for three or four days a week, and spent the remainder of the week at the studio in Carmel.

That September, I flew Adam to Oregon, and on our way I suddenly realized... I looked over at Adam and said: "Wow, I moved in with my grandmother right before I made a career move, right before I quit drinking, and now I'm living with her again. I went back to her to get something, but I'm not quite sure what it is yet." Without saying a word, the white haired, eighty-two year old man just looked at me and smiled. A few months later, I resigned from my job and moved to Carmel. Funny how I returned to my Yahweh-fearing Grandmother to find the unspoken courage to step into a new life.

So anyway, the desolation I felt today was the same desolation I felt on the northern Oregon coast, after I had dropped Adam off to play tennis, a few months before I left that particular old world behind. It was windy today. I arrived in Kinvarra, which is south of Galway City, on the opposite side of Galway Bay. I continued the drive along the western coastline through Burren and once in Black Head, the narrow coastal road turned south.

The scenery was breathtaking, beautiful, yet remote and desolate. I happened upon a cow that was walking in the middle of the narrow road and slowly pulled up behind her, hoping for her to give way. I was cautious about trying to nudge her off of the road; it was too narrow for forgiveness and the rental car wasn't much larger than my stubborn adversary. The cow wouldn't budge or change her pace one bit, so I slowly putted behind her, reached for the camera, and took a few snapshots.

By the time I arrived at the Cliffs of Moher, it was two o'clock. The weather was sunny with a few high clouds, but the wind was gusting in excess of twenty-five miles-per-hour. I put on my jacket after leaving the car, hoping that the wind would blow yesterday's stale smoke out of the coat. I had an achy feeling in my guts; emptiness echoed through my bowels. It wasn't sadness, not all of it anyway. It was much greater than sadness or a simple disappointment. It wasn't anyone's fault either, not even mine.

I parked next to two girls and spoke briefly with them as we walked toward the cliffs. They were from Spain. I'd seen them a few miles out before arriving at Moher. They were hanging a u-turn thinking that they'd missed a turn, but fate had brought them to their destination in spite of their disorientation. Next, a busload of teenage children pulled into the park. They turned out to be Frenchies, a bunch of pushy little bastards who tried to inch their way in ahead of other spectators trying to take in the view.

The cliffs were haunting, very dramatic. It was a harsh coastline. Shear ledges dropped several hundred feet down where the surf crashed against the walls. Hundreds, if not thousands of birds nested in the crevices of the walls. I wished for wings, for the wind to carry me away.

Most of the area where spectators normally went to view the cliffs had been quarantined and taped off because of the foot and mouth epidemic. The wind blew right through my jacket and sent a shiver coursing through my bones. After spending ten minutes taking in the cliffs, and acting like, what I most despise, a tourist, I walked back towards my car, stopping in the visitor's center to buy a small bottle of water. I was down to thirteen pounds. I had to find a bank soon.

I decided to drive to Limerick. The damn Irish radio station kept playing *Uptown Girl*; it was a remake by some new rock group. I hated that goddamn song and it wasn't because I was in a bad mood; I never could stand the damn thing. A few miles after leaving the Cliffs of Moher, I hit a pothole, and it jerked me out of my goofball state.

My mood, my victimhood, I was stuck in the women's quarters that Sophia spoke of at the Mary Magdalene seminar. I was mulling around in my shitty state, avoiding something of greater importance, much like the state I'd been muddling around in for the past several years, afraid of having to become something new, afraid of stepping into a new dream, afraid of being born.

I drove to Limerick, and found a vacant parking spot a block from the city center. At an Internet café I checked for messages and had two from Kelli. One said she was going to Insomnia for morning coffee, inviting me to join her if I was around, and the second message was just a report on how she'd had too much coffee and was suffering an insomniac attack. I didn't respond to either message. I didn't come to Ireland to have an e-mail relationship with the girl next door.

If she wanted to commune with me, she'd have to call. I was pissed, felt as if I had gotten the run around and didn't like it, even if I was there on my own invitation. Then I began to wonder if I'd actually included my mobile number in my last message to her but quickly recovered from my doubt, leaving it to fate.

I walked out of the Internet café, found a teller machine, and withdrew a hundred pounds. It felt good to be walking instead of driving. After the cliffs of Moher, it also felt good to be in a larger city with its resources and people, even if I didn't utter a single word while there. Galway was nice, but Loughrea was too small, not enough life bubbling up from within it, and the Cliffs of Moher, as dramatic as they were, felt like death.

I found a Bewley's, ordered a black and white coffee, and went upstairs to sit in the non-smoking section. It was a joke because all the smoke from everywhere else infiltrated the room like a fog. There were three, hot, long-legged, brunettes with fake tits puffing away in the smoking room across the way. That's really why I was sitting in the non-smoking section. This had been a day of disconnection, a despairing day, a day without hope, a day I won't soon forget, life's one long birthing.

Kelli hadn't called, but her e-mail had made me feel a little better; knowing she was actually thinking of me helped. I tried to figure out what it was about me that scared women. Was I an oddity that stirred their curiosity but spooked them too much to approach me? The world seems full of wounded people or perhaps it's just me seeing them all through my own wounded eyes. But even if I am seeing them from my own point of view, the world still seems full of lonely, wounded, disillusioned souls, each having given up hope of finding love and communion with another. It's possible that even people, who appear to be happy and full of life, have just learned to live with their unhappiness. Maybe that's it! Maybe the happy people have learned to roll with things, learned to keep on keeping-on in spite of life's disillusionments.

I looked at the opposite corner of the room. There was a man close to my age, possibly a few years younger, pen in hand, writing in a notebook. Was he substituting penned disillusions for life? A middle-aged woman walked in and sat at a table in front of me. She had a pot of tea and a slice of cake. Perhaps this was how she dealt with her emptiness. She was a lovely woman, took care of herself, and was in excellent shape, but today, maybe that's what it took for her to make the exchange.

Then there were other crazy people like this guy I knew who hopped a jet to Ireland, hoping to capture a lass he'd met and visited with for only a few minutes at a coffee shop back in the States, all a futile effort to fill up the hellish emptiness in his guts. Eating, drinking, drugging, shopping, fucking, consuming, consuming, and consuming even more. We're a world full of people consuming in order not to be consumed by that growling terror, that deep hungry pit of emptiness within each of us that constantly threatens our very existence.

I've been down in this pit several times before, and every time I pay a visit to this place I believe it to be the last, but, for some reason, I find myself here once again. It's never actually gobbled me up, though. It doesn't want to consume me like I wish to believe; it simply wants my attention, communion.

Today felt like doing time. Imagine that, doing time in Ireland. Maybe that's why Joyce's bones are buried in Zurich. I wonder where they'll bury my bones, or do I really give a shit, probably in a cemetery full of women who have been spooked to death by man.

I'm tired of this searching genre, this old dream. I'm stepping into a new dream, building myself a home, a cabin somewhere, my own retreat. Maybe I'll buy one, maybe I'll build one, or maybe just rent one for a while. Whatever I do, it has to have a fireplace, my laptop, and my laser printer. I don't need much, just a cabin somewhere, a place to craft my trade.

It feels right, a peaceful, spacious place, where I can wake up in the morning without anyone around... well, perhaps my lover but other than Her, nobody else. No one picking on me; no old lady landlord hovering over me, monitoring my every move, my coming and my going, my woman habits, my fucking bowel movements. Maybe it's right for Kelli to have returned home to Ireland, just as it's right for me to return home soon. Perhaps we've come together for the last time.

It is amazing how I can go from utter despair, to acceptance, and then right back into despair, all just by rolling over a bump of scar tissue in my psyche. Remnants of the past are rooted deep. Logic and reason are great tools when it is time to deal with the known, but what runs me is the unknown, and these tools have little, if any, influence when it comes time to pay a visit to the realm of the mysterious.

Walking to my car, I noticed a hotel and checked on a room. They were full but phoned another house and found me lodging. I passed on the offer. Something didn't feel right. It might have been Limerick. It was too big, kind of reminded me of a little Dublin. I really hadn't been there long enough to make a valid assessment, but I decided to leave just the same.

I set off on the drive from Limerick to Killarney, thinking that I might stop in Castleisland if I grew tired. I did stop, but only for gas and then continued on toward Killarney, only half-an-hour south. I drove into the city center. It was almost dark and difficult to get an overview and feel for the place. It appeared to be a pleasant city, much smaller than Dublin or Limerick. I got caught up in a couple of roundabouts and ended up spinning off out of town southbound, towards the Killarney National Park area.

It was close to nine when I spotted a sign for a B&B. I couldn't see the place from the main highway so I turned in to check it out. It was a farmhouse setup that was close to a river and catered to fishermen. The foot and mouth disease scare had even put a stop to fishing in Ireland. There were vacancies, so I took a room but was too late for dinner. The woman who ran the home sent me back up the way a couple of miles to Mallow Road, to a roadhouse called Darby O'Gill's.

All but one of the entrances to Darby O'Gill's were closed off. It was easier to maintain the disinfectant mats for people to walk on before entering the establishments. These mats were everywhere, entrances to businesses, hotels, parking garages, and countless other locations, all in effort to prevent the spread of the foot and mouth disease.

Oddly enough, the door that Darby O'Gill's used was the one that led through the bar. The bar had five or six local fellows hoisting pints and shooting the shit. It got quiet when I walked in.

"The lady back at the River Valley Farm House said I might still be able to get dinner here," I suggested to the bartender.

"I only have roast lamb or roast beef."

"That's fine. I'll have the lamb."

"Dining room is right through that door," he pointed.

I found a large lounge area that had a bar that was twice the size of the room where the locals gathered. I took a seat and the bartender brought a place setting.

"What are you drinking?"

"Water with gas will be fine."

"Would you like some chips to go along with dinner?"

"Sounds good," I answered. I liked how he called them chips instead of French fries. I was all for taking any credit I could away from the French.

While waiting for my meal, I had a look at the dining room that was adjacent to the lounge. It was a hall-like setting and looked as if the room was also used for entertainment. There was a framed poster on the wall, actually a few of them. One was a movie poster with a Leprechaun dancing a jig, advertising the production of Darby O'Gill and the Little People. It started to come back to me, about there once being a movie or television series that starred Sean Connery; the Little People were Leprechauns. This must have been the area where the movie had been filmed or possibly the place that had given the film its name?

My dinner came, sliced roasted lamb, mashed potatoes, peas, carrots, mint jelly, and chips, and I ate every last bite. The check only came to a mere seven pounds sixty pence. I told the bartender to add a couple of pounds to the tag for himself, and handed him my credit card. I signed the tag and left via the local's room. Once again I enjoyed the silencing effect that my being a stranger caused. I drove back to the farmhouse.

I'm beyond tired. I sleep at night, but the emotional ride over the last few days has worn me down. Why didn't I get a phone call from her the night we were to have dinner? Something about this whole Kelli thing smells.

Maybe it's guilt, maybe she's addicted to guilt. She might be one of those people who have to fail others in order to get her fix. I noticed how often she apologized for things, about not writing longer e-mails, about the weather, about not being able to offer me a place to stay, and about several other little things, that to me are unimportant. Perhaps she has the need to feed on guilt, about not being enough, setting things up to fail and causing disappointment in order to be guilty and in turn be forgiven. It's a cycle, an old dream: failure-guilt-forgiveness-failure-guilt-forgiveness-failure...

Even in her e-mail earlier this week, the first thing she mentioned was to forgive her for not showing up to dinner. Who the fuck was I to grant forgiveness to her anyway? Addicted to guilt, to being bad, to being not-enough, addicted to being wrong; I wish.

I have a habit of wanting to be the cause for everything around me, but I doubt that her inability to meet me has much to do with me. Did she really need to stand me up the other evening? In doing so was she able to reclaim a lost part of herself that had little, or nothing, to do with me at all?

It's that whole trickster thing. I remember when I had just started seeing a woman a few years back, and I caught her lying to me. It threw me into this self-righteous: "Who in the hell do you think you are? You think I'm flippin' stupid or something?" Then I realized that she had to lie to keep herself, she had to lie or believed she had to lie in order not to sell out and it had nothing to do with me, or about her being bad or wrong. It was just her problem and how she related to herself and to man.

She believed that she had to lie to a man to get and do what she wanted, when in reality she needed to do nothing with the exception of what was right for her. She didn't have to lie to do what she wanted to do; she just thought she did. She had married a man who controlled her with money and the illusion of security, or I should say she let him control her that way. She finally found the courage to leave the marriage and the externalized patriarchal dominating dream she'd been living in for the past several years. But, she was still living out the dream inside of herself, and my being a man had invited her projection.

Man suffers just as much as woman from this patriarchal catastrophe, from this imbalance. Both sexes have become lonely and estranged from each other because of the images we carry of one another. Man makes woman into what he believes her to be, and woman makes man into what she believes him to be, neither able to see beyond their own tainted views.

So, anyway, someone else's lying or misleading me isn't about me, or even a reflection of their perception of my intelligence. It's not a personal insult; the cause is often another's fear.

April 11, 2001 - 1:30 p.m.

I'm standing outside of the Bantry library. The staff breaks for lunch from one to two; I'm waiting for them to return. Bantry is a harbor town on the western coast, south of the Beara Peninsula, at the southern base of Bantry Bay, in County Cork about an hour south of Killarney and an hour and a half west of Cork. I drove from the farmhouse in Killarney National Park to Bantry this morning and have been here for a couple of hours, writing a few postcards. It's a beautiful sunny day, the first I've seen for awhile.

Kelli left two phone messages on my mobile this morning. I thought I had turned on the phone when I got up earlier to use the toilet, but for some reason it was off when I got out of bed the second time, so I missed both calls. Those goddamn Leprechauns are sneaky little bastards, I'm telling you, and quick too.

Kelli's first message said she was going to a bookstore somewhere in Dublin. She'd be there until around eleven and invited me to join her if I was in the area. The second message said that she realized that she had probably hurt my feelings and didn't blame me for not calling her back; she understood that I might want to maintain my dignity and that she wouldn't bother phoning anymore.

I phoned her but got her voice mail, so I left a message telling her that I was en route from Killarney to Bantry. She phoned back but I was traveling through the mountains and missed her call. Her message said that she and her mother planned on coming to Killarney in a couple of days for the Easter holiday weekend, said she had an uncle near Castleisland they planned to visit. She went on to say that he was ninety-two and just had a leg amputated, literally had one foot in the grave. Then she started telling me all about a concert taking place on the Monday after Easter. She sounded so excited.

Hell, I was good and confused, not that I wasn't before, but this just added to my bewilderment. Was she excited that I'd actually returned her call, about her upcoming visit to Killarney, or about the possibility of seeing me again?

I'm not holding my breath, though. Yeah, I'd love to see her, but something just isn't right; something's missing. A part of me says to stick around and fight, and a part of me says to leave her alone, that she'll only bring grief. I decided to handle it all by sitting back and hanging loose, let whatever is to happen during my last few days here in Ireland, happen.

I'm also going to allow Kelli to influence me even if it doesn't unfold according to my wants and desires. In other words, I'm going to let her be my guide. I'll follow her unpredictability and see where it leads instead of fighting fate. I don't want to judge her based on a prejudice, nor do I want to view her as woman who's cheating me out of something.

Anyway, now I'm in Bantry, waiting for the library to open so that I can check my e-mail. The library is up on a hill. A small stream descends from farther up and curves around the library like a moat and powers a paddle wheel that is twenty feet from the entrance. Across the street, a backhoe is digging up the remnants of a building that's been torn down. It's noisy and warm. I've had to take off my sweater. After I check my e-mail, I plan to drive to Cork City.

April 11, 2001 - 10 p.m.

Kelli phoned while I was still standing outside of the library. We finally connected again.

"Hello, Malcolm; it's Kelli."

"Hi Kelli, good to hear your voice again; I was a little worried about you."

"I'm surprised you're even talking to me."

"Would you rather I didn't?"

"Would you?" she asked, answering with a question.

"You know I want to talk to you."

"Where are you?"

"Bantry."

"That's where the concert is Monday. It's so weird that you're over where we're headed in a few days."

"I'm sorry about all this noise," I said, having a hard time hearing her. "There's a paddle wheel on the river here and a backhoe across the street making all kinds of racket."

"Would you like me to phone you later?"

"Hell no, I finally got you. You're not getting off that easy," I teased.

"Listen, I'm really sorry for the way I've treated you. I..."

"Kelli, you don't need to explain."

"Yes, I do owe you at least that. How long do you plan to stay in Bantry?"

"I think I'll go back to Killarney. I spotted a few nice B&B's just north of town."

"Well, my mother and I are coming there Thursday. We want to visit the uncle I spoke of in Castleisland. We won't be staying with him, though. We'll probably get a room somewhere in Killarney for the weekend. I was hoping that we could get together if you're still around."

"I'm sure I'll be around. I really like it over here on this side of the island."

"Oh, great, then I'll phone you when we arrive."

"Call anytime, Kelli."

"Okay, I'll see you in a few days..."

It was nice to talk with her, again. It felt even better than receiving the e-mail from her telling me that she was sick and that she'd call when she was feeling better. After looking over my on-line messages, I set off for Cork City, taking the southern coastal route that actually ran inland a few miles from the ocean.

The western coastline was beautiful, but for some reason it had a harshness: had a way of putting a chill in my veins. The drive to Cork provided a view of some magnificent countryside; it had a warmer feel with rolling hills that smoothed into flatlands, green flatlands with bigger trees, it reminded me of spring time in the San Joaquin Valley.

Kelli's message earlier this morning said something about

maintaining my dignity. I don't have to lose my dignity just because I choose to continue engaging her. My dignity is my own, not to be defined or maintained by another's actions. I've been guarding against having my dignity or anything else taken from me for years, living in fear of being taken advantage of by others, and I'm tired of living this way. For quite some time now I have unsuccessfully been trying to move into a place of vulnerability.

I reclaimed something by going back to that wounded place, that hellish emptiness I bathed in yesterday while driving, at the Cliffs of Moher and in Limerick. Things that happen in the world aren't about me. People's actions and reactions might have an effect on me, but it isn't happening to me, because of me or because of who I am, and the flip side is also true. I might have an impact on others because of choices and decisions I make in life, but it isn't a personal attack on them. How we human beings relate amazes, yet grieves me; our unconscious entities really call the shots, keeping us apart, or bringing us together.

Cork is another large city, not the size of Dublin, but larger than any other city I've visited so far on this trip. It's located on the southern coast. I found a parking garage in Cork City. It was below a shopping mall, similar to all the other shopping malls I've encountered in Ireland. I found a café Kylemore, like the one in Galway City, and used the pisser. The food didn't look too appealing, and the café had cigarette smoke billowing from every direction, so I left the mall and walked along a side street hoping to find a place to get a bite to eat.

Halfway down the block, I spotted a sign that said Kafka's and found it to be a restaurant. A young woman with a beautiful smile showed me to a table and presented me with a menu. The place was full of young college girls who had gathered around several tables chattering, smoking, eating, and answering their mobile phones. I only saw two men in the place, sitting at a table together, studying or reading, but not exchanging words, quite the opposite of the women.

The restaurant was dark inside. The walls painted a bluish-purple. It had a bohemian feel. It was like being underground somewhere, or in a cave. I studied the menu, bouncing back between the fish and chips and the pepper steak sandwich. The woman who seated me returned to my table.

"Are you ready to order?"

"I think so. Is this fish a dinner or a sandwich?"

"It's a dinner."

"Okay, how about this pepper steak?"

"That's a sandwich on a baguette. It's strips of steak with grilled onions, mayonnaise, and salad on top."

"Can I get it without the onions?"

"Not a problem."

"Okay, I'll have the sandwich without onions, and I'd like to add the sautéed mushrooms."

"Okay, and to drink?"

"Do you have iced tea," I asked, realizing it had been over a month since my last glass of iced tea.

"No, we do have some herbal teas, though."

"I'll have a sparkling water."

"Sure thing," she said, as she finished jotting down my order.

"Who's this place named after?" I asked.

"Oh, it's some English or German writer. I can't remember his first name."

"Franz."

"Yes, that's it," she confirmed, smiling.

I wanted to ask her if she knew about the secret raven, but saved my breath. I'd have just taken on the same role with her that old lady Shams did with me. She loved to corner me and ask me questions from an era gone by; knowing damn well that I had no idea what she was talking about. She really asked to confirm her higher learning and superiority over me. She'd revel in my ignorance and then shake her head in disgust, certain that I was missing out on life. Her parting shot as I walked out of her door for the very last time was something about me chasing a bluebird.

"What do you mean by a bluebird?" I asked.

"Oh, you don't know that story?"

"No, I sure don't."

"Well, you'll just have to go back and finish school to find out," she replied in her self-righteous, all-knowing tone, holding her hand up and pointing her index finger into the air. Mrs. Shams had missed her calling: she should have been a proctologist.

I spared the waitress what I suffered from that old bitch over the last year. My sandwich came with onions, so I sent it back. They picked the onions out and returned it to me. There was still one small piece left sitting on the top. I wanted to hurl it across the room into the kitchen or onto a wall, but refrained and simply flicked it out onto the table. I ordered a small side of chips and some more water. The meal wasn't that great, the only part worth a damn was the chips; I should have ordered the fish. I paid the bill and walked out to find a fish and chips right next door. I settled on Kafka's too quickly. Oh, well, I was happy to have been able to step into his underworld for a meal, even if it wasn't all that tasty.

I made my way back to the parking garage and tried to pay the fee at the automated ticket machine, but the damn thing was on the blink. It must have been acting up, because an attendant was standing there when I put my money into the moody contraption.

"What color is your car?" The attendant asked, as he opened the machine and made change.

"Red."

"You don't need a ticket. You've paid. What kind of car do you have?"

"I don't know. It's a little red rental car," I answered.

"Alright, I'll call ahead and tell them to let you through," he explained.

Ten minutes later, I drove up to the gate, pushed the intercom button and advised them that I had paid. The gate lifted, and I drove into the five o'clock Cork City traffic.

The Irish most definitely have a style of their own. They're unique, yet lacking a certain refinement, which I find very refreshing. Maybe it's not so much that the Irish lack a refinement but more that they don't hide behind pretension. They're kind people, warm like the Florentines, but certainly different. The Italian people have a way about them, a certain style and self-assurance that seems to be missing in Ireland. If it isn't confidence that the Irish lack, then at the very least it's a lack of understanding about how to live with their prosperity. The Florentines are natural; they have their own style. They aren't cocky or arrogant like the French. The Italians just seem to have solid identities; they're adapted, not carrying a hidden rage, or anything else that might be unexpressed.

I pulled into the flow of traffic, unable to find a road sign to point me back in the direction of Killarney, so I followed my gut. I looked out and noticed the sun settling toward the west. My intuition had again served me. A few blocks later I spotted the sign confirming what I already knew.

My pride is keeping me in Ireland, that and my defiance. I set out to meet Kelli again, to make something of it all, and by golly if I go down, I'm going down swinging. Then again, maybe it isn't my pride, maybe it's the part of me that hasn't been able to stand up before and swing like I'm now swinging. The part of me that needs to stand up and say: "No, I'm not walking away from this. This woman's worth fighting for."

Popeye, that's who the Irishmen reminded me of, sailors, tough old boys who have spent a good part of their lives battling the elements, the seas. "I is who I is and that's all that I is; I'm Popeye the sailor man." Maybe they don't lack confidence or anything else for that matter. Maybe the Irish just don't give a damn what others think.

I drove back to Killarney and found a B&B five minutes north of the city center, the Dagda House. The woman who answered the door showed me to a room, her two daughters, two and four years old, at her heels. The room looked new, had a wonderful view out to the west, and a queen-size bed. I told her I'd take it and turned to the stairs to get my bags.

As I was about to go down, the oldest of the girls said something to her mother about me being alone. The mother explained that the girls were used to seeing couples rent the rooms. When I returned with my bags, the husband was waiting for me with a book to point out some of the local highlights.

He mentioned that I might possibly want to take a drive out to Dingle while I was in the area. He started telling me about how to get there, about how I'd need to make a certain turn that was so many miles before the city center. Right after the man had given me directions, his wife came out of the kitchen and corrected the distance to the turn he'd just given me by adding a couple of miles to her husbands estimate; then she returned to her chores.

"A lot of these places are closed off to the public because of the foot and mouth outbreak," the husband explained, shrugging off his wife's correction.

"Isn't that tragic?"

"It's been blown way out of proportion," he explained, and then proceeded to tell me how he was in agriculture. He worked for a company that manufactured milking machines.

I also learned that he had built the house himself, and it was a very nice home indeed. He was proud of it, and he damn well should have been. The wife walked into the entryway where the husband and I were visiting and offered me tea. I accepted her invitation, and she returned to the kitchen. The little girls were vying for their father's attention. They were in a room adjacent to the entryway yelling for their daddy to come watch a Barney video while he was carrying on about all that had gone into building their home.

The father showed me into a room that doubled as a dining and living room. I sat down in a good, comfortable armchair while he stood in front of the fireplace giving me some more details on the finishing work of the house. The place was spotless.

"How long have you lived here?" I asked, looking at the wedding pictures of the couple that were up on the fireplace mantle.

"Let's see. I think six, no, almost seven years."

"Next month will be eight years," his wife corrected, as she placed a tray with tea, bread, and biscuits in front of me.

"I'm not so good with numbers," he confessed, not a bit annoyed by his wife's interruption.

They excused themselves to be with their children and left me to drink my tea. Photos of the two little girls at various ages since their birth were hanging on the walls or sitting on furniture throughout the room. This was their home and they left no one in doubt of it, even if they did entertain guests. The place was impeccable, yet lived in and comfortable. It felt as if

I had arrived home. I yawned several times, and that's always a good sign that I'm letting go and relaxing.

"And how are we doing?" the wife asked, having returned to check on me.

"Everything's fine, thank you."

"What time would you like to be having breakfast in the morning?"

"Oh, I don't know for sure. Nothing too early though: maybe nine-thirty or ten."

"Okay, that'll be fine, then. Do you like the traditional Irish breakfast: eggs and bacon?"

"You know. I've been eating a lot of that over the last few days, and it's just too much. I'd rather just have cereal and toast. Oh, and maybe some fruit."

"Okay, cereal, toast, and fruit it is then," she confirmed, before withdrawing into the kitchen.

I yawned a few more times and settled deeper into the armchair. The owners of the house are probably a few years younger than I am. Their life could very well have been mine. Family life doesn't seem so bad, not as it once did. It almost appears inviting. I finished my tea and then went up to my room to phone Kelli. Her voice mail answered, and I left the name and number of the B&B, telling her it was a nice place and rooms were available in the event they were concerned about finding a place.

Kelli returned my call a few minutes later. She thanked me for the information, and we visited for quite awhile. It was one of our nicest exchanges. We might not have spent much time together, but it seems that we have moved through an area that has cleared the air between us, possibly opening a space for our coming together in a more comfortable and honest fashion.

April 12, 2001 - 2 p.m.

I'm upstairs in the Scribe's Rest, a little restaurant above a bookstore in Dingle. There are three large peninsulas in this area. The northern-most of the three is the Dingle Peninsula, the middle the Iveragh Peninsula, and the lower being the

Beara Peninsula. Killarney is a town that is inland of the Iveragh Peninsula, so it is a nice central point to have a room. The town of Dingle is located several miles out on the Dingle Peninsula, but not all the way out to its western tip.

Hold up your right hand in front of you, open your hand and extend your fingers to the left. Now close your thumb and pinky and leave the middle three fingers extended; the top finger is the Dingle Peninsula, the middle finger is the Iveragh Peninsula, and the lower finger is the Beara Peninsula. Killarney is on your hand, just past the base of your middle finger. Okay, now close the Dingle Peninsula and after that close the Beara Peninsula; what remains is my favorite Peninsula. There, now you have something else to use your fingers for, although I haven't found it necessary to share my favorite peninsula with many motorists so far on this trip.

I entered the Scribe's Rest and tried to close the door behind me, but someone was pushing it open from the other side: a middle-aged woman. I held the door open for her to pass and then tried to close it again; this time a child was pushing from the other side. I held the door for the kid, too. I looked around before trying to close the door for the third time and noticed several people giggling over the door scene.

"I'm sure there's more coming," someone remarked.

"I got a feeling you're right," I said, letting go of the door and backing away, holding my hands out in front of my chest as if I was pushing away some unseen force.

I left the Dagda House for Dingle around eleven this morning. It was a foggy, drizzly day. About twenty minutes into my journey I came across two girls thumbing a ride along the country road. I pulled up to them, and rolled down my window.

"Where you headed?" I asked, checking them out.

"Dingle," they answered in unison.

"That's where I'm headed. Hop in," I said, and started to clear some things from the front passenger seat, but before I could, they had both slid into the back seat. I didn't mind, probably made them feel safer.

"I'm Malcolm."

"I'm Josephine," the blonde answered.

"And I'm Laura," the brunette answered.

"Where're you girls from?"

"Frankfurt," the brown haired Laura answered.

"Germany, huh?"

"Yes," they both giggled.

"You speak good English."

"I was an exchange student in Wisconsin," Laura explained.

"Oh yeah, my sister in-law is from Wisconsin. You girls go to college?"

"High school," Laura answered. "It's our last year," she added.

Shit, they were young enough to be my daughters. They were on holiday, touring Ireland, and staying in youth hostels. They had spent all their money shopping and, against their parent's knowledge and wishes, were hitchhiking their way across country; they'd traveled from Cork to Killarney yesterday.

Both girls were beautiful young women. Laura had straight, mid-length, auburn-brown hair that was pulled back into a ponytail; her ice-blue, wolf-like eyes were attractive, but intimidating. She was wearing a workout suit that had black bottoms and a light colored top. She had a black scarf wrapped around her neck and black tennies. Her father was a pediatrician and her mother a psychologist. Laura didn't mention any boyfriends.

Josephine, on the other hand, did have a boy back home. She was a curly, wavy blonde with green eyes, but her eyes didn't cut through me like Laura's. She was wearing black pants, a black top, and white tennies. Her hair was also pulled back into a ponytail. Josephine's father worked for a television station and her mother was a schoolteacher.

Laura had previously spent five months in the States as an exchange student, and just last year, both girls had volunteered for two months in Belfast, working in a facility for handicapped children. Their English was exceptional, but it appeared that Laura was a little more proficient; she answered most of my questions, anyway.

The car was low on petrol, so I planned to fill up at a station along the way to Dingle. It was so misty that it was hard to have a feel for where we were heading, even if we did have a map. I followed the road signs and turned left, but it felt like we were going right back to where we had come from.

We'd been driving for about thirty minutes when the low fuel bell sounded, and magically, a filling station immediately appeared. It was just a country market out in the middle of nowhere that sold petrol. It was timely for more than just fuel. Concerned that I might have taken a wrong turn earlier, I wanted to confirm that we were indeed on the road to Dingle. I went in to pay for the fuel and learned that we were heading in the right direction.

"You girls are brave to be hitchhiking."

"We aren't afraid, because we don't have any money to steal," Laura explained.

I didn't respond, but their naïveté concerned me. Money, hell, they were only eighteen and had yet to experience the betrayal of man. Money was about the last thing that should have concerned them. I know of a few women who have lost their bodies, not to mention their souls because of their innocent natures leading them into compromising positions.

Thirty minutes later, we pulled into Dingle. It's a small port town with several knickknack shops that cater to the tourist trade. It was still misting. I parked and told the girls that I'd be returning to Killarney at three o'clock and to meet me at the car if they wanted a ride. Then we went our separate ways. I set off to explore the village, figuring two hours would be enough time to see a few things and have a snack.

I walked into a few of the knickknack shops looking for a souvenir to bring home to Alexis, Adam's daughter, but nothing caught my eye. Before picking up Josephine and Laura, Kelli was floating around in my mind. I was playing with the fantasy of taking her back home to California. I must be nuts. Hell, I don't even know her, was stood up by her for dinner less than a week ago, and now I'm toying with the possibility of clunking her over the head and dragging her home.

That kind of blind thinking has gotten me into some of the biggest messes in my life. Unfortunately, not thinking blindly has also been the greatest contributing factor to a life filled with boredom. I'm ready for trouble. My biggest problem has been the avoidance of problems.

I'm trying to convince myself that I am the voice of God, and have been sent to Ireland to rescue Kelli from this beautiful, yet misty, rainy, cold country that she picked as her retreat. She told me that she had gone to California to mend a broken heart after a failed marriage, and here I am trying to weasel my way into what I hope is now mended, just to break it all over again, and if not that, then to have mine broken. What the hell do I care if she breaks it anyway? I'm long overdue. It's been so long since I've had a broken heart that I don't even know if I still have one.

The rain stopped, but the clouds were still hovering over Dingle. I was unsuccessful in the souvenir shops and grew impatient with my search, but decided to try just one more. Actually it was almost decided for me. I found myself in a herd of people who had somehow settled on visiting this one shop all at the same time, and I was caught in the middle of the frenzy. I walked through the door and found the shop overflowing with patrons, so I turned around to leave, but the herd behind me kept pushing through as if it were feeding time at the troughs. The people flowed in around me like water around a stump sticking out of a river. There I was again, stuck between the coming and the going.

"I have all I can handle," the woman who ran the store announced, trying to make her way up front to stop the incoming traffic.

"So have I," I answered.

"Sorry," the woman replied, concerned that she might have offended me.

"It's no problem," I assured her, and pushed my way up stream and out through the door.

There was nothing in that store that would have interested me any more than in the other two shops I'd just visited. I had just lost track of myself, and for a moment had fallen into the masses. I walked up the street a bit and turned down a side road. I came upon a bookstore, and through the window spotted an attractive brunette behind the counter who drew me inside to have a closer look.

"Hello," I said, greeting her with a smile.

"Hello," she echoed back with a beautiful smile. "Can I help you find anything?"

"No, thank you. I'm just looking around."

She smiled again and nodded without saying anything, and I had a look about the place without really seeing a thing, besides her. Then I walked up to the counter.

"Do you have any notebooks?" I asked, already knowing they didn't.

"No, we sure don't. You can try the newsstand up the street," she suggested.

"I'll do that. Thanks," I lied.

She was a beautiful woman in her mid twenties with green eyes. Her straight hair was cut in a bob. She was wearing green pants and a white, low cut-top. She was sitting on a stool behind the register, leaning forward, resting her elbows on her knees and her posture was making her already plump boobs all the more inviting.

"You live here in Dingle?"

"For another week; this is my parent's store. I've been away at school for the last five years. I just finished up and came back for a short stay."

"Where you off to?"

"Australia."

"Oh, you'll have a good time there."

"You're right I will. I always have a good time," she answered confidently.

"As you should," I confirmed, while imagining what having a good time with her would be like.

We visited for a while longer. She'd been to the States once. Her stepfather was from Los Angeles. I told her about San Francisco, Monterey, Big Sur, and encouraged her to visit California sometime. I wished her luck in her travels and said goodbye. I left, walked by several other stores and stopped. I turned around; she was too damn cute not to give her my e-mail address, so I pulled out a business card and walked back to the bookshop.

"Here you go," I said, handing her the card. "Now you've got a friend if you ever make it over to the States again."

"What's your name?" she asked, smiling and taking my card.

"Malcolm."

"Malcolm, I'm Judy," she said, extending her hand.

"It is a pleasure, Judy," I answered, taking her hand, and then feeling somewhat embarrassed, I smiled and left for the second time.

Continuing my uncharted walk around the village, I came across the Scribe's Rest and climbed the stairs for a coffee and the un-closeable door act. I'm sitting on a stool at a bar that lines the wall with a window view, sipping my coffee and watching people pass below.

April 12, 2001 - 10 p.m.

It was close to three when I left the Scribe's Nest, making my way back to the rental car. I took a shortcut, but ended up getting lost and was ten minutes late. The girls were waiting for me. From a distance it looked like they were either eating or smoking, and, as I got closer, I saw them putting away a loaf of bread and finishing the last bites of what must have been a sandwich.

"Did you have enough time?" I asked, thinking that they might want to look around a while longer.

"Yes," they both answered in unison as they looked at each other and giggled.

"Do you want to stay longer?"

"No, it was boring," Josephine quickly answered.

"Okay, then," I laughed. "Do you need to get back, or would you like to take in some sights out around Slea Head?" Slea Head was farther west, out on the tip of the Dingle Peninsula.

They looked at each other without immediately responding, and then Josephine asked: "Can we take pictures?"

"Of course you can. All you have to do is speak up when you want to stop," I explained, wanting them to feel comfortable.

"Okay, Josephine answered, and then the two of them looked at each other and giggled again.

They both climbed into the back seat of the car and I took my position behind the wheel. I started the car and then laughed to myself. "After all, you girls have your own car and driver for the day. You might as well take advantage of it," I teased, and they responded with their giggling thing.

So, there I sat in my red rental car with two young women, or some might say old little girls, I being their unpaid chauffeur for the day. I didn't mind, though. The thought of making it with one of them did cross my mind. Hell, I wouldn't have stopped to offer them a ride if they hadn't been such beauties. My thoughts went no farther than that, though; they could easily have been my daughters. I find it distasteful for older men to take advantage of youth's innocence, and these girls at least appeared to be innocent.

We rounded the corner out of Dingle for Slea Head, and I decided to voice my concern: "Okay, ladies. I've got one thing to say, and I'm going to say it and get it over with," I announced to get their attention. "Now, I know you're on holiday away from your parents, and you certainly don't need anyone filling in for them, but hitchhiking isn't safe! You could have been picked up by some goofball who ended up raping and murdering the both of you. It just is not safe!"

"Yes, we know..."

"Alright, enough of that," I interrupted. "Let's go have fun and take some pictures."

We continued our drive along the narrow coast road. It was foggy and misty, but when a break in the weather did come, the scenery was dramatic. Hill's covered in green forage ran up to the cragged cliffs that descended down to the ocean. There were old farmhouses with barns and small dairies. The hillsides were covered with sheep. Lambs would race to their mothers, poking up underneath the ewes, frenzied-like, searching for their mother's milk, as if they had to steal it away from her.

We came to a place where a river literally ran down off a mountain, across the road, and then down the lower mountain. Instead of building a bridge or putting in a tunnel to divert the water flow, the road was just built through the river. Hesitantly, I drove through the water and came out on the other side unscathed.

"You girls have brothers or sisters?"

"I have two sisters; they are three and four years old, but we are all from the same parents," Josephine answered.

"And I have two brothers. One is twenty-three and the other is sixteen," Laura added.

Both girls had plans for college. Laura entertained the possibility of working with handicapped children, but she wasn't sure yet. I congratulated her on the uncertainty, actually encouraged her not knowing.

Josephine had aspirations of becoming a speech therapist, and seemed quite content in her knowing, and I congratulated her on her clarity. They both planned on traveling for a year after high school, before starting at the university.

We made several stops along the road to take some snap shots of the scenery, but after a while grew tired of the stopping and starting and became much more selective of our stops. When we descended out of the foggy mountains and into the valleys, things were quite beautiful, but not sunny like the postcards at the news agency portrayed; the scenery was still breathtaking.

Driving around in the fog was mystical. It was hard to tell where we had been or where we were going. For all I knew, we could have been driving in circles. We talked about what it was like living in our countries of origin and other fun things about life; it was kind of like a question and answer forum where we got to know a little bit about one another. Having the girls company was sweet, like spending time with daughters I never had. We came across another river that crossed the road.

"Wow, check this out. Another river," I said, still amazed at how it flowed right over the road.

"I think, maybe, it's the same one," Josephine suggested.

"I think, maybe, you are right," I answered, noticing that the geography had an uncanny resemblance to where we'd crossed earlier. We had been driving in a circle, seeing the same thing twice, and not even recognizing it, or I hadn't recognized it anyway. It was so misty that where we had passed not long before had taken on another form.

"I'm glad you girls were paying attention."

They giggled, and I wondered how long ago they had figured out that we were retracing our path. I did a three-point turn right in the middle of the flowing water, and then backtracked out of Slea Head, this time successfully finding the turnoff to Dingle.

I was getting hungry, had actually been hungry for some time. I hadn't planned on our drive taking so long. Josephine asked to stop at some pottery barn along the way so that she could use the facilities, and I was all for it, figuring I'd find a candy bar inside. There was plenty of pottery, but not a speck of food.

After our brief stop, we resumed our drive towards Dingle. They finally asked about me, about my life. I spoke a little of my failed marriage, but mostly of my life as a tractor peddler.

"I'm the oldest of four boys," I explained.

"No girls?" Laura asked.

"No, but I was supposed to be a girl. They had my name picked out and everything."

"What was your name supposed to be?" Josephine asked.

"Tamara Renée."

"I like that," Laura said.

I then went on to tell them what it was like having been raised in an all boy family and that I went from there into the tractor business where I was surrounded by men. Then I told them how I'd left my career, moved to the coast, started taking college classes, and how most of the friendships I had developed were with women, but that I was frustrated because none of them had become my lovers. "On the other hand," I went on to say, "if they had become my lovers, I wouldn't have been able to learn from them what I've learned. Frustrating as they were at times, all these friendships were leading me back to myself."

I explained my trip to them, about flying to Zurich, taking the train to Florence and meeting the women at the Mary Magdalene seminar, about the train ride and my short stay in the south of France, about Saintes Maries de la Mer, and then hopping the plane from Paris to Dublin. I didn't tell them anything about Kelli, though, for fear of looking like a fool.

We passed through Dingle and, teasing them, I offered to stop in case they were worried about having missed an attraction earlier that day. That's when I realized that a few hours had gone by since we left for Slea Head, but it might as well have been a hundred years that passed. We drove on to Killarney, and I told them that I was writing this book, and they wanted to know if they'd be in it.

"Yeah, you girls made the book for certain, but you have to pick a new name," I explained, looking into the rearview mirror to catch them both beaming a smile. "So pick a name. Now's your chance to be called anything you like, and *you* get to choose."

The girls loved it, and that's how Josephine and Laura came to be. Why not? I liked the idea. Who says we have to be what we've been told to be, or called by a name that someone else chooses for us? The whole idea of having to accept what another person assigns stinks!

There should be a certain time in our lives when we are allowed to return the names given us by our parents, and this should be honored without having to suffer the fear that we might offend our creators. As far as I'm concerned, it should be a law, a universal law that when we turn eighteen we can legally choose our name, our identity. Better yet, why not at the age of twelve, or even earlier. Hell, we're the ones who have to live with ourselves. Claiming ourselves would be a powerful statement, a right of passage of sorts, where we would become autonomous, to chose who and what we will be.

The girls were all excited about making the book, and I was excited for them. It was all meant to be. If I had happened on the spot where I found them a minute sooner or later, Josephine and Laura probably wouldn't have been there. We'd come together for a reason: for me to father them, and for them to daughter me. Guess I was a compensated chauffeur after all.

"I don't know about you girls, but I'm hungry."

"Would you like a sandwich?" Josephine offered. "It is black currant jelly and butter. They aren't in the best shape, but..."

"No, but thank you," I answered, but then it didn't sound so bad. As I mentioned before, I have a hard time receiving things, at first anyway. "You know what? Maybe I will try one of those sandwiches." Why not? I was hungry and they were offering. It gave them an opportunity to contribute, and it gave me an opportunity to receive. In a way, it had fulfilled the whole experience, like breaking bread together. A beautiful way of culminating the communion we had shared together throughout the day.

The youth hostel was on the outskirts of Killarney, a few miles from the city center.

"You can drop us off across the street," Laura suggested.

"No, I can take you all the way there," I answered, as I pulled onto the access road that led to the grounds. We exchanged e-mail addresses and then said goodbye.

I had women coming out of the woodwork. I wonder if Laura and Josephine were angels, sent to be with me, keep me safe and provide company as I skirted around the jagged edges of Slea Head this afternoon? They might very well have been sent to provide sustenance in my time of need. I'll know when the picture I took of them is developed. I've heard that angels, like Leprechauns, can't be photographed.

April 13, 2001 - Dream

I had returned to the States, and met my friend Bruce. It was almost as if he expected me to be troubled, which I was. It was about me stepping from one woman to the next. I was frustrated, but when I was talking to him about it, I realized that it was no longer a problem, because it had become conscious to me, and I didn't have to live that out anymore.

Also something about fishing or hunting somewhere, don't remember the details, also, something about settling my bill at the Dagda House. I'd stayed 4 days and the bill was 88 pounds. I gave them a hundred and didn't want change.

April 13, 2001 - 3 p.m.

I'm having a late lunch in Killarney. I woke up before ten, showered, came down for my light breakfast of cereal and toast, and then drove to town. Staying on the outskirts of the town for the past two nights, I've yet to give much time to Killarney itself, so that's my plan for today, to hang out in town.

I've been driving an awful lot, too, over a thousand miles in less than a week: Irish miles, on the other side of roads that are rough and narrow and behind the wheel on the opposite side of the car, to boot.

There was a vacant parking lot a couple of blocks north of the main street, so I parked and walked into the city center. Killarney isn't a big city, but it isn't a small village either. It has most things that a big city has to offer, but with a small town feel, and I like it.

My first stop was at a drugstore to buy some hand lotion. My hands are chapped and peeling. They had a small bottle of Tea Tree Oil lotion that I chose because it was small and fit nicely into my pocket. My next stop was the Killarney Bookstore. I found a book on Celtic myths and purchased it. I then asked them to hold the book, so I wouldn't have to lug it around while in town.

My next stop was at a tour-booking office where I inquired about reserving a seat on the TGV from Paris to Zurich. My flight was scheduled to depart Dublin on Monday, so it was time to attend to these details.

"We can't do that here," an older gentleman explained.

"Any idea where I can get this done?"

"I'd check with a travel agent," he answered.

"But it *is* Good Friday, you know, and I doubt that you'll find anything open on Good Friday," the woman standing next to the man added.

"Okay, thank you," I answered, wanting to ask her what she was doing open on Good Friday, but I held my tongue.

I then ducked into a coffee house called the Bean, and ordered an Americano; it was one of the best I've had on the trip. Kelli phoned last night and told me that her mother was getting a new car and they decided not to set off on their drive until this morning. I guessed her to be en route and expected her to phone when she arrived in the area, but I wasn't holding my breath.

I wasn't anxious because I was quite certain that I'd see her again after our conversations on the phone and because of the dream I'd had where I was playing ping-pong against the woman and then we became partners. I don't know why, but that dream put me at ease with all that has been happening.

I miss California. I'm looking forward to getting home. I'll travel again, but I've been away long enough to know that California is my home. I also noticed that many of the Irish women have flat asses, and I don't see how I'd make it in Ireland being the ass-man that I am, not to mention all the wind and rain.

It's another cloudy overcast day. All the picture books and postcards show otherwise, but I've yet to experience more than a few hours of sun in the past week. The sunniest it's been was the day I flew into Dublin, and then again the day I was in Bantry, but that was just for a few hours.

The Irish people appear to gray prematurely, the men do anyway; I guess the women use coloring. I'm not sure if it's the result of their lifestyle or heredity. Then again, maybe I'm a fortunate soul, living a charmed life but not knowing it.

A gay guy walked down from the Bean's upstairs seating. I haven't seen many gay guys in Ireland, none with that feminine side that they often like to flaunt, anyway. It doesn't seem like a country that encourages a gay lifestyle, not an open one anyway. This isn't a judgment, just an observation.

I haven't seen many women touting boob jobs, either, but one gal who worked in the Bean was bouncing her new set around, proud as could be. She was in her mid-forties and walked pigeon-toed, a short gal with wire-rimmed glasses. Her long blonde hair was held up in a clip with a red ink pen stuck in her hair-bun. Unfortunately, she had a flat ass. She was running around the place making double-time while the other help moved in low gear. The Bean had filled up for lunch.

When I looked around, it seemed that everything, including the patrons, had turned black and white, photograph-like. It was as if the place had frozen still a century ago. The people could have all been boarding a ship for Ellis Island. Their faces reminded me of pictures of Irish immigrants I had seen in history books. I was looking forward to becoming an immigrant back to the States as well. In less than a week I'll be America-bound, ready to start a new life.

Some people really can let go of things, just drop them and walk away, no matter what the cost. I like to think of myself as having this freedom, but I don't. I have the habit of clinging to old images, old ideas, fruitless hopes, and this rigidity has robbed me of greater possibilities. I'm beginning to see this now, and desperately want to make up for lost life, time gone by, and now that I cling to this desperation, this hope of reconciling with myself, I wonder what else I might be missing?

We all go to the grave with some regrets, for life unlived, choices not taken. As humans, we just can't have it all, and accepting this as truth has been one of my biggest downfalls. I want it all. I want to be my own man, run my own life, and yet I want to crawl home to mama, back up into the warm safe spot from whence I came.

I'm ready to return to mother America, back to the familiar places, to people I know, to restaurants or coffee houses where I feel comfortable taking up space for days, months, or even years at a time. I'm ready for a massage, a roll in the hay with an old girlfriend, enjoying a hamburger without having to worry about Mad Cow disease, and organic California greens. And I'm sick and tired of this whole foot and mouth thing; it's beginning to remind me of the 2000 U.S. presidential election.

The kids in Ireland are all beautiful, teeming with life, but many of the adults seem to be missing something. Something's missing in their eyes; it's hard to find a smile, a real smile from the heart. I know it's there, because I have been warmly received by everyone here, but they wear these serious, distant looks, as if they are living somewhere outside of themselves. Maybe it's a retreat, a sort of womb to return to. I guess we all need a womb at certain times and places in our lives.

It will be nice to return home without an agenda, return to my Mac PowerBook and LaserWriter, Ford Expedition, California girls, and freedom to retreat to wherever it is that will allow me to finish what I've started.

Frank Sinatra was playing on the radio: *That's Why the Lady is a Tramp*. I'd been in the coffee house for quite a while; it was time to move on. I decided to check my e-mail and also see if I could find a bargain flight on-line that would take me directly from Dublin to Zurich; that way I could avoid a return to France.

I answered a few e-mail messages but was unsuccessful in finding a flight from Dublin to Zurich, so I decided to stick with my scheduled departure on Monday at noon. I walked around town again, retracing my steps to see if I might have missed anything of importance, but found nothing new.

I did notice something rather queer, though. Several different children were crying wherever I walked. A crying theme was going on, in the shops and out on the streets. These kids were all unhappy about something. Maybe about their parents dragging them into town, shopping, doing things kids probably weren't too interested in doing unless they got a treat of some sort for their sacrifice, but that usually only came with good behavior, or I should say behavior that matched the demands of their parents. I wondered what the cries might be asking for: a treat, a toy, a candy, a hug, to be heard, recognized?

I just walked into a restaurant for a late lunch, and ordered the special, cod and chips. It comes with potato leak soup and a drink. I can't find any potatoes in the soup, but it's tasty, just a bit too salty. I tore a baguette into pieces and dropped them into the bowl. The news is blaring from the radio. I'm sick of hearing the news, not only is it boring, it's redundant. Nothing much is happening in Ireland that's worthy of news, but then again, I feel the same way about the media in the States. It's all hype, a bunch of bullshit.

I still haven't heard from Kelli today. I recall a fortune cookie I once received. It said something like - for a person in wait, an hour seems an eternity. That truth was worth more than the lottery numbers printed on the flip side of the fortune strip.

The rooster has crowed, the temple's veil has torn, and this squealing bearing that's seizing up in the cooling system compressor is driving me out of my fucking mind. I'd rather listen to the unanswered cries of a child. I hope to have enough strength on Sunday to roll the stone away.

The cod and chips hit the spot. They filled my belly and relieved my edginess. Almost all the food in Ireland has been great, but it won't take a great famine to get me to set sail for America. They're a fiery bunch, that's what the Irish are.

I've finished my meal, but for some odd reason I'm still sitting here listening to that annoying squeaky compressor bearing. There must be some unconscious attraction I have for unwarranted suffering. That goddamn bearing is a lot like the women I've picked to have in my life. They drive me fucking batty, but I long for them. I'm leaving, can't stomach this shit any longer.

April 13, 2001 - 10 p.m.

When I left Killarney this afternoon, I drove out of town, back towards the Dagda House but turned left at the first roundabout and followed the signs to the Ring of Kerry. I wasn't going to drive the whole Ring but wasn't ready to retreat into my room either, so I continued driving west. I noticed a huge gap in the mountain range to the south. Light was shining through it, the most light I'd seen all day. Damn, did I want to fly! If my little red rental car could have sprouted wings, I'd have taken off and flown right through that pass on into never-never-land.

I turned south on the next road and noticed a sign that said Gap of Dunloe. That had to be what was drawing me in. If it wasn't the gap, then it was most certainly the vortex created by the Atlantic Ocean's vacuum on the other side. I might have been a bit off trajectory, but I was still within the gravitational pull of my origins.

I drove until I came to a sign that said road unsuitable for passenger cars, so I parked and walked into a café to use the facilities and to buy a bottle of water. Returning from the toilet, I pulled up a chair and took out my notepad. A critical inner-voice told me I had no business writing, that time was ticking and that I should be out taking in more scenery, but I ignored the illegitimate.

Fuck, I wasn't there for fun. I was there to work, and if not work, to write. I raised my head, and noticed a young woman looking my way, probably wondering what I was all about; wondering about my scribbling in the notebook. *I bet she doesn't have a clue that she's looking at a soon-to-be-famous writer,* I thought, then laughed out loud and continued with my fantasy.

Big fucking deal, what will fame do for me that everything else has failed to provide? I was jacking myself off to feel better, just like I jacked off all the way over here to Ireland. I could fly to the moon in the space shuttle and still wake to my dick in hand. Fame, hell, I'm just trying to trade-in my lost youth, praying to it, like I prayed to all the other illusive idols in my life: still trying to fill up that emptiness.

I'm surprised that I don't miss my time with Adam. I may not be connecting with Kelli, but I am connecting with myself and having one hell of an adventure on my own. For all I know, Kelli standing me up might have been one of the best things that happened to me in a long time.

Hell, if not for Kelli, I wouldn't be on this jaunt. That's how it often goes for me, too. I'll be off chasing what I think I can't live without and end up getting something altogether different. But, I never know it until enough time has passed so that I can objectively see what, to others, has been obvious all along.

The road might have been unsuitable for cars, but I decided to trespass on foot. I left the restaurant and walked out towards the road, into an area where a horseman was working on a horse's shoe. There were several carriages for hire and they were soliciting my business as I passed them. I declined and continued on along the road until I came to a sign that restricted entry into the area because of the foot and mouth disease. I thought about continuing on in spite of the posting, but decided to heed the warning.

I drove back to the Dagda House. I had picked up a card on my way out the door this morning and found out that the husband's name was Niall and his wife was Brighid. It appeared that Niall had yet to arrive home from work, and Brighid was outside watching the kids play.

"Hello," Brighid said, greeting me as I climbed out of the car.

"Hello there," I answered and smiled cordially. "Letting the kids burn off some of their energy?"

"Yes, and Lord knows they have it," Brighid said, rolling her eyes and head back.

"How old are they?"

"Lady Elizabeth is four, and little Louise, there, is two."

"Well, they're really beautiful children," I complimented.

Both little girls had brown hair and big blue eyes. I could see a streak of orneriness in Elizabeth's baby blues, but Louise had nothing but innocence shining from her eyes. Niall drove in, following the driveway around to the back of the house to park. He came over to where Brighid and I were visiting.

"Good evening," he said, seeming excited to see me. Brighid walked away to check on the children.

"Hard day?"

"Oh, not too bad." He worked for a company that built automated milking machines for the dairy industry. We visited for a bit while Brighid gathered up the children and took them into the house. I learned that Brighid's mother had a dairy farm just two places south of their home, and her father and brothers did custom farming. Brighid and Niall had purchased the land from her mother, and then built the house themselves. Niall said they would never have been able to afford it any other way.

The wind came up and we found shelter in the entryway of the home to avoid a chill. Elizabeth and Louise were playing in the room just off the entryway where they watched videos. Elizabeth must have heard us talking, and curiously walked out to be around us. She walked up the stairs, straddled a rail post and hung her legs over it, just above her father's head. Niall continued telling me about his work, and I looked up to find Elizabeth sticking her tongue out at her father without him even having a clue. She eventually grew tired of failing to capture her creator's attention and came back down to the playroom.

The phone rang and, a few minutes later, Brighid came out to get Niall.

"My father needs help with some electrical problem when you have time," Brighid explained.

"That's just great. A whole day of taking care of people's problems, and now I've got to go down and take care of my in-laws as well," he complained as Brighid walked away.

"It works both ways," she retaliated, just before the kitchen door swung closed.

Lady Elizabeth ran out of the playroom and down the hallway towards the back of the house, as a cry from little Louise grew louder.

"Elizabeth," Niall called out, but she had long gone into hiding.

We talked a bit longer, and Elizabeth came out of her hiding place, climbed the stairs, and once again, dangled her feet right over her father's head, and stuck out her tongue. I looked up and started to laugh, cuing Niall to look up at Elizabeth.

"You know papa doesn't like that, little lady," Niall reprimanded, having caught her in the act.

Her tongue disappeared into her mouth, Niall resumed our conversation, only to catch her again minutes later. "Elizabeth, you know the story about the little girl who lost her tongue doing that," Niall reminded her, as she sucked her tongue in very quickly, shaking her head. "Yes, she did so," Niall added.

"Tell me the story, then," Elizabeth demanded.

I couldn't hold back any longer and busted out into laughter. Elizabeth was a sharp one; she'd led her father right into that one, and at only four years of age, to boot.

I retreated to my room, and watched the clouds roll in from the west. I phoned Aerlingus to see if I could change my flight from Dublin to Zurich, instead of Paris, but they didn't offer such a flight. It looked as if I'd be leaving as planned on Monday to Paris.

I hadn't heard a thing from Kelli all day. Who was I fooling; she wasn't interested in me. I didn't know what was going on with her, and it really didn't matter. Maybe she was a compulsive liar on top of manic-depressive and borderline tendencies, or maybe it just wasn't the time or place for her to consider a relationship with me, or maybe she simply had no desire. There were only two things certain at that moment: we weren't together, and I'd never again see the day's sunset that was melting into the horizon below the clouds.

At eight-thirty, I went to town for some dinner. On the drive in, Kelli rang my mobile.

"Hello, Malcolm?"

"Hi Kelli."

"Malcolm, listen, we've just arrived in Killarney."

"You made it, huh?"

"Finally, it took us forever to get here. What's the name of the B&B where you're staying?"

"The Dagda."

"You're not going to believe this, but we're right next door," she explained. "I thought I saved your voice message yesterday, but I lost it somehow and couldn't remember where you were staying. I thought it started with a D or something like that." She told me the name of the B&B that was supposedly next-door, but it didn't sound familiar, and I was driving into town, so I couldn't step outside to confirm her suspicion. I explained that I was on my way to dinner, and we decided to wait until the morning to get together.

I'm a mess, all over the place, feels as if a roller coaster is surging through my veins. I'm out of control and don't like it. Is this love, being out of control, or better yet, something that can't be controlled? I'm nervous as hell, and excited all at the same time.

When I got in this evening, I shaved off the beard I've been growing for the last few days; I can't seem to make up my mind about the damn thing. I'm excited, but want to squelch my emotions; I don't want to set myself up to be disappointed. But, at the same time, I also long to let the excitement spew from within, abandoning my need to control whatever it is that I'm fighting. I desperately want to let loose, but I'm so afraid of exposing myself, of being turned away, rejected, or worse yet, accepted.

April 14, 2001 - Dream

First, there was a black and white picture show of Jacqueline's grandfather. Jacqueline is a woman that I fell for, but she ran; she was just getting divorced. He, her grandfather, harvested cotton. The dream, or picture show gave me the idea of doing that, and the next thing you know, I was negotiating with my old manager in the machinery business, and the salesman who replaced me, about possibly buying a brand new machine.

I remember asking Thad, my ex- manager, if they had a new one in stock and he said no, but that he could get one, and I told him to check into it. And I remember wanting to check into a lease and interest rates and I... I don't know... I was excited because it would be a way to make money and not be a slave to it all year. It would just be the seasonal thing.

Next, I was riding around with, Abel, the salesman who had replaced me and then I was somewhere at the bottom of these steps. I was getting ready to walk up them, and I asked him what the interest rates were. You know, to check into that, and I was remembering the down payment of almost 25% (I sobered up at twenty-five) and trying to do the calculating in my head with the interest rate at like 3.8%. (I left my machinery career at thirty-eight, maybe that was a sobering experience, too.)

Then I was in the community of Westley, where I used to work. I was telling a couple of people about the idea I had, and I was thinking how I could harvest for these brothers who farmed, how they would probably hire me to work for them, and it would be a good paying account, it would be a good account all the way around, a good thing for them and a good thing for me. I was telling their foreman about the idea and he was all excited. Yeah, yeah, yeah, yeah, he was interested in that and then I was with him, and I remember one of the brothers was in the background of the dream, and he was even kind of for it.

The next thing I knew I was pulling onto... up behind the foreman's brother, his youngest brother who had a white truck with a trap wagon behind it, and he was where the fuel pump was, and I needed to get fuel. So we drove up and we had to... he had to move. He had to get out of our way, so we drove up and I was with the foreman, and we had to ask his brother to pull up, and that's where everybody else, the foreman's brothers, and the brother who was one of the farmers were. The foreman's brother got in and pulled the truck up, and... or I got in and started... it was a diesel and it had glow... glow-plugs, you had to wait for a second to start it, so I did and then started it and we pulled forward and then I woke up.

The foreman's brother is the same image I had in a dream when I quit John Deere. He was flipping me off when he was changing a tire, and I was checking out this beautiful girl in my dream. It was over two years ago. He was the trickster in that dream. Oh, and the brother who is a partner is Parsifal-like, the innocent fool.

April 14, 2001 - 9 p.m.

It happened! We actually were able to come together

again. I called Kelli this morning, met her after breakfast at the Killarney Great Southern Hotel. I even met her mother who is also quite a stunning woman. Now I know where Kelli inherited her beauty.

Instead of having tea, I suggested that we walk. I thought Kelli might have some things to say and I wanted to be walking at her side instead of sitting across from her in what might appear to be a place of judgment.

"Did you know it was a full moon last Saturday?"

"Yeah, I think so."

"It was. I remember standing in Blackrock waiting for you in a state of confusion, and I looked up and saw it coming and going behind the clouds. I just started laughing. I knew that something else was going on, something much bigger than me."

"I'm so sorry. I'm surprised that you're even talking to me."

"I'm not telling you this to make you feel bad."

"I actually started walking there that evening..." Kelli started to explain.

"I had given up on you earlier in the day when I didn't hear from you. I got into my rental car and drove south to Wexford. When I got your message, I was in this computer store checking my e-mail. That's when I called you and rushed back all excited that we were actually going to get together again."

"I've got to put on my glasses. I can't look you in the eyes right now," Kelli said, as she reached into her pocket for her sunglasses.

"You can look me in the eye. I'm not saying this to make you feel bad. I'm just telling you what happened to me then," I said, putting my arm around her shoulder and giving her a quick squeeze.

"When I was walking to meet you for dinner that evening, I started thinking how I'd met you in Carmel, and how I was going to Spain, but that didn't work out, and how all this time has passed, and I'm still staying with my mother, and I don't even have my own place yet..." Kelli explained.

"I knew it. I just knew something like that was happening to you. That's why I wanted to come here. Remember when I said it was like we weren't finished yet, that I felt we had to come together because we weren't finished exchanging whatever it was that we had met for in the first place?"

Kelli nodded, as we continued our walk towards Killarney's lower lake.

"Perhaps you were going through some sort of reorientation. That's why you got sick and couldn't meet me for dinner. Thank you for following yourself. That was an important thing you did."

"I just felt so awful, and then I thought how selfish. I mean, it's not like I have a family or kids of my own that have to count on me. I don't work for some big business where they have to rely on me, and then I couldn't even meet you like I said I would."

"Like I said Kelli, thank you for following yourself."

"I think it has something to do with being the oldest child. I'm like a cat when I get sick."

"You want to be left alone."

"Yes, you know."

"It was the moon that clued me in the other night. I was standing there, worried what might have happened to you. I called…"

"I had my mobile phone turned on. I don't know why it didn't ring through to me. Often times it doesn't give me a chance to answer," she explained, as if she needed to justify herself.

"I believe you. That's why I'm here. You don't strike me as someone who would jerk me around."

"I'm not. That's why I feel so bad."

"Well, you can feel bad all you want, but there's no need on my behalf."

"I interrupted you about the moon," Kelli said.

"Oh, I was just saying how I was all bummed earlier in the day. Then I got that message from you about looking forward to dinner, and I got all excited and hurried back to meet you on time. You weren't there and I thought perhaps you were upset that I was late. You didn't answer your mobile when I phoned, but I still waited around hoping to hear from you. After a while, I looked up and saw the full moon beaming from behind the clouds and started to laugh."

"Laugh?"

"Yeah, that's when I knew something magical was happening, you not being there had nothing to do with me. It was far greater than my miniature world."

"I do hope you know that."

"Well, I did at the time, but then I went in and out of it for the next few days; it was good for me. It brought me back to myself. I had to go back to those places of doubt, places that I thought I had dealt with and mastered. I had to reconnect with those lost parts of myself. I mean, I had to go to some pretty lonely places..."

"I'm so sorry..."

"Kelli, thank you."

"But..."

"You know, I think there's already enough guilt and shame in this world. I really don't want to be a part of all that crap. So like I said, if you want to go on feeling bad about all of this, go right ahead, but it isn't going to be on my behalf."

We continued our walk to the Killarney's lower lake, walked out onto a cobblestone dock that had been built into the water, and sat down to visit. The wind was blowing lightly. Kelli asked about Adam, about our friendship, and we talked about that for a while. She recognized how Adam knew that I needed to be loved in a certain fashion, and how he was able to do just that.

I then learned of how, years ago, Kelli had been married and lived in England, and eventually left the marriage with only two suitcases. That was when she returned to Ireland. She heard about the Esalen Institute and went to a party that a friend insisted she attend. She went, by chance met someone who had recently spent some time at Esalen, visited with this person for ten minutes, and left the party. It wasn't long before Kelli was Esalen bound, her one-month stay extending into years.

The wind started to pick up, so we decided to leave the dock and move on. We arrived at the Killarney Lake Hotel, located right on the shores of the lower lake. Kelli and her mother had booked a room there for the next two nights.

"I had my doubts about seeing you again, but a couple of nights ago I had a dream. I was playing ping-pong with a woman, and then for some reason we became a team..." I teased her, saying something about us being a match made in heaven. "Now you don't have to take that literally, but it showed me what was going on inside of me, it showed me how the masculine and feminine energies inside me were relating. Once I had the dream, it was like I relaxed. For some reason, I knew that we'd come together again," I explained as we walked towards the hotel.

Kelli listened without responding to my dream. We made our way into the hotel through the back entrance, and found a seat next to a fireplace where we warmed ourselves and ordered tea. I talked about the loneliness I had felt for the last few days, how I missed my home, about wanting to rent a cabin somewhere in the States, a cabin with a fireplace, and making it my home, at least for a while.

"I don't know. I'd just like to feel stable for a while."

"Whatever stable is," Kelli responded.

"Yeah, in three years I'll probably still be looking for stability."

"And in thirty years we'll be all hunched over, with canes, still looking for stability," Kelli said, laughing about the image she had dreamed up.

I thought about Adam. At eighty-five it appeared he no longer searched for stability; it was more like he'd given up the illusion of its attainment. If there was anything that Adam had taught me, and he had taught me much, it was that life was ambiguous.

After tea, Kelli and I walked back to the city center. The wind had died down and it was sunny. Walking, we were solicited by several horsemen who were offering discounted carriage rides.

"I'd bet a large sum of money I wouldn't be getting these offers if I was walking alone," I teased.

"They might offer to take you for free," Kelli quipped.

We teased and joked with each other on our walk back to Killarney, teased about Leprechauns and other things Irish.

"Now remember, if you spot a Leprechaun, don't blink," she giggled.

"That's exactly what I did wrong last Saturday. I blinked and she got away!"

"And you didn't even get to make a wish."

"Oh, now, don't you bet on that one," I quickly answered.

Kelli then told me about her brother's friend. Years ago, he had dressed up as a Leprechaun; some tourist company had hired him. "It was when the tourism industry in Ireland was just getting started. A bus would be hauling a group of people through one of the more boring stretches where my brother's friend had been hired to run across the road or through a field to shake things up a bit."

"You Irish certainly have a way of your own," I answered.

We walked into town, and picked up the book I'd forgotten at the bookstore the day before. Then we decided to take a ride out towards the Ring of Kerry.

"Would you like some air?" I asked, rolling down the driver's side window.

"Sure, I'll take all the air I can get, but I must warn you, I have a habit of hanging out of the window like a dog," Kelli teased.

Winding through the countryside, I asked Kelli about Jasper, a Boxer dog she once mentioned in an e-mail letter. Kelli reminisced about how one of her Boxers had gone into heat and was visited by the Dalmatian from down the street. They ended up with a litter of spotted boxer pups.

"I had an Irish setter," I announced.

"Yeah, I bet you did," she said, as if I should have come up with a better one than that.

"No, really I did. She was my eighth grade graduation gift."

"Okay."

"When she went into heat, my brother Freeman and I went out and found a stray male Irish setter and brought him home. That dog didn't know what he was in for. Probably thought we were going to sell him into slavery, but he ended up being thrown the biggest bone he'd had for a while. I guess she did too, though."

Kelli smiled without responding.

We continued our drive. It was a beautiful day, although I wasn't focused on what was happening outside of the car. We talked about art, images and dreams. Kelli spoke of her travels down to South America and spending time with the indigenous

Indians of that region.

Somehow, I began to speak about my cousin, John Thomas, who had died when he was just seven. I was just a few months older than John Thomas. For years, I was unaware of the huge impact his death had on me because of the guilt I felt for having survived. Then I started talking about Gian, a friend of mine whose grandfather had passed away a year earlier, about how I made sure I connected with him on the day of his grandfather's funeral. I remembered how lonely it was when John Thomas died, how much I needed an adult to reach out to me, to recognize me, to tell me it was all right to be alive.

"How do you spell Gian?" Kelli asked.

"G-I-A-N."

"That's so odd. You're not going to believe this. Well, maybe you will. My ex-mother-in-law gave me a locket when she was dying. Inside the word 'Gian' is engraved. I've never heard the word since, and I have no idea what it means. She literally handed it to me right before she died," Kelli explained, as a dog that looked like a Boxer darted across the road several hundred feet ahead of us.

"Did you see that?" I asked.

"It looked like a Boxer."

"A huh," I nodded, and then shut up.

Our magical drive came to an end around four that afternoon when I pulled into the Killarney Lake Hotel. I parked and accompanied Kelli into the lobby.

"I'll be around for a few more days," Kelli said, preparing to say goodbye.

"I'll call," I said, waiting for her response, but got none. "Shall I call?"

"Yes," she nodded. Then we embraced and said goodbye.

Before retiring to my room, I stopped at a restaurant in Killarney for an early dinner of Shepherd's Pie and chips. After eating, I checked my e-mail at a café a couple of doors down from the restaurant and found a most welcome message from Adam saying that he missed me.

When I returned to the car, I noticed a missed call on my mobile, so I checked the voice mail. There was a message from Kelli saying that she'd had a nice time, and enjoyed my company.

She invited me to join them for dinner the following evening after they had returned from visiting her uncle in Castleisland. I called her.

"Hi Kelli."

"Oh, hi, Malcolm."

"I'm sorry I missed your call. I stopped for an early dinner. Listen, I had a wonderful time today, as well. I'd love to get together with you again tomorrow."

"Good. I'm not sure when we'll be back from Castleisland, though."

"Just phone me. Actually, call me anytime."

"Okay, good, then I'll see you tomorrow."

"Tomorrow it is."

April 15, 2001 - 5 p.m.

I slept so tight that I didn't know where I was when I woke up. It was as if I'd just arisen from the dead. I phoned Kelli, leaving a message on her voice mail saying I was going down to breakfast and that she could phone later, or I would.

Down in the dining room both tables were filled. I'd been spoiled. This was the first time there were other guests at the Dagda House beside myself; robbed of the titty once again. There was actually an empty seat at each table, but I didn't care to socialize in the morning nor would I invade the space of others. I hated imposing as well as being imposed upon. Besides all that, I didn't like to share.

I sat in an armchair on the other side of the room, thinking that one of the parties might soon finish. Then it felt as if I may be causing them to rush, so I walked up to my room and sorted through my dirty laundry, not wanting to be hovering over the other guests in anticipation of getting my shot at the titty. Fifteen minutes later, Niall knocked on my door to say that a table was free.

I ate cereal, toast, and a banana, and returned to my room. I was scheduled to fly out of Dublin to Paris tomorrow at noon, and wanted to check into continuing my stay. The holidays in Ireland extended over to the following Monday, and I didn't want to risk being trapped in traffic and missing my flight. I also wanted to be in a position to spend more time with Kelli if the opportunity presented itself.

Again I tried to change my Dublin-Paris flight to Zurich, and again was unsuccessful. I didn't want to spend another three hundred pounds when I had already paid for the ticket to Paris, as well as a rail pass. My flight from Zurich back to San Francisco left at four-twenty in the afternoon on Thursday, the 19th, so I ended up changing my flight from Dublin to Paris from Monday at noon to Wednesday at seven in the morning. That way I'd have time to catch the TGV at noon in Paris and be in Zurich at ten that evening, giving me a night in Zurich and a time cushion in case something went wrong.

After shuffling my flight and phoning the rental car company to inform them that I'd need the car for an extra two days, I drove into Killarney, and walked into the city center for coffee at the Bean House. I ordered an Americano and sat close to the entrance. Some man in his mid to late twenties came in, ordered a piece of pie to go and then sat down at the table in front of me to read the paper.

Not long after the guy sat down, a buddy of his showed up and they greeted each other with a "hello mate." They were quite excited to see each other, and must have had plans, because shortly after their greeting, the two pals were on their way out the door, and one of the girls working behind the counter had to remind the first mate that he had yet to pay for his pie. It was an honest mistake, a mere distraction from his excitement. The poor guy turned red with embarrassment, and his friend's laughter along with mine didn't help matters. He paid the bill with money and his fine with embarrassment, and was out the door in a flash, most likely never to return.

Kelli phoned while I was having coffee.

"Hi Malcolm, it's Kelli."

"Hi Kelli. How are you?"

"I'm fine. We're almost in Castleisland. We passed by the Dagda House earlier. I think I saw you in the window. Were you wearing something white?"

"Yes, my sweater. I was on the phone changing my flight from tomorrow to Wednesday."

"Oh, I didn't realize you were leaving so soon."

"Yes, and it was too soon. I was feeling cramped, you know, but I got it all squared away."

"Good. By the way, Happy Easter."

"Oh, thank you. Happy Easter to you, too."

"I don't know how long we'll be here in Castleisland. It's been so long since my mother was last here that we aren't exactly sure where he lives, and we didn't phone ahead because we want to surprise him."

"What's your uncle's name?"

"Uncle Jack," Kelli answered. "And what are you doing today?"

"Right now I'm having a cup of coffee at the Bean House in Killarney."

"People watching, huh?" she laughed.

"You know it," I answered, laughing along with her. She had my number, probably had it long before ever meeting me.

"Listen, Malcolm, I'll call you when we get back to Killarney to set a time for dinner."

"Sounds good, have fun."

"You too."

"Good luck finding Uncle Jack."

"I'm sure we'll need it..."

The Bean was pretty dead when I first arrived, but business began to pick up. I was seated in a non-smoking section, which was a privilege for me while in Europe. In California, smoking isn't allowed at all in restaurants; Europe is quite the opposite.

I was actually spending Easter in Europe, and in Ireland, to boot. I thought about celebrating in Belfast, but Kelli wasn't up that way. As much as I hate to admit it, I'm in Ireland for Kelli, or at least my believed desire for her. I wonder how much longer I'll be chasing her? Where will she lead me next? What in the hell am I doing here anyway? I know what I am doing, searching. I'm searching for what's been sought after for centuries, perhaps since the beginning of time, that is if time even exists: the Holy Grail.

Some goofy fuck with a half-ass Amish-cut beard and his wife sat at the table that the pie-thief had vacated. The fuck-head was full of himself, one of those bastards who had all life's answers. He was in his fifties, and had a crew cut; a chubby fuck wearing a gray wool sweater. His wife sat with her back to me. A friend of theirs joined them, another man, probably divorced, a tall, thin, lengthy fellow, a few years younger than the Amish-fuck. I took them for teachers by what I could hear of their conversation. I couldn't make out everything, only parts of their rhetoric.

The fat-fuck started comparing something in Ireland with America, something that seemed trivial, an excuse just to be making noise. He said something that he thought was funny and then let out this loud belly laugh, following it up with "Americana, Americana... I'm tired of hearing about the Americans."

The fat leprechaun fucker forgot where his ancestors had flocked to in times of famine and other economic hardships. Laugh all you want you chubby fuck, just don't blink next time your life goes to the shitter. I'm not suggesting that America is the world's savior, but there have been plenty of times when she's been there to offer a helping hand to those in need.

Their conversation shifted to where the skinny teacher had the wife and her cackling husband sitting silent and hanging on his every word as if he were Christ just arisen from the grave. Occasionally, chubby fuck would look over to me, like he was concerned that I might be listening to him, then he'd turn back to chew on his buddy's... the prophet's tongue.

I'm going home in a few days. It's right that I've been in Ireland for this length of time. I finally connected with Kelli. Even if nothing comes of it, it's right for me to have stuck things out and stayed around to give us the chance to come together again.

Kelli isn't as fucked up as I wanted to make her when things weren't falling into my lap, my universe's order. But I'm not going to make a home in Ireland, not even attempt to do so, even if she does decide she wants to have something more than a friendship. No, I have to get home to take care of business. I have bills to pay and I've an airplane to sell so that I can pay my bills.

Maybe I'll move to Lake Tahoe when I return to the States? I used to spend a lot of time there and loved it. Yeah, that sounds good, maybe I'll find a place on the backside of Kingsbury Grade, on the Nevada side, down around Genoa, at the base of the Carson Valley, or maybe over on the Northshore, somewhere around Tahoe City. Hell, I don't know. All I know is that I have to get back to the States soon to wrap up the loose ends that have been dangling for the last few years. I need to find a home for the Bonanza, and for myself. I might even take a job, or not.

The know-it-all, cackling, chubby-fuck and his party left, so I decided that I could probably stomach some lunch. I ordered a tuna melt. After eating, I checked my e-mail at an Internet café across the street, and went on over to the Killarney Great Southern Hotel. There was an open seat next to the fireplace, the same seat I sat in while waiting for Kelli just yesterday.

A man was playing the piano in the lobby. Music filled the air; it was peaceful. I still can't get over all the flat-assed Irish women. It has to be genetic; what else?

Jenny, who didn't have a flat ass, which didn't matter because she didn't like to fuck anyway, had sent an e-mail. I had tried to get her to bed for six months, and it had all been in vain, her excuse being that she'd lost her sex drive. The harder I tried to help her find it, the more misplaced it became.

Anyway, Jenny's e-mail said she thought she was starting a mid-life crisis. Starting, hell, she was a mid-life crisis. She wrote how she'd had a hormone test and that she was in menopause. She said it was nice to have finally discovered the source of her discontentment. Hell, she was only thirty-years-old. She told me that I was her menopause man. What a fucking honor; I never even got a blowjob out of the deal!

She was just another woman who doesn't know how to have me, but doesn't know how to let me go, either. That's been my story for the last couple of years: all kinds of women in my life, just none that can give all of themselves to me. I tried to sit and wait without hope or desire. I've been dancing in the realm of a silent void, in a space of terror; yet, it isn't bravery or by choice. It is either that or death, and I'm too damn afraid of dying. I suppose this aloneness has a purpose. I'm making my way through some sort of passage, but it's hard to evaluate something while caught in its throes.

It's time to stop selling myself. I have nothing more to

prove, no need to impress, not even myself. If love is earned, it's nothing more than chattel, something that can be traded: one illusion swapped for another. I no longer have the time or desire to chase this futile recompense.

My whole life has been centered on selling myself, convincing others of my worth, and when they bought, I was convinced that I had value. So, if I no longer have the need to sell myself, then what will be my new form of living, the motivating factor in my life?

The piano echoed through the halls of the Great Southern. It's music! That is my motivating factor, art, the revelation of the chords that resonate through the halls of my inner universe. Do I sing? Of course I do. I sing, dance, laugh, cry, scream I love you, and I hope you fucking die, all to an unknown, yet so terribly prevailing God.

I've been dancing in hell for the last few years, dancing to the symphony of chaos, to the chants of demons, crying to the prince of darkness, Yahweh, to set me free. I want so badly to leave this heaven or hell, to return to my old familiar home. I want to live again, I want to love, and I want to play.

A little redheaded Irish boy came whisking in through the revolving door. He ran twenty feet past the entryway, stopped, and grabbed his privates, trying to decide which of three hallways would take him to the nearest toilet. He ran down the hall to the right, but the bathroom wasn't there, actually it wasn't down any of the three hallways; it was through a door in an adjacent room. The boy came back to the three-way intersection, I pointed to the fourth direction and off he went, running as if he was chasing an ice cream truck.

That lucky little guy has a lot of years ahead of him, years of looking, searching, and for much more than a simple toilet, although right then finding the toilet was probably one of the grandest treasures he'd stumbled upon in awhile.

People continued to reel in through the revolving door, walking directly to the fire, consciously or unconsciously being drawn to this source, and the piano man continued playing as souls from countless generations danced to the celestial tunes in the lobby of the Killarney Great Southern Hotel and throughout the rest of the world as well.

Making the passage through the revolving door, I stepped out into another world. It was sunny; a few clouds floated over like stray sheep. I was waiting, as I had waited for my ex-wife, for her presence, her loyal undivided attention, which I never did receive, just as I had waited in vain for Lauren, Jacqueline, the menopause girl with the succulent ass, and my mother, too.

I walked into an outlet shopping mall across the street from the Great Southern. The mall was full of people spending their Easter Sunday afternoon consuming.

What am I really waiting for; something to be different? Maybe the waiting keeps me going, gives me a reason to keep living. Maybe it has, but the wait now seems to be more of a thief as opposed to the Great Mother.

Perhaps it's time to go into the waiting, to see who it is, what it really wants? No one can stop this relentless cry, no one but myself, by communing with this unknown deity. It might only need recognition instead of avoidance; it might only have the need to be heard? It might actually prove to be my helper?

Who are you bullshitting you silly fuck? You're just trying to make yourself feel better.

Maybe I am, but I need to test it, find out for myself. It's possibly an unexpressed energy, an entity needing a voice that is allowed to laugh or cry, an entity that might only want to step out of its isolated hell and into communion with another. Maybe this is all right, no wrongness in it at all.

Maybe that's what everyone in that mall was trying to buy back, a piece of themselves, pieces of their scattered souls. And, then again, maybe they weren't, maybe they weren't having my experience, maybe they were content unto themselves, and the solitude, this being alone, is my own terror.

I returned to my room at the Dagda House. In allegiance, clouds of sheep float over from west to east. I'm staring into a mirror that hangs over a desk. My face is fat, my eyebrows need trimming; ten years have sailed by.

I'm not a tractor salesman any longer; I'm not married. I'm nothing that I once believed myself to be. Yet, I have to be more than a nothing. I'm alive, breathing, eating. Or am I? It feels as if I might be dead. My heart still beats. I have to count; somehow, somewhere, there must be a place for me? I'm searching, trying to justify my life, looking for a reason, an excuse to exist. I need something, someone to give me permission to be. "Yahweh, are you dead?"

God isn't who he once was. He's just as much gone as the person I once was. Where'd you go? Where'd we go? How can I even expect to be communing with who you once were, who I once was, who we once were? I'm no longer an iron peddler; we're divorced. We've changed, grown apart, can no longer relate and have no need for each other any longer. We have fallen from grace, out of relationship, out of love, and into hell. I've died, and along with me, God has died, too.

That's my emptiness, a longing for communion with God, but I have no image of my longed for new lover, other than my need for Her to meet and receive me where I am, to love me, take me by the hand and walk with me, kiss me, make love to me. My God, She's a woman!

April 16, 2001 - 3 p.m.

The wind is crisp, cold. I'm sitting in the square across from Bantry Bay, under the outstretched arms of a statue that could possibly be Christ, or the image of another venerated saint calming the seas. I feel peaceful. When Kelli and I parted last night, the possibility of our coming together again was left open. She had plans of attending the concert in Bantry. I didn't want to invite myself. She said that I was welcome to join her, but I didn't want to impose. Kelli and her mother were meeting friends who are to accompany them to the concert, so I left it for her to call when she knew more of what was happening, giving her the space to invite me later if it felt right. It's now three in the afternoon, and I've yet to hear from her.

We finally met at the Killarney Lake Hotel at seven-thirty last night. She and her mother got lost trying to find Uncle Jack's place, and once they arrived, found that he had recently been taken to the hospital in Cork City. They never did get to see him, although they may drive to Cork tomorrow to check on him.

We decided to stay at the Lake, because Kelli had been

driving all day, and it was a warm and accommodating place anyway. I had expected her mother to join us, but when Kelli came down from the room she mentioned that her mom might join us for tea later, but that wasn't certain. We sat in the lounge area and ordered some sandwiches. Her mother eventually did join us. Kelli told her about my attending the Mary Magdalene seminar with the twenty women.

"It's not certain that Mary Magdalene really was a whore," I commented.

"Perhaps she was, and that's why Jesus fell in love with her? Maybe he wanted an experienced woman?" her mother suggested.

"You know, I kind of like that idea," I said, a bit taken back by mom's response.

"What's the matter Kelli? Are you above all this?" her mother asked, as Kelli looked on with a smile trying to hide her look of uncertainty. She appeared to be concerned with what her mother might be coming up with next.

"I understand that these men didn't become sexually active until they were in their twenties," Kelli answered, avoiding her mother's question.

"Yeah, so he needed an experienced woman because he had a lot of catching up to do," I joked.

"Tell me Malcolm, what was it like, being with all those women?" Mom asked after our laughter settled.

"At times I felt privileged and other times I asked myself: 'what in the hell am I doing here?' Most of them were psychologists, you know," I answered, knowing that Kelli's mother was a psychologist herself.

"Well, here in Ireland, we like to say the psychologists are the ones who are all fucked up!" Mom explained, and we all roared with laughter again. We were laughing so much that I think we were disturbing some of the other guests, but maybe that was my own thing.

After a brief visit and some more hearty laughter, Mom excused herself. Then I told Kelli that I was there, as a voice that had been sent to ask her to return to California, and that it was a voice beyond my ego. Man, if that wasn't a bullshit line, shoot me.

She continued to listen to my rhetoric, and I could tell that she was getting tired. Occasionally a silence fell and then we would pick up on something else. We were both tired, but I didn't want to leave, and yet, I didn't want to talk anymore either. I felt as if I was pushing for something but just wasn't sure for what.

One thing that I did notice was how we kept getting interrupted. It was as if something was trying to block our communion. People would walk up and want to sit with us. Two girls wanted to sit at our table and smoke, and another couple wanted to have a drink, neither of them stayed. They just engaged us long enough to rob us of what was being exchanged or trying to be exchanged. It was weird; it happened several times. In reflection, her mother in some ways had also brought an interrupting confusion to our table.

We were forcing conversation, and this seemed to cause greater fatigue for both of us. We decided it was time to turn in for the evening. We hugged goodnight and I lightly kissed her cheek. I became embarrassed after having kissed her, and quickly slid out between the crowd in the lobby and through the front doors of the hotel. I drove directly back to the Dagda House and went to bed.

I felt as if I should have pushed for more, perhaps a kiss on the lips. It was the same feeling I had when I was visiting with her; that feeling like something was going unsaid, unexpressed. It must be my imminent departure, the possibility that I might never see her again. One voice was telling me to push, make a move, but a stronger voice said to wait. The embrace I received from Kelli this time was the most powerful and grounding hug I had received from her yet; it felt as if she was really standing within herself and able to receive me.

Lying in bed, I reflected on the evening. I'd like to convince myself that I don't need anything else to happen, but I damn sure want something else, or I think I do anyway. Sitting with her in the lounge at the Killarney Lake Hotel, I didn't want to go back to the Dagda House, nor did I want to keep on talking. I wanted to commune with her in a different fashion. I simply wanted to cuddle up with her in silence, or did I?

Then I knew that the kiss on her cheek was enough. It was

right to allow a space, so that the amalgamation of our spirits can take place. If that proves successful, then perhaps we'll be able to commune in another fashion. I've had sex with a fair share of women, but it isn't just sex that I want with Kelli. It would be nice for certain, but...

So it's three in the afternoon, I haven't heard from her. I've pretty much left it up to Kelli to phone. She told me where and when the concert is, but it still doesn't feel right to just show up, so if I don't hear from her again, I won't attend.

April 16, 2001 - Midnight

I decided to drive out to Sheep's Head, the farthest point on the southern peninsula of Bantry. It's a narrow peninsula, kind of like the pinky, but not really. It's below the Beara Peninsula, the ring finger; these two peninsulas form Bantry Bay.

My disappointment was returning, but I wasn't devastated. I wasn't quite sure how to have her in my life, even if she did want to be a part of it. Kelli is gorgeous, smart, witty, sexy, and everything else I've ever dreamed of, but she doesn't know where her life is going. Hell, she just left California and now here I am trying to drag her back, and all fueled by selfishness. Hell, I don't know what's to become of me either, my life is just as much in a transitional state as Kelli's life is, and on top of that, we live on opposite sides of the world. My heart's aching to be back in the States, but even more it's aching to have a woman in my life, aching for love.

The drive out to Sheep's Head was breathtaking. The farther I drove the narrower the road became until the passageway was only wide enough for a single car. Driving became work, calling for much of my divided attention as it bounced back and forth between the road, and what-ifs. I could hear seagulls cawing and screeching, much like my guts were. I felt so alone, a man without a home. I wondered if I'd ever feel at home again? I ached; oh, did I ache. What the fuck was wrong with me?

I stopped at Sheep's Head. Actually I didn't have a choice as the road came to an end. It was desolate and windy. There was a lone house on the point. The mountains sloped several hundred feet down to the bay. To the south was another desolate peninsula.

There was a snack-bar trailer at the end of the road. A man was treating his two little girls to a pop and snack. He was trying to get them moving back into the car so they could get on the road. It wasn't really a place for kids. It appeared he was a divorced man who occasionally had the kids on the weekends. The countryside and scenery was magnificent, but, as a child, I'd have found the drive quite boring because there was nothing to do, nothing to look forward to after having arrived. I purchased a bottle of water, took a few photos, and climbed back into the rental car for the drive back to civilization.

I parked on the square in Bantry and walked into a hotel to check on possibly renting a room. There were vacancies, but it didn't feel right to commit to a room just yet. I walked back to the car and sat inside, staring out into the square in front of me, at a statue of a man by the name of Tone who was some sort of historical figure. I was feeling sorry for myself again, feeling exactly how I didn't want to feel.

Then it hit me. I was getting what I wanted. If I believed that Kelli didn't want to be with me, then I wouldn't be with her. I was creating my own hell. My negativity invited a negative. I wasn't open to her when I was in this hellish place, or to any woman for that matter. As long as I remained there, I would continue to solicit the same response. It was a self-fulfilling prophesy; a response to the morphic energy that was oozing from within me.

Again, I was lying to myself. If I really wanted to see Kelli, I'd have gone to that concert, I'd have been there, and instead of being honest with myself, I put the blame on her, for not calling me, not inviting me. I had gone into my funk, wanting to make it her fault because of her lack of response to me. I was putting my funk out onto the world, because I wasn't willing to be responsible for myself. When I put the funk out, I got it back, and when I put something else out, that something else is what I got back. I don't like labeling it positive or negative, but whatever it's called, it was still a form of energy that I emitted and the world reflected back to me. Yeah, energy, instead of naming it good or bad, right or wrong, positive or negative...

Let's just say I got what I put out. What comes out of me is what comes back to me.

I wasn't with them at that concert because I didn't want to be there, yet I was blaming Kelli. I really wanted to be alone, with her alone, and if I couldn't be with her that way, then the hell with it, and that was exactly why I was alone, that was exactly why she hadn't phoned.

I left Bantry and drove back towards Dublin. I took the back roads, avoiding all the traffic, the grand finale of the Easter weekend. A fox darted across the road. I love foxes. Next, I passed through a group of men on the outskirts of Mallow. It appeared to be a gathering after a funeral service. It was just a bunch of men standing around outside, in a yard along the side of the road.

The next curve was sharp. The camera slid off my lap, hit the seatbelt button and it unlatched: a case of cause and effect. Things are linked, timing and all, everything has to be set up in a certain perfect-like order for a seatbelt to actually become unlatched, or stay latched. And that's not only the case with seatbelts; things have to click.

April 17, 2001 - Dream Fragment

A woman, possibly Kelli... she was angry. I'm not sure why, but she was angry, and it was a side I had yet to see of her. Is she angry because I am leaving and not pursuing her any longer? This is my Kelli, the Kelli within, but could it be my friend Kelli as well?

April 18, 2001 - 2:30 a.m. - Wednesday Morning

At eleven Monday evening I stopped at a hotel in Abbeyleix, about an hour from Dublin. After haggling over the price, I paid for a room. I had breakfast yesterday, Tuesday morning, and then checked out of the room in Abbeyleix. Purposely, I left my Wolverine work boots behind in the hotel room. I'll soon be returning home, and I don't need to be lugging around an extra pair of shoes. Besides, I can only wear one pair at a time, so getting rid of the work boots lightened my load. Pulling out of the hotel parking lot, I phoned Kelli.

"Good morning."

"Malcolm, good morning."

"I looked for you last night at the concert."

"Yeah, I kind of felt like I was imposing, so I decided to start my drive back to Dublin."

"You wouldn't have been imposing, but we were late getting there. It was a mess. We got lost just like when we went to look for my uncle in Castleisland."

"Getting lost in this country isn't hard to do," I laughed.

"Where are you?"

"About an hour west of Dublin. A place called Abbeyleix."

"Oh, my, you did start back. We're just leaving Bantry for Cork. We're going to try to find Uncle Jack before making our way back to Blackrock. I would like to see you again before you leave."

"I need to go to Dublin and find a place to reserve a seat on the train, and it sounds like you might be several hours away. Why don't you phone my mobile when you get to Blackrock?"

"Okay, I'll do that."

I finished the drive to Dublin, and then spent almost four hours before finally succeeding in making a reservation on the TGV from Paris to Zurich. It took an hour to find an agency that was tied to the computer system that could actually make such a reservation. Then it was another hour before I was able to speak to an agent as they were short-staffed; it took the agent almost two hours to figure out how to process the reservation. They had a new computer system, and no one seemed to know how it worked. It nearly took as long to reserve a seat, as the actual train ride will be.

I almost left three different times. Right when I was ready to walk, they assured me that it would only be a couple more minutes; what they really meant was a couple more hours. They finally placed a phone call to the main office in London and someone walked the clerk through the program step by step. Once they had the magic formula, I was on my way in no time, and eight pounds ninety pence later I had my reservation. I ended up with a seat from Paris to Lausanne, and then changing trains for Lausanne to Zurich.

I hoofed it back to the parking lot, which was south of the Liffey, near the end of Grafton Street by St. Stephen's Green. After spinning around a few roundabouts, I miraculously whipped out southbound and drove to Blackrock. I snuck in through an exit and parked in the same parking lot where I'd parked the evening I was to meet Kelli for dinner.

After sorting through my plane and train tickets and other important travel documents, I started walking to the center of Blackrock, which was only a block away. I noticed two pretty girls in the window as I passed a hair salon, so I stopped my gait towards Insomnia where I'd planned to have an afternoon coffee. They didn't look busy, so I decided to see about a haircut.

Leon was gorgeous; I mean hotter than hot. She was not yet thirty, a blue-eyed brunette with the most beautiful body I'd seen in quite some time. Her breasts were magnificent. Well, I actually didn't get to see them, but she was braless, her top was this thin black spandex-like material. They were perfectly round, about the size of medium grapefruits... I mean, her nipples were beckoning me, and she had time to cut my hair. She had an ass to die for as well, and it wasn't flat, far from it. Actually, it had the perfect tilt. She had a smile to die for, too. Leon was perfect. Her assistant washed my hair, and then brought me a cup of tea, with cream. Maybe there are some women left in this world who really do like men?

I was right about the men graying prematurely in Ireland. Leon confirmed my observation. I told her that I had just turned forty a few months ago, and she mentioned that most Irish men at forty had quite a weathered look.

"Yeah, the men seem like real men here. None of that sissy stuff," I said, testing her response.

"They like to think they're tough anyway," Leon answered, sounding as if she knew that men had another side that they preferred to keep hidden.

It made me laugh. It wasn't just an Irish trait.

"How's that?" she asked, as she stepped back to let me have a look at myself in the mirror.

"Great," I answered. It was the best haircut I've had in years. Not only did I like how she looked; I even liked how I looked, and that was a miracle in itself.

"Now there's no need to rush off. You can stay and finish your tea."

"How much do I owe you?"

"Fifteen pounds."

"Here you go," I said, handing her twenty. "I don't want change, but I would like to borrow your phonebook," I added. I needed the phone number for the hotel at the airport to book a room.

From my mobile, I phoned the hotel while finishing the tea. They wanted a hundred pounds for the night, the next closest place was in Swords, north of the airport where I'd purchased the mobile phone several days ago; they wanted sixty pounds for the night. I booked with neither of the hotels; I'd be damned if I was going to pay that much for a room. I probably should have had the same impatient attitude and walked away from the agency that had reserved my seat on the TGV earlier this afternoon.

After dragging out my teatime and admiring my haircutter's finer features for as long as I thought respectable, I thanked her and made my way to the center of Blackrock. I noticed a lot of pretty girls, more per capita than most of the areas I'd visited. Pretty girls are everywhere, but a greater concentration of them seemed to be hanging around Blackrock. It made sense; it was an area where the well-to-do resided. I ended up at Café Java, across the street from the Wicked Wolf.

I thought about phoning Kelli, and her 'fucked up' psychologist mother who I'd have no problem falling in love with as well. Hell, I think I already have.

I ordered a café mocha and settled into a booth. I was beginning to relax, now that I had my reservations all in order. I didn't particularly want to leave Kelli behind. I was just getting to know her, but things had to be taken care of back in the States. I still needed to sell the airplane, and bills had to be paid, things that just wouldn't take care of themselves no matter how much I willed them to be gone.

I phoned Kelli, got her voice mail and left a message. What did it matter if I saw her again or not? Nothing different was going to happen, not that I could foresee anyway. My guess was that the mother-daughter team was at least two hours from Blackrock, maybe more.

When I get home, I'm going to shit-can more stuff. I have some furniture to sell, and several articles of clothing that I've never worn, things that can use a new home. I'll have a garage sale at my grandmother's house. She lives on a busy road that will attract the bargain-hunters in my hometown. It's the same home where countless dreams of my youth took place and molded me. Yahweh will be there for damn certain. Oh well, I'll use him to keep an eye on the petty thieves. My storage unit is full of remnants from the past that need to go, too. I'll keep the memories, but that old shit, that garbage in storage is as good as gone.

Damn, there were more beautiful women running around Blackrock than ever, and like a hand in a glove they all seemed to fit into those nice, tight, black pants so well. If the nice plump hinies keep filling the gloves, I'll soon have to change my hypothesis on the hereditary flat-assed Irish woman syndrome. Things have changed. It doesn't take much to resurrect my hard-on, and that feels good. Saturday has passed; Easter morning's rock has been rolled away.

I left the Java House shortly after a brief downpour. The wind was blowing clean brisk air. It was a different air than I had breathed the evening I'd paced the very same streets looking for Kelli. It was a salty ocean breeze, a fishy scent, but nothing obnoxious. It was actually quite nice. It smelled like life, brought me into myself, right into that moment.

I retrieved the umbrella from the rental car in case of another downpour, but left my jacket behind. It was cold, but I wanted to feel the cold. There was something about the air, its crispness, its scent that was infusing my soul with new life, and I wanted to make sure that I was fully exposed to these elements.

I thought about the work boots I'd left behind in the hotel room in Abbeyleix. I had a jacket I considered leaving in the room as well. I never really did like the jacket all that much. It was a brown field coat with a leather collar that I'd purchased from a vendor while in the machinery business. Even though it was nice looking and had only been worn occasionally, I wasn't all that fond of it. I didn't like how it hung over my body, just didn't feel right. My conservative side is what kept me from leaving it behind with the boots. There was that haunting voice: "That jacket cost too damn much, and its too nice to leave behind. Bring it home and give it to your father."

For the last few years, I've been giving things away. Slowly but surely, I've been prying my fingers from what I once believed to be near and dear to my heart. The coat wasn't near to me, but I was clinging to something else that still was: an old life, images and beliefs, things that reeked of death.

Kelli phoned. She was still a couple of hours out. She and mom were having a bang up time together. She told me that they'd gotten twisted around on all the one-way streets in Cork.

"It must be that fucked up mother of yours," I teased, not quite sure how'd she take to my play.

"I'll pass that on to Mom," Kelli answered.

"Take your time. I'm already in Blackrock, and I'm not going anywhere. I'll be here whenever you arrive. I've had a crazy day, but things are finally in order. I'm relaxing now, getting ready to have some dinner."

"Okay, I'll call when I get into town."

I stepped into a pub called Shehaan's, found a comfortable seat close to the front door, and ordered a shrimp appetizer, some chips, and sparkling water. I was getting a hard-on just thinking about Kelli, about the whole thing. Our missing one another and then coming together was becoming a ritual. Not having her was driving me mad, making me want her all the more. I wondered if I'd ever have her, if I'd ever get to smell, taste... have her until she shivered speechless, until she begged me to stop, and then curl up and pass out, cupped inside of me.

Kelli phoned again after I had ordered dinner. It was noisy inside of the pub, so I walked outside to speak with her. She just wanted to know where I was so that her mother could drop her off when they arrived in Blackrock.

After eating dinner, I ordered another sparkling water. Other than with Kelli the first day we met in Dublin, and dinner at Darby O'Gill's, I hadn't frequented any pubs. I considered having a drink. It's been fifteen years. I wondered what it would be like, could I get by with one or two or end up getting smashed and waking in the gutter, or better yet, the Dublin jail. I could see it, that cackling Leprechaun would end up leading me on a wild goose chase, I'd blink, and end up treading the stale waters of the Liffey, either that, or swinging from the top of the Eiffel tower pissing down on all of the Frenchies.

Dionysus had me by the scruff of the neck for long enough; I stuck with the sparkling water, and let some old boy at the bar do my drinking for me. This guy was sucking down pints like they were lemonade on a hot southern muggy afternoon. After a while, the old boy changed from beer to whiskey. My, oh, my, did I remember those days. I usually ended up taking the back-roads, praying the whole time to be delivered from evil, and then waking up the following morning and trying to backtrack in my mind the path I'd taken home in my drunken stupor the night before.

At the other end of the bar was a group of three women and one man who was old enough to be their father, possibly even a grandfather. They'd also been pounding away the pints. They were lost in some deep conversation, probably drunken business gossip, or some family soap opera drama that was taking place in their absence, or imaginations.

A couple walked in, ordered a beer and sat down at a table with ten chairs, just the two of them. They sat at one corner of the table, facing each other, nose to nose, their knees tightly knit together. They had their own little soap opera going on, but it appeared to be real, but who knows?

Kelli phoned at ten. She called from home and suggested that we take a walk as she'd been pent up in the car for most of the day and thought a stretch would do her good. She left the house walking east, and I left the pub walking west, both of us on Garysforth Street. We met somewhere in the middle.

It was cold out and Kelli was bundled up in a heavy jacket. Her blonde hair flowed out under a gray fleece beret and her blue eyes sparkled. We embraced and then I followed her lead west on Garysforth and then south to a pub. Kelli found a seat while I walked up to the bar to order a spritzer for her and lemonade for me.

"What time is your flight out tomorrow?" Kelli asked, when

I returned with our drinks.

"Seven in the morning."

"Oh, my goodness, I hope I'm not keeping you."

"Not at all."

"Where are you staying?"

"I'll drive to the airport and get a room. I've already made arrangements to leave the car there," I explained. She must have thought me to be out of my mind. I was leaving early in the morning, it was eleven at night, and I didn't even know where I was staying.

I learned quite a bit about Kelli that evening, about her marriage, how she'd fallen in love, married on a whim, and why it didn't last. Kelli's past wouldn't permit her heart to give in to a second whim. After her marriage fell apart, she left on a tour of South America, spent almost a year with the indigenous people and after that came to Big Sur.

It was just after midnight when we started back towards her home.

"I thought I might come here and fall head over heals, madly in love with you, but it didn't happen," I confessed as we walked.

She smiled as we walked in silence for a minute before she responded. "That whole thing about falling in love is something. Why don't we ascend to love instead?"

I started to say something more about not falling in love with her, before actually being able to understand what she had just said. "If I had fallen in love with you, I might not have been able to really see you."

"They say that when you fall in love with another person, you're really falling in love with a part of yourself," Kelli suggested.

"Oh, yes, that magical other, finding in them what we can't see within ourselves."

Kelli turned to me and smiled.

"I've lost it Kelli: that whole illusion of falling in love."

"I seem to have a way of disillusioning people."

"It's not you. It happened quite a while ago. The problem is, I keep trying to return to that old lie, but I can't," I explained, Kelli slowing the pace of our walk as we approached a corner.

"I have to go here," Kelli said, as she nodded to the group of townhouses across the street.

"I'll take you there," I said, and crossed the road, walking at her side. I started to rattle on about love and stuff, but caught myself. "I guess there's a time to shut up isn't there?" I asked. Kelli didn't have to respond; I already knew the answer to my question. I quit talking, and we walked the rest of the way to the complex's gate in silence.

"This is it," Kelli said, as she stopped at the gate and turned towards me. We embraced, and I kissed her cheek. "Travel well," she said, holding her hands together in a prayer like fashion, lifting them to her chest in a namaste and then bowing.

"Thank you. I'll be talking to you," I said, continuing to look into her eyes for a few more seconds before we parted.

I started to walk away and turned to have another look. Kelli had already passed through the complex gate, and had turned to look at me as well. We waved to each other, and I continued my walk.

Ten minutes later, I slid the key into the ignition switch, fired up the red rental car and pulled out of the parking lot in Blackrock to begin the drive to the airport. It was twelve-thirty. My plane left in six and a half hours. I considered skipping the room thing and catching a few hours sleep in the car before turning it in.

I drove out of Blackrock towards the M50 that would loop me right around to the airport. I somehow missed the turn off and drove toward the heart of Dublin City center. I decided to stay with the city route because, like breadcrumbs, there were airport signs to guide me to my destination. I followed the crumbs and eventually came to a roundabout that was unclear about which exit would lead me to the airport. On a whim, I took the turn to the right, but after having done so, could no longer find the airport signs. I turned around and returned to the roundabout, this time taking the left exit, and again, no breadcrumbs. The airport signs had brought me to that roundabout, so the only other option was to continue on straight after making the half-circle, so that is exactly what I did after returning to the crossroads for a third time.

The middle road proved fruitless as well. By then I was

completely disoriented and said the hell with it and decided to let fate guide me. I thought about the little kid who came running into the Killarney Great Southern Hotel holding his privates in hope of finding the bathroom down one of the three hallways. There was no one to guide me to the hidden fourth passageway. Lost, I drove through the city streets and finally came to a sign that said Blackrock. I was only a few blocks from where I'd said goodbye to Kelli. There was a Jury's Hotel up on my right advertising forty-nine pound rooms, so I pulled in. The door was locked, but an employee spotted me.

"Do you have any rooms?"

"I'm not sure, but I'll get someone up here who knows. It'll be just a minute," he said, and then walked off to attend to his duties.

There was a group of ten or more people sitting in the lounge. They were pretty smashed, and one woman was singing an Irish tune at the top of her lungs. For being drunk, she was pretty damn good, too. Within a few minutes, a young man stepped behind the front desk.

"You're looking for a room, are you?"

"Yes sir. Have you got anything?"

"Yeah, it'll be eighty-nine pounds, not including breakfast."

"What about the forty-nine pounds you're advertising outside?"

"Those rooms are all sold out, but what the hell, I'll let you have it for that. After all, the nights damn near over anyway," he offered. It was one-thirty. I signed in, parked the car and dragged my bags to the elevator.

Something just isn't right. It doesn't take four hours to reserve a train seat. Besides that, I have no desire to return to France to be insulted. I'll get home another way, possibly via Germany. I don't care if I miss my Zurich flight. It's only one hundred fifty dollars to change the ticket; money, as well as time, is quickly losing its dictatorial influence.

I don't know what I'm doing, but I know what I'm not doing; I'm not leaving Ireland, not yet anyway. I'm also getting tired of toting around my goods in this goddamn old broken down suitcase. Things are going to get lighter from here on out.

All that really matters right now is that I get some rest. What in the hell am I doing? Where am I going? What's my name? I need a good dream to point me in the right direction. Fuck! That's all I've got to say: simply, fuck!

April 18, 2001 - 8:30 a.m.

"Hi Kelli."

"Malcolm, are you on the plane?"

"No, at Jury's..." I answered, and then went on to explain what had happened. "I'm going to see about booking a flight in a few days. I'll call you when I know what's going on."

"Sounds like we might have dinner yet," Kelli suggested.

"I hope so. I'll call you."

April 18, 2001 - 12:30 p.m.

After phoning the rental company to inform them that I still had the car, I left my room at Jury's, and in it, my big, broken-down, limping suitcase with the missing fourth wheel.

I had gone through and sorted out the clothes that I wanted to keep from ones that I had grown unattached to and threw my undesirables into the sick suitcase. I pitched my dirty socks and underwear into the trash, and told the housekeeper that I was leaving the suitcase, and that she could have all that was in it. I even left the damn field coat behind. Sorry dad.

The housekeeper told me where I could find a laundry just a block from the hotel, so I dropped off my dirty clothes and headed towards Café Java for a late morning coffee. I pulled into a shopping mall where parking was free for the first three hours. It was a block north of where I had previously been parking.

I walked through the mall and out onto the main street of Blackrock. There was a travel agency just a few doors down from the mall, so I went in to check on a possible flight. There were three women working, but they were all on the phone, and after waiting more than ten minutes without making eye contact with even one of them, I walked out. Just a few doors down, I found another travel agency, where an attractive and cheerful young woman met me as soon as I walked in. I knew I'd find love; it was just a matter of walking through the right door.

"Can I help you?"

"I don't know. I missed my plane this morning, and I'm going to need to get back to the States one of these days without it costing me a million dollars," I explained.

"When do you want to leave and where in the States are you goin'?"

"San Francisco, sometime within the next week."

"Okay, let me see what I can come up with for you," she said, as she started plugging away on the keyboard. "Okay, I can get a one-way flight on KLM Airlines from Dublin to Amsterdam, and then Amsterdam direct to San Francisco for two hundred eight pounds."

"What day will I be departing?"

"The twentieth."

"That's too soon. How about on the twenty-fourth?"

"Let me see if that fare is available then," she answered, already plugging away on the keyboard. "Yes, it's available for the twenty-forth. Would you like to book it?"

"Can you hold it for me?"

"I can hold it for twenty-four hours."

"Okay, hold it. I haven't had my coffee, and I'm not all here yet. I'm going to walk down to Café Java, and when I'm finished there, I'll stop back in and let you know what I wanna do."

I gave her my name so she could hold the flight and went over for my coffee. I ordered a café mocha. I hardly ever drink café mochas, but for some reason chocolate was working for me.

It was going to cost one hundred fifty US dollars to change my Zurich flight, and forty US dollars to change my Dublin to Paris flight. Two hundred eighty pounds was three hundred twenty dollars, so for an extra one hundred thirty dollars, I could skip the French and the eight-hour train-ride to Zurich in one fell swoop, but, most importantly, I'd possibly see Kelli again.

After my café mocha, I returned and purchased the ticket.

Now all I had to do was find a room, turn in the rental car, and e-mail my family to let them know I'd extended my stay. If they had yet to believe I've fallen in love, they would with the next e-mail I was to send; a disappointment that later they'll lovingly accept.

What really amazes me was that my travel dilemma has been remedied so inexpensively, and easily for that matter. Maybe roundtrip tickets aren't always the bargain they're made out to be, just an illusion to make you think you were getting a good deal. I've purchased two round trip tickets on this trip and have yet to use one of them, and it doesn't look like I ever will.

While traveling, I've lost the obsession I had about my health and mortality, a pleasant change. Money is also losing its neurotic grip on me. I'm living; it's as if something has broken free inside of me, as if I've become unshackled.

I'm not supposed to leave Ireland. I'm not finished here, not yet anyway. The signs presented themselves to me yesterday, but I fought them. The next few days will probably prove to be interesting. My stay is perfect; it will give me a chance to see Kelli a few more times. She's scheduled to leave for the Middle East on the twenty-sixth, two days after my rescheduled departure.

April 18, 2001 - 9:30 p.m.

After booking the ticket, I returned to Café Java for a sandwich and another café mocha. Then drove to the tourist office in Dun Laoghaire where I had originally booked the rental car. I was able to book an en suite room at a place called St. Jude's B&B on the southern outskirts of Dublin City, near a place called Pembroke Park, between Donnybrook and the Ballsbridge areas where I can use the train or bus as transportation. I drove by to pick up my laundry and on to St. Jude's to check in and drop off my now lighter load.

The car rental company had its main office in Dun Laoghaire, so I returned the car there, and hopped a bus, stopping at the Dun Laoghaire mall. I entered the luggage store to find the same sales woman who had pointed me in the direction of a B&B a few weeks back.

"Hello," I said with a smile.

"Weren't you here a couple of weeks ago?"

"Yeah, you helped when I was looking for a room."

"I thought that was you," she smiled.

"I finally got rid of that broken down bag of mine, and I'm going to need something else. I'm just not sure what, though."

"Is it just to get stuff home?"

"Pretty much."

"Go to a department store. You can get something for a lot less there."

"You were so kind to me that I thought I'd give you my business."

"Oh, don't be silly now," she said, as she walked behind the counter and started closing out the till. It was almost six o'clock, and she wanted to go home. We visited a few more minutes and then I said good-bye so that she wouldn't mess up on her count.

I found an Internet café a block from the mall and e-mailed my aunt Adrienne who was supposed to pick me up at the airport in San Francisco. I wrote that I'd extended my stay and would get back to her with my new arrival time. Told her that I needed to rest in Dublin for a few days and wanted to spend some more time with Kelli. If that doesn't set the rumor mill spinning, nothing will.

I had an e-mail from my mother and replied with the same message I had sent to my aunt about my extended stay, but skipped the part about wanting to spend more time with Kelli. I paid the Internet fee of three pounds sixty pence and left the café.

It was cold. I wished I hadn't so hastily discarded the field coat. The windbreaker and the sweater I wore underneath it weren't cutting the chill. I headed back towards the mall and turned the corner to walk down to the port area where the train station, better known as the Dart, was located. The wind swept in from the ocean and came straight up the street that I had turned on to access the Dart, literally chilling me to the bone. I braved it; I had no choice. Well, I did, but having just given a jacket away, I wasn't going to run out and purchase a new one.

I thought of an old client of mine who had all the money in the world, but was too tight to spring for a jacket because he said the damn things cost too much; he was a flippin' multi-millionaire. I've become who I once mocked, minus the millions, that is.

Eighty-five pence bought my Dart ride from Dun Laoghaire to Blackrock. I phoned Kelli while riding on the train, leaving a message to say I'd be around for a few more days and to phone me if she had time and wanted to get together. I didn't want to impose upon her as she had a project that had to be completed before she left for Palestine.

I got off the train. Walking up towards the main street, I noticed the backside of the Wicked Wolf and considered hanging out at the pub for a while. Instead, I crossed the street to an Italian restaurant, taking a window seat.

Two older women were seated two tables from me. The one with her back to me was in her seventies, but had her hair dyed blonde and cut like a woman half her age; she wore a fur coat and smoked a cigarette. The woman facing me was a brunette in her mid to upper fifties. She wasn't an unattractive woman, but the Tiparillo she smoked robbed her of what her age had yet to thieve away.

I had meat lasagna and salad for dinner, and the Irish don't mess around when they say meat; it was loaded with minced beef. Dessert didn't appeal to me, but I did top my meal off with a cappuccino that was light on the froth, but tasted quite good. The hot drink was in preparation for my impending return to the cold world, something to warm my innards before stepping out into that icy chill on my way back to Ballsbridge.

The wait for the train was less than ten minutes. There was no attendant at the ticket window, just a sign that said to pay at the destination window. The train car I selected had few passengers. Did Kelli find me attractive; did she even consider me a potential lover? Did I even come across to her that way? If so, it had yet to be confirmed. Do spiritual people still enjoy sex, or do they transcend such trivialities? God, I hope not, yet I am beginning to doubt the possibility of once again having a lover in my life.

It was a twenty-minute walk from the Lansdowne train station to St. Jude's. My scrotum was sucked up so tight around my balls that you'd have thought I'd been hot tubbin' in a thirty-three degree Jacuzzi. My nose was running when I walked into my room. I pulled some tissue from the toilet paper roll. The roll was pulling from behind, so I flipped it over to pull from the top; it's the little things that bug me.

I thought that our coming together would have turned into some mad passionate love affair that could some day be the basis for a movie, but it hasn't turned out that way at all. It's all right, but it would've been nice if things had turned out differently. My ideas and expectations, those I like to pretend don't exist, might have gotten in the way? Might have, hell, they did, and not just in the way things happened with Kelli. They're also getting in the way, filling a space, so to say, and not allowing my life to ebb and flow.

It's my fifteenth night in Ireland. Why am I still here? I mean, besides the whole Kelli thing. I gave the jacket away, and now it's turned freezing cold. Why the hell did I do that? I'm just another dumb-fuck who got carried away. Maybe it's normal to feel this cold after having shed a layer of skin? What's it like for a snake? Can those cold-blooded reptiles feel the difference? And the sheep when they're sheared every year, what's it like for them? They must feel a disparity. Perhaps that's why I've stayed: to feel the Irish wind, its sting, to feel what it's like to be exposed out on that remote mountainside, having just been sheared.

April. 19, 2001 - Dream

I went to see Thad at his house. Thad was my manager in the machinery business; his health is failing. He was doing things in his garage. I asked how he felt. He looked good. He was getting out of one of his cars or trucks. (Perhaps getting out of an identity?) He showed me how he was beginning... how his body was changing. His neck looked real long for some reason. He looked distorted. He showed me what it was doing to his neck and said that it was affecting his heart; that he could feel his heart changing. He was sad; his disease was killing him. He said something about going to church. I said something about stopping by, but not being sure. He said I could stop by.

Then Fritz was in the background of the dream. Fritz was my manager before Thad. I don't remember much of what was going on, but Thad seemed sad. His mortality had changed him.

Then it was like I was somewhere with him and a child of some sort, a child who may have been eight to twelve years old. We were somewhere... Thad wanted to be... at an auto parts store or something. I stepped into the store next door and tried to use the pay phone. It was giving change, but the dimes were bent up, curled up, distorted. I tried to phone somewhere. The call didn't go through, but I got a quarter back, a quarter that wasn't distorted, and we left.

Then we were at this place where Thad went for medical assistance, but the place was at the church of my youth. He was angry, had been sick for three years and he still had not been able to recover. He was dying, frustrated, and sad.

Then he was like a young boy, eight to twelve, and he got a ball, maybe a soccer or a football and started kicking it around, playing, and he started to come to life. It was like re-energizing him, renewing him. It was like he forgot his problems and they went away, were no longer problems.

Perhaps this has something to do with my conservatism, my conservative way of living, of holding on to things, of not allowing the old to go, so that something new can move, flow into my life. This has something to do with allowing my life to flow, play, open, and entertain what I believe to be impossible.

April 19, 2001 - 11:30 a.m.

The people at St. Jude's told me that it was a fifteen-minute walk to Dublin City center. After breakfast I began the hike. Once to the center, I checked my e-mail at an Internet café that I had stumbled upon two days ago, when I was looking for a place to reserve my train seat. After checking my messages, I left and walked around a corner to find the church that had been converted to the tourist center. I wasn't as lost as I thought I had been the other day.

I ended up back at Bewley's on Grafton Street, the same place I'd met Kelli two weeks earlier, only this time we had no plans to meet. I ordered a white coffee and asked them to make it mostly black; I didn't feel like too much milk, just a taste was all, to tame the bitterness.

I felt tired, even though I'd had a good night's sleep. I suppose it was more of a relaxed feeling as opposed to being tired, a kind of laziness that takes over after eating a good meal. I was trancy, feeling like I wanted to fall asleep and into a dream.

A little boy walked up next to me. He was waiting for his mother, older brother and sister to come through the food line. Chest first, the little guy started banging himself into the counter. He was only a foot away from me. His sister spotted him in action and came to rescue him from his self-destructive behavior. I smiled at them and the sister gave me an odd look before walking over to their mother to report on the boy's actions.

I'm sitting upstairs in Bewley's this time, in the Atrium café. It must be a non-smoking area, because I'm actually able to smell the scent of a woman's perfume instead of the stale smoke I've been sucking up for the last month. I'm waiting for the place to turn crazy with the lunch rush. It's slow in the making, but it isn't quite noon yet. People really seem to take to the streets at noon in Dublin, which only adds to the endless bustle of this city. Dublin reminds me of San Francisco, the feeling more than the aesthetics.

While at the Internet café, I sent Kelli a message that said she could call to join me for coffee or dinner, but not to feel obligated because I knew she had a lot to get done during the week. Someone's perfume just drew a sneeze out of me. Noon bells are ringing outside, reminds me of my youth and Sunday morning's call to worship.

The dream with Thad, I'm not quite sure what to make of it. I think it has to do with living outside the constraints of my conservatism. His healing took place on the steps of the church, just outside the door I used to exit from the sanctuary after the service. It was where we'd meet friends after the sermon, where parents and grandparents would gather to visit.

Thad seldom if ever spoke up. He let things sit, hoping that they'd resolve themselves. He held things in, seldom stood for anything, hardly ever voiced his anger or frustration, let alone did anything about it. In the years that I worked with him, he hardly ever played. He used to rebuild cars and go to swap meets with his buddies, but, once I took his sales territory over and he took the office job and moved into town, his whole life centered around his job. He was in bed around eight and up at four-thirty, and after his hour-long drive to the office, was there by six, and often didn't get started on his drive back home until five-thirty or six in the evening. On top of all that, he was running someone else's business for a fixed salary, with an occasional bonus that was begrudgingly handed to him only for exceptional years.

My calves are sore from walking so much. I may catch the bus down the street near Trinity College and ride it to Blackrock. It's the same bus stop where I snuck that second hug from Kelli two weeks ago, the day that I first met her here at Bewley's. It'll be nice not to walk or drive, just sit back and enjoy the ride.

I'm supposed to be flying home today. Home, do I really have one? The tiredness and yawns after breakfast this morning might have been an invitation to come home, home to myself, to inhabit this body. I suppose my body is really the only home that needs my concern, and you-know-who went and gave away his coat. "How about a little sunshine, Yahweh? Come on; have a heart won't you?"

At home there's a jacket I purchased back in the States. It's a canvas shell that can be worn with a sweater or vest. I really like the jacket, wish I had packed it. It fits just right, not too big, not too small. The damn thing wasn't that cheap either, but that didn't keep me from buying it. I saw it, liked it, and bought it. It was just that simple. Money didn't dictate the run of my life that day.

A Bewley's employee just brought a satisfaction questionnaire to my table. They want me to rate their level of service; they want my opinion. It scares me when people start passing around surveys like this, reminds me of the business world I've left. If you have to ask, it's already too late. If you have to ask someone else to define your business, or life for that matter, it's no longer your own. It's wearing someone else's jacket.

April 19, 2001 - 10 p.m.

I left the survey blank and walked out into the crowd on Grafton.

On the way to catch the bus, I found a bank that exchanged my Swiss francs and Italian lire and found myself ninety Irish pounds heavier. I probably got screwed on the exchange but don't care. I have no plans of returning to Switzerland or Italy soon, although I'm not quite sure why I'm letting plans dictate anything; plans can change in the twinkling of the eye.

I have a fifty-franc French note that I considered wiping my ass with, but then had second thoughts about exposing myself to such cruelty. Besides, the note bears the image of Antoine de Saint-Exupéry's Little Prince, and I've elected to keep it in honor of the spirited *Puer Aeternus*.

I caught the number seven bus in front of Trinity College, dropped one pound fifteen pence down the change slot of the mechanical ticket dispenser and tore off my ticket. Blackrock was much quieter than Dublin and in the words of an Irish man who had helped me determine the correct bus fair: "much safer, too." I don't know what he meant, if he was serious or joking, but it doesn't matter anyway.

I got off the bus and walked into the same mall that I had parked below yesterday. In a bookstore on the second level, I found a book with aerial photos of various places throughout Ireland. Paging through the picture book, I realized that I'd visited many of the documented locations over the last couple of weeks. It was nice, gave me an objective, birds-eye view of where I'd been.

Leaving the bookseller, I noticed a health food store across the way. Inside, I found some honey wheels: Dutch cookies called Stroopwafels. The cookies consist of honey-like syrup that is pressed between two thin waffle-like wafers that are two and a half inches in diameter. My grandmother and great-grandmother both used to make them. They're quite a treat and hard to find in the States, so I indulge whenever I happen upon these sweet memories.

The next stop was at the travel agency. My ticket isn't supposed to arrive until tomorrow, but I wanted to confirm my flight time so that my aunt can make arrangements to pick me up in San Francisco. After confirming my itinerary, I walked half a block down the street to Café Java for a double café mocha. Like I said before, I'm not a big chocolate drinker, but this place makes one hell of a mocha, and I'm beginning to develop quite an affection for this sweetness.

Two women in their thirties and three children came into the café. One was a blonde with a bobbed haircut; she was ringless, and in pretty good physical shape, too. The other woman, a brunette, was pregnant and appeared to be the mother of all three children. Two of the kids were girls between eight and ten. The little boy, a toddler, sat in a stroller while the rest of them had lunch.

The toddler grew restless and after the crew had finished lunch, the mother picked him up to give him his due, and that's when the blonde got up to pay their bill. The brunette looked up as she soothed the child and spotted her friend.

"Don't take her money, I'll pay for that," the brunette spoke up with the squirming boy in her hands.

They ignored her.

"Really, let me get this one," the brunette insisted.

They continued to ignore her, and she looked at me smiling with a can-you-believe-this look. I smiled back, and her embarrassment grew as she protested again. When the brunette was protesting the second time, I noticed that she had a tongue stud. With three kids and pregnant with her fourth, she obviously knew nothing of the tongue studs utility. I won't so easily fall prey to the fantasy of having my way with a tongue-studded woman in the future.

Could Mary Magdalene have sported a tongue stud? I'm certain to burn in hell for even considering such an ordeal, and at the very least lose the pleasure of having a woman accompany me to bed for at least the next decade. Tracy Chapman's *Give Me One Good Reason* from her *New Beginning* album was playing in the background.

A young couple sat in the corner, smoking cigarettes and kissing all with the same breath. Outside, the wind was still delivering its chill, the clouds continued their overhead march eastward towards other worlds, and occasionally the sun teased with a smile, bringing me the image of bikini clad round-rumped women strewn across the California beaches.

I'll arrive home a few days shy of May. I'm ready for summer, for shorts, for smokeless restaurants, for my cabin in the mountains where I can sun myself by day, burn logs in the fire by night, and make love to the next beautiful woman who dances her way into my life. With so many lady friends, sooner or later, one of them is bound to come around. Maybe my absence will have awakened a hidden passion that lies dormant in one of the many beauties.

The radio was now playing the J. Giles band's *Angel in the Centerfold*. I grew restless and hopped the Dart to Dun Laoghaire. Once there I walked around, checking out parts of the town that I'd yet to explore. I also e-mailed Aunt Adrienne my arrival time into San Francisco before catching the bus to Donnybrook.

I had a nice dinner at Roly's Bistro, which was only a five-minute walk from St. Jude's. I stepped off the bus too soon and had to walk an extra thirty minutes. As recompense, I decided to treat myself at Roly's. Of all the beautiful women who were waiting tables, I had to pull the gay waiter straw. I ordered a pan-fried Hake fish that was served with mashed potatoes and melted goat cheese, along with a side order of spinach in honor of Popeye.

There was a hot young blonde in her mid-twenties serving. The first time she walked by my table, she glanced over and gave me a polite smile. The second time around, she took a long stare, almost as if she thought she knew me. The third time, as she walked by to deliver a dish to the table next to mine, she didn't bother looking my way at all, not even a hint, but she didn't need to. Her second look had done the trick; it warmed my belly like a shot of whiskey.

I considered walking over to her and introducing myself, giving her my mobile number, and asking her to meet me for coffee at Bewley's in the morning. I left without saying a word. I was going home in a few days and had no business starting something that I couldn't finish, and I wasn't into playing games just to see what I could get away with, besides also being afraid.

When I was making money, I had confidence. I'd have

walked up to her and introduced myself. Selling tractors and making money is how I once defined my value, but I don't have that false image to cling to any longer. It's been more than two years since I left that old life behind, and as time has passed, it all seems so trivial, but there are moments that I long to have something to color my face with, some image to hang my hat on that will resurrect that lost sense of self-assurance.

April 20, 2001 - Dream

I had returned home from Europe. I was going into an insurance agency. A place where I had a policy of some sort, but I didn't think they knew me - a new me? I just thought they... you know, I had a policy there with them, but didn't think they knew who I was. Anyway, I drove up. They were in a home, out in the country along the coast - west coast of California, a home similar to the two and three story B&B's where I've been staying in the countryside of Ireland. I drove up and it looked like it had been raining. The place appeared to be abandoned or maybe they had moved? It was kind of odd. I pulled in. It was slippery, and my truck was sliding, and it spun around. It wasn't a U-turn because there wasn't enough room to make a U-turn. The slipperiness helped me; the sliding helped me to get turned around. In other words, it was kind of a pain in the butt, but then it turned out to be something that was... that helped me.

I walked up, went inside, and I said hi and before I could say anything else they said: "Oh, hello, Mr. Clay." They remembered me. They knew who I was. I told them that I had just arrived back from Europe that very day, and I was going to be traveling again, and I just needed to make sure I got my things... some things in order with them, and I took care of some business concerning my policies. I told them I had been in Europe for six weeks and was tired, and also something about... I was going to talk about having written a book, but then I didn't. I, for some reason, didn't go there.

There were two men: a taller guy and a shorter guy who might have been a little younger than me... the taller guy... I met them before... just didn't think that they'd remember me. They weren't somebody I notice from the waking world.

These two guys could be Darrell and Manuel, the guys who bought an Insurance Company in Westley, where I once had a policy. I once wrote a letter threatening to sue them for not taking care of business, and they ended up paying for my entire policy - a homeowner's policy- for one year.

Then I was having dinner with a young woman who was... she was my lover or she was going to be my lover because... I say that because I kissed her - she didn't fight it. She wasn't closed, but she wasn't overly expectant. She wanted to get to know me before she started kissing me, which was okay. Somehow in the dream, I had gone to a restaurant with her and... oh, she was almost like cautious, but I didn't care. I had these feelings, and I was just expressing them without worrying about what she thought. I was old enough and confident enough that I just didn't care.

April 20, 2001 - 10 p.m.

Waking to the buzz of an intercom that was soon blaring out a call to breakfast, I thought my heart would pound it's way right out of my chest and on up through my throat. There's nothing more disheartening than to be jolted out of REM sleep. "Fuck you Yahweh! What happened to the sun, anyway?"

I shouted back that I didn't want any breakfast, and the voice over the intercom came back and said that was fine. It reminded me of my mother coming in and waking me for school. I was pissed; breakfast and school are both illegitimate reasons for waking a resting soul: "And so are you, Yahweh!"

Yesterday, someone knocked on my door to get me down to breakfast. I was already awake and moving around, so it didn't bother me so much. I had a hunch when I registered that this might be a problem as there were certain times when they served breakfast, and they made sure that I marked a slot. Checking that box was like setting an alarm clock, and I hate alarm clocks.

The only alarm clock I'm interested in hearing is the one inside of me that sounds when I have had adequate sleep, or a good old-fashioned wake up call from a woman who has slid under the covers to gently welcome me into a new day. The latest time for breakfast was nine-thirty, so that's what I chose, although I'd have preferred ten or ten-thirty.

Unable to go back to sleep, I showered and was just about to leave when someone knocked. I eagerly answered to set the record straight on the intercom trick.

"Yes," I said, after swinging open the door. It was the woman who cooked and took care of cleaning the rooms. She was a friend of the woman at the tourist office who had booked my room at St. Jude's; they sang in the choir together.

"Just checking the rooms; do you need any towels?"

"I'll be out of here in a few minutes and then you can have it," I answered. She was in a hurry, as if she was on a time schedule.

"Okay, is everything else all right?" she asked, possibly sensing my agitation.

"No, it's not. I don't want to be called on that damn intercom unless this house is burning down. I keep odd hours, and don't like to be startled out of my sleep. I don't even turn the phone ringer on until after noon at home."

"I'm sorry. That was the woman who owns the place."

"I don't care who it was. Getting bolted awake like that sets my whole day off into a panicky frenzy."

"I'll make sure she knows not to call you."

"And don't worry: I don't care if I miss breakfast."

I might have been a little harsh with her, but if I'm going to spend another night at St. Jude's, the intercom thing has to be straightened out. If the illegitimate thing sounds off again, I'll cut the goddamn wires. "You hear that Yahweh; I'll cut the goddamn wires!"

My next home will be quiet, a place where I won't be bothered. The woman had blamed my disturbance on the owner, but it was more about getting me up and out of my room so that she could tend to her duties and get on with her day. Well, that was all fine and dandy for her world, but it was fucking with mine. I'm sure she got the message, though. She knew my growl might very well turn into a roar; a roar that even scares the shit out of me at times.

I walked into Dublin and checked my e-mail before even having a cup of coffee. Had a message from Kelli saying she'd received my voice mail, but that it was garbled and she couldn't make it out. She said she had dinner plans for Saturday and Sunday, but could meet me Friday, which is tonight.

I also had a message from my aunt saying that she'd be there to pick me up at the airport, said she was leaving for a week the day after I arrived and that I could have the house all to myself. To a homeless man, this is like finding a pot of gold at the end of the rainbow. It'll be perfect for my assimilation back into California life. I'm looking forward to having my own vehicle and having my feet planted on familiar ground.

I left the Internet café and phoned Kelli, making plans for an early dinner in Blackrock, and then started walking back toward the St. Stephen's Green area to find some coffee. I ended up in a place called Samsara, a pub on Dawson street, a road one block south, paralleling Grafton Street, but with much less foot traffic.

I sat in the foyer, in a huge lounge chair in the window where I could watch the world spinning by outside. Beyond the foyer was a dark, brick walled room of enormous depth that appeared much narrower than it actually was; the long room seemed that it might extend all the way to Grafton Street. There was a huge stained-glass window at the far end of the church-like sanctuary.

I ordered an Americano and fish and chips. Now, that's my kind of breakfast, my kind of living, and on my time schedule. The waitress was very friendly. She told me about Dalkey, the town where she'd been raised. She suggested that I visit it before leaving Ireland. It was just a couple of stops south of Dun Laoghaire on the Dart. She said it was a wonderful little village. I could tell that she'd grown up there by the sparkle in her eyes; it was as if she had returned to her childhood playground and was dangling on a swing as she described the landscape of her youth.

After lunch I waived to the friendly waitress. "Can I get you something else?" she asked.

"No thank you. What's your name?"

"I'm Niamh," she answered, extending her hand.

"Niamh, I'm Malcolm; it's a pleasure to know you."

"Ah, the pleasure is mine. Malcolm, I'll be right back with

your check."

"Here you go Niamh, put it on this," I said, handing her my credit card.

Niamh walked back into the sanctuary and returned shortly with a credit slip to be signed.

"Niamh, here's a card with my phone and e-mail address. Now you've got a friend in California if you ever get out that way."

"Ah, thank you, Malcolm. That's very kind of you."

"I'm serious, too. I expect to hear from you if you ever make it that way."

"Listen, Malcolm. Tomorrow night I'll be in Dalkey, at the Laurel Tree. Stop by if you can make it."

"I might just do that."

"One thing though; it's kind of a family affair. So if you do stop in, act surprised. You know, like you're a long lost friend, and we've just run into each other by accident."

"Okay, I got you," I said, smiling.

After lunch, I caught the bus to Donnybrook, and stopped at St. Jude's to change sweaters before starting my walk to Lansdowne Dart Station. The day had turned sunny, but the wind still persisted. A couple of houses down and across from St. Jude's, there was a two-seater Mercedes convertible with the top down. A chill ran through me, the same chill that has been piercing my bones for the past few days. That car belonged somewhere else, somewhere warm.

At the corner, I turned east on Herbert Park Road, which cut right through the center of Pembroke Park. There were two Pakistani boys, ten to twelve years of age, doing gymnastic tumbles on the grass. Their father stood with a soccer ball under his right foot. It looked as if he was waiting for the kids to quit messing around and give him their undivided attention.

Continuing the walk, I came upon flowerbeds full of blooming bright red tulips, occasionally spotting the yellow of a stray daffodil. The flowers reminded me of a yard in Santa Cruz where, once a year, hundreds of bright red tulips bloom and light the landscape ablaze.

Approaching the main street that led into Dublin's city center, near Roly's Bistro, there was a Y in the road where a

Garda had stopped a car. The cop was writing something down while visiting with a redheaded woman. As I got closer, I noticed a motor scooter and an older gentleman. They must have had a minor mishap, as neither of them appeared to be injured and both seemed quite calm.

I turned north on the main street and walked by the American Embassy. I imagined myself working there in one of the offices that had a window facing outside into the world of Ireland. Not long ago, our National Lunatic had been there. The lucky bastard can hop onto Air Force One any time his little old heart desires and in a matter of a few hours be anywhere in the world. Fuck him; he sold his soul for that power. Besides, I can hop on a plane whenever I damn well please and go anywhere I want, and without anyone else even giving a damn, let alone knowing.

A block past the American Embassy, I turned east again and crossed the street, and a few blocks after that was at Lansdowne Station. I paid my eighty-five pence tariff to ride the train to Blackrock, and passed through the turn stall, following four teenaged girls to a covered canopy. I sat down on the opposite end of the bench where they sat and took in their giggling banter. They were talking about stories from different books they'd read.

One of the girls was holding a book of short stories about cats. It looked boring to me, reminded me of something my ex-wife would enjoy. The southbound train, the one that would have taken me to Blackrock, pulled into the station on the opposite side of the tracks. Not paying attention, I had blindly followed the teenagers and had failed to walk through the passageway below to the boarding platform on the other side.

Knowing that I'd never make it across in time, I watched the train depart and then casually stood up and walked to the passage way, knowing that I'd be the object of some humiliation when I emerged on the opposite platform. Sure enough, when I popped up on the other side, the four girls all broke out into a chatty laughter. The next southbound train showed up eight minutes later, and I left the swirling whirlwind of meowing felines behind.

When I got off the train in Blackrock, I heard music, an

accordion and a horn, coming from the main street. I was about to sit down on a bench just up from the Dart station, behind the Wicked Wolf, when a black woman with long braided hair walked past towards the train. She looked familiar. I watched her round the corner towards the station, and then it hit me: she worked at the travel agency, and I was supposed to have picked up my ticket today.

I made it before the agency closed. The ticket had arrived. I was greeted by an agent who had never helped me, but for some reason remembered me. Love, I tell you, I went to a place that knew love.

"You must be here to pick up your ticket?"

"Yes I am. The name's..."

"I remember you Mister Clay," she said, reaching to a file behind her desk. "I've got your ticket right here," she said, turning to me with a smile. "Here you go," she said, opening the folder and going over my itinerary.

"Okay, looks good."

"Safe travels Mister Clay," she said, still wearing her bright smile.

"Thank you very much," I answered and left. I had twenty minutes before Kelli was to meet me at Café Java, where we were to choose a restaurant, if she showed. I decided to buy another pack of Honey Wheels since the health food store was only a few steps from the travel agency.

I was sipping a café mocha, sitting in a corner seat at Café Java, when Kelli walked by and spotted me from outside. She came in and gave me a hug.

"Listen, I'm not stopping yet. I have to run down to the art supply in the mall before they close."

"Take your time. Would you like me to order you something to drink?"

"When I get back," she answered, as if I didn't understand that she wasn't there to stay.

"Okay, see you in a while."

Twenty minutes later Kelli returned with a bag full of goods. She was wearing a pair of black leggings under a gray dress, and a black leather coat. She was dressed nicely, but she could have been in sweats and a T-shirt, and I'd have still worshipped her.

"Can I get you something?"

"Yes, but I'd like to go somewhere else."

It was five, and we planned on an early dinner, so we set off to find a restaurant. We first stopped at an Italian place, but they didn't begin serving until six, so we crossed the street and walked a block south to a restaurant called Dali's and found out that they too didn't serve until six. We ended up in Shehaan's, the pub that I hung out in while she was returning from Cork. After finding a seat, Kelli ordered a spritzer and I had my usual sparkling water.

I started telling her about characters who often, as if I were their long lost friend, just walk into my life and tell me their life's story. "I'll just be sitting somewhere, like right here, and they'll walk right up to me."

"They trust you."

"I guess, but they don't even know me."

"Well, it's something."

"It doesn't bother me. I mean, hell, I'll probably never see them again. They're not like some people I know who keep singing their same old poor-me life drama over and over again. Those are the one's who drive me nuts. When they walk away, it feels like I've had a gallon of blood siphoned out of me."

"I call them energy vampires."

I told Kelli about being zapped from my sleep by the intercom. "The quickest way to piss me off is to wake me from a perfectly good dream."

"I can't imagine you getting mad."

"Oh, it's there."

"Show me. Make a mad face," she teased.

"I can't fake a mad face," I laughed.

"Come on, try."

"Really, I've got to be mad," I answered, continuing with my embarrassed laugh. "I had this girlfriend once who was a shrink," I said, trying to skirt around having to make a mad face.

"Oh, yeah," Kelli smiled, knowing that I was trying to sidestep the topic.

"Yeah, she told me that I was an angry man and that I needed to get rid of my anger."

"Whatever happened to her?"

"I told her that she was nuts, and I dumped her," I answered trying not to chuckle, but I couldn't contain myself, and we both broke out in laughter. "Hell, I like my anger. As far as I'm concerned it serves me."

"I agree, just has to be put in the right direction."

"It's being angry and trying not to be that's more of a problem," I continued.

"Yes, like if you're angry and acknowledge it, you can put the energy into something creative," Kelli confirmed.

"Yeah, like a great painting, instead of holding it all in and then unconsciously reacting to it and hurting another."

We talked for a while longer, and after a couple of drinks, decided to try for dinner again.

"Where would you like to go?" I asked, as we walked out of Shehaan's.

"It doesn't matter that much to me," Kelli answered.

"Well, you pick," I said, slowing to walk a step behind her, allowing her to lead."

"No, you can pick," she said, as she rounded the corner toward Dali's, the Italian place being in the opposite direction.

"Okay, let's try Dali's," I suggested.

It was just after six when we walked in and not a soul was in the restaurant, but the host haughtily told us that they were booked up for the evening, so we walked back to the Italian place and were seated immediately. Kelli ordered the cannelloni, and I had the veggie lasagna.

We talked about my marriage, but mostly about my failed love affair with Lauren.

"What happened?"

"I left. She kept going back and forth. One day she'd be getting divorced and the next she was staying married. I couldn't take the uncertainty of it all, so I left. Damn, I was in love with her, though."

"Whatever happened to her?"

"That was six years ago. I completely cut off all contact with her. I mean, it hurt too much to keep going back into that mess."

"She really moved you. So you don't know if she went back

to her husband?"

"She didn't. A few months ago I decided to phone her."

"So you have talked to her?"

"No, I got her message machine. It was one of those machines with two different mailboxes. There was one for her and her new man, and the other box was for her two boys and his son."

"Maybe it's her brother."

"No, she doesn't have a brother," I smiled. "It doesn't matter anyway. I didn't really want to be with her."

"But you're in love with her."

"I'm in love with her image. When I phoned and got the message machine to learn that she didn't go back to her husband, it really hit home. Maybe I could have had her."

Kelli nodded without responding.

"I mean, if I had really wanted to be with her, I'd have waited. I'd have kept in contact with her, and I might have been the guy whose name was with her on the answering machine, but I didn't and I didn't because I didn't want to. It was never about her, about her not knowing what she wanted or about her getting a divorce. It was about me and what I wanted, and not being able to accept it, so I made her out to be the problem."

Kelli was quiet. The last time we came together, the night before my originally scheduled departure, she had shared more about herself, and I got to listen, but it seemed that I was to do most of the revealing this evening.

We got to talking about energy vampires again. When people were stuck, they'd look outside to others for guidance, or still worse, depend on someone else to carry out what they couldn't do.

"I know a lot of people who see me living my life and they're attracted to me because I'm doing what they want to do, what they dream of, only they're still living in that old dream, clinging to the same excuses that keep them from cutting their ties and getting on with their own lives."

"And they come around wanting something from us because they don't want to take the risk themselves," Kelli confirmed.

"I hate it. I mean, they're human, and I don't want to dishonor their humanity, their existence, you know, but at the same time, I can't live their lives for them."

"It's like you don't want to write them off, but you don't want to lose yourself in the process," Kelli acknowledged.

"Sometimes, I just back away. I don't write them off forever, but I don't call them back. You know, keep a distance. Then when it feels right, I'll call," I explained.

"That's when a real relationship can begin," Kelli added.

"Yeah, there's been enough time and space."

"And they realize they can be your friend without clinging to you."

After dinner, Kelli took a napkin and a pen and asked me to draw some images that were part of a symbolic game. Then she interpreted what they might mean according to where I'd placed the symbols and the different sizes that I'd given them. Somehow, she interpreted that I chose wisdom over love from my primitive rendering.

"If you were going to have dessert, what would you order?" Kelli asked.

"I'm not sure. How about you?" I asked.

"I must confess that I'm not perfect. I'm a chocoholic. So, if I were to have dessert..."

"So you'd like the chocolate cake, huh?"

Kelli confirmed with a nod and an excited-little-girl look.

"Good, and I'll order the crème caramel. And tea for two?"

"But of course," Kelli confirmed with her luscious smile.

Kelli was beautiful, simply beautiful. I admired her as she delighted in the chocolate cake. Her satisfaction was much tastier than my crème caramel.

A Richie Valens song was playing. "I was thinking about how some people come into the world, create something beautiful and then are gone, dead so young," Kelli said, after she had finished her dessert. It made me think of Saint-Exupéry. I pulled out the fifty-franc note and showed her the picture of the Little Prince, mentioning that Saint-Exupéry had also died young.

"Kelli, come back to California," I bravely suggested.

"I have to finish this Palestinian project."

"Come back to California," I repeated.

"I can't think about that right now. I have to stay focused."

"Yes, you can. Finish the project and come home."

"But..."

"Come home," I interrupted, not interested in excuses.

She smiled. "I'm not running," she defended.

"I didn't say you were."

She smiled again, this time at the slip of her tongue. It was after eight. I excused myself to the restroom, and gave the waiter my credit card on the way, signing it when I returned.

"Come on, it's getting late. It's time to run," I teased.

"How about if we walk?"

"Okay, walk it is."

As we walked down Garysforth Street, back towards the condominium, we teased each other and talked about whatever randomly came to mind. I kept throwing in the come-back-to-California thing, too. "Go to the Middle East and rescue the part of you that needs rescuing there, come back to Dublin and reclaim what you've returned here to recover, and then come back to California."

"San Francisco is nice, but not in the middle of town."

"How about Marin?"

"Yes, Marin is nice. I just don't want to be in the middle of the city, around all those wires and things. The area around Mount Tamalpias is nice."

"Okay, that'll work; just come back," I urged, feeling like the old salesman who had finally found a trinket of attachment that would allow me to close the deal. Kelli didn't seem to be disturbed by my pushiness.

"Oh, did I tell you about my Grandfather, my dad's father, the Cherokee Indian?" I asked, as we turned the corner to walk the last stretch to the condo.

"No, I don't think so."

"He never placed a foot into any of his children's homes."

"Why not?"

"He came to their houses, helped them work in their yards, put up fences, and built things, but he never once set foot into their homes."

"But that sounds so unfair."

"We went into his house all the time though, but he was the elder of that home. My father told me that he wouldn't come into his children's home because he felt that they were the elders of their own homes, and he didn't want to interfere."

"So it was out of respect," Kelli said, as we walked up to the gate.

"For something sacred," I answered, and nodded.

We embraced, I kissed Kelli's cheek, and then we stepped back, still holding hands and facing each other.

"Okay, now go to Palestine, come back to Dublin, and then come home to California, but please be safe, because I really want to sit across the table from you again and watch your beautiful face eating chocolate cake."

"You're so sweet," Kelli said, and then we embraced again once more before my departure. "You be safe, too," she said, as I walked away.

I nodded without looking back to her. I followed a trail that cut through the park behind her mother's house, leading me back to Garysforth Street. I was full of myself, just knew I was working my way into her heart. I walked away with confidence this time, knowing that I'd see her again.

I left the park along Garysforth. On my way back to Blackrock Dart station, there was a man with two King Charles spaniels.

"May I pet them?" I asked, as they approached.

"Certainly. What part of the States you from?" he asked as I knelt down to pet the spaniels.

"California. You've got some sweet pups here."

"Aren't they? I love it out your way. If I could go back twenty years and start again, it would be in California."

"Well, I met this beautiful Irish woman in the States right before she returned home to Dublin, and that's exactly why I'm here."

"To take her back to California? You shouldn't have such a hard time doing that, now should you?"

"Well, I don't think it should be that hard either, but so far, I haven't finished the mission."

"Oh, keep the faith. I'm sure she'll come around."

"Thanks a lot, huh," I said, and then shook his hand before walking on toward the city center.

The ticket office at Blackrock station was closed and the main gate was rolled down, so I snuck through an open gate and hopped the train without a ticket. Eight minutes later, I stepped off at Lansdowne station, swinging the bag of Honey Wheels like a kid slinging his brown bag full of goodies that he failed to finish during lunch because of having one thing on his mind: the playground.

I strolled down the tree-lined street that led from Lansdowne back toward St. Jude's. It was dusk, almost dark when I heard shuffling in a driveway of one of the many Edwardian homes that made up the neighborhood. It was a pair a mallards, a hen and a drake; they flew up out of the driveway, clearing my head by just a few feet.

I flashed on Kelli; did mallards mate for life? It sure was odd having a pair of ducks fly up out of a driveway in the middle of a city, nearly scalping me, and then flying off into the dark of night. It seems that more than Mallards were floating around in the air this evening.

April 21, 2001 - Noon

Today is old-love day, but, in a way, different from all my past old-love days. The memories are fond instead of harsh. I have no regrets for having loved and lost. I also have clarity about what I am and am not willing to live with, and it has nothing to do with trying to make right or wrong of all my good old-loves gone bad.

I've loved women who spooked and ran, and I've done the same myself. I have loved from a place of innocent, infantile naïveté, and I have loved from a place of maturity. I have loved from a place of anger, and I have loved from a place of compassion. I have clung to old images, loving too long, and at other times severed myself from what I was nowhere near ready to let go of.

I'm on Dawson Street again; this time in a little coffee shop half a block down the road from where I had lunch yesterday at Samsara. I'm sitting at a tall table, at a window seat watching the pretty blue and green-eyed girls stroll by. Occasionally, I get caught. Sometimes our eye contact carries over into an extended gaze, other times the exchange is like a ricocheted bullet.

One woman looked inside and we locked onto each other for

at least five of her strides before she had to look ahead of herself preparing to walk out into traffic. Her eyes brought me back to the image of Jacqueline. I've actually seen Jacqueline's blue eyes and rosy cheeks in many of the Irish women I've passed on Dublin's streets. I really felt something for Jacqueline. She was the first woman that I potentially could have opened my heart to since the Lauren thing fell to pieces six years ago.

Jacqueline was just divorcing, just as Lauren had been when our love affair had started. I'm sure she was afraid of getting close and opening herself up to any real sort of heartfelt exchange. It seems I've developed an affinity for women who have suffered the wrath of patriarchal domination. Jacqueline certainly had been wounded, much of it her own doing, an unconscious doing, but her doing just the same. She had let guilt and duty override her truth. It's one thing to be the recipient of another's rage and abuse, but it's something else to stand there and take a beating, and that's what I meant by it being of her own doing. I guess we all have a hard time stepping out of those old dreams.

Across the street Niamh is walking up to the newsagent. She's walking briskly and smoking a cigarette. She's a thin gal, isn't wearing a jacket, and it's damn cold outside. She's an attractive woman, yet certainly has a tough side to her. She's probably seen a few things in her day. Seen hell, I mean experienced a few things. Compassion accompanies her edginess though, and wisdom; having weathered more than one harsh Irish winter shows in the depths of her green-eyes, yet there's a joy that pours forth from them as well. Niamh appears to be a woman who has found meaning in her suffering: a meaning that has allowed her to continue living life in spite of its unwelcome adversities.

Niamh just walked out of the news agency and is standing on the sidewalk staring across the street to what I believe is an art gallery in the building next door. I just stood up to walk outside and shout out her name as if she was a long lost friend, but now I hesitate because something isn't quite right. Now she's stepped back into the news agency. Now she's walking out and across the street appearing to be drawn to something behind the window of the art gallery. She's standing right outside my window. I just tapped on the glass and she looked up. I could read her lips saying my name.

"Malcolm, nice to see you again," Niamh said, as she poked her head in the door.

"Nice to see you, too. I saw you at the news agency across the street."

"Yes, I had a little break, so thought I'd get out for a walk. Listen, are you coming to Dalkey tonight, Malcolm?"

"I'm not sure Niamh."

"Well, if you are, we'll be at the…"

"Laurel Tree," I interrupted.

"You got it Malcolm, but remember, it's a family affair, so make it a surprise like you just bumped into me."

"Niamh that'll be no problem at all; I can fake it real good." I winked, nodded, and smiled.

"Okay then, maybe we'll see you tonight."

"Maybe."

"At least stop in down the street for a coffee in a bit," Niamh invited, having sensed that I probably wouldn't see her at the Laurel Tree.

"I'll see you in a while."

"Okay, I need to get running. Bye now, Malcolm," she said, as she hurried out the door and fell into a brisk stride.

April 21, 2001 - 10 p.m.

Shortly after Niamh left the bar where I was having my coffee, it started to sprinkle and the place soon filled with people. I ended up sharing my table with a woman who had just bought a sandwich and was sitting outside eating when the rain started. The woman asked to sit with me and then respected my silence, but I started to get uncomfortable just the same and noticed myself sagging into the seat of the bare wooden bar stool. It began to feel as if the walls as well as the floor and ceiling were closing in on me, like some kind of torture chamber. I left and walked to Samsara and that great big comfortable lounge chair in the front window.

My seat awaited me at Samsara. One of the girls who had served me the day before took my order for tea. It wasn't

Niamh, but another gal who was a bit younger and moved quickly, almost too quickly. I settled into the chair and yawns began moving up and out of me; my body's reaction to the environment and its surroundings never ceased to amaze me.

The ceiling in Samsara seemed to be three stories high. The doors were tall enough to take in three of me stacked on end. The foyer had a warm comfortable feeling. The entire building had been decorated with an oriental flare. I didn't feel the need to vacate Samsara after a certain amount of time in order to accommodate new patrons; there was so much space. When I did leave, it was because something moved me from within, not from the nudging of humanity.

I thanked the server for delivering my tea and then asked how she was doing; she didn't respond. It was as if she was deaf. She was awake, but unreachable. A middle-aged balding Caucasian man and his daughter, a toddler, came in and sat in the lobby not far from me. The little girl appeared to be Asian, or half Asian. The father ordered a dark brew for himself and an orange juice for the little girl. Everything remained quiet until shortly after their drinks arrived, but then the little girl began to cry.

"It's alright, you just spilled your juice," her father said, trying to comfort her. "It's okay."

It seemed that the poor little toddler was upset or ashamed that she'd had a spill. Her sense of shame or embarrassment really grabbed my attention. How young we learn to judge and place value on ourselves by our actions, even if it is an accident as small as spilling a drink; it certainly had no reflection on this little girl's true essence.

Then again, maybe she wasn't feeling ashamed or embarrassed one little bit. Maybe she was angry or sad about losing the treat she had so innocently enjoyed. *That long lost titty; no point in crying over spilt milk,* I chuckled to myself.

I yawned again and looked out the window to check on a few more of the pretty, and, this time, not so pretty girls. A double-decker Dublin City tour bus with an open top drove by. Even with the scattered showers and chilly weather, the opened canopy of the bus was still filled with curious souls. Niamh walked into the front lounge section without taking notice of me.

"Hello there," I said, trying to get her attention.

"Oh, hi. Hello, Malcolm. How long have you been here?"

"A while."

"Indeed you have," she said, looking down at my empty teacup. "I've been working in the back, bringing boxes of liquor up from downstairs," she added, brushing the dust from her black slacks before walking off to attend to more of her duties.

After Niamh left, the deaf waitress walked up to have a look out the window. I said "hello," trying to get her attention, but she didn't respond and walked away. What was she looking for, hope? Where had she drifted? Where did she really long to be?

She came back to the window again, and I was finally able to get her attention. "Excuse me. Can I order some fish and chips?"

"Okay," she answered in a nasal tone. She wasn't Irish, probably Eastern European.

"And I'd like some more hot water for my tea and a glass of cold water with a lime please."

"Okay," she answered, again in her nasal tone, English most likely a second language.

Time passed, and no hot water, although another server brought my glass of cold water, but it had a lemon instead of a lime. I received the lemony water without making a fuss, but when the nasally gal walked by the next time, I asked her what had happened to my tea.

"Oh, I thought you were finished."

"No, I asked you for more hot water."

"I'm sorry, I will get you another tea."

She didn't waste any time getting the tea and my fish and chips came shortly thereafter. "Can I have some catsup please?"

"Yes," she answered and went after my request.

She returned, appearing to be more frantic than she had been and set the catsup down on the table, noticing that I had no place setting. She left and promptly returned with my silverware.

"What is your name?" I asked, trying to reach her.

"Anna Marie."

"Thank you, Anna Marie," I said in a tone that finally reached her.

"You're welcome," she said with a smile of relief. She had finally returned to herself. "Now, I am going on a break," she announced.

"Good," I replied, as she smiled again and then disappeared. Waitresses, waiters, servers, anyone in that industry had to grow tired of people's countless demands, even if none of it was personal.

Into my tea, I squeezed the drops from the lemon that came with my fish and chips. I've now slept through breakfast for two days straight. It feels good. I'm moving back into my natural rhythm. I sipped the tea. It had a fishy twinge, but it was a far cry from a chowder.

Anna Marie returned after her break to check on me. "Are you a writer?"

"Oh, yeah, I'm fine," I answered thinking that she asked me if I was alright. "Oh, you asked if I was a writer?"

"Yes," she answered in her nasal voice, nodding.

"Yes, I am, and I really like it here because it's open, full of space so that things can come to me."

"Yes, I know what you mean. I am a singer and sometimes when I write, things come to me when I am in an open space."

"It has room to move through us then," I answered.

"Yes," she answered, nodding and smiling a confirmation of human connection before she walked away to attend to her other duties.

Outside, the horses clip-clopped by pulling carriages; it had been raining consistently for a couple of hours and considering their covered carriages, the horsemen's business had picked up. Watching them pass was like stepping back into a lost age, until one of the carriages drove by whose horseman had the reigns in one hand and holding a mobile phone to his ear with the other.

Earlier, while on Grafton Street, I noticed a store full of leather coats but kept walking. I was cold, and could easily have purchased one from an economical standpoint, as well as from necessity, but principle kept me from indulging. Just knowing that I could do things had become satisfaction in itself.

There was a Dr. Scholl's foot store on Grafton, so when I left Samsara, I returned to the store to see if they might have a remedy for my aching feet and shins that have taken quite a beating over the last several weeks. I ended up purchasing arch supports and foot spray. I then caught the bus back to Donnybrook and walked the few blocks to St. Jude's.

Once in my room, I removed my shoes, tossed the socks into the trashcan and soaked my feet with the cool refreshing spray. I then stretched out on the bed and closed my eyes. After a brief rest, I slipped the arch supports into my shoes and walked to Donnybrook to catch the number forty-six bus back to St. Stephen's Green. I should have invested in the supports before leaving the States.

I checked my e-mail but had no messages, so sent some instead. Sent a few to friends back in the States to let them know I'd extended my stay and would be home the following week. Leaving the Internet café, I stopped and stood under an awning on the sidewalk for at least thirty minutes. I didn't know what to do or where to go, so I just stood there waiting for something to move me, for a sign of some sort to come along and guide me to my next destination, but nothing happened.

Sometimes, when I stood around like that, things just came my way, but not this time. Emptiness began to take hold of me. It was an emptiness that I'm quite familiar with, but at the same time, I hadn't the least bit of interest in entertaining the beast. I wanted to walk away from myself, but paid heed anyway, knowing that brushing the discomfort off to the side would only bring more agony. I stayed put under the awning for a bit, trying to remain open, to see where She wanted to go.

Eventually, I ended up walking south, past Grafton Street and Dawson Street, turning west on the next road that paralleled Dawson. I wasn't ready to eat, and I wasn't ready to turn in for the evening. The road was boring, full of shops that were closed, not even a bookstore to fall into. The pubs didn't appeal to me; the idea of hanging out in a pub just to be somewhere reminded me of the lifeless, phony banter and camaraderie that I once sought in the bars back in the States. Maybe the pubs were full of soul for others, but I didn't want to have to drink to invite the spirit.

I thought about Kelli. Who was she having dinner with tonight and tomorrow evening? I don't think she has a man in her life, but I'm not sure. Whenever she has mentioned meeting a friend, it has always been another woman. I never asked; it was always information that she volunteered, which was now beginning to ruffle up a bit of my own paranoia.

What I'll tell another isn't so revealing; it's much more about what I don't tell. I look beyond words, at the actions and reactions of others, at their congruence or incongruence, at the myriad of ways in which we humans communicate. Hell, for all I know she could be fucking Bill Clinton for these next two evenings while I'm hanging out with the other lost souls at Bewley's on Grafton. Then again, I could be wrong. Maybe it's Hillary; God I hope not.

So, Bewley's and a white coffee it was. The date was with Her; the same date I'd been on for the last forty years. There was a ton of single women eating alone, just like me. I've chosen this life; I'm afraid that living any other way will rob me of something. I've chosen to eat alone, sleep alone, dream alone, and in the morning, wake up alone. I've chosen it all, and as much as I want to blame a Godforsaken God and Woman, I am the creator of my own universe.

If I had tried it once, I had tried it a hundred times. I fucking hated my ex-wife when we split, and I hated her because I needed to hate her; I wanted to hate her. I wanted her out of my miniature world. I wanted to be left to chase a new illusion, only to be disillusioned once again, and again, and again. And now, here I am in Ireland, hunting for a flat-assed cackling Leprechaun to deliver me from evil, from myself.

As sad as it all is, something magical is really my only hope, because the relics of my physical world and my old dream have left me circling in the same holding pattern. Whenever I think I have made a change, I find that I am still taking off and landing on the same runway. What I love the most, I most despise. God, Woman, I love her, hate her, and I'll be hanging at the foot of her cross long after I've become ashes, long after I've gazed upon my final sunset.

So, how can I ever live again with a woman, let alone myself? How can I not tire of lapping up one woman's juices from now through eternity? Fuck! I want to scream the whole world into a silence. I want to reach down into my throat, jerk my fucking heart out and beat it until it falls into a new rhythm, a divine rhythm that matches Hers, the celestial feminine, in hope of... well, just in hope.

Will I ever be able to sit still and simply contain this madness that surges through me, this craziness that leaps from one synapse to another, this insanity that courses through my veins, oozes from my pores?

I couldn't love her. I couldn't love and accept Lauren for who she was or where she was in her life. I couldn't love and accept her ambivalence, her suffering, her humanity, her hanging on the cross, her descent into Saturday's abyss, her hell, her heaven, her everything, just as I couldn't accept myself.

I went through the line at Bewley's for another black and white. At the register, some gay guy took my money. Maybe the priests were gay and they'd taken the vow of celibacy as a compensation for their sexual orientation, maybe they'd become priests to avoid a perceived sin and the threat of eternal damnation; and maybe not. I sipped my coffee and looked around Bewley's. I found nothing but the faces of derelicts.

April 22, 2001 - Dream

Something about meeting or having a dinner date with Francesca, my high school sweetheart.

April 22, 2001 - 2 p.m.

After having showered and dressed, I opened my door and sat on the end of the bed to slip on my socks and shoes. The housekeeper stuck her head in and asked if she could take care of the room. I told her that I'd be out momentarily. They had failed to clean the day before. The room wasn't dirty, but they could have at least made the bed, must have been afraid of waking me?

I caught the bus at Donnybrook, still uncertain of my mood.

I walked to the back of the lower deck and sat two seats from the back row. It was quiet. I like quiet Sunday mornings; they lack a tension that the other six days of the week carry. At the next stop, a group of eight women in their sixties climbed into the bus, and after paying their tariff, all came to the back of the lower deck and huddled around me.

The whole bus was full of empty seats, but they had to crowd around me and start that goddamn cackling - so much for a tensionless Sunday morning. They started clucking excitedly about where they wanted to shop and about a bunch of other pointless, horseshit possibilities. I left... no, I fled from the bus at the next stop, considerably short of my originally intended destination of St. Stephen's Green, but quite certain of the mood that possessed me.

Hoofing it the rest of the way to the city center, I encountered an old man walking hunched over with a cane, shuffling forward, a few inches at a time, some of his steps even seemed as if he were going backward. If that's part of getting old, I want no part of it. I looked at him and smiled, and received a smile back from the old boy. Was it an emotional condition, a physical condition, or possibly both?

Samsara didn't open early on Sundays, so I continued my walk to find that the place I'd had coffee the day before was also closed. I crossed the street to a self-service diner that made hot and cold sandwiches and other treats. I ordered a coffee and took the stairs up thinking that it might be quieter, but there was a group of motorcyclists, all dressed in leathers, holding a club meeting, and smoking up the room to beat hell. I went back down and found an empty seat at the counter.

It's starting to hit home, my ambivalence, that is. I like to look around, check out all the pretty girls, dream about them, and keep my options open, but then I see couples spending time together on the weekends, and I dream about having that again, too. I like to piss and moan about being a single man, mostly to myself, but it's still pissin' and moanin'. All bullshit set aside, I like being alone, having the freedom it brings.

I'm frustrated with myself for not being able to find it within me to seduce Kelli, for not being able to find an opening in her that invites my kiss. I'm not looking for a woman just to sneak an occasional fuck. I'm searching for a woman whose scent will lead me back home every evening, the same scent I'll wake to the next morning, my nose nestled in the hair that flows from this sleeping beauty. I want it; just don't know how to have it.

My illusion of falling in love has vanished, but maybe that isn't such a bad thing? Maybe my image of love has been lost, so that it can be replaced with a new image? Maybe love doesn't have to come crashing down on me to be love? Maybe love isn't the big bang but, instead, a river flowing and all that's required of me is diving in with abandonment, the absence of having to reach any certain destination or of love having to take on a fixed form? Maybe I don't need a recipient to receive and mirror love back to me as much as it is only important to be a part of it?

The cafeteria wasn't doing it for me. The only thing that looked appealing were the potato chips they served with the sandwiches. My feet, legs, and lower back ached. I'm sick and tired of chasing Leprechauns; the little bastards are slicker than snot.

I walked back to St. Jude's after purchasing a souvenir for Alexis. I began pulling clothes from the dresser and started to pack. I was restless, ready to leave Dublin. I felt lonely, too. I've been the one pursuing Kelli, and occasionally she'd meet me, but it wasn't coming back the other way, or at least I didn't sense her to be all that interested. I've been initiating everything, not once have I received an unsolicited phone call or an invitation from her.

April 22, 2001 - 5 p.m.

After packing, I caught the bus back to Dublin and sat down in another self-serve café in the St. Stephen's Green Mall. Two men in their twenties sat down at the table next to me; one had light brown hair and the other was blonde. The brown haired one had a tough look to him, a careless-little-boy look, like a kid who ran into walls and then bounced off them as if they weren't even there. He looked like he'd make a good rugby player. The blonde fellow was thinner than his comrade, and had more of a smooth, polished look, the kind of guy who bathed twice a day and never wore the same pair of pants two days in a row.

The brown haired fellow took a drink of his bottled water, and then made a face like he'd just swigged sour milk. "This damn water is all fruity. I just wanted plain water."

"There's regular water over there," I said, butting into the conversation.

"Yeah, I know," Brownie answered. "I spotted it after I paid for this stuff," he said, with one opened bottle sitting in front of him and one that was still sealed.

"Trade the one you haven't opened yet," I encouraged.

"You think so?" he asked.

"Yeah, hell yeah, they'll let you. What do they care?"

"Yeah, why not?" Blondie added, as Brownie was already standing up to make the trade.

"That other shit you were drinking has that fake sugar stuff in it," I said, as Brownie returned with his bottle of real water.

"Aspartame?" Blondie asked.

"I don't know what you call it, but I had one the other day. Tasted like shit."

"Yeah, you don't want to drink that crap," Blondie said to Brownie. "I go around giving lectures on how unhealthy that stuff is for you," Blondie said, turning to me.

"Well, what I don't get is why you let your buddy here drink almost a whole damn bottle of the stuff?" I teased.

Brownie rolled up his nose in disgust. "Lots of pretty girls here in Dublin, hey?" Brownie suggested, changing the subject to something more palatable.

"Not bad, huh," I confirmed.

"Not at all," Blondie quickly answered, making sure he got to participate in the fun and games.

"Where you guys in from?"

"London," Blondie answered.

"How'd you get here, fly?"

"Yeah," Blondie confirmed.

"Aerlingus?"

"Yeah, got a great deal, too," Blondie answered.

"About a hundred twenty pounds," I guessed.

"Yeah, about that with the taxes," Blondie answered.

"Well, was it worth it?"

"Oh, yeah," Brownie chimed in. "We dropped our bags at our buddy's and went straight to the pub."

"Sounds like you boys don't mess around."

"Not a bit," Blondie answered. "Our buddy lives right across from one of the pubs."

"Bet that came in handy."

"Real handy," Brownie answered, nodding his head up and down rapidly and grinning like a kid who was about to get a scoop of his favorite ice cream.

"We went to another pub last night, though, and we'd have never made it back if we didn't have our buddy with us," Brownie explained.

"She said she wanted to see me again," Blondie boasted, finally having to flex his muscles.

"Yeah," I said, waiting for more details.

"Yeah, and I told her that I was leaving tomorrow. Then she told me that she never fucks on the first date."

"You should have told her you'd leave and come back in an hour," I teased.

"I told her that we met at eleven and that it was past midnight and that should count for two days."

"And?"

"And I don't have to work until Wednesday. I'm thinking..."

"About staying," I interrupted. "For forty pounds you can change your ticket. Believe me, I know, I was supposed to leave last week."

"She had on stockings that were her panties and everything. She showed them to me. She said she always wears them when she goes out without a date, or on a first date, but on the second date she only wears the kind that go halfway up, nothing else underneath," he explained, raising his eyebrows.

"Yeah, I'll bet she does," I laughed. That girl had dangled the bait and this young man had swallowed it all, hook, line, and sinker. "What are you doing here, then?" I asked.

"We have all kinds of girls in London," Brownie chimed in to rescue his lost counterpart.

"Yeah, that's right, and they chase *you*, there," Blondie

reasoned. "That's why I'm not so worried about that one girl; plenty of it at home."

"I see."

"Where're you from?" Blondie asked, wanting to get out of the hot seat.

"States."

"Where?"

"California."

"I was out there last year. Spent eight months touring the country," Blondie said.

"Yeah, I'm going home on Tuesday."

"You here on business?" Blondie asked.

"I'm here because of a woman, but I suppose you could call it business," I answered. "Met her in the States, right before she was leaving to come home to Dublin; I've been e-mailing her for months. Finally came over to see her."

"Did it work out for you?" Brownie asked with that excited little boy grin.

"Oh yeah," I lied, smiled, and nodded.

"Alright," Brownie said, as they both nodded their head in agreement, following cue to my coy grin.

"What do you guys do in London?"

"I lecture on health and work at a hotel," Blondie answered.

"How 'bout you?" I asked Brownie.

"I work at the hotel, too."

"We're not from London, though. We're Australian," Blondie explained. "We've been over in London living with an aunt for the last year."

"But it's about time for us to get our own place," Brownie added.

"Yeah, they're getting a bit bitchy," Blondie said.

"I see," I answered.

"So, you gonna see this girl again?" Blondie asked.

"I don't know, maybe," I finally answered honestly.

"You been married before?" Blondie asked, as if he sensed something.

"Yeah, I've been married before," I answered like an old bull.

"So you're not worried about that." Blondie said.

"That's the farthest thing from my mind. A guy's fucked whenever he thinks that there's only one woman in the world for him."

"So you're just having fun?" Brownie asked.

"You got it," I nodded and winked. Then I blew a bunch more smoke their way. Told them how I had been fucking four women for a whole year.

"You never got caught?" Blondie asked.

"No, their ages ranged from early twenties to late thirties, and they all ran in different circles. One even lived an hour away. I fucked all four of them at least once a week, and some of 'em twice, and it lasted for over a year."

"And they never caught on to you?" Brownie asked.

"No, never did, but I moved, and everything went to hell after that. Now look at me, I'm chasing a woman halfway around the world in hopes of getting lucky," I smiled.

"It comes and goes, doesn't it." Blondie said.

"You got that right," I answered.

"Are you married now," Brownie asked.

"No sir, I'm not..."

We shot the shit for a while longer. The boys were brothers. They asked me to guess who was the oldest, and I guessed wrong. Blondie was twenty-eight, and Brownie would be twenty-six in just a few days, Tuesday the 24th actually, the day I'm scheduled to depart from Dublin. I'm done calling on Kelli. If we're to talk again, it'll be on her invitation.

April 22, 2001 - 10 p.m.

After leaving the St. Stephen's Green mall and the bullshit session with the Australian brothers, I stopped by Samsara to see if Niamh might be around. I didn't see her. I did, however, find two blondes seated farther inside the sanctuary than I preferred to sit. I walked in and sat one table from them. There were two guys at the bar and four other men sitting five tables away from the women. The blondes knew they had an audience; it was almost as if their beauty had set up this invisible force field that kept all these men at bay. They sat at least twenty feet removed, gawking at the women and drooling all over themselves. I, on the other hand, like one of Cinderella's jealous, evil stepsisters sat right next to the beauties and ignored them.

A waitress walked past, ignoring me, so I stood up and started for the bar. She quickly turned around and told me she'd be right with me. I ordered sparkling water with a lime as another blonde walked up to the table and joined the two hotties. It was my lucky day; now there were three beauties for me to snub. They probably thought I was queer or something, but I couldn't have cared less.

I sipped my water, ignored the hotties, and thought about my good friend Devin. I had nicknamed him Slick. He became one of my best friends after my divorce and after the Lauren thing fell apart. Slick was as loyal as the day is long, all six and a half feet of him. He weighs a husky two-fifty plus, has short blonde hair, and his blue eyes are nestled into his baby face. He's nine years my junior.

When I met Slick several years ago, he was a reserve deputy sheriff and a law student with political aspirations. He packed milk delivery trucks at night to earn his wages until he wrapped his turquoise-jade colored Ford Taurus around a light pole on his way home from the milk plant early one morning on the last day of the year. That's right, he literally ended the year with a bang. The wreck reduced his identity to a law student with political aspirations, minus the jobs.

We started hanging out a few months before his wreck. He pulled up in his new car as I walked out of a local Coffee house on Halloween morning. Slick wanted to haul me to a resort up in the mountains, about an hour's drive.

"Hey Malcolm, what's going on?"

"Not much Slick. Some pretty fancy wheels you got there."

"Leased it; it's great. Come on, I'll take you to lunch up at the pass."

"Pick me up at my house; I don't want to leave my truck here to be stolen." At the time, they stole Chevy extended cab pickups like I once stole pomegranates.

Devin picked me up at my house a few minutes later and we were off to the hills.

"Wait 'til you see how this thing corners."

"Oh yeah," I answered, not quite sure what I was getting myself into.

"It halls balls, too. Look how this console flips open for your mugs."

"I thought your heart was set on an Eddie Bauer Ford Explorer."

"It was, but it wasn't in my budget and they gave me a hell of a deal on this Taurus."

"It's a damn fine car; you just surprise me," I answered.

"You'll see why when we get into the hills."

It handled all right. It was a fine car indeed, but my concern wasn't with the Taurus; it was with the driver. I was riding with a twenty-six year old reserve deputy sheriff who thought he was invincible. In my youth and beyond, I had wrecked plenty of cars and done a lot of other dumb things, but, being thirty-five-years-old at the time, I was beginning to sense my own mortality; Slick didn't. He passed cars and cornered curves at twice the posted speed limit. I was a nervous wreck when we finally arrived at our destination.

The drive home was about the same: reckless. When we pulled into town and were almost home, he tried to beat a car out of its position where two lanes merged into one. He beat the other car out of the pole position alright, but only by the hair of his baby-faced chin.

"Did I ever tell you about the time I got picked up for drunk driving?" I asked.

"Sure did."

"Did I ever tell you what happened to the cop about six months after he got me?"

"No."

"Well, you see Slick, he was slick, too."

"Whadaya mean?"

"He was this young, fair haired, blue-eyed CHP who was on a mission to put every drunk on wheels behind bars."

"So, that was his job."

"Was his job, but he was making it more than a job. He was trying to prove himself."

"So what?"

"So he was chasing a car down the highway one day. It was an out-of-control, high-speed chase and he decided to pass a car on the right shoulder. Hit a parked motor grader head on. I was working out in his hometown on the day of his funeral, drove by the cemetery when they were burying him. I thought to myself how he'd slowed a lot of us drunks down, just couldn't do it for himself."

We pulled into my driveway just as I finished the story; a story I didn't think Slick heard.

"Hey, thanks for lunch man," Slick said, as we shook hands.

"Thanks for driving. Enjoy those new wheels, huh. But be careful."

Devin wrapped it around the light pole two months later, busted pelvis, busted back, and a crushed left arm. Six weeks in the hospital and three surgeries over the next several months changed him. When I visited him in the hospital the first time he was pretty doped up.

"Hey Slick, how the hell are you?"

"Not too good, Malcolm."

"At least you still have your good arm," I teased.

He grinned. "That's about the last thing on my mind right now."

"You might as well take advantage of these sponge baths; that way you can save your arm for when you're home alone."

"You tried to tell me, and I didn't hear you."

"Hey Slick what's the help like around here? Don't be hoarding 'em all to yourself, now. I hope you're keeping your best buddy Malcolm at the top of your overflow list."

"You got to pay your dues before you get to shop in this place."

"I wouldn't expect any less from you, Slick. Guess if I was in your shoes I might not be so generous either," I teased.

When Devin got out of the hospital and started feeling like getting out of the house, I'd pick him up and hold him captive, forcing him to have to listen to my long winded spells. He called it bullshit, but he liked it. Life's just a great big bullshit session anyway; that's what makes it so much fun. I was hauling Devin around getting him healed up and he was healing me up by being my biggest fan. I just about had the big fucker brainwashed until the time we were driving back from Lake Tahoe.

"Hey Slick whacha got going tomorrow?" I asked, knowing that he had an open calendar.

"Nothing, why?"

"I need to get the taxi up to Tahoe, so I'll have wheels there when I fly in for my winter ski trips. I was hoping you could drive it while I follow you in my pick-up."

The white 1986 Chevy Caprice with a dark blue Landau top had been nicknamed, 'The Taxi' by a colleague whom I had bought it from.

"Sure, what time you want to leave?"

"After lunch tomorrow, I'll get us a room, and we'll drive back the next day."

"Malcolm, I haven't got the money for that."

"Won't cost you a dime; I'll get a room at the Ridge Tahoe: a nice room with two queen size beds. We'll have a good dinner and then you'll sleep like a baby. Just don't forget your ear plugs."

"I can't let you pay for all that."

"Devin, you're doing me a favor. If you don't do it, someone else will, and I'm still going to spend the night. I'm not driving there and back in one day. Besides, we'll have a hell of a lot of fun and you'll get to take in some different scenery."

We left the next afternoon, dropped the car off at the airport, got to the Ridge Tahoe around six that evening and checked in to our room with two queen size beds just as planned. We had dinner in the steak house down in Minden at the Carson Valley Inn, and with full bellies got a good night's sleep.

"Get your ass up you snoring mother-fucker," I yelled the next morning. If he snored it was news to me, but I wasn't going to let him know any different. Besides it gave me a good excuse to talk to him that way.

"What time is it?"

"Nine-thirty, get your ass in the shower."

"What's your hurry?"

"I've got to find a good looking woman to flip off today."

"You what?"

"You heard me."

"You mean, like give her the bird?" he asked, with a sleepy confused look.

"You got it big boy."

"You're sick, but probably serious," he said. Slick knew that I was just twisted enough to be telling the truth. He doubted me most of the time until he saw me carrying out my threats. I was volatile enough that he at least considered my sincerity.

"Damn serious."

"What do you hope to gain?"

"You've never done it?"

"Why would I even consider such a thing?"

"For the reaction, the attention."

"You *are* fucked up, Malcolm."

"Beats the hell out of being ignored. I mean, you might piss 'em off, but at least you've got 'em for a minute, which is more than you get from a wave or hello."

Devin just shook his head on the way to the shower. We had lunch at the Tahoe Keys, outside on the patio of the Fresh Catch Restaurant, before heading home. While we were winding down 88, I started giving the bird to the oncoming traffic.

"What the hell are you doing?"

"Flippin' 'em the bird."

"Why?"

"Because it feels good, and because it's too much trouble for them to turn around to come stomp our asses." I gave every passing car the finger for several more minutes, belly laughing the whole time and it felt damn good, too. Slick didn't know what to make of me, but I caught a sparkle in his eyes.

"I got to take a leak," he soon announced.

"How about the Burger King on the other side of Jackson, about fifteen minutes. Will that work?"

"Sounds good."

Fifteen minutes or so later we pulled into the Burger King, and I took the bathroom first. When I came back, Devin was in line to order. For Slick, the titty had become a Pepsi.

"Hey Slick, I'm going around back to Baskin Robbins."

I got my cone and returned to Burger King just as Devin came out of the door, jumbo-size Pepsi in hand, wearing a great big grin and a twinkling beam in his blue eyes.

"What's going on?" I asked, as we started towards the truck.

"I just pissed all over that fuckin' bathroom."

"You what?"

"I just pissed all over that bathroom. I pissed in the sink, I pissed on the floor, and I pissed all over those nice fresh rolls of toilet paper. How'd you like to show up there havin' to take a shit," he boasted, all proud of himself.

As he was bragging about pissin' the Burger King, we stepped out into the driveway of the parking lot towards the truck and this good-looking blonde rounded the corner and almost hit us. Actually, she didn't almost hit us, but came close enough for the sheriff-turned-fugitive to draw and brandish his weapon.

"Did you see her turn around? It worked," he said, as if he'd just pissed on another roll of toilet paper.

"What the *fuck* you doing?" I asked, shaking my head.

"I flipped her off."

"What the fuck you flippin' off a good lookin' woman like that for?"

"Hell, she almost hit us, man."

"She did not. And she was beautiful! Man, I can't take your ass anywhere."

Slick gave me a you-son-of-a-bitch grin, and without a word, climbed into my pickup to finish our drive home; every five or ten minutes I'd just bust over, doubled-up belly laughing.

"I can't believe that you actually gave her the finger."

"What's even sadder, you began to orchestrate the whole thing from the time you woke my ass up this morning. You know what Malcolm, fuck you!"

After just one drink that was stretched into an hour-long gossip session for the three blondes, some guy walked into Samsara and greeted the three hotties. He was a queer fucker for sure; although, he did manage to get the three gorgeous blondes to follow him out of the front door. If he wasn't a queer, he was their pimp, or both.

I wasn't calling Kelli anymore, just wasn't calling. After ordering another lime and soda, I went to the pisser. Walking back to my seat, Niamh spotted me. She was behind the bar.

"Malcolm, how are you?" she asked, as she washed some dirty dishes.

"Good, Niamh, how 'bout you?"

"Oh, pretty good, besides my having to wash dishes that the day shift shoved under the counter."

"Got you a little game going on, have you?"

"You know how it is Malcolm. Listen, you missed a smashing party last night."

"Bet I did. I just didn't feel right barging in on a family affair, you know."

"Oh, it was bigger than I ever expected. A bunch of my cousins even showed up."

"A good time, huh?"

"Oh, it was grand. Even had a belly dancer."

"Whose idea was that one?"

"I asked Mom, but she claimed she had nothing to do with it," Niamh smiled.

I returned the smile and then backed up to my seat. Niamh was sweet, a real buddy, but she still had that edge that wouldn't let anyone get too close. I sipped my soda while a man working behind the bar brought a green bottle of liquor down to the end where the waitresses picked up their drink orders, close to where Niamh was doing the dishes.

"Hey Malcolm," Niamh called out, "Come on over here. We're about to have a little entertainment," she said, motioning me over to where the bottle of liquor was sitting. I got out of my seat and walked toward the bar. "Ian, this is Malcolm, he's over visiting from the States. He's been hanging out here for the last few days. Malcolm, this is Ian. Ian's the manager here."

"Nice to meet you, Ian," I said, extending my hand.

"Ah, the pleasure is mine," he answered, as he gripped my hand firmly and gave it a good shake. He was a thin fellow, too, and also like Niamh, was very present, stood right within himself as he conversed. Neither of them seemed to be lost in their minds to another world. Ian had thin brown wavy hair and was in his early to mid thirties. He wore wire-rimmed glasses and stood no taller than five-eight.

"Well, Malcolm, you're just in time for a small bit of entertainment," Ian announced, as he filled a couple of shot glasses with the green potion. He then took a napkin and tore it into strips, rolled them into wick-like pieces, and dipped one end of the wick into the shot glass to soak up some of the juice. Next, he drank the shot and, with a cigarette lighter, lit the wick, held it an inch from his lips and spewed out a stream of fire that extended well beyond three feet.

"Wow," was all I could say.

"Learned it from some American bartenders who were visiting not long ago," Ian explained, as he wiped his mouth with the back of his left hand.

"You swallow that stuff or use if for fuel?" I asked.

"Hell, no, I don't swallow that crap."

"What is it?"

"Some French stuff they make out of wormwood. They say it has THC in it. I guess drinking a couple of shots is supposed to be like smoking that silly stuff, but I wouldn't know, you know," Ian explained with a grin.

"Like getting high, huh?"

"Yeah, but like I said, I wouldn't know," he teased, as he lit up a cigarette.

"You better be careful about lighting up and inhaling anything just yet," I kidded.

"Oh, I never inhale," he giggled.

"Yeah, we had a president like that once."

"Oh, yeah, fucking politicians, I call 'em," he said, as he checked out two attractive young women who walked into the sanctuary.

"Not bad, huh?" I asked.

"Oh, I never look at stuff like that, Malcolm" he joked. "I'm the manager around here. No fun for me, you know."

"You never look at what?"

"At what? Oh, yeah, you got it." Ian nodded and grinned, before dragging on his smoke.

Ian was a riot. Another fellow walked up as we visited. He had short, dark, kinky hair and spoke with a French accent. Apparently, he had been taking fire-breathing lessons from Ian. He made a few unsuccessful attempts; needless to say, only after I had stepped back four or five feet. The rookie Frenchman was spraying booze all over the place. With Ian coaching him, he was finally able to blow a flame that extended about a foot, and after that Niamh put the bottle away, and the Frenchman wandered off.

"Say, Ian, where'd they come up with Samsara."

"Oh, the owner of this place has three daughters. One of them is named Samantha and another is Sara. But they say Samsara is a Buddhist word for Groundhog Day."

"Groundhogs Day?"

"You know, like that movie with Bill Murray. Has something to do with living things over and over again until you achieve perfection. Something like that, anyway."

"Okay, I think I gotcha now."

"He's got another daughter, too; Rebecca. They're naming the restaurant after her. Beck's Tiger, like the Celtic tiger. Malcolm, wait here a minute. I'll go after the article so you can have a look," Ian said, right before he hustled down to the other end of the bar.

He returned with a small leather day planner, pulled out a newspaper clipping and handed it to me. There was a picture of the three daughters, all hotties, and an article about the newly opened bar and restaurant.

"Ian, these girls are something," I said, raising my eyebrows and giving him an evil grin.

"Now, Malcolm, there's a lot of things I'll do, but fucking with the boss' daughters isn't one of them. Hell, I could lose my job."

"Ian, some things are fucking well worth getting fired over."

"Ah, Malcolm, you know, I'd say you're on to something here," he answered, with that I-never-inhale grin.

April 23, 2001

I phoned the hotel at the airport before checking out of St. Jude's and the price to stay had gone up from one hundred to one hundred thirty pounds. After settling my bill with St. Jude's, I set out for Donnybrook with two of the three bags I originally had with me: my small roller suitcase with its wheels still intact and a small carryon bag that contained a camera, tape recorder, travel documents, and several other incidentals.

From Donnybrook, I rode the bus to St. Stephen's Green. I sat across from a tall brunette who was holding a bottle of sparkling water. As she opened the bottle, water started spewing out from under the screw cap.

"Bumpy ride, huh?" I asked.

"I guess so," she smiled.

Grafton Street was quiet by Grafton Street standards, but I still had to dodge people on my way to the Internet café. I had a message from Angus; his wedding is in a few weeks, so in my return message I assured him that I'd be home in time to stand up with him.

I also had a message from Adam, telling me that my friend Hilton had stopped in to visit him in Monterey and that he had a pretty lady by his side. I sent a message to Hilton saying that he could run but couldn't hide, and that rumor had traveled halfway around the world about him having a new lady friend.

I also wanted Hilton to know that I had extended my stay in the event that he needed to contact me. In addition to being a good friend, Hilton is the attorney who's been looking after my affairs while I'm away. If the Bonanza sold, I wanted Hilton handling the transaction. He'd have already sent word if anything had transpired with the airplane. It was just fun to throw a curveball his way.

I had no message from Kelli, nor had I received a phone call. I hated to be such a stubborn soul, but it was important for me to step back. It wasn't a game, just a test. I'd been the one pursuing her all the time and it now had to become reciprocal for me to continue engaging her.

After leaving the Internet café, I noticed a small restaurant a few doors down and was drawn in by its bohemian appeal. It was a health food place; a vegetarian restaurant with tattooed servers who had dreadlocks or their heads shaved. Reggae music played in the background. The help at the restaurant reminded me of several people I'd met on the California coast. They liked to puff a little weed occasionally; I still hung out with them even though I'd given up the smoke when I quit the booze.

I think about getting high sometimes, in my dreams I

actually still do, but in my waking life, I only daydream about it. I wonder what I might have lost by giving up that lifestyle? The life I'm now living seems so narrow and rigid. It really has been a long time since I've let down, turned off all that serious shit that bounces around in my mind, just to let something else, like a higher order of things, take over.

In some ways, my sobriety has become something I hide behind, believing myself to be superior and above it all or inferior and unable to fit in. It's become my excuse to withdraw into my own little world where I don't have to judge and compare myself to others.

After sobering up, I defined myself in the working world. That's where my social needs were met. My success in the business world was validation enough for most and gave me enough confidence to skate by in the other realms of my life, but there was a falseness to it all. It wasn't an intentional lie, more of an unconscious compensation for a deep-seated sense of inferiority.

I had coffee, a powdered sugar-dusted scone, and a fresh-out-of-the-oven chocolate chip pear muffin. I tried to order lunch, but they weren't serving for another half hour. The coffee was my favorite, just like what I'd get in the States, a dark, rich, French roast. The scone was good, but the muffin, even though it was still warm, lacked something. I normally wouldn't have had two baked sweet breads, but I was hungry. My belly did the ordering this morning.

Within an hour, the place was packed, and I had yet to get up to order lunch for fear of losing my seat. People kept coming through the door in waves. I felt a little guilty taking up a table all to myself, but the guilt didn't overwhelm my desire to be there. Four, twenty-something-year-olds sat at the table next to mine, and a fifth joined them and asked to sit across from me. I welcomed her presence, figuring it would no longer appear that I was hoarding the table.

I didn't bother listening in on their conversations, wasn't even interested. They were all nice looking kids, but I just didn't have the desire to step into their lives. Selfishly, I was much more interested in living out my own drama. I was tired; it was as if I was doing the last day of my sentence. About the only thing that would reel me in from my state would be a phone call from Kelli.

I noticed a woman who looked like the wife of an old client. He had met his wife and after a few dates quit calling her because he felt that she wasn't interested in him. Time passed and then she finally phoned him. That was what it took for him; eventually they married. He was a great big pain in the ass, got his feelings hurt with every changing breeze, but just the same, I understood him.

I understood his wound and his stubbornness, and the older I get the more sense the stubbornness makes. It weeds out the bullshit, separates fantasy from reality. Being in the second half of life, I no longer have the time, nor do I care to live a fantasy life filled with good intentions.

People kept packing into the place; I felt cramped and needed space. I decided to check on the availability of my seat in the window at Samsara. Grafton Street was now in full bloom. I spotted another woman who looked like another friend's wife. Funny how I could be a world apart from family and friends yet still spot their images and feel their presence in another. It was almost as if they had a double.

Niamh greeted me as I walked through the tall doors of Samsara. A gentleman server tried to take my order immediately after I'd settled into my familiar seat, but I put him off. I moved to the seat on the opposite side of the table, to the empty seat I'd been sitting across from for the last several days, deciding to have a different view from my perch and watch the foot traffic coming from the west as opposed to the east.

The door from the kitchen into the lounge had closed and Anna Marie, with both hands full, stood by waiting for someone to come by and open it for her. The damn thing only swung open in the opposite direction and she couldn't unlatch it with both hands full, no doubt an architectural design flaw. I got up and opened the door for her.

Anna Marie was a beautiful young woman. She was short, with long brown hair that was held up by a clip. She had green eyes, and a petite, pointy nose. After delivering the order she had in her hands, she returned to check on me. Again, I ordered the fish and chips and water with a lime. Anna Marie went to place my order and shortly after, the gentleman who had tried to serve me when I first arrived returned to my table.

"I'm sorry sir, but we are out of limes," he announced. "We do have lemon, though."

"Lemon will be fine. Thank you."

He returned with my water a few minutes later and left. I was about to take a drink, but, like a fingerprint at a crime scene, I detected the remnants of a woman's lipstick imprinted on the rim of the glass.

"Sir," I called, loud enough to catch the server before he walked back into the sanctuary.

"Yes," he said, returning to my table.

"Will you bring a new glass please," I said, pointing out the lipstick.

"Right away, sir," he answered, before leaving with the tainted goods. As he scurried away, I thought: *A kiss, I've just been kissed.*

The man returned with a fresh glass of water, and Anna Marie followed shortly after with my fish and chips, this time with a smile. After lunch, I ordered tea and sat back to watch the pedestrians. The woman who I had seen while at the Bohemian restaurant, the woman who reminded me of an old client's wife walked by and shortly after that, the same girl who had the fizzing bottle of sparkling water on the bus earlier this morning walked past as well. Dublin's a huge city; funny how certain images return to me, while others pass my way only once in a lifetime.

Anna Marie didn't look happy. She seldom smiled, seemed to be working at Samsara out of duty. That huge door leading to and from the kitchen that she had to constantly muscle her way through wasn't helping matters, but there was more weighing on her than just that heavy door. No doubt she was a hard worker, but her heart was elsewhere.

"Anna Marie," I said, to catch her attention as she walked from the kitchen.

"Yes."

"Where are you from?"

"Romania."

"Do you like it here?"

"I am here," she shrugged. "For a year, I was in Spain."

"Spain, huh; how long have you been here?"

"I don't know," she answered, thinking I was asking how long she planned on being in Dublin.

"No, when did you arrive here in Dublin?"

"Oh, last year."

"So, a year in Spain, and a year in Ireland."

"Yes, that is right."

"How about the States?"

"It is my dream, but I don't think it will ever happen," she answered with a despondent tone and a hopeless look.

"It can happen," I reassured. "Here's my card. If you come to California, I will help you find work. What do you like to do?"

"In Romania, I was a teacher," she said, her eyes lighting up. "For three years I was a teacher, but then I came here to learn English."

"And maybe you'll come to the U.S. to teach Americans to speak Romanian."

"I don't think they want to learn how to speak Romanian."

"I know a Japanese woman and a woman from Kosovo who are both teaching Americans to speak their language. There are two language institutions where I live," I encouraged, trying to help her see past her limited view of things.

"Maybe," she answered, sounding hopeful, but with the negative doubt still running her from behind the scenes.

"You keep that card, and if you come to California, I'll help you."

"If you even remember me," she said, as she walked away.

"Anna Marie," I said, in a commanding tone. She turned as if I wanted some sort of service.

"Anna Marie, right?"

"Yes," she answered hesitantly, with a confused smile."

"I'll remember you Anna Marie."

She turned and walked to the bar with my card in hand. Then she started talking to a man who worked there as a busboy, possibly her partner. She showed him the card and started telling him something and then she pointed me out to the fellow.

Tomorrow I'll be airborne en route to San Francisco. I won't get much sleep this evening, but that will be fine, a few hours will do. Then maybe I'll be able to sleep on the plane and have a smooth transition back into California time, back into my old, yet new life.

* * * * *

Kelli phoned just after three. She said she finished ninety percent of her work for Palestine, and wanted to know if I was around Blackrock to meet for coffee.

"What time?" I asked.

"I need to have some copies made. How about half past four?"

"I'll see you then."

"Oh, wait," Kelli stopped me before hanging up. "There's a coffee shop in the mall next to the art supply store. I'll meet you there. Wait for me if I'm late. Sometimes there's a line for the copy machine."

"Why don't you meet me at the Wicked Wolf instead."

"The Wicked Wolf?"

"Yeah, the pub across from Café Java. I've wanted to check it out, but keep getting sidetracked."

"It's across from Café Java, right?"

"That's it."

"Okay, I'll see you there when I finish making the copies."

"Don't rush. I'll wait for you."

I settled my bill at Samsara, and walked back into the sanctuary to say goodbye.

"Well, Niamh, I probably won't be seeing you again."

"So, this is it, huh, Malcolm?"

"This is it," I answered, as she came out from behind the bar.

"It's good to know you Niamh," I said, reaching for her hand. Instead, she kissed my cheek.

"Say, Niamh, how do I get out of here and to the closest Dart station?" I asked, a bit set back by her gesture.

"Ah, Malcolm, that's an easy one," she answered, almost as if she had anticipated this *very* question. "When you walk out the front door of Samsara here, you'll go left down Dawson Street until you reach Trinity College. Then follow the wall around to your right and stay on that path. It'll wind a bit, but stay on that path and eventually you'll see the bridge where the train crosses. It'll take you about ten minutes."

"Okay, Niamh, sounds easy, and I can always ask for help if I get lost."

"Listen Malcolm," Niamh commanded in a firm, direct tone. "Just do exactly as I say: follow the path and you'll have no problems."

"Okay, I'll trust you Niamh," I answered, and trust her is what I was about to do.

Ten minutes later, I tugged my bags through the gates of Pearse Station, purchased a ticket, and stood on the loading dock for no more than two minutes before boarding the southbound train for Blackrock.

We had made one stop and were pulling from the station when I heard a swishy, fizzing sound from behind and quickly turned to trace the source. It was a young woman who was opening a bottle of sparkling water. It wasn't the same woman who I had encountered earlier on the bus and who I had again seen passing by Samsara, but it was a woman her age. Her bottle had also overreacted to an unknown source. The day was taking on the theme of doubles.

Less than half-an-hour from the time Kelli phoned, I got off the train at Blackrock station. Having some time before meeting her, I walked over to Wicked Wolf for a mineral water.

About thirty minutes before Kelli was to arrive, a tall balding man in a wool sweater walked right up with his hand extended for me to shake, so I shook it. He was drunk, but seemed harmless.

"I had a nervous breakdown," the old boy explained as he stood over me from my left side.

"Good," I answered.

"Well, I don't know if it's so good, but I did end up having myself a few pints this afternoon."

"Even better," I encouraged.

"So you're an American, are you?"

"Yeah, I sure am."

"What's your name, son?" he asked, extending his hand for another shake.

"Malcolm."

"Malcolm, huh... I like that. Mal, you know there's a Saint Mel, now don't you?"

"That wouldn't be me," I proudly announced, and laughed a hearty laugh.

"Saint Mal, I'm O'Kelly. My friends call me Kelly."

"Pleasure to meet you O'Kelly," I answered, as he sat down at my table.

"I like Americans. Got a lot of family there. Where're you from?"

"California."

"Ah, California, huh? San Francisco?"

"Below it," I answered, not telling him that I lived in Carmel.

"You know, I was a movie star before I had a nervous breakdown," he explained, and then started rattling off a few famous actors that he supposedly co-stared with. "Ah now, that old Clint Eastwood, he's alright, you know. I guess he's the mayor of Carmel, but there's nothing there, you know."

"What's that?" I asked, wanting him to repeat what he'd just said about Carmel.

"Carmel, there's nothing there I tell you."

I nodded my head, not quite sure how to respond. He started talking about how he shouldn't have stopped for the drinks, but that he was just having a hard time.

"O'Kelly, I want to buy you a pint, and I need your help."

"Saint Mal, how's that?"

"I've got to run over to the travel agent down the block to pick up my plane ticket," I lied. "I'm supposed to meet a woman here in a few minutes. I'm wondering if you'll watch my bag and keep an eye out for her until I get back. She's a beautiful blonde. I won't be more than twenty minutes."

"Mal, tell me, how beautiful is she?" he asked in a drunken slur with a sneaky grin.

"She's fucking beautiful, O'Kelly. Believe me, you won't have to guess when she walks through that door."

"Mal, that's no problem. I'm happy to be helping you out," he answered, as I motioned for the waitress to come take our order.

O'Kelly ordered his beer, and I left ten pounds on the table for when the waitress returned with his freshly pulled pint.

"Okay, O'Kelly, I'll be back within twenty minutes," I said, slinging the small carry-on over my shoulder.

"Take your time now Saint Mal. There's no hurry," O'Kelly assured, as he lit a cigarette, leaned back in the chair, and crossed his legs. "Oh, say, Mal, what might this beautiful lass's name be?" O'Kelly hollered, as I walked for the door.

I stopped and turned around. "Kelli," I answered, with a great big smile.

"Whoo whoo," O'Kelly cooed. "Okay, Mal, I'll make sure she doesn't get away," he added with a wink.

I smiled, nodded, and walked out the door. I walked across the street to Café Java, and ordered a mocha to go and sat down a few seats back from the window, waiting for Kelli to walk up to the Wicked Wolf. I spotted her walking on the sidewalk; right near the payphone that I had frantically called her from the night that she had stood me up for dinner. I watched her beautiful image take the last few steps up to the door of the Wicked Wolf, and once she'd gone inside, I walked out of Café Java, crossed the street, made my way around to the backside of the Wicked Wolf and then down to the Dart station.

I purchased a ticket to the Tara Street Station, which was one stop past Pearse Station, close to Dublin City Center, and the River Liffey. Within fifteen minutes, I boarded the train, and found a seat. At Pearse Station, a young mother and her little boy boarded the train and sat across from me. The little boy was restless and whining, crying about something that his mother ignored, hoping for her child's attention to shift to a new desire. My mobile phone rang as we slowed to stop at Tara Street Station, the little boy still carrying on.

"Hey kid, you've got a call," I said, handing him the phone before stepping off that train.

Epilogue

April 24, 2001 - Dream

I was bringing a new pair of pants home to my brother Angus, and I was dribbling a basketball. I was in a jovial mood, as if I had regained control of my life, or maybe not control as much as having found a new confidence.

Also by Mel Mathews:

LeRoi

Menopause man

www.malcolmclay.com

LeRoi

ISBN 0-9776076-0-7

The most intriguing thing about Malcolm Clay was his battered MG. And now, with a cough of black smoke, even that had quit. Fortunately, the car had breath enough to limp up to the only two buildings in town: the garage and the diner across the street. Neither looked to have much reason to exist. No one was around. Maybe the mechanic was in the café getting a coffee. Maybe he'd had a heart attack from one strip of bacon too many. Maybe the place was an abandoned set left over from a bad remake of *Our Town*. "I've died," Malcolm thought, "and purgatory is the back road to Pumpkinpatch." There was nothing to do but wait since his cell phone had lost a signal about the same time the car had given up the ghost. He slumped back into the seat of the MG, then stood back up. "Well," he said to himself as he headed towards the diner, "if I'm in hell, I might as well find a bag of marshmallows, a pack of hot dogs and a wire coat hanger."

LeRoi is a story about blame and fear. Come along on the ride as Malcolm Clay stumbles upon what has secretly been running his life.

"This is a story of a man who is not afraid to be who he really is. Its authenticity and vulnerability made me laugh, cry, and wonder if I also have the courage to live an authentic life. A good read that is painfully sweet, honest and hopeful..." -- Sharon E. Martin - Atlanta, GA --

"I've read few novels written by men that have such keen insight into the struggle for truth and intimacy. To admit one's frailties is unusual. Malcolm Clay manages to do that in the most unusual of places, which is revealing in itself. One need not go on a trek to India or elsewhere to discover one's Self. Sometimes our greatest teachers are working the tiller at a diner..." -- Dana Lucas --

Menopause Man

ISBN 0-9776076-1-5

"Over here," he announced, holding up her leash.

"Come on Diana," she said, walking over to retrieve the dog. Malcolm kept petting Diana to keep her from running off. He wanted to make sure Lance got a good crack at the master, not to mention that he desired the same for himself.

"Hi there," Malcolm greeted the master as she reached for the leash.

"Oh, hi there," she answered in a soft, listless-like tone.

"How are you?" Malcolm asked to hold her up for a few more seconds.

"Fine thanks. Come on Diana," she said, smiling half-heartedly as she led the pup away.

"See you later," Malcolm said, as the couple walked towards the parking lot across the way. "What do you think of Diana?" he asked, looking up at Lance with a big grin after dog and master had crossed the street.

"How do you know Diana's name?" Sheila was quick to ask.

"It's my job," Malcolm quipped.

"Yeah, right! Your job," Sheila said.

"She's got the most potential of any woman I've met around here, yet."

"She is pretty damn cute," Sheila conceded.

"Cute. Hell, she's hot!" Lance chimed in.

"I'm partial to the dog, myself," Malcolm smiled.

"You *are* a dog," Sheila snapped. "I know what you're really after," she added, punching Malcolm's shoulder.

"What's her name?" Lance asked.

"Diana," Malcolm answered with a smart-ass grin. "Weren't you listening?"

"Not the dog, the woman."

"I don't know."

"But you know her dog's name?" Sheila asked in a give-me-a-break tone.

"Yeah, she came and jumped up onto my lap one day."

"Right," Sheila said, shaking her head.

"The girl or the dog?" Lance asked grinning.

"Really," Malcolm said, holding back his laughter to Lance's question. "I was sitting right up there on that bench," Malcolm said, pointing to the porch. "The pup just trotted right up those steps and hopped up into my lap."

"How do you know her name's Diana?" Lance asked.

"I asked."

"But you don't know the woman's name?" Sheila chimed in.

"I didn't ask," Malcolm answered in an impatient tone.

"Why not?" Lance asked.

"She wasn't ready to tell me."

"How do you know?" Sheila asked.

"I just know, all right? I can sense these things, you know."

* * * * *

Like a lot of people, he'd developed the habit of looking for love in all the wrong places. He really wasn't all that bad of a fellow. Yeah, he was selfish and self-absorbed, but Malcolm Clay had some redeeming qualities, too.

Something had changed, something he couldn't quite put his finger on, and it was driving him, as well as a few others, half nuts. He might have been chasing his tail, he might have been making mistakes, but he was still trying. One thing was certain: Malcolm hadn't given up!

Fisher King Books can be purchased online at:

www.fisherkingpress.com

or by calling:

1-800-228-9316